Lack of Jurisdiction

G.K. Parks

Copyright © 2014 G.K. Parks

A Modus Operandi imprint

All rights reserved.

ISBN: 0989195872
ISBN-13: 978-0-9891958-7-4

For my best friend

OTHER BOOKS IN THE ALEXIS PARKER SERIES:

Now available:

Books in the Julian Mercer series:

ONE

"So were they impressed that we have a former federal agent on the job?" Paul Eastman, my supervisor at Personal Defense National, asked when I dropped the signed forms from the Secret Service on top of his desk. It seemed a bit extreme that PDN had to be vetted by a government agency before being allowed to work as a third party contractor during a two day international business and diplomacy convention which was being held at one of the prestigious five-star hotels in the city.

"I'm not that impressive," I remarked.

He smiled. "Somehow, I doubt that. Keep in mind, Alexis, I've read your résumé. There isn't a single thing about you that isn't impressive, from your education to your career to your references." Something flitted across his features briefly. "Have you completed your evaluation of our security plan for the hotel? I hired you to consult on our emergency protocols, but unfortunately, it seems your role has turned into that of a glorified courier."

"I'll get it to you by the morning. Now that we have approval, I want to do a final walkthrough before the Secret Service locks the whole place down."

"Okay. I'll make a few calls and let them know our

consultant will be stopping by later tonight."

"Sure." I turned on my heel, not wanting to do anything else for the rest of the evening, but I didn't have a choice. Thankfully, once my report was finished, I wouldn't have anything to do until the background checks were completed by the government agencies. "I'll e-mail you my findings," I called over my shoulder, not waiting to be dismissed. Eastman seemed like a decent guy, and I didn't think he wanted to stand on ceremony for our impromptu meeting.

After completing my final analysis of PDN's protocols in relation to the hotel layout, I went home, typed my report, e-mailed Paul, and went to bed. Sleeping wasn't one of my talents, and nightmares were a far too common occurrence. Tonight was no different, and after being forced to explain my reason for resigning from the Office of International Operations earlier today, a familiar nightmare played out in my subconscious mind.

Agent Michael Carver, my old partner, was in the back of the ambulance. Agent Sam Boyle was dead. They didn't even bother to put him in an ambulance after the explosion. It was my order that sent the two of them and my mentor, SSA Mark Jablonsky, into that warehouse. The bomb exploded, and now, I was next to Michael, clutching his hand and watching helplessly as he struggled to breathe. His eyes fluttered, and he flatlined. Jerking awake, I was covered in a cold sweat and screaming.

After the two year anniversary of their deaths, Mark suggested that I stop punishing myself, accept what happened as beyond my control, and move on. I tried. Things were looking better, but with the mandated psych consults required to work as a third party contractor for the government, the depression was back. Although, I was assured by a professional that it was part of the grieving process, and since I never dealt with it properly, this time around, it was kicking my ass.

Thankfully, I had a great support system in place and a job to keep me occupied. Being a private investigator and security consultant sometimes came with lulls in work, and I was grateful that now wasn't one of those times, even if I could have used a break. My last case ended less than a month ago after I sustained a bruised spine, five broken ribs, and almost lost a close friend. Maybe some time off would have been better than signing on to consult for a personal security company.

With any luck, my current job with PDN would be peaceful and nonviolent. Security analyst and corporate consultant might be boring, but they rarely involved blood, guts, and gore. And a break from the violence might be just what I needed.

* * *

"Agent Parker, do you copy?" the radio squawked in my ear, and I snorted at the absurdity. Agent was a vastly inappropriate title.

"Copy," I replied into the radio, running up the steps to the control room to make sure the camera feeds weren't disrupted by the most recent power outage.

PDN was conducting drills at the hotel since my role had been expanded from consulting to monitoring foreign diplomats and evaluating the vicinity for any threats. It sounded like work for the Secret Service, but since the point was to avoid an international incident and the place would be crawling with foreign dignitaries and business types with their own security details, it didn't hurt that we were filling in as rent-a-cops. My reason for being here was simple. First, I was hired by PDN as a freelance consultant, and second, my personal goal was to find balance in the private sector. Ever since I quit my job at the OIO, I tried a little bit of everything, personal bodyguard, police consultant, insurance fraud investigator, stalking cheating spouses, corporate consultant, et cetera, but none of it was the same as being a federal agent.

There was something wrong with me. I needed to solve crimes and arrest people. It's who I am, or rather, who I used to be. Evidence collection, building a case, and filling out hours upon hours of paperwork were all tedious hassles of law enforcement, but I missed it. Maybe I just missed the agents we lost. But until I found closure, I could rub elbows with government employees as an independent contractor. The only real difference was the badge, or so I kept telling myself. There was a time the badge was my only desire. It was everything, and now it was basically nothing. Unfortunately, I never found anything to replace the deep-seated need to be a federal agent. My current job titles left something to be desired – namely arresting people. It must be a justice thing, knowing the boundaries and where the lines were and not to cross them. Private sector work didn't have clearly defined lines, and I'd crossed them a few times over the course of the last couple of years.

"What the hell's taking you so long, Parker?" Paul Eastman hissed in my ear. "Did you get lost on your way to the control room?"

"Sorry." I sighed, realizing I was stuck in my own head. "Cameras are functioning. Nothing odd to report."

"Good. Let's keep it that way."

"Roger. I'll continue to monitor the area from here. Teams one and four should be conducting their walkthroughs within the next ten minutes."

"Afterward, sign off in the lobby and call it a night."

"Yes, sir."

"Hey, Alexis," he suddenly broke from his stiff radio protocol, "I know these practice runs are boring, but it's important. We have to devise contingencies for every possibility. It's how PDN works and why the Secret Service gave us the contract for this international conference. If your head's not in the game, I need to know."

"I'm focused."

"You better be." The radio let out a staticky sound, and then he added, "Going radio silent."

"Copy that."

I remained in the control room, watching the row of screens. Eventually, the unit assigned to guard the perimeter came into view and physically checked the exterior. A couple of minutes later, a secondary team assigned to the emergency stairwell appeared on monitor seven, ensuring all the doors were properly sealed. After watching the two teams go from monitor to monitor while performing their duties, I went downstairs to the lobby, signed the sheet, and disconnected the earpiece and radio. Before I could make it out of the small security office, Paul came up behind me.

"Alex," he nodded to the sheet, "any problems to report?"

"None." I met his eyes, wanting to go home and not get chewed out for the delay in responding earlier. I was distracted, but it wouldn't happen again.

"Care to explain?"

"Don't call me agent."

He narrowed his eyes slightly, and I realized it was a test. "Your psych evaluation indicated you were having some personal issues concerning your previous career."

"I always have personal issues. But guess what." I forced a fake smile on my face. "They're personal, and in no way will they interfere with my job performance."

"Can I ask you a question? According to your résumé and personnel file, you've been through some serious shit, but you always come out on top. So how come something from way back when is giving you pause now?"

"You read the report?" He nodded, waiting for me to say the words. "I didn't deal with it at the time, and now, I'm in a position to accept it and move on. A lot has happened since. This shouldn't be a hindrance any longer."

"I'll see you tomorrow. One more practice until the real thing."

"Can't wait." Feigning enthusiasm, I gave him another fake smile and left the building.

On the drive home, I contemplated the gig and took a detour to my office. Something was bothering me about the building set-up, and I wanted to check the blueprints. Since PDN hired me as a security consultant, I needed to assess their plans and implementations again. However, from the role I'd recently been assigned, it seemed obvious Mr. Eastman thought that I was just another one of the guards he could order around and harass with personal questions, which didn't mesh well with my personality since taking orders wasn't one of my many talents.

The location chosen for the upcoming conference was

one of the most elite hotels in the city. Level upon level was blocked off for nothing more than foreign dignitaries, their entourages, and their security details. For the most part, they weren't my main concern. Each diplomat had their own protection. Bodyguards, trained military personnel, and the like would ensure their safety. Plus, the Secret Service had actual agents patrolling these areas and fulfilling the every whim of ambassadors, politicians, and diplomats. PDN's role was much less pronounced. Even though we were all temporarily considered Secret Service agents, we were third party hired guns to maintain the peace on the main levels of the hotel. Actually, since I was hired to consult for a third party, did that make me a fourth party? My head spun with that possibility, so I got back on track.

The reason for this meeting of the minds was to work on an international business proposal combining technology and transportation to improve the international rail system in Europe. Along with dignitaries, the European Union was sending their greatest and most influential men and women. Basically, whoever possessed the finances to pull the strings behind the curtains of government would be present. Most were billionaires with deep pockets and their hands in everything from energy to weapons to consumer products. It wasn't that different from the types of business people I was used to dealing with at Martin Technologies, except the powers that be at my former corporate gig looked like a lemonade stand compared to the people at this conference.

I did my best to avoid the details concerning the point of the conference. All I needed to know was that I was hired by PDN to evaluate their plans and techniques and ensure everything ran like clockwork. That was until the Secret Service made all PDN personnel, consultants included, undergo the official government vetting process and evaluation. Now I could consider myself on temporary loan to Homeland Security. Maybe I still wanted to be a federal agent, but not like this. Someone gag me.

PDN had been in the personal and corporate security business for a few decades. Their plans were efficient, well thought, and the same ones used since the company's creation. There was no reason to mess with tried and true, but that also meant their tactics could be easily discovered. After an initial review, I suggested some slight modifications. Paul Eastman, the man in charge of this operation and the one who hired me, took my advice and beefed up security. He even went so far as to implement some of the emergency procedures I created when I was the security advisor at Martin Technologies. However, those plans were meant for a single office building with regular employees. This was a hotel with guests, staff, and hundreds of visitors daily. The building wasn't as secure, and that was a main concern for the actual government agencies to deal with. PDN was small potatoes compared to the three letter acronyms scouring the building and checking every guest and employee's background.

Instead, I focused my attention on the stairwells. When I was monitoring the walkthrough earlier, I noticed a few doors in the basement that supposedly led to nothing. After searching the online databases, particularly the fire department's database for building codes, I realized that the hotel's original foundation was expanded after an extensive remodel in the 1980s. Despite the thirty-something year difference, there was another subbasement underneath that originally connected to the underground metro system. Crap.

Dialing Eastman, I checked the time. It was after ten, and I was tired of burning the midnight oil. Sleep when you're dead, Parker. When the call went to voicemail, I suggested he reconsider the implemented basement security in light of these new details and hung up. Placing the phone back in its cradle, I hit the flashing red button and listened to half a dozen messages on my office answering machine.

Mark Jablonsky, my friend and mentor from the OIO, called to check in. He was worried about me after my last case and failure to be reinstated at the OIO. We didn't talk about it, but attempting to pass the government's physical requirements with five broken ribs probably wasn't the soundest decision a person could make, particularly after accidentally being drugged a couple of weeks prior to that. Then again, there was the very real possibility that was subconscious self-preservation to keep me from returning to something I swore I'd never do. Sabotage might just be my only saving grace.

After calling him back and reassuring him that I was fine, I listened to the rest of the messages. The majority was telemarketers, but Luc Guillot, the vice president of Martin Technologies, left a message in regards to my previous stint working for them. The last message was from James Martin himself. He was the CEO of MT and the love of my life. We'd been to hell and back, and he still didn't run for the hills. Smiling, I listened as he warned that Luc would be calling soon for business reasons. Then he asked when we could see each other since he was going away on business next week. Unsure of what Luc wanted or how long the modifications would take once Eastman considered my request, I didn't bother to call Martin back since I didn't know what my schedule looked like. Scribbling a note to call Guillot first thing in the morning, I locked up the office and went home.

My one bedroom apartment was quiet and depressing. After reheating some leftovers, I curled up on the couch with my dinner and flipped mindlessly through the channels, failing to find anything to watch. Turning to a late night show, I finished eating, put the plate on the coffee table, and slumped further into the cushions. When infomercials came on, I changed the channel, pulled the blanket off the back of the couch, and fell asleep to the TV. When morning came, I turned off the TV, tried to work the kinks out of my neck and back, feeling the slight pinch of still healing bones, dropped last night's plate in the sink, set the coffeemaker, and took a shower.

By the time I emerged, I wanted nothing more than to curl up on the couch and go back to sleep. Face it, Parker, you're depressed. My internal voice commented while I poured a cup of coffee and phoned Guillot. The stupid mandated therapy sessions from PDN made it worse. Normally, I was excellent at compartmentalizing, but this was one of those stare down the enemy situations. And for the last two years, I'd been hiding from the enemy. It was time I got over this. Perhaps moving on really would be for the best.

Pushing pointless thoughts away, I listened to the MT assistant inform me that Guillot was in a meeting, and he would have to call me back. That wasn't helpful, so I dialed Martin's cell. He was always busy; that was just a side effect of being a workaholic. Luckily, being his girlfriend came with a few perks.

"Hey, sweetheart," he cooed. "Did you get my message?"

"Yes, but I'm not calling because of that. I'm calling because of whatever Luc wants. What's going on?"

"You don't work here anymore, so it's entirely up to you if you want to address this issue."

"What issue?" I hated it when he was intentionally vague.

"There's something wrong with one of the emergency protocols within our security system. The entire MT security system, not just this building, and Guillot was hoping since you devised the plans that you would consider coming back to evaluate the situation."

"How long?" I didn't want to work for MT when I was sleeping with the big boss, even though Martin did all he could to separate our private life from our professional one.

"A month or two. I don't know. You'll have to ask him."

"All right." I sighed. "I'll call him after four, and with any luck, he'll be available then. Right now, I have to convince someone else that security needs further revisions. Why is this the story of my life?"

"It's better than killers and kidnappers, isn't it?"

"I guess," I hedged. He knew how neurotic I could be, so there was no need for qualification on that statement. "I promise we'll get together before you leave, but I don't know when yet. But I'll see you soon."

"I'm holding you to that, Alex." He lowered his voice. "Stay safe. I love you."

"I know. Me too."

TWO

Standing in the basement, Eastman and I were assessing the security situation. The three questionable doors were sealed shut, but anyone with some spare time and a blowtorch could get them open. A few of his guys were reviewing the blueprints, and one of the local fire chiefs came by to explain the architectural changes.

"Was the city planner busy?" I remarked, snarky as always. "What about someone from metro? They probably know the old subway lines better than most."

"Odd," Eastman glanced in my direction, "there wasn't any mention of insubordination in your employee records."

"Probably because it's just so prevalent it didn't need to be expounded on." I smirked and flipped to another page of building schematics. "Obviously, there isn't much we can do to permanently shut the doors. As far as anyone knows, they're already sealed."

"But you disagree?" Eastman raised a questioning eyebrow, and the fire chief let out a snort.

"She's right, y'know." He flipped through the database on his tablet. "We fielded a couple of calls a few months back. There were abandoned tunnels, closed off for years, that we discovered dozens of people living inside. Nothing remains shut forever."

"Chief, do you think a couple of your guys can take us down to check the doors from the other side?" I asked.

"Fine by me." He radioed to a few of his men to drop by and escort us through the abandoned system.

"Maybe you could post a few more guards in the tunnels," I suggested to Paul, "that way the doors are secure from both sides."

"It's no wonder people don't mention what a pain in the ass you are since you're actually a decent consultant."

"I was surprised too." I grinned, and he rolled his eyes at the comment. "Other than that, I'd say PDN is set to monitor the perimeter and assist the Secret Service. I didn't find any other obvious flaws in your planning."

"Great," he remarked, nonplussed. "Let's take a walk, Alexis, and we'll check out those doors together."

"Whatever you say, sir." My personality has a habit of getting in the way. Flippant comments and sarcasm were the two most powerful weapons in my arsenal, and as of yet, there was no discernible on or off switch to the jibes. Thankfully, Eastman was only a stickler for procedure and not for what some may construe to be disrespectful banter.

Led by a couple of firefighters who seemed less than enthused to be our tour guides, we made our way through the city's underbelly. Using a nearby maintenance shaft, we gained access to the abandoned tunnels that led to the hotel's sealed subbasement. On the way, one of the chattier firemen asked why we were interested in sealed doors that led to a sealed floor, and Paul gestured that I should answer that question. Unfortunately, I didn't have a great answer, even though it still seemed reasonable to me.

"It's a possible security threat. C'mon, guys, you have all those fire codes. How many of them can you guarantee will lead to a fire?" I questioned.

"They all could," one of the men answered, realizing the point of my analogy. "Fine. I'm just thankful you're not consulting for us." He glanced back at my boss and then at me. "No offense."

"None taken," I replied as we reached the third door. "Why don't you take a crack at this one?" The firefighter yanked on the door handle then took a crowbar and tried to pry it open. It was bolted and sealed. After a minute of metal clanging, he gave up. "How long would it take to get one of these doors open?"

"With the proper equipment, under eight minutes," he responded.

"What type of equipment would you need?" Paul asked while I surveyed the dimly lit, abandoned subway tracks, checking for other maintenance paths and entrances.

"Some heavy-duty equipment," the firefighter began, and I caught the gist of the gear needed to burn through the metal door.

Honestly, the doors didn't pose much of a security risk. My earlier assessment might have been premature. After climbing back up the maintenance shaft and resurfacing in the light of day, I thanked the men and headed back to the hotel with Eastman.

"Satisfied?" he asked, knowing our outing proved that his current security plans were still viable.

"Yes, but I would suggest posting a permanent guard in the basement, just in case. It's rather unlikely, but you never know."

"Did I hear you volunteer?" He smiled, and I realized my stint working for PDN would now include sentry duty for three derelict doors in addition to everything else. Oh well, you win some, you lose some.

"Apparently," I growled as we went inside the hotel to perform a final set of drills before the conference tomorrow.

I shadowed the teams as they conducted their equipment checks, door checks, and security implementation review. Then I went upstairs to the control room and watched as everyone performed as planned. Constant roving sweeps, patrols, and a strongly visible security presence was the role PDN was playing. The actual government agents were keeping much lower profiles. They hoped to blend in with the business and political types in order to better ensure security. Hell, we were basically decoys.

"One more time on the contingencies for power outage,

medical emergency, and fire," Eastman instructed on the comms, and his teams performed as expected. If only real life were this calculating, there wouldn't be any problems. But real life was messy. There was nothing surgical or practiced about what could happen, and I just hoped that everything would go off without a hitch. Any hiccups in the plan would most likely be dealt with by someone's private security or a government agent. We were window decoration that marched well and looked good on paper. "Great job. Reconvene in the main conference room for our final briefing." The radio squawked, and I remembered just how much I loathed two-way communication.

As the Secret Service agent described in extreme minutiae what PDN's role was and how to avoid impeding the actual agents, I checked the time. It was a little after 4:30, and I wanted to step out to call Guillot. The longer the droning continued, the more I realized just how pointless PDN really was. We were toy soldiers in a sea of former Special Forces. It was sad and somewhat disappointing, but these were the types of gigs consultants ended up with. Waiting impatiently for the briefing to end, as soon as the room opened to questions, I ducked out, dialing Guillot on the way.

"Mademoiselle Parker," he answered, not surprised to hear from me thanks to Martin, "how are you?"

"Monsieur Guillot," I replied, knowing he enjoyed some familiarity with his native language on occasion, "I'm bogged down with a job at the moment, but your message sounded urgent. What's wrong with the security implementations?" Several months ago, I was assigned to completely overhaul the security system from equipment to training. Obviously, whatever went wrong was my fault.

"There's an issue with the elevators," he began, struggling to find the proper method of describing it. "We were conducting our monthly check, and a few of the security officers brought this to my attention."

"Okay, I'll need to see the report they filed. Is Jeffrey Myers back on guard duty?" Myers was head of security, and he was easy to work with. "I can speak to him and figure out how complicated the issue really is."

"So you'll fix it?" Guillot sounded surprised.

"Well, it was my screwup." I took a breath. "That is, if you trust me to fix it."

"Of course. Shall I have HR draft a consulting contract?"

"Not yet. Let me see how complicated the issue is before MT hires me again. I feel like I burned some bridges when I left."

"Nonsense." He lowered his voice. "There's always a place for you here, regardless of your relationship with James."

"Yeah, well, I don't like mixing business with pleasure, but I'll be by to correct this problem later in the week. My schedule is booked for the next few days, so it'll probably be Thursday afternoon or Friday morning." While I spoke, a few Secret Service agents left the room, signifying the briefing was concluded.

"D'accord. The report will be in the security office, awaiting your arrival."

Disconnecting, I turned around to find Paul waiting for me. He narrowed his eyes and watched as I shoved my cell phone into my pocket. "I take it you didn't have any questions for the Secret Service."

"They've been doing this awhile. I think they have it under control." I hesitated before adding, "What else do you want from me? I've reviewed your procedures, double-checked all your employee backgrounds, and cross-referenced them to the foreign parties. Everyone is clear. The plan is clear, and all systems are go."

"Come with me," he instructed, leading the way down the corridor and to one of the suites in the hotel. He slid the keycard through the slot and held the door. Entering, I gave him a quizzical look, and he shrugged. "This room was rented so I could stay close in case there was any type of problem."

"And people think I can't separate from the job," I quipped.

"Take a seat." He gestured to the couch, and I sat primly. "Do you drink?"

"On occasion. I don't have a problem in case that's what you're asking."

"It wasn't." He pulled a can of beer from the mini-fridge and held it in my direction, but I shook my head. "Just for the record, neither do I." He popped the top and took a sip before sitting in the chair across from me. "Your résumé is impressive. It seems you could have your pick of consulting work anywhere you want. And with the scuttlebutt I've been hearing from the government employees, I'd say you could get your old job back in a heartbeat." I stared, not wanting to voice a protest when I was still unaware of the point of this dialogue. "So tell me, what is PDN really doing at this international business conference?"

"Putting on a good show. I'm sure you must have realized that."

"That was my first inclination, but after they made everyone go through the government background checks and psych exams, I thought maybe I was wrong." Judging from his tone, he found the thought of his team being solely for show disheartening.

"Everyone coming and going has to pass the same background checks, just look at the hotel employees and caterers, but I'd say it's safe to assume that your role in all of this is miniscule."

"When did you realize it?" he asked.

"The moment the Secret Service said they were still monitoring the situation."

"Then why'd we check out those doors this afternoon?"

"Sometimes, the government agencies still miss things. Honestly, I believed the doors could be a possible breach point, but after our tour through the tunnels, it seems unlikely."

"Are there any other breach points that you noticed?" he asked, taking another swig from the can.

I stood and went to the window, noticing his luggage in the corner of the room. The guy must have been staying at the hotel so he'd be around to deal with any possible problems or threats, and I just told him it was for nothing. Like I concluded, lack of an official role really sucked.

"Everything is covered by one security entity or another. Maybe the roof would be viable, but that would require a helicopter. The large windows on the sides of the building could also pose a danger, but that would mean targeting a specific individual in a gun's scope or a breach by a team with extensive rappelling capabilities. Frankly, if any of those things occur, duck and cover because the situation will turn into a bloodbath." Turning around, he didn't seem shocked by my commentary.

"So we're window dressing," he finished the can and put it on the table. "You know, Alexis, I tried to join the military ages ago, but I couldn't get in on account of an irregular heartbeat. Then I tried to join one of these government agencies, but I was rejected for lack of experience and education. Finally, I applied to the police academy, and they rejected me for the same reason the military did. Private security is all I've ever known." He shut his eyes and shook his head. "Just once, I'd like to think something I do actually makes a difference."

"Don't sell yourself short." I wasn't one for pep talks. Too much doom and gloom ran through my veins. "There's no way of knowing what kind of an impact your job may have made. Hell," I glanced around the room, "who knows what's gonna happen at this conference. With any luck, everything will run smoothly, and if it does, just remember, that's probably because you ran countless drills and made sure all the contingencies were in order."

"Yeah, like that does anything."

"An outward show of security can be a great deterrent. That's why convenience stores sometimes leave broken surveillance cameras posted on the walls. If someone thinks they're being watched, they won't steal anything."

"And you think the same principle applies here?"

"I know it does. And so does the government agency that approved PDN for this gig. They wouldn't have asked for your help if they didn't need it. So remember that." I collected my purse from the couch. "Was there anything else you needed tonight, sir?"

"Not unless you wanted to join me for dinner. The room service here is killer."

"I'll pass. See you tomorrow at oh eight hundred." I opened the door. "I'll be the one in the basement, making sure the sealed doors stay sealed." As I pulled the door shut behind me, I shook my head and let out a growl. Since when did consulting require cheerleading, pep talks, and being asked to dinner? He was lucky my firearm was locked in my car after the day I had.

THREE

My entire body ached. Standing in the same place for hours on end wasn't recommended for anyone with ribs still on the mend. Although it had been a month since I damaged my already broken ribs, it set the healing process back to the beginning, so it'd probably be another two weeks until the soreness abated. In the meantime, my entire back and torso hurt. I strolled through the basement, glancing at the emergency exit and the maintenance room. There was no reason to think anything was amiss, and I'd been down here for the last six hours without any strange happenstance occurring.

When I arrived at the hotel this morning, I was briefed before ensuring everyone at PDN was positioned properly and the comms were up and running. Since then, I'd been in total seclusion. The only activity I witnessed was the occasional hotel employee running some mundane errand inside one of the storage rooms. Everything else was quiet. Deciding to give my legs and back a rest, I did a final check of the area and slid to the floor.

It was only three p.m., and I was bored out of my mind. Not to mention, I was tired, hungry, and in a pissy mood. Shift change was in an hour, and I was counting the minutes until I could take a break. Granted, it wasn't much of a break. I'd get an hour off, and then I was on guard duty until six this evening. The day's business conference was scheduled to end at that time. The guests would depart to their rooms or go about whatever travel itinerary they had planned, and I could go home. At least the seclusion was a nice reprieve from listening to the droning of business proposals and the same information being repeated by dozens of translators.

While I waited for my relief to show up, I listened to a few radio transmissions regarding one of the caterers. Someone forgot their security badge and was denied access to the event. PDN was handling the situation, and eventually, the man was turned away. He left without too much protest, probably because he didn't really give a shit about catering. Not that I could blame him. Since there were no other significant transmissions following that incident, I didn't think his attempt to infiltrate the business function was a ploy to assassinate one of the delegates.

"Alexis," I tilted my head toward the voice, "ready to go upstairs?" Eastman asked. He led one of the newbies down the stairs to take over my position while I went on break. "Reyes will fill in." He raised an eyebrow as I stood and headed to meet him. "Is there anything he should know?"

"Don't get caught sitting down on the job," I replied, winking at the man and following Eastman up the steps while I pulled the radio free from my jacket.

"How are you holding up?" Paul asked, pushing the elevator call button. "Is the monotony getting to you?"

"No, I'm fine." I glanced at him and noticed a grin on his face. "What?"

"Nothing. It's not often I find my guards sitting on the floor. Y'know, there are chairs in the hotel."

"The basement is lacking in furniture," I retorted. "Plus, I was assessing different vantage points. And for the record, you didn't hire me to be a guard. Sentry duty wasn't in my contract."

"I suppose it wasn't." He glanced at his watch as the elevator opened on the conference level. "Give me your radio and go home." He held out his hand.

"Sir?"

"I'm not punishing you." He leaned against the elevator doors to keep them open. "You're right. You're not a guard." His eyes studied my posture. "Old injury acting up?" He nudged his chin toward my arms, wrapped around my ribcage.

"You could say that, but it's okay. I'm not about to leave you shorthanded. What kind of consultant would I be to cause a breach in your security protocols?"

"I have three guys on standby, and like you said yesterday, the basement isn't a feasible entry point. But if you're so insistent on helping out, then you can come back tomorrow afternoon and monitor the security feed. Deal?"

"Deal." I handed him the radio and stepped to the side as he exited the elevator. "What time?"

"Noon."

"See you then." I pushed the button for the lobby and waited for the doors to close. At least I didn't have to stay in the dusty basement and be bored for the rest of the day.

Instead, I went to the MT building to get a jump on their current security issues. Entering the building, I set the metal detectors buzzing. I forgot my handgun was in my purse, but thankfully, Jeffrey Myers was working the security desk. He smiled and waved away the two guards that attempted to intervene.

"Sorry, Jeffrey," I blushed, getting caught in a compromising position for the second time today, "I came from work and forgot to leave the heavy artillery in the car."

"It's not a big deal. I don't think you're planning a hostile takeover."

Chuckling at the business humor, I took a seat next to him behind the security counter. "Mr. Guillot called the other day about a security issue with the elevators. I didn't realize I'd be available this quickly or else I would have called first. So what's the problem?"

Jeffrey went to a filing cabinet and pulled out the binder of emergency provisions, flipped through the tabbed pages, and laid it on the desk between us. "As you know, the elevators automatically lock in the event of a fire and go into fire service mode." He flipped through the diagrams.

"And as is required by the state licensing board, fire department, and the protocols you developed, we've implemented that they return to the lobby and open unless smoke has been detected on that level in which case they will open on an alternate level."

"Right, we selected four as the alternate because of the stairwell and freight elevator options in addition to easier access to the service entrance." I skimmed through the sheets, unable to determine what the problem was.

"Exactly. It seemed like a great plan," he hesitated, "but apparently the problem occurs when the elevator doors open and then smoke is detected afterward. It sets off the sprinklers."

"Okay, and...?"

"And once the sprinklers kick on, the elevator locks because of the electrical preventatives in place."

"Shit," I cursed, rubbing my eyes, "does it do it on all levels or just the lobby?"

Jeffrey's eyes went wide, and he sighed. "I didn't think to check."

"Obviously, there's a lot of that going around." I flipped through a few more pages. "What about manually overriding the system once it's locked? Have you tried that?"

"The complete shutdown of the electrical system prevents a manual override," he replied. The point was to prevent an accidental electrocution or fire, except this was still the case even in the event of a pre-existing fire.

There had to be some other way around the issue, but I couldn't find it. Fuck. There was no easy fix. Either the electrical security preventions in place had to be changed, or the elevator's response system needed to be modified. The only thing left to do was figure out which was a better solution.

"Do you mind if I sit here and think about things for a while? If I'm in your way, I can go."

"No, stay put. You're not bothering me. I just figured you'd be more comfortable in your office."

A laugh escaped my lips. "I hate to break the news to you, but I don't work here anymore. I haven't worked here in four months, maybe five."

"That explains why I haven't seen you around." His brows furrowed. "Why are you doing this?" He tapped the binder.

"It's my mess to clean up."

"It was an oversight, Miss Parker." He graced me with a reassuring smile. "No one blames you. Stuff like this happens."

"Well, I'd feel better knowing it's fixed. Blunders on my record don't bode well for future job opportunities."

"Why did you leave MT?"

"Personal reasons," I replied. "I should let you get back to work. Maybe I'll have a talk with maintenance. Can I borrow a visitor's pass? I still have my old I.D. card, but I'm guessing it's inactive."

Jeffrey pulled a pass from the drawer and handed it to me. "I think your card is still programmed, but if you need some assistance, just holler."

"Thanks." Clipping on the pass, I went to the elevator, intent on speaking with maintenance to come up with a plan of attack for the current dilemma.

Maintenance was little help, but they gave me a few numbers to call for electricians and elevator operators. I returned to the security desk and made a few calls, asked dozens of questions, and eventually dialed the fire department for their input. After performing my due diligence, I phoned maintenance to share my findings.

Absently doodling on the corner of a sheet of paper while I waited for someone to take me off hold, it seemed the problem might have a simple solution. We might be able to reprogram the manual override without changing too many of the safeguards already in place. It was worth a shot.

"Miss Parker, are you still there?" the technician asked as soon as he came back on the line.

"Yes. What's the verdict?"

"It seems your plan is feasible. We should be able to rewrite the code and modify the systems so the sprinklers don't cause a complete electrical shutdown in the building. If we reroute the elevator functions to a separate system, then they won't be affected and the protocols established will remain in place."

"Really?" That was easier than I thought.

"Well, theoretically, yes."

"All right, run a few diagnostics, write up the proposal and e-mail a copy to me. I have to get approval before we implement anything, but I'd like to know all the details and finer points before I pitch it to Mr. Guillot and the Board." Apparently, I escaped one business meeting to put myself directly in the line of fire of another one. No wonder I enjoyed consulting for the police better. Crime was so much easier to handle.

"Yes, ma'am. When do you need it?"

"The sooner, the better. If it's at all possible, Friday morning at the latest."

"I think we can swing that. Have a good afternoon."

"Thanks, you too." Hanging up, I leaned back in the chair and snatched the abandoned cup of coffee off the security desk. With all the calls and notes, I forgot all about my caffeine fix. Gulping down the remainder of the now cold coffee, I shut my eyes and inhaled. I worked in this building every day for a little over six months and sporadically on and off for a year before that, but somehow, it felt foreign. Spotting Jeffrey returning from an errand, I collected my notes and unclipped the pass. "I appreciate the desk and the coffee." Maneuvering around the counter, I dug around in my purse for my car keys. "Fair warning, I'll probably be back Friday."

"No problem." He winked. "Maybe I'll just have to call in sick."

"But you're my favorite security guard."

"I'm everyone's favorite security guard. And it's executive security guard to you." He smiled, and snickering, I pulled on the monogrammed brass door handle and exited into the late afternoon sunlight.

FOUR

"It looks like you're having fun," Paul Eastman said as he entered the control room. "Anything substantial to report?"

"The furniture isn't much more comfortable than the floor," I remarked, glancing at him before returning my gaze to the row of monitors. "Other than that, nothing out of the ordinary."

"Good." Pulling out a chair, he sat next to me. "Are you feeling better today?"

"I'm fine." Small talk wasn't one of my favorite things. I much preferred silence, even awkward silence.

"Alexis," he scooted closer, and I caught the vaguest whiff of something fermented, "I'm just making some friendly chitchat so the hours pass faster. You have to give a guy something to work with." When I failed to immediately fill the brief pause in conversation, he continued. "What is it? GSW? Stabbing?"

"Broken bones. Ribs. Again." I snorted. "They healed much faster the first time, but they aren't an issue. Just sore sometimes." My prattling seemed more awkward than the silence, and I wondered why he was showing such an interest. I'd only known him for the last couple of weeks since getting hired on at PDN.

"How'd it happen?"

Despite the fact I didn't want to talk about it, I couldn't come up with a good enough reason not to. "My last job involved going toe-to-toe with a steroidal bull of a man. Asshole tried to snap me in half."

"Ouch."

"You could say that." In order to get him to stop asking questions, I posed one of my own. "When do you think the conference will end? Have they reached an agreement or understanding of what they hope to accomplish with the proposed railway?"

"They're merging transportation lines across the European continent. It's supposed to be some type of bullet train. From my understanding, yesterday, they decided on a design. Today, they're determining which nations are responsible for the building and maintenance."

"No wonder we have diplomats and business tycoons at this meeting of the minds," I commented more to myself than Paul, "it's politics and business."

"That's a pretty damn accurate summation." His chair let out a squeak as he readjusted in the seat. "I was wondering if you'd like to grab a bite after the surveillance is through for the night."

"My boyfriend and I have plans," I lied. Although, I really did need to make plans with Martin soon.

"I wasn't asking you out. Why don't you have him meet us?"

"Sorry, but no." A million excuses ran through my head, but there was no need. No was no. It didn't require any additional qualifiers or explanation.

"I know this must seem like prying, but are you dating James Martin of Martin Technologies?" I spun in my chair to face him, my mouth practically falling open at this complete intrusion of my privacy. How the hell did he know this? Paul laughed nervously. "I'm not stalking you or anything like that. But Martin Technologies was listed on your résumé, and I have a few friends on the Board. When I called to check your references, well," he looked embarrassed, "we got to talking."

"Is there a point?" My tone was icy.

"No, just curious."

Studying him, I was certain he was lying, but I had no basis for proving it or confronting him. Until now, Paul Eastman didn't set my radar buzzing, but given that he was asking about Martin, I was suspicious. "Bullshit." If Paul fired me, then so be it. "What do you really want?"

"Whoa, hey," he held up his hands in surrender, "take it easy. I was just asking." Glaring at him, he realized I wasn't buying it. "And," he hesitated, "I overheard the head of one of the engineering companies talking last night after the conference. It was hours after you left. He wanted a meeting with Martin Technologies about an unrelated business proposal. I thought maybe I could convince the CEO to have a chat with him."

Narrowing my eyes, I scrutinized Eastman, but I couldn't determine his motivation. "So you're such an altruist that you thought you'd help the guy out? I don't believe you." I also didn't believe that he happened to overhear something like that. Coincidences didn't happen like this.

"Maybe I mentioned something about having a connection to the company. Perhaps there was some talk of a finder's fee."

"Unbelievable. Is this the only reason you even hired me?" I was always afraid people would use Martin to get to me, but apparently I thought of myself much more highly than the rest of the world.

"No. Your credentials are amazing."

We sat in the uncomfortable, tense control room for another few minutes, but I was fuming. I needed a minute to regroup before I said or did something I would regret. Maybe I was overreacting.

"Sir," I wanted to throw something, "pay attention to the monitors since I need to take a break." There was no question, and as soon as the words left my mouth, I was out of the room.

Pacing the hallway, I wasn't sure how to react or what to do. Something was fishy, and I didn't like it. Unfortunately, I was stuck until a business agreement was reached. As I stormed down the hallway, one of the Secret Service agents stopped me to ask if I was okay. After explaining that everything was fine, I went back to the control room and sat down.

"What happened to monitor nine?" I asked, noticing the picture was fuzzy and the screen kept flickering. At least it was a nice distraction.

"I don't know. Maybe one of the cables is on the fritz." He picked up the radio and asked someone on level seven to check it out. "Apparently, this place is falling apart without you."

"Where do you get the audacity to try to use me to—" I began, but the radio squawked with a cry for assistance. The words were barely even out before the comms went dead. Great. "Stay here," I growled, halfway out the door.

The Secret Service agent disappeared down the corridor, and I followed. If the government agents were responding, then this probably wasn't a drill. Seriously, I left the control room for less than five minutes. All hell should not be breaking loose right now. From what I gathered, the conference was still underway, so whatever it was must not be that dire since it didn't disrupt the moguls from making more money.

After descending three flights of stairs, I burst through the stairwell door to find a man swinging from a metal fixture with a thick electrical cable wrapped around his neck like a noose. One of the PDN guards was vomiting in the corner as the Secret Service cordoned off the hallway.

"Who is he?" I asked, hoping someone would have an answer. I didn't recognize him, but that didn't mean a thing. He could be one of PDN's guys, a federal agent, private security, a hotel employee, one of the diplomats or businessmen, or someone completely random.

"No I.D.," one of the agents replied. At least someone was brave enough to check for a pulse and the man's wallet. "The more important question is is this self-inflicted." He spun and met my eyes. "Get your people out of the hallway before they contaminate anything else and keep it quiet. Until we have time to process this and gather information, no one's leaving."

"Aye, sir," I replied, managing to corral the two PDN guards out of the hallway and back to the stairwell. "All nonessential personnel will monitor the area and stop anyone from leaving. Our two guys that found the body will wait in the conference room for your instructions."

The agent nodded, radioing the orders to all the other private sector guards as we made the trek upstairs. At least radio communication was up and running again.

"What did you see?" I asked. Mike Talbot and Kenneth Anderson were the two PDN guards that discovered the body. Kenneth was the one with the weak stomach, and Mike looked ready for a fight. Apparently not everyone who comprised the guard squad at PDN was hardened paramilitary. "Did anything strange happen before you discovered the body?"

"Nothing, ma'am," Mike replied, and I gritted my teeth, hating the term ma'am. "We were conducting our normal patrol. We'd already walked it a dozen times when Mr. Eastman radioed that something was up with camera nine. When we diverted to check it out, we found that man hanging from a nearby power cable. I think the electrical interference temporarily shorted out the radio."

"Not the camera cable?" I asked. Even though I knew for a fact it was a separate cable, I wanted to test Mike's recollection. Most people didn't pay attention, and their subconscious would fill in details, oftentimes inaccurate details.

"Different cables. I believe those are utility cables, jutting out of the ceiling tiles."

"Okay," I nodded, "anything else you remember?" Mike shook his head, and I turned my gaze to Kenneth as the elevator opened. "Are you okay, Mr. Anderson?"

"Yes, ma'am."

"Okay, guys, it's Alex, not ma'am." I led them down the hallway to the conference room where we had been briefed two days ago. "Stay here. I'll be right back." Tossing a quick glance at them, I asked, "Do either of you need anything?" They shook their heads, but Kenneth looked far too green for his own good.

This was ridiculous. The place was crawling with agents,

private hotel security, and a slew of bodyguards. No one should be swinging from the rafters, particularly not in a swanky hotel and especially not in one that was bursting with security personnel. Who was this guy? How long was he hanging there dead? And was it suicide or murder? Goddamn.

"Alex," Eastman called as I entered the control room which was now packed with Secret Service agents, "what's happening?"

"A body was discovered on the seventh floor. COD and TOD are unknown. Are they calling the police?"

"I don't know. A couple of the federal agents came in and asked questions about the monitors and then shoved me out of the way, so they could watch the surveillance feed. Do we know what happened or who died?"

"No." Spotting the Secret Service agent I followed to the scene entering the office, I made a beeline to him. "What do we know? Was he still warm?" It was a morbid question, but I was under the impression that the camera distortion must have been timed to fit in with the hanging, self-inflicted or otherwise. Therefore, when the corpse was discovered, it still should have been warm.

He narrowed his eyes. "I can't say much, but it wasn't recent." He glanced at Eastman. "The two of you were in the control room and radioed for the team to check out the camera. Go wait in the conference room with the other two PDN employees. We'll send someone in to question you once we figure this mess out."

There was no point in protesting, so I exited the room without another word. Paul asked a few questions and protested the roles we were relegated to, but by the time the elevator doors chimed, he was next to me.

"What happened?" he asked.

"You tell me," I growled, entering the elevator and hitting the close door button. "I only left you alone for a few minutes, and when I came back, monitor nine was on the fritz. What the hell happened in those three minutes I was gone?"

He snorted. "You really think I had something to do with this? In case you've forgotten, Ms. Parker, I'm in charge of this team and fortifying hotel security. So why the hell would I orchestrate a murder?"

"You tell me."

"I didn't do it. And as soon as we're dismissed, turn over your I.D. and get the hell out. You're fired."

"Actually, I quit." I shoved the radio and temporary security pass at him. "And if you come anywhere near me or Martin Technologies, I will take out a restraining order and file stalking charges against you."

"God," he muttered, "I can't believe that I ever hired someone like you. A paranoid, delusional, psycho bitch."

"Keep talking and I'll add a few more items to that list."

As soon as the elevator doors opened, I stormed out. Death made me bitchy, and my ex-boss was at the top of my suspect list. First, he came into the control room, smelling of liquor and asking inappropriate questions, and then he supposedly missed the disturbance on camera nine, and now there was a dead man inside the hotel. Maybe that was paranoia, but I preferred to call it cautious.

Opening the door, I stepped inside. At least in the conference room, Mike and Kenneth could act as a buffer. The room was windowless and isolating. Were the cops on the way? Who was taking point on the murder, if it even was a murder? So many questions needed answers, and here I was, unable to get them and not permitted to leave. My role at the hotel was over. Either I was fired or I quit, and oddly enough, my mind was focused on which of those would be the case instead of the corpse on level seven.

Eastman kept his distance and made small talk with the other two PDN employees. Kenneth was no longer green, but he was a ghostly shade of pale. The fact that his boss kept dithering on about sports scores wasn't helping to take the edge off. Typically, I would have offered whatever sage advice I had based on personal experience, but I didn't want to interact with Eastman or anyone he was talking to. Mike seemed to catch on to this because he would glance in my direction every so often. The minutes ticked by, and the faintest sound of sirens echoed in the distance.

Another hour later, and I wondered if I imagined the

sirens. Then I spotted a uniformed police officer at the conference room door. He spoke a few words to the Secret Service agent who accompanied him. Then he opened the door.

"Ms. Parker? May I have a word?"

"Absolutely," I replied, standing.

Eastman glanced up, looking startled. "For the record, gentlemen, Ms. Parker is no longer a PDN employee. Nothing she says is representative of PDN or its mission."

The law enforcement officer ignored Paul, and I rolled my eyes, resisting the urge to comment further. It would be childish to sink to his level. I was better than that, and there were more important concerns, like the dead guy swinging from the utility cable.

FIVE

"Detective Jacobs would like a word with you," the cop said, escorting me to the stairwell. When the door opened, Jacobs was speaking with a group of Secret Service agents. After a few minutes, he excused himself and came toward me.

"Parker," he smiled, "funny running into you here."

"What? Were Detectives O'Connell and Heathcliff too busy to make the drive themselves?" I quipped. Jacobs was one of the cops at the precinct, but not someone I worked with. Maybe we said hello in the hallways a few times, but that was it.

"Don't ask." He rolled his eyes. "We've identified the deceased, but at this time, we're not sharing information with any outsiders. Suffice it to say, he's the night clerk, but given the current international conference, they asked if he could pick up a few extra shifts." He flipped open his notepad. "What can you tell me?"

"I don't know the guy. When the camera went wonky, I followed a Secret Service agent and discovered the body."

"No," he shook his head, "what can you tell me about the security personnel that was hired?" He lowered his voice. "Specifically, the guards that discovered the body."

"I don't know much. Everyone went through extensive background checks and psych evals before being granted security clearance by the government. We've all been vetted, so you should ask whoever's in charge of that."

"What was your spat in the elevator about?" He looked up from the notepad, finding a look of surprise on my face. "I did a preliminary review of the security footage around the time the body was discovered."

"My boss, well, ex-boss decided to infringe upon my private life in an attempt to make some under the table deal with one of the businessmen at the conference. I don't take too kindly to being used."

He nodded and made a few notes. "All right, thanks. Officer Sarcone will escort you back to the conference room. And, Parker, try not to put anyone in the hospital while you wait to be formally questioned."

"Then don't make me wait too long." I tossed a sly grin at him and went upstairs. My reputation and smartass attitude were both well-known throughout the police department, so I wasn't worried about Jacobs taking my hollow threat seriously.

"What did they want?" Eastman asked as soon as I returned to the conference room.

"To say hi." I rolled my eyes. "What do you think they wanted?" Since I didn't work for him, there was no need to be respectful.

"When are they planning to question us?" Mike interjected, probably afraid he'd have to separate the two of us. "It'd be nice to get back to work or go home. Shit, it'd be nice just to get out of this room."

"Soon," I muttered, sitting at one end of the table.

Shutting my eyes, I leaned back and visualized the scene. There were too many unknowns. And asking Mike or Kenneth any questions would potentially compromise their interviews, so I resisted. The room remained silent, and my mind wandered to questions concerning jurisdiction. Since the deceased was a hotel employee, the ME would have to determine if it was murder or suicide before the local authorities could investigate. However, with dozens of potential international suspects and Secret

Service agents already onsite, I'd wager Homeland Security or the FBI would step in and take over.

"How the hell are you so goddamn calm?" Eastman asked, and I opened an eye and assessed him. "Yes, I'm talking to you, Alexis. There's a man a few levels away that died on our watch, and the four of us are being treated like suspects. Aren't you going to do something about this?"

"Nope." There were a million arguments I could make and accusations I could throw at him, but there was no point. You can't argue with stupid, just like you can't argue with pompous, and Paul Eastman was a stupid, pompous ass. "I have no jurisdiction here. I'm not even private security anymore."

Before Eastman could say something he'd probably regret, the door opened, and a man dressed in the standard dark suit walked in. "Sorry to keep you gentlemen waiting." He noticed my presence as an afterthought but didn't bother to amend his apology. "I'm Agent Walton, FBI." He held up his identification before taking a seat at the conference table. "From what I understand, two of you found the body."

"That's correct, sir," Mike spoke. "It was me and Kenneth that went to check out the area after Mr. Eastman reported the camera was acting strangely."

"Okay." Walton jotted a note. "Why don't the three of you get some coffee and stretch your legs while I ask Mr.
..."

"Mike Talbot," Mike supplied.

"Mr. Talbot a few questions." Not needing to be told twice, I left the conference room. Kenneth followed close behind, but Eastman prattled on about who he was and how his people shouldn't be questioned without his presence or representation from PDN.

"Buy you a soda?" I offered as a few uniformed officers monitored our movements like we were wanted fugitives.

"I don't want anything." Kenneth shook his head. "That was some freaky shit. It looked like something out of a horror film."

"Eh. I've seen worse, but let's not talk about any of that." Okay, so the only thing I actually wanted to talk about was the scene. Crime solving was my most beloved pastime, rivaled only with being a wiseass. "How long have you worked for Mr. Eastman?"

"Since he's been at PDN, but I've been there longer. Let's see, four years in private security," he made a face, squinting in recollection, "and this is the first time anything freaky has ever happened. Most of the time, we guard a building as it undergoes renovations or get hired on as temps when new businesses begin or require added security, like this." I nodded, glad that he found something less morbid and relevant to talk about. "How long have you been consulting on security matters?"

"A little over two years, and before that, I had a badge and gun. This is all I've ever known, so strange doesn't really register." Hopefully, he would find my words reassuring, but before he could say anything else, one of the police officers escorted Kenneth away to be questioned by a detective. "It's going to be a long night," I muttered, leaning against the wall near the conference room.

The next six hours were filled with nothing but questioning and waiting. The four of us were separated for the interviews to be properly conducted, and everyone with a badge wanted a crack at us. The local police department was considering this a homicide. The FBI was investigating in the event it turned into some type of federal or international crime. The Secret Service was conducting its own internal examination to figure out who screwed up and which heads would be on the chopping block. Frankly, I was surprised the OIO, Homeland Security, the NSA, and every foreign government who had a citizen present in the hotel also didn't come to question us.

"Ms. Parker," Agent Walton said, entering the room and dismissing my current inquisitor, "all PDN employees are relieved of duty for the duration of the conference."

"Well, I'm sure Mr. Eastman has mentioned that I'm not included in that particular subset any longer."

"You've picked a strange time to quit. Is there a reason for it?"

"Personality clash, I suppose. He thought he could use my background and private connections to enhance his pocketbook. We disagreed."

"I see." He shook his head, not wanting to get into the juvenile nature of my current unemployed status. "In the meantime, we're taking everyone in for more formal questioning. Whether you're a PDN employee or not, you're still a material witness."

I smirked. Material witness and feasible person of interest, but comments like that could lead to handcuffs and a reading of my rights. Instead, I smiled appeasingly and stood. "Lead the way, SAC Walton."

The questions were the same. Basic and rudimentary. It didn't matter if we were in a conference room in the hotel or inside an interrogation room at FBI HQ, this was the preliminary interview. Eventually, the investigators would determine if a crime was committed, which of us had means, motive, and opportunity, and then the questions would start to sound much more accusatory. At the moment, they were your garden variety, 'where were you', 'can anyone verify your alibi', and 'did you know the dead man.'

Aside from the questions which were delivered separately by each law enforcement body so the same things were being asked in triplicate, there was nothing else to do but wait. Thankfully, my inquisitors were still being pleasant since I had yet to become an actual suspect, so they took my dinner order, kept my coffee mug filled, and allowed as many bathroom breaks as I liked. Maybe playing nice did have benefits.

After another lull in the questioning, I glanced at my watch. It was morning, and I'd been here all night. On the one hand, I could leave anytime I wanted since I wasn't under arrest, but I didn't want to piss off the investigators. Or at least that's what I kept telling myself. In actuality, I wanted someone to request my expertise and offer me a job. Maybe it was a pipe dream or a delusion based on lack of sleep, but in the past, I'd consulted for the police department and FBI. And since I was familiar with PDN, the conference, and a couple of the Secret Service agents and their mission, it would make sense to seek assistance from an inside man, so to speak.

"Ms. Parker," Jacobs entered the interrogation room with two steaming mugs, "I'm sorry for the delay. I'm sure you didn't expect to spend all night in this room."

"Well, I also didn't expect to encounter a dead guy in the hallway. Shit happens." I inhaled deeply. "Any idea how much longer this will take?"

"You're free to go whenever you like," he whispered, leaning in.

"Yeah, I know, but it seems like someone might need my help." I tossed a glance at the two-way mirror, wondering if anyone was paying a bit of attention. "Did you catch the case, or is it out of your jurisdictional line?"

"I'm not sure yet. My boss, Lt. Moretti, is having a chat with Agent Walton in order to make that determination, so needless to say, one way or another I still have to get the proper paperwork filed." He grimaced.

"Well, I'm at your disposal." Hint, hint.

"I appreciate that." He began on his report while I drank some more coffee. At this point, I might float away. "Why did you leave the control room a few minutes before the mechanical difficulty with the camera?"

"Eastman and I got into an argument, which I've already explained, but suffice it to say, I stepped out to get some distance and air. The Secret Service agent on our level can vouch for me."

"Yeah, I know. I just wondered." His brow furrowed, and it seemed we might have the same thought. "Who initiated the argument?"

"Honestly, I don't know. I blame Eastman, but it was my reaction that led to heated words," I elaborated, recalling as much of the conversation as possible. "At first, I thought he was asking me out, but then things went in a completely different direction that I never expected."

"Did he have any prior knowledge of how to push your buttons?" Jacobs asked, chewing on his pen cap.

"Detective, just ask the question."

"Do you think Paul Eastman purposefully caused the argument so you would leave the room and miss the homicide taking place in the hallway?"

"So it was a homicide." I bit my bottom lip, considering

everything I knew. Mostly, I realized how much I didn't know. "Maybe he did. Off the record, my immediate thought was he was involved, but I have no hard evidence."

"Tell me what your duties were during the conference," Jacobs said.

"Monday, I was assigned to guard the sealed basement doors, which was sort of my idea, but then Paul sent me home early that evening. Today," I shook my head, "sorry, yesterday, I was positioned in the control room." My days were jumbling from being up for close to thirty hours.

"Okay, that could be anything or nothing. Once we sort this out, I'm sure we'll have more questions." He pushed his chair back and stood. "I'll see who drew the short straw, and if this is a police matter, then you're free to go. I'll be back in a few." He left the room, and I sighed. Ten minutes later, he opened the door and jerked his chin at the exit. "Take off, Parker. This is our show, and someone from the precinct will be in touch tomorrow or the next day with a follow-up. If you remember anything in the meantime or run into problems, give me a call." After handing me his card, he disappeared into the next interrogation room, and I wandered out of FBI HQ. At least I was free from the invisible shackles of a federal building.

Being completely exhausted but too keyed up to sleep, I took a taxi back to the hotel and picked up my car. Then I stopped by my office and ran backgrounds on Paul Eastman, Kenneth Anderson, and Mike Talbot. No one had a criminal record. Afterward, I searched for any news stories on last night's murder, but there was nothing but a brief paragraph about a hotel employee dead at the conference. It wasn't even described as murder. That would probably change in the coming days.

The conference itself was concluded. An American engineer was hired to design the plans, workers from each nation would work on that particular part of the railway, and an international corporation was in charge of the actual train construction. Everyone wins. So if the conference was a success, it was hard to fathom that the death of the night clerk had anything to do with it. So who was he? Why was he killed? And why did his murder coincide with the European business conference? None of it made any sense.

Hell, I didn't even know the guy's name. There was no reason I should be investigating. Curiosity killed the cat, and I'm sure it would do the same to me. Locking up my office, I drove home, listening to my missed voicemail messages on the way.

SIX

"Jesus," I flipped the safety back on my gun and put it on the table with slightly shaking hands, "what did I say about showing up when I'm working?"

Martin sighed and rolled his eyes. "Alex, if I had a nickel for every time you've pointed a gun at me, I could go crazy at a vending machine." Running my hands through my hair, I took a deep breath. "Plus, I left you a message. Didn't you get it?" The smirk on his face was irritating. "I thought things between us had changed, and you weren't keeping me at arms' length anymore while you were working."

"Old habits die hard." I glanced at his overnight bag. "What are you doing here?"

"So you didn't get my message?"

"All it said was you were stopping by before you left on your trip." Scrunching my brow in frustration, I felt the exhaustion setting in. "When are you leaving?"

"Tomorrow morning. I finished at the office early, packed a bag, and came here. Marcal will pick me up at eight a.m. and take me to the airport. It's okay that I'm here, isn't it?"

"Yeah, it's fine, but I've been up for the last thirty-something hours. I need a shower and sleep." Not bothering to elaborate, I found a change of clothes and shut myself in the bathroom.

Stepping under the steamy water, I was tired, frustrated, and otherwise just plain old blah. Lathering my long brown hair, the ramifications that I was fired hit hard. Some job. Eastman was a piece of work, and PDN was a joke. However, there was a dead body, dozens of federal agents crawling all over the hotel, and my job was to go another round of interviews whenever the police called. Joy. And to top it off, Martin was leaving tomorrow morning for the next three weeks.

"Hey, are you hungry? I was thinking of cooking, but if you'd rather order in, we can do that instead," he said when I exited the bathroom.

"I don't care."

He studied me for a moment, and his gaze settled on the crumpled blanket on my sofa. "Still depressed? I know how much you love sleeping on sofas, but Mark says it's a sure sign you're depressed and to seek professional help immediately. Thankfully, I'm a professional." He smirked as the devious thoughts swam through his mind on ways to cheer me up.

"Don't even." I didn't want to talk about it. Talking about it was what led to the problem in the first place. "I spent all night in interrogation, and I'm exhausted. Now isn't the time for that conversation."

A smile crept onto his face. "Putting the screws to the bad guys?"

"No. A body was found. So guess who's suddenly a material witness and potential suspect. Oh, and to top it off, I was fired."

"What?" Everything I just said made little sense, and he was flummoxed. Curling up on the couch, I elaborated while he made lunch or dinner or whatever the hell it was. When it was ready, he put it in front of me, and I picked at it. We ate in silence for a time until he cleared his throat. "Alexis," he hesitated, and I looked him in the eye, "why don't you come back to Martin Technologies full time?"

"Because your initials are monogrammed on the front

door. Not to mention, I screwed up the security protocols and have to fix them. Don't worry, I'm not charging you my consulting rate since it's my fault." Wow, I was batting a thousand. I was fired from PDN. I couldn't get my old job back at the OIO. I screwed up at MT, and there hadn't been any private investigator gigs in a few weeks. "I give up."

Without another word, I went into my room and crawled into bed. There was no point in coming out. Nothing good could come of it. I shut my eyes and curled into the fetal position. As I drifted closer to sleep, Martin climbed into bed and wrapped his arms around me.

"We'll talk about this later," he whispered, kissing my hair.

A while later, the phone rang, and I opened an eye to make sure it wasn't mine. Martin grabbed his cell and went into the living room. From his half of the conversation, I could tell it was about his business trip. I didn't even know where he was going or why he was going. Some girlfriend I was. Maybe that should be added to my current list of failures. Instead of getting out of bed to start making that list, I fell asleep and woke up in the middle of the night.

Martin was next to me, and the illuminated three a.m. glowed in the darkness. I stared at him, watching the slow rise and fall of his chest. I was a workaholic, and so was he. The difference was he was a CEO with a corporation. I was an unemployed loser. It made it difficult to drown my sorrows in work when there was no work to be done.

Around five, Martin shifted and opened his eyes. "Since when are you awake this early in the morning?"

"Since I went to bed sometime yesterday afternoon." I snuggled against him. "Don't go." The words left my mouth, and I felt idiotic for saying them. He held me tighter, obviously confused since I always insisted we put our careers first. "Stay here. The two of us can hide in my apartment forever." I laughed, playing it off as a joke.

"Really? What about food and other necessities? Your fridge and pantry are sadly paltry."

"Delivery. Lots of delivery."

"We would run out of condoms pretty fast and then what?" For once, I was glad he was a morning person and could joke around at five a.m. At least his annoying habit was good for something.

"We'll have Marcal pick them up and deliver them since your driver would need something to do."

"So we'll just hide in your tiny apartment for the rest of our lives?"

"Yes."

He chuckled. "Alex, I don't believe you for a second. You'd go crazy."

"I am crazy."

"Fine, I'm calling your bluff. If you're completely serious about this, then I'll call my accountant, liquidate my stocks, sell my company, and never leave your side." He nudged me with his shoulder. "But we're not staying here. If you insist on hiding indoors, then we're going to my place. It's bigger and comes with a pool, home gym, plenty of rooms, and a much better cable package. So you'll just have to move in with me."

"I don't want to move in with you." This was an old argument. I practically lived part time at his place anyway. Depending on work, various injuries, and other issues, I would spend anywhere from a night to a couple of weeks there on a fairly regular basis, but that didn't mean I wanted to move in permanently.

"Hence, the flaw in your otherwise brilliant plan," he teased.

"Damn."

We fell silent for a few minutes, and I wondered if he was going back to sleep. But then he interrupted the quiet. "I have to go on this trip, but if you need me here, maybe I can rearrange some things and cut it short."

"No. It's fine. I'm fine. You should go, and I'll hide in my apartment all by myself."

"Why don't you come with me? You're not working. I'll be busy, but it'd be preferable to not seeing you for the next three weeks."

"I can't. I have more questions to answer for the police department, and I have to fix the elevator issue at your company. When did life get this hard?"

He snorted. "It'll be okay." He shifted so he could see

my face. "What I will never understand is how someone could fire you. That guy must be an absolute moron. You're an amazing consultant, and before that, Mark always said you were an amazing agent. This Eastman schmuck has no idea what he's missing."

"Is that flattery I detect?"

"See, and a damn fine investigator too." He smirked. "If your ribs are up to it, I'm wondering how much more flattery it will take to convince you to drop your panties. After all, I'm going away for three entire weeks."

I smiled. "The ribs are okay with it, but keep talking. I might need a bit more convincing."

*   *   *

After Martin left later that morning, I went back to bed. There had to be a way to shake the funk I was in. My career stagnated, and the last time this happened, it was self-inflicted. It had been an escape from the job, the death, the mayhem, and it was the clean break I needed. However, my current predicament wasn't any of those things. I wasn't trying to escape; I tried to return. Unfortunately, that wasn't meant to happen mainly because, in all honesty, I liked being my own boss, taking different gigs here and there, and I knew Martin worried. Too many close calls and we were both fairly neurotic when it came to the other's safety.

"What to do. What to do," I mumbled, burying myself further in the sheets. Since the few friends I had at the precinct weren't assigned to the current murder investigation, I couldn't insist of insinuating myself into a consulting role, and Det. Jacobs didn't get the hint. PDN fired me. Perhaps I was insubordinate, and maybe I overreacted. But where the hell did Paul come off thinking I would land him a finder's fee because of my previous employer and current love interest? No, something still shady about that situation. Even Jacobs thought it was fishy.

Could Paul have choreographed the murder and ensured I would be removed from the situation? After all, we had a rather strange conversation in his hotel room a couple nights before. And why was he staying in the hotel in the first place? Plus, what about that under the table deal? How did he make contact with one of the European business tycoons, and why would they want access to James Martin or his company?

So maybe that last bit was my paranoia getting the best of me. It happened, and sometimes, it was difficult to decipher where the crazy train started and where legitimate concern ended. Granted, I wasn't always the most rational person on the face of the planet, and emotions were known to get the best of me on occasion. Mostly, I acted overzealously to protect people I cared about, but this didn't feel like one of those instances.

I stretched, feeling the tenderness in my torso, but nothing popped or cracked. Maybe I could eke out a few miles on the treadmill to help sort through the endless string of questions my psyche posed. Changing, I started out slowly, gradually increasing the speed as I thought about the entire three weeks I was employed by PDN, the lengthy checks the Secret Service conducted on its private contractors, and the dead hotel night clerk. If Eastman was dirty, there should have been an indicator in his past. Someone would have noticed and caught on, right?

Pounding out the miles, I needed to know the deceased man's name. Who knew he was scheduled to pick up a few extra shifts and work days? The telephone halted my questions and stopped my impromptu workout which began as an easy jog and turned into an all-out sprint.

"Parker," I huffed, unsuccessfully attempting to regulate my labored breathing with only shallow breaths.

"Hello, Ms. Parker, this is Officer Sarcone from the police department," the voice responded, sounding completely business appropriate. "Would you be willing to answer a few more questions concerning your employment with PDN?"

"Sure." Maybe we could do this over the phone since the PD didn't want to hire me.

"Great. Can you come by the precinct at two o'clock tomorrow afternoon?"

"Yeah, okay. Hey," I paused, wondering if it was worth asking the question, "do you know what the dead guy's name is?" That was a somewhat irreverent way of asking the question, but being in law enforcement for any length of time tended to have a desensitizing effect.

"I'm sorry, ma'am. I'm not allowed to disclose any information on the current case."

"It's just a name. I'm not asking if you have any suspects or if an arrest has been made or what evidence you've found." Okay, that was overstepping. Tread lightly, Parker, my internal voice chastised.

"Two o'clock tomorrow." There was an uncertain hesitation, and then two whispered words. "Alvin Hodge."

The line disconnected, and I put the receiver down. Oh, Romeo, what's in a name? My mind played through Juliet's soliloquy which I had been forced to memorize in high school as I wiped my sweaty palms on a dish towel and took a seat in front of my computer. It was time to see what I could discover about Mr. Alvin Hodge. It was the closest thing to a work distraction I had, even if no one hired me to work on the case.

SEVEN

Alvin Hodge was born and raised in Portland, Oregon. He had two ex-wives, four unpaid traffic tickets, and lived in a decent neighborhood in the suburbs. Not exactly what one would think of when discussing homicide victims, particularly since he drove an eco-friendly automobile. I tapped my fingertips against the keyboard, trying to come up with something relevant to type into the databases. Even though the murder seemed hotel related at the very least and conference related at the most, I still ran backgrounds on his two ex-wives. Typically, lovers whether past or present had the strongest motives for murder, but Sally Hanson lived thousands of miles away in Portland. Moving on to ex-wife number two, Rachel Romanski was a local yoga instructor with no criminal record. I would drop by and ask a few questions, but she didn't strike me as worthy enough to be considered a person of interest.

After wasting an hour on an absolutely fruitless endeavor, I showered and heated some leftovers. Halfway through lunch, there was a knock on my door. Opening it, I was surprised to find Paul Eastman outside.

"You must really want to see how quickly I can file

harassment charges," I growled. "I'm assuming you used company records to learn my address, and I'm pretty certain this can be construed as stalking."

He stared blankly at me. "I came to apologize. I left a few messages on your office phone and stopped there first, but you were out."

"Wow, you really want to make sure that stalking charge sticks, huh?" I moved to shut the door, and he stepped forward, blocking it from closing with his foot. "I'm within my rights to shoot an intruder if I'm in fear of my life. So in two seconds, I'm going to scream bloody murder. I would suggest you leave before things escalate beyond that point."

"I want to hire you," he blurted out, taking half a step back.

"You fired me two days ago, remember?" I glared daggers, wondering if anyone would believe I was afraid of this guy enough to warrant putting a few holes in him.

"I don't want you back at PDN. I want to personally hire you. The police have been questioning me. They think I'm involved in that man's death."

"Well, are you?"

"No. I don't even know who died." He looked down the empty hallway of my apartment building. "Can I come inside so we can talk about this?"

"No." I moved to shut the door, but he didn't budge. "Fine, if you want to make an appointment, I'll meet you at four thirty tomorrow at my office. And if you come to my house again, you won't be walking away."

"I'll see you tomorrow afternoon." He nodded curtly and turned toward the stairwell.

Slamming the door shut, I locked my two deadbolts and went to the window to make sure he left my building. His appearance was beyond inappropriate, and it left an uneasy feeling in my gut. But on the bright side, I had some idea where to continue my computer search for leads on the deceased.

After a couple hours of internet searching, half a dozen phone calls, and a stiff drink, I gave up. There was no reason for me to dig into Hodge's death. No one hired me to do it. Okay, maybe Paul wanted to hire me, but I wasn't too keen on the idea. After my search for other possible suspects in the Hodge murder turned up empty, I shifted gears to focus solely on Paul Eastman.

Everything he said in his hotel room seemed true enough, and he didn't have a record. I even phoned a few guys at the OIO to see if he had a file without a conviction. Sometimes, crimes were dropped for lack of evidence, inappropriate arrest or search, or whatever, but that wasn't the case. Despite his stalker-like behavior, strange urging for under the table business dealings, and failed attempts to join the ranks of law enforcement, he wasn't a criminal. And if he was, then he was smarter than I gave him credit for.

"It's time to reevaluate your behavior," I grunted, recalling words various shrinks might have said to me over the course of the years at various psych evals and mandated job required therapy sessions since I personally abhorred psychology and would never seek it out on my own. "What do you hope to accomplish?" I snorted, hating psychobabble and confused why I was tormenting myself with it. Unfortunately, my sick, deranged psyche had a point. I was a backseat driver, and being relegated to material witness in the middle of a homicide wasn't acceptable on any level. I needed a real case.

"Thank you for calling Martin Technologies. This is Jeffrey Myers speaking. How may I assist you today?" he asked pleasantly.

"Hey, it's Alex. I have some unexpected free time this evening and wanted to run some drills before I read through the revised maintenance proposal. How much will you hate me if I come in tonight and set half the alarms off?"

"Do you need help?" he asked, sounding hesitant.

"No. I can lock down the elevators and accidentally set off the sprinklers on my own. Actually, we should probably disable the sprinklers because I don't think Mr. Guillot wants a flood in the building, especially since he's in charge while Mr. Martin's traveling."

"Okay, how 'bout I make a few calls to the security firm and police department, giving them the heads up concerning your impending drills? Then I'll hang around until you show up, disable the sprinklers, and let you have the run of the place until the night shift arrives."

"Sounds great."

"All right. Just do me one favor and ask Mr. Guillot for permission before you turn this place upside down. Some of us still work here." The teasing was evident in his voice.

"Fine." I pretended to be annoyed and hung up. Then I dialed Guillot and asked that he send word to Jeffrey before he left work today.

At least I found something to occupy my time. Changing into something slightly more work appropriate, I reviewed the elevator schematics and protocols one more time before setting out. On the bright side, tonight's check would help prove my theory to modify the system, and if something went awry, there would be plenty of time to correct it before pitching the new implementations to the Board. Plus, it'd be a great opportunity to work on my stealth tactics and clandestine maneuvers. Hell, maybe I should become a burglar since this private investigator/consulting thing wasn't going very well.

* * *

"Ms. Parker," Luc Guillot greeted. It was after five, and he was standing at the security desk, chatting with the guards. "I'm sorry to rope you into more corporate work." His eyes twinkled, remembering my proclamation that I wasn't cut out for this type of career. "Is there anything I can do to make sure these exercises go smoothly?"

"As long as all relevant authorities are notified, it should be fine." I tossed a look at Jeffrey. "We're disabling the sprinklers to prevent any flooding or leaks."

"Okay. If you need anything, you have my number." Nodding, he said good night to the security guards and left the building. A few of the guards packed their belongings and followed him out.

"Is anyone still upstairs?" I tilted my chin at the elevator banks.

"Three guys are still in marketing, but I notified them

that any alarms that sound are just a practice drill, and the elevators won't be operational for the rest of the evening. So you shouldn't encounter any problems," Jeffrey insisted. He slipped his jacket on and made sure the office door was locked. "Also, after speaking with Mr. Guillot, your MT I.D. card has been reprogrammed with complete access. Everything you need is operationally available at your fingertips."

"Thanks. Enjoy your night."

"You too." He snorted, amused, and went to the front door. "Just don't ransack Mr. Martin's office."

"I wouldn't dream of it." I winked. If I wanted to ransack anything, it would be his house, but there wasn't much fun in that since he would consider it a precursor to moving in together.

Swiveling in the chair, I opened the relevant files, entered the proper commands into the computer, and went to the elevator. Perhaps there was a way to bypass the locking function without redoing the entire system or placing the elevator on a separate system. I stepped inside, glad that the MT building had a wireless network to access the alarms via tablet. At least if I got stuck in the elevator, I could bypass the security. However, since I was often paranoid and a little crazy, I made sure my cell phone was shoved in my pocket. It never hurt to have a back-up. Now, if I was really crazy, I would have taken a crowbar into the elevator in case the doors needed to be pried open. Faltering slightly before pushing the button, I decided the crowbar idea really didn't seem that crazy, but I would risk it anyway.

Pressing the button to the seventeenth floor, I waited for the elevator to arrive at the top level of the building. Then I stepped out, activated a few of the alarms, and used the fire service mode to open the doors. Stepping inside, I pressed the close door button, and the descent to the lobby began. So far, so good.

The doors opened in the lobby, and I hit the smoke alarms and sprinkler key to fool the system into thinking the sprinklers were activated, even though they were currently disabled. The doors were forced shut. The elevator lurched slightly upward, apparently intent on heading for the fourth floor, and halted half a second later. The abrupt stop threatened my balance, and I grabbed the handrail. Sighing, I checked the tablet for an update on the situation.

After resetting the alarm function using the tablet, I manually entered the reset code and turned the key inside the elevator to return it to normal functioning. The elevator descended a couple of feet back to the lobby, and the doors opened. That wasn't particularly productive.

Starting over, I repeated the process a few times. Everything worked properly as long as the sprinklers didn't turn on. Once they did, the elevator car would lock wherever it was, even between levels. The between levels was the most troublesome factor, and in the event someone was disabled or injured, the elevator had to be functional.

Repeating the process with the freight elevator, it didn't encounter any of the same issues, and I realized it was because they were on separate systems. Crap. I let out an unhappy sigh, went back to the main elevator, and started over, mentally coaxing the system to obey the few tweaks and modifications I made as I went. After several hours of riding elevators, recalculating the security systems, and all the lurching up and down, I was nauseated and pissed.

The simplest solution was to remove the smoke sensor from the elevator that way it would go down to the lobby and remain there in the event the sprinklers were activated. It was the easiest solution and possibly the best. Furthermore, in the event of a real emergency, the freight elevator could be used as transport if the main elevator was already disabled.

"Ma'am," one of the men from marketing asked, emerging from the stairwell, "whenever you finish, do you think you can turn off the emergency lighting?"

"Oh, sorry." Hitting a button, I returned the lights to the normal brightness. I turned off the blaring sound but didn't think about the lights. "I guess I'm not making your jobs any easier."

He laughed. "Thanks." He went back to the stairs, and I decided to call it a night. Making sure all the systems were reactivated, the sprinklers were working, and the security station was locked up, I waited another twenty minutes for the night guards to arrive, and then I went home. On the bright side, my entire day wasn't wasted checking into a murder that the police didn't want my help with.

EIGHT

"I'm sorry to make you do this again," Jacobs offered, letting out a long exhale and flipping through a few forms inside the folder, "but start at the very beginning. Why did you apply for a job at PDN, and when did you begin working there?"

"Roughly three weeks ago, I heard PDN was looking for a consultant to evaluate their protocols. And after my last case, I needed something that wouldn't be physically demanding." I shrugged. "Anyway, this was supposed to be easy. The Secret Service hired PDN as a private contractor to assist in protecting the international diplomats and a couple of congressmen who were attending the conference. Originally, PDN wanted their security plan evaluated, and since I had previous experience devising the remodeled security for Martin Technologies, it seemed like the perfect fit."

"Okay." Jacobs glanced at me, hoping for a more Cliff notes version of these facts. "How did you go from evaluating security to providing security?"

"I wasn't really providing security. The day before the conference, I went through a final check of the hotel with Mr. Eastman. We completed numerous drills, and something struck me as odd. The original foundation was expanded, and the subbasement led to some abandoned subway tunnels. It seemed like a potential risk." He gestured with his hand that I move the story along. "Anyway, turns out I was overanalyzing the risk, so for my efforts, Eastman assigned me sentry duty on Monday, the first day of the conference."

"So until then, you weren't supposed to be on-site during the conference?"

"Well, since the Secret Service vetted all of us, I was supposed to be in the control room, watching the monitors, but instead, I was tossed downstairs." I saw the question in his eyes and added, "Yes, it was on Paul Eastman's order. He also told me to go home early that day. At the time, I was stiff and sore and didn't give it a second thought."

He sucked in some air between his front teeth and scratched his chin. "Do you remember anything strange happening Monday?"

"No. There was the occasional hotel employee running to the storeroom or service room or whatever's down there, but I was rather isolated." I shrugged it off, recollecting the hours alone and the boredom. "Oh wait, there was a caterer that forgot his identification, but they didn't allow him access to the hotel. Or at least that's what I heard over the comms."

He nodded. "Then Tuesday, you were upgraded to the control room?"

"Yes." I closed my eyes, remembering meeting with Paul in his hotel suite Sunday night and then the way our first conversation began on Tuesday.

"What is it?"

"Eastman was renting a room at the hotel. He took me there the day before the conference began, hoping to exploit my connection to Martin Technologies by putting the CEO in contact with one of the European businessmen for an alleged finder's fee. He said he didn't have a problem with alcohol that night, but I think he was drinking before he came into the control room on Tuesday." My eyes darted around the room, remembering minute details. "He tried again to gain access to MT's CEO by extending an invitation to go out to dinner Tuesday night. That's why we argued and what caused me to storm out of the room. When I came back, monitor nine was messed up, and he didn't know why. Or so he said." It didn't sound like Eastman was trying to get me to leave the room, but he was distracting me.

"Interesting distraction tactics," Jacobs said, reading my mind. "But it's circumstantial at best." He stood and collected his notes. "Thanks for coming down here." When I didn't budge from the chair, he asked, "Was there anything else?"

"Paul showed up at my apartment yesterday. He's concerned and wants to hire me to prove his innocence."

"Huh," he scratched his head, "well, have fun being a P.I. but don't get in our way."

He strode out of the interrogation room, and I rubbed my eyes. I missed working with Detectives Nick O'Connell and Derek Heathcliff. Hell, even Thompson was a little more into the give and take than Jacobs.

On my way out, I glanced forlornly at the empty desks in major crimes, but there were no friendly faces. Continuing to my car, I checked the time, stopped for lunch, and took my food back to my office. After my enlightening conversation with Jacobs, I was having doubts about Eastman's involvement and guilt. Then again, there was still something incredibly suspicious about the guy when it came to Martin. I wasn't ready to rule him out as a killer, but I was willing to play nice and hear him out. The more information I had on the situation, the better off I'd be. Knowledge could only aid my rational thought processes in making a decision. Plus, I didn't have anything better to do.

"Ms. Parker," Eastman said, entering my office and glancing around, "or can I refer to you as Alexis? We were friendly before you started giving me the cold shoulder."

"Have a seat, Paul," I replied, forcing my tone to remain neutral and detached. "Why don't we start at the beginning?"

"Well," he gave me a half-assed smile that didn't make it to his eyes, "I was born in a small town in Maine." My glare would have killed someone smarter. "However, I'm guessing that's not the beginning you were referring to. Maybe you'd rather I start with the smartass brunette who sauntered into my office building less than a month ago and asked for a job." The retort was on my lips, but he soldiered on. "Fine, we'll start with PDN entering the bidding wars for the government contract."

"And we have a winner."

"Look, PDN is just a job. I've been doing it for three or four years now. It pays the bills, has great benefits, and gets me close to the action. You remember our discussion from Sunday evening, I assume." I nodded. "Great. It's nice to know someone was paying attention."

"I've been paying attention, and I would suggest you cut the bullshit and get on with your story."

"Seriously, Alexis, what happened to us? We were friendly at work. Hell, I thought you might actually be a friend, a person to confide in. I let you lead me by the nose on that cockamamie stunt through the subway tunnels, and then I assigned you guard duty. But you pull a complete one-eighty, and I don't know why. What gives?"

"Excuse me?" My jaw dropped. "You think you were doing me some grand favor?"

"Wasn't I?" He genuinely looked confused. "I've read your résumé. You like to think of yourself as a cop, so I let you play the part to feel useful." I blinked, not sure which of those incorrect statements to attack first. "No one could honestly believe that doorway in the subbasement would lead to anything, but you seemed so adamant about wanting to appear useful."

"It was a risk," I rebutted, wondering why I was even arguing over moot points.

"Whatever you have to tell yourself to get through the day. From the few MT board members I spoke with, it's quite apparent you loathe corporate work, so letting you play guard was just me being a nice guy. And the thanks I get is you accuse me of something sneaky and underhanded, continuously insult my professional work ethic in front of my subordinates, and then to top it off, you practically threw me under the bus on the murder charge. Oh, and let's not forget your accusations that I'm harassing and stalking you."

"Since you're obviously delusional and believe all that insanity you just spewed, why are you even here? This is for paying clients, people who actually believe I'm not some hack and that I can solve their problems."

"Because if you're insane enough to think some ancient door is a threat, then you won't leave a single stone unturned when it comes to investigating an actual crime, and seeing that I'm not the killer, there's no harm in paying you to figure out who is."

"Wow, apparently I'm neurotic to the point of having some type of obsessive compulsion for investigating and assessing threats, or so you believe."

"Tell me I'm wrong."

"You're wrong about pretty much everything."

"All right then." He stood. "This was a waste of my time." He went to the front door, pushing it open.

I was steaming mad, but my mouth moved on its own volition. "Wait." He turned, the obvious victory playing across his eyes. "You'll pay my daily rate, plus expenses and incidentals, and I want to know what your interest in Martin Technologies is."

"How much are we talking?" he asked smugly, stepping back into my office and taking a seat, crossing his legs in a very self-satisfied manner that I wanted to knock out of him.

Scribbling a number on the back of my business card, I slid it across the desk. "Why were you renting a room at the hotel during the conference?"

"I told you I like to stay close to the job."

"I want the real reason." But he didn't respond as he flipped my card over in his hands as if considering the proposal. "If you make me start guessing, you won't like the result."

"Actually, I like that idea very much. I'll tell you what," his grin was evil, "if you can tell me why I was there and it's correct, I'll hire you. And if not, then maybe it'd be best if we stay away from each other."

"Damn, now you have me over a barrel. I can either work and collect a paycheck, or I can be rewarded with an even greater prize of never having to see you again." I took a breath. "You were at the hotel to make contact with someone. I'd guess it was a few of the business tycoons. Maybe it was a job search. Maybe it was a booty call. Hell, maybe it was to sell secrets. I hear corporate espionage is lucrative nowadays. But let's be real honest, whatever motivation you like to tell yourself is legitimate is horse shit. It's really because you like to drink a little too much."

"I don't have a problem."

"Right. That's what you said in your hotel room. And since I'm being so brutally honest, the drinking thing is probably the least of your worries right now."

He glowered. This exercise in evaluating my deductive skills wasn't helpful. There was little to work with, and with the limited details I knew of Paul and the conversations we had, there were only so many conclusions I could draw. Obviously, he wasn't fond of any of them, but he didn't storm out of my office in a huff, so I must have hit the nail on the head. I was still determining if I was pleased or upset that he didn't leave when he took a slow, deep breath and produced his wallet.

"Do you take credit cards?"

"I'll bill you. But first things first, what in god's name drove you to request a meeting with James Martin?"

"Can't we start with a general apology, some mending of fences, and maybe grab a beer?"

"Maybe drinking should be off limits while you're in my company. And since you're still sitting here and you haven't been harmed, I think enough fences have been mended for the foreseeable future. We can agree to act like adults, so now, as an adult, would you be kind enough to answer the question?"

"It's more complicated than it seems."

"Well, it's a good thing I cleared my schedule." He still looked uneasy, so I added, "We'll start with an easier question. Did you hire me simply because of my connection to Martin Technologies?"

"No."

"After I passed the background checks and you inquired about my references, was that when you changed your mind about my usefulness?"

"No."

"Okay," I sighed, feeling my patience wane and a kink develop in my neck, "then be a dear and explain when everything changed."

"Nothing changed. I just thought you'd help a guy out." Leaning back in my chair, I swiveled slowly back and forth, waiting for an elaboration. My interrogational skills were stellar, and I could break him. Too bad I didn't have a cup of coffee to sip slowly while eyeing him over the rim. "It was Bernie's idea."

"Is that your imaginary friend?"

"No." He narrowed his eyes, silently communicating that my sarcastic remarks weren't professional or particularly mature for someone in their early thirties. "Bernie's the marketing director at Klaus Manufacturing." Something darted across his face. "You might as well know, Alvin Hodge introduced us." I stopped swiveling and jotted down a few notes. "If you don't believe me, ask Alvin yourself."

"Paul, Alvin Hodge is dead."

NINE

"I'm only going to ask this once. Were you involved in Mr. Hodge's murder?"

"Alexis," he let out an exasperated sigh, "no. I don't even see how the authorities can believe it's murder. From what Mike and Kenneth said, it sounded like an apparent suicide."

"Okay," I narrowed my eyes, "what makes you think Hodge was suicidal?"

"I never said I thought he was suicidal." He shook his head, blinking rapidly. "After days of questioning, I can't believe no one ever told me who died. When I asked, they said it was a hotel worker. They probably thought I must have known who it was and expected me to slip up and say his name. Shit. The authorities asked for my fingerprints and DNA. They seriously think I would do this to my friend?"

"Did you cooperate?"

"Whose side are you on?" He pushed his chair back, stomping around my office like a child throwing a tantrum. The only problem with the theatrics was he didn't have anywhere else to turn. "Alvin was my friend." He met my eyes, seeing the skepticism reflected there. "Okay, maybe we were more acquaintances than friends. Kinda like you and me, before you started hating me that is."

"I don't hate you. I don't particularly trust you, and thus, I'm not getting any warm, fuzzy feelings when I think about you. But I'm pretty much indifferent." I still desperately wanted to know the reason for his desire to meet with Martin. "C'mon, this is a truce. So take a seat, and we'll have a heart-to-heart." He seemed jittery, and his hands were shaking slightly. Maybe it was the news of his friend's death or because he might have a problem with alcohol. Rescinding my earlier proclamation, I took a beer from my office mini-fridge and put it on the desk in front of my client chair. I wasn't AA, and his helpfulness would be impaired if he started going through the DTs. Maybe I was jumping to conclusions, but after he came into the control room smelling of liquor, I suspected he was a functioning alcoholic. And why else would he keep insisting he didn't have a problem? "Peace offering, but only if we get back to the matter at hand."

He went to the bottle and picked it up, spinning it by the neck as he read the label. "This doesn't mean I have a problem," he stated coolly, expertly popping the top off by hitting it against the desk. He took a long sip and put it down, shutting his eyes and relishing in the cold liquid. "Thanks. Dealing with all this has been so stressful."

"Yeah." I leaned back in my chair and toyed with the computer mouse, attempting to look productive while I waited for him to open up. Silence was one of the most useful tools an interrogator possessed.

"So," he put the bottle back on the desk and adjusted in the chair, "nice place you have here." I tore my eyes from the computer screen, abandoning the game of solitaire. "Alvin and I have known each other for about a year. PDN uses the hotel to put up VIPs every now and again. We've never had anyone that important to guard, but we'll get the occasional B or C list celebrity who claims to want to avoid the paparazzi. Alvin worked the night shift, so whenever I stopped by to check in on the security detail, he'd offer a more realistic viewpoint of the situation. Occasionally, one of our clients would order a few hookers or ask the concierge for an eight ball or some coke. Things PDN didn't want to be involved with."

"What does that have to do with the night clerk?"

"He'd run interference. The concierge made the connections to procure the contraband, and then Alvin would call up to my security team and claim there was someone suspicious or an issue downstairs. That way, during delivery, we'd have plausible deniability."

"Does the concierge have a name?"

"I don't know who's working there now. The hotel went through a few. It's policy not to have questionable characters running things inside these fancy hotels, even though they all do it."

I rifled through a drawer. Placing the notepad in front of him, I pulled a pen from the cup on my desk and jerked my chin at the paper. "Make a list of names. PDN clients, hotel employees you've encountered, any whores or drug dealers you remember, and don't start spouting out the confidential status of PDN's clientele. Frankly, it's you or them, and unless you have a better idea of who might have an axe to grind with Hodge, then I suggest you start writing." He nodded and picked up the pen. That was the easiest request I ever made. "How much of this did you tell the police?"

"None of it."

"Why not?"

He continued to write, but his face contorted as he thought about it. "Because I only answered the questions they asked. And they didn't ask any of this. They asked about the conference, Mike and Kenneth, PDN's job, and why I was staying at the hotel." He looked up. "Did you tell them that?"

"Yes, but if it makes you feel any better, they would have found out on their own. With a murder, it wouldn't take much to subpoena the guest registry. In fact, I'm sure Detective Jacobs already has."

As he wrote, he periodically glanced up. "What gave it away?" he asked, rereading the last few names he had written down before turning the notepad to face me. "I mean your record is impressive, but anyone can look good on paper if you know the right people, go to the right schools, and create the right kinds of connections." He let out a snort. "No judgment, but people in our line of work know how to conduct a proper background check and collect a few dirty little secrets." He smiled. "It took almost three hours before I figured out you and James Martin are a thing, and that involved asking the right people the right kinds of questions. So who gave you the insight on my extracurriculars?"

I still didn't know what Paul was talking about, but the comment set my radar buzzing. Martin was always part of his plan, and that scared me. Thankfully, Martin was globetrotting, far away from all of this.

"No one." I spoke carefully, not wanting to tip him off to my confusion. One of the accusations I made earlier must be correct. "But your actions speak louder than words, both written and spoken." I lifted the list and skimmed through the names, failing to find any I recognized.

"Serves me right. After I invited you to my room that night, I could tell you were serious about this job. I should have guessed you'd realize what I was up to, but I thought if I played it cool, you'd assume I was flirting with you." I cocked an eyebrow. "Maybe I should have been straight with you, and then we wouldn't be having this discussion now." He let out a bitter laugh. "I never imagined my life would turn out this way. And PDN pays pennies compared to what our clients make. Really, what's the harm in trading some favors and information to the highest bidder? No one is supposed to get hurt. It all adds some friendly competition to the market. Hell, if two competing companies make the exact same item, the price will be driven down to something affordable. I'm doing a service to the ninety-nine percent that are busting their asses and can barely make ends meet."

I smirked. Corporate espionage. Ding, ding, ding. We have a winner. "Initially, I wouldn't have pegged you as stealing secrets or selling secrets, particularly not after that sob story from Sunday night. And frankly, someone should hand it to you. You passed the government background checks with flying colors which means you don't affiliate with questionable characters, there aren't abnormal money transfers in your accounts, and I'm guessing not many people would have given your hotel reservation a second thought. Clearly, you're not as stupid as you look."

"Thanks, I think." He frowned suddenly. "Are you planning to turn me in?"

"It depends. Hodge was part of this, wasn't he?"

He nodded, looking grim. "I didn't kill him. I've never hurt anyone. Everything I do is victimless."

"Right, you think you're Robin Hood or something like that, except you have no problem lining your pockets with your ill-gotten gains." I stood up and leaned my hips against the edge of my desk. "What was the plan? When was it devised? Who was involved? And don't you dare hold anything back."

"If you're going to use whatever I say against me, then we're done. I don't need more charges to deal with."

"I'll only divulge what's absolutely necessary for the apprehension of Alvin Hodge's killer. Whatever deals you've brokered, information you've stolen, and companies you've screwed over in the past might be necessary to figure out who murdered Hodge, but it might not be imperative to the police department's case." He remained tight-lipped, so I tried another approach. "Tell me what kinds of schemes you and Hodge were concocting during the conference."

He was hesitant but realized it was the best deal he could get. "Alvin gave me the room number for Bernie, the representative for Klaus Manufacturing. He put us in contact last week. It was Tuesday, so six days before the conference."

"Does Bernie have a last name?"

"Bernard Muller, marketing director." He finished the beer and tossed the bottle into the trash. "We were working out a business transaction."

Without any plying on my part, Paul went into detail about his meetings with Bernie and the role Alvin played. Eventually, the dots connected. Klaus Manufacturing was one of the smallest companies represented at the conference. The only reason they were invited was because of the technological advances their R&D department was making with alternative energy sources. If they could power this transcontinental train system for next to nothing, then they would join the big leagues. The only problem was whether or not their research was viable. Things still considered theory or experimental weren't favored by skeptics or, in this case, the bigger businesses fighting for their own spot.

Bernie was the executive marketing director. He was excellent at creating flashy, business savvy presentations and selling product. But he was also a realist. He didn't believe that their unproven energy source would be accepted, and he was right. Having decent business sense, he figured there was no reason to waste the trip and thought to enter into a lucrative venture with a smaller corporation across the pond, or whatever term the Germans used to refer to the Atlantic Ocean, and since James Martin was known for being ecologically friendly and fiscally responsible, Bernie set his sights on Martin Technologies.

"Who did you talk to?" I asked, kicking my leg against the desk absently. "You said you asked a few board members about my past experience, so how come one of your contacts couldn't hook a meeting up for Bernie?"

"Maybe I embellished a little." He let out a long exhale. "I sweet talked one of the ladies in HR to reroute my call to someone in a top position. The closest I came was to one of the lower level board members. Marcy something."

I rubbed my face. "Rule number one. Don't lie to me. You do it again, and I'm walking." I sighed. "Let me guess, she mentioned I was hired as a consultant because I was already romantically involved with James Martin."

"Yeah," his eyes darted back and forth, and he held his mouth at a strange angle, "I take it from your tone there's something inaccurate about her statement."

"When I met her, I was his personal security. Our relationship was a cover story." I rolled my eyes. "All of this was based on bad intel you received, and because of that, I ended up quitting my job at PDN. Un-fucking-believable. Are you sure any of the corporate espionage you've sold was even accurate?"

"Why are you mad about this?" He looked completely confused. "Shouldn't you be thankful that I was wrong and that people airing your dirty secrets don't even know what the hell they're talking about? If anyone should be pissed, it ought to be me. I'm the one who was working a bad angle," then he scrunched his face together, "except I wasn't because you are dating him."

"It doesn't matter. None of this is relevant to anything." At least Luc wasn't the questionable board member, and we needed to get back to the Klaus Manufacturing and Alvin Hodge issue. "So you couldn't sweet talk Marcy into getting you a meeting?"

"I barely managed to get her to acknowledge you were dating the CEO," he finally admitted. "And that was after an hour on the phone, asking for all your qualifications and every single interaction she had with you. I asked when you first met, how you met, where you were, who else was there. Y'know, leading questions."

I put my hand up. "All right, fine. It doesn't matter. What I'm not clear on is how Hodge knew to hook you up with Bernie."

"After I ran your background, it seemed your corporate connections could be of use. I mean we were dealing with plenty of industries, domestic and international, so it made sense. I told Alvin to keep his ears open, and if anyone mentioned Martin Technologies, to keep me in mind."

"But he was the night clerk. How would he hear any of this?" Paul's story wasn't making much sense.

"Because he always worked closely with the concierge and was close with everyone at the front desk. It's easy to find out what people want. Phone numbers, contact information, directions even, and it wasn't like Bernie was keeping this a secret."

"Why didn't Muller just arrange a meeting with MT himself?"

"Because Martin Technologies refused his request. From what he said, there were a few dozen conference calls in the last two months between Klaus and Martin Tech. Klaus wanted to get an American company to back them.

At least that was the goal before the conference, but when that proved unlikely, Klaus Manufacturing figured their best bet was Martin Technologies since the newest line is all about clean energy. But even MT said the technology wasn't feasible, and it wasn't the type of project they were interested in at this point. So Bernie thought if he talked to the man in charge face-to-face, then things would be different."

"So he didn't discuss any of this with Martin over the phone?"

"Not that I know of."

"Do you know who he talked to?" I asked. Paul thought for a moment but shook his head. "Okay, where's Bernie now?"

"I haven't heard from him since Sunday night. I imagine he was busy with the conference. I was supposed to tell him if I could arrange a meeting once the conference ended, but then this happened with Alvin." He froze, aghast. "Do you think Bernie did this to Alvin?"

"I have no idea." I paced the room, thinking through the connection from Alvin to Paul to Bernie to Martin. "What was Alvin supposed to get out of this deal?"

"We were going to split the finder's fee," Paul said, realizing that might go to motive. He blanched and swallowed a few times, sweating and shaking.

TEN

Too many possibilities, too many problems, too little sleep. That practically summarized my entire existence, and it was still the case. After meeting with Paul Eastman and discussing the murder, I was less inclined to believe he was a killer. Frankly, it seemed he just happened to get lucky when he discovered my romantic attachment to the CEO of Martin Technologies which didn't bode well for any of the companies or entities he sold stolen corporate espionage secrets to. Granted, if forced to choose between being good or being lucky, the correct answer is always lucky. So perhaps he was blessed with an insane amount of luck, and all his stolen secrets were accurate. But somehow, I doubted it.

But since it seemed incredibly unlikely that Paul was the killer or in cahoots with the killer, that left everyone else. Alvin Hodge wasn't as upstanding as his record indicated since he liked to play in the grey areas when it came to his work life. Although, it was still on the lighter side of the spectrum. Making a few extra bucks to look the other way or pass along a few messages wasn't normally something that resulted in death, unless you were an international spy or a hitman, and as a general rule, they didn't drive eco-friendly vehicles. Or at least that's what James Bond and

Jason Bourne would have me believe.

After Paul left my office late that afternoon, I dialed Det. Jacobs. Even if I wasn't getting paid to assist, it couldn't hurt to help him do his job. I provided a brief synopsis of Paul's story, leaving out the unimportant details. Jacobs said they were looking into matters, and unless I found something concrete to incriminate a suspect, I should mind my own business. So much for being helpful. Briefly, I considered going over his head and talking to Lieutenant Moretti. The former acting-captain was back to his normal position, and my assistance might give him that additional bump he needed to be groomed for a permanent captain spot. But all I had was conjecture, and that wouldn't be beneficial to anyone at this point in the game.

I placed a call to Interpol and asked for a full workup on Bernard Muller and Klaus Manufacturing. They still owed me a few favors for my help identifying and detaining an international contract killer, so there was no reason why I couldn't cash in a few of my chips. The information would be available by Monday, so until then, my research was limited. I considered checking with the hotel, the Secret Service, and maybe speaking to a few of Alvin Hodge's contacts and his ex-wives, but the police would be doing that. And I didn't want to get arrested for obstruction. That meant my only potential leads were the names Paul provided.

After running a quick background and ascertaining the locations for the bulk of PDN's clientele, who were just famous enough to have their upcoming gigs or locations posted on various blogs, promotional websites, and the gossip pages, I didn't believe any of them were responsible for Alvin Hodge's death, particularly since they weren't in the vicinity of the hotel during the conference. The only remaining names on the list were PDN and hotel employees, and the police would be checking into them.

Switching gears, I read through my e-mail, locating the report I was promised on how to rectify the MT security situation. After reading through the intended process to fix the elevator in the event of a fire, I compared it to the notes I made from my test run the previous night, rewrote it in a more corporate appropriate fashion, and phoned Luc Guillot. It was Friday, and there was a good chance he left for the day, particularly since he and Martin worked all last weekend. When the call was redirected to the answering service, I left a message to schedule a meeting for sometime soon to discuss ways to correct the problem and hung up.

As soon as the phone was back in the cradle, I reconsidered and dialed the main MT number, hoping to get a chance to speak with someone. MT was my in with the business world, and I could use it to my advantage to discover some more facts about Muller and Klaus Manufacturing. Except with the CEO away on business, it appeared the rest of the board members ran from the building as soon as five o'clock rolled around. I should have known better than to expect anyone to still be working at six thirty on a Friday.

There should be something I could do in the meantime, but nothing wanted to cooperate. Out of ideas, I scribbled down a few addresses and locked up the office. Someone had the answers, and since I was actually being paid to investigate, there was no reason my job couldn't begin with some surveillance.

My first stop was the hotel. Security was prevalent, but since a deal was struck, there were far fewer VIPs hanging around. Mostly, I noted the obvious police presence. Assessing my options and the time, I let the valet park my car, and I went into the hotel bar for a drink. With only standing room remaining, I found a spot near the corner, ordered a gin and tonic, and scoped out the room. Some young professionals were out after work, meeting with friends or colleagues to knock a few back. A few people were on dates or looking for someone to keep them company, and as I made a final visual sweep, my eyes came to rest on someone with an entourage. Bingo.

Picking up my drink and handing the bartender a twenty, I sauntered over, watching the two bodyguards immediately make me. I smiled, took a sip, and continued on my intended path. "Were you here for the conference?" I called over the chatter. The two men in off-the-rack suits stepped in front of me, blocking my path to the intended target, but he was intrigued.

"Da," he responded, "do I know you?"

Slowly, so as not to cause a panic, I slipped my old MT I.D. card out of my pocket and held it up for inspection by the *Blues Brothers* impersonators. "I was observing. We weren't part of the bidding wars, but I thought you looked familiar." He smiled. Honestly, I wasn't sure who he was, nor did I actually care, but he might know something useful. And since the police and Secret Service weren't hounding him, he either had diplomatic immunity or no ties to the deceased. That didn't mean he didn't have ties to Paul Eastman, Bernard Muller, or Klaus Manufacturing. "Who do you represent?"

"SMI. Out of Minsk." He ordered the guards to step aside and let me closer. "It was a bloodbath, watching the way those deals were made." The accent only made his annoyance sound like a guttural growl.

"Tell me about it." I took a seat at his table. "I'm sorry to barge in on you. I just changed into something casual and wanted to relax and enjoy a drink. But it's standing room only, and you had an empty chair."

"No reason for a pretty woman to drink alone." He smiled. "I don't turn beautiful women away."

"Aww, you're sweet." For once in my life, I wished I paid more attention when Martin dealt with this corporate nonsense. "What did you think about Klaus Manufacturing?" I didn't know how to ease into it because I didn't know what actually transpired at the conference, so I might as well get straight to the point.

He muttered something long and derogatory in his native tongue, so I only caught a word here or there. I could speak enough Russian to function in most difficult situations, but corporate was barely a language I understood, even in English. On the other hand, I could curse in over a dozen languages, so there was that.

"My sentiments exactly." I smiled and downed my drink. Your move, comrade.

"You speak Russian?"

"Nyet." I snickered. "Have you ever dealt with Klaus

Manufacturing before? They've been pestering everyone on the Board to take a meeting with them, and I can't imagine what it is they have to sell."

"Shit. They sell shit." He gestured to a waitress, and the next thing I knew, two shot glasses were on the table with a bottle of vodka. "Drink." He poured liquor into both of our glasses, and I regretted ordering the gin. We drank, and he poured again. I knew the custom. If I could keep up, he'd keep talking. "They've been testing their clean energy," he said with a level of disdain. "It blows up in their faces. They try again. And again, accidents happen."

"Is Mr. Muller still staying at the hotel?"

"No. He ran back home with his tail between his legs." Well, at least now I knew I wasn't going to get a chance to speak to Bernie, so my Russian pal would have to do.

"Have you seen their specs?" Drinking and not eating wasn't smart. Furthermore, I needed to remember whatever he said. This was such a bad idea.

"Everyone has seen their specs. They passed along the papers like they were propaganda. But I've seen their reports." He narrowed his eyes. "They were at the conference. You said you were at the conference too." He seemed suspicious why I wasn't already aware of these facts.

"Right." I shrugged. "It all blended together once the negotiations began." I laughed and touched his arm before he could pour another shot. "Like I said, I was sent to observe, not pitch our product, but so many translators and issues concerning energy, expense, manufacturing," I let out a soft sigh, "you were there. You know what I mean."

"Yes, I do." His eyes drank me in, and his look changed to something sexual. "No more business talk. Do you have a husband? You aren't wearing a ring."

"No." I was about to excuse myself when he leaned back and smiled.

"Come, you can play with me and my girlfriend."

"Thanks, but no thanks." I stood, having learned more than I wanted to about this guy's sexual preferences and just enough to have some solid ground to stand on when asking about Klaus Manufacturing. "Do svidaniya."

He nodded slightly and watched as I walked away. That was progress. Exactly how much or how useful was still a question, but it was something. And something was always better than nothing, wasn't it? Stopping by the ladies room to purge as much of the excess alcohol from my system as possible before it could metabolize any further, I strolled through the hotel to see if I could gather any other information that might be helpful.

The staff refused to answer my questions about Alvin Hodge. I had no jurisdiction, and my P.I. license never made much of an impact. Hotel security wasn't eager to speak to me. And the few federal agents still lingering and the obvious police presence discouraged any illegal snooping. Failing to gather anything interesting, I did notice a few thick cables running from the ceiling tiles down the wall and through the floor. They were only visible near the main elevator, and after walking around a few levels, it was clear they were only visible on certain floors and in very few places. It was the same type of cable that Hodge was hanging from, but what was it for? Maybe it'd be on the hotel blueprints and schematics. Thankfully, I had access to those after my extensive review of PDN's plan.

"Maybe you're not so rusty, Parker," I said to myself, deciding I was sober enough to drive home.

It felt good to be doing something, even if I wasn't entirely certain what that something was. Furthermore, I was relieved that Eastman seemed clean. At least, I thought he did. Sure, he played around in the grey area of illegal activity, and he drank too much. But I didn't think he was malicious. One less person I could mark off as a danger was always a good thing. Tomorrow morning, I would sift through the information, figure out which leads to follow, and form a plan of attack. But I did enough for today. And the only thing I wanted to do now was go home, crawl into bed, and not think about any of this for the next eight hours. But as usual, the universe has an obvious vendetta against me and my wonderfully laid plans.

"Alexis Parker?" one of the two uniformed police

officers asked as I emerged onto the sixth floor of my apartment building.

"At your service," I remarked, giving them both a curious glance. "Can I help you with something?"

"Ma'am, we need to ask you a few questions."

"Okay." I unlocked my front door and invited them in. Phones were invented for a reason, but apparently these two cops didn't get the memo. "What's going on? I spoke with Detective Jacobs earlier today. Did he forget something?"

"Maybe you should take a seat."

"Maybe you should get to the point." I didn't like this. Something was wrong.

"According to your interview notes, you were stationed in the basement of the hotel during the conference," one of the officers read as he conferred with his notes. "Was anyone else down there on Monday between noon and two p.m.?"

"I was the only PDN employee present, but various hotel personnel were in and out of the basement for whatever the reason." The two officers exchanged a glance, but I couldn't figure out what the point of the question was. "Why? Is there a reason this is suddenly so important?"

"What about other security personnel? Did any federal agents or private security check the basement?"

"Not that I'm aware of. Is there something I should know?" I narrowed my eyes, hoping one of them would decide to volunteer some information.

"No. That was it. Thanks for your time," the second officer said, and he opened my front door. "Someone will be in touch if there are any further questions that you need to answer."

"Officers," I followed them to the door, "next time, save yourselves a trip and make a phone call."

"Yes, ma'am," one of them replied, even though my helpful hint seemed to irritate him.

Arriving home to a few police officers outside my door didn't sit well, so I did the only thing I could think of and phoned Jacobs. "Detective," I began when he answered, "why were two officers at my door five minutes ago?"

"Parker," he let out an exhale, "since it's you and we all know exactly what you're capable of, you might as well know, we discovered a breach in the subbasement, and a second body was discovered this afternoon below the hotel."

ELEVEN

I am so sick and tired of death haunting me at every turn. My federal agent days were plagued with close calls and the occasional corpse, but for the most part, they weren't that typical. It's not like I was a homicide detective, so expecting a dead body wasn't part of the job description. The private sector was supposed to be even less dangerous. No more death for me, except that seemed to be the norm. It was a constant tossup between discovering a body, someone nearly killing me, and being stuck in a situation where taking a life was the only option. This was the part of the job I wanted to escape when I took a sabbatical from crime, and here I was again.

Jacobs wasn't including me, probably since there was a good chance that I was a person of interest. No one else thought of the doors or insisted on taking a team down to the old tunnels, asking questions on breaching the sealed doors, and then determining that they weren't a risk. Obviously, my original inclination was accurate, or someone working security at the hotel was paying more attention than they should have been. Despite the fact that earlier today I determined he wasn't involved, the only name that came to mind was Paul Eastman, especially after

Lack of Jurisdiction

considering his frequent absences, connection to at least one of the vics, and some of the underhanded things he did. Great, now I was working for a killer.

Picking up the phone, I dialed Det. Nick O'Connell. We were close, and he would be straight with me about the case. Unfortunately, he and his partner were wrapped up in a robbery turned multiple homicide, and he didn't know anything about Jacobs' investigation. After promising to see what he could dig up when the dust settled, we disconnected.

With limited information, I made a list of every person from PDN that was assigned to the hotel, the few Secret Service agents I recalled, the fire chief and the two firemen that led us through the tunnels, and any of the hotel staff that might have been in the basement on Monday. The police would want the list eventually, so I e-mailed it to Jacobs. This wasn't my show. I was simply cooperating, even if it was one of the things I barely knew how to do.

After completing the list, I opened the file from my meeting this afternoon and read through the information Eastman provided. Assuming he wasn't responsible, someone on his list might be. After cross-referencing those names with the list I made for Jacobs, only the PDN and hotel employees overlapped. With little else to do, I made a few brief notations on what I learned from the SMI rep at the bar, dug up whatever I could find on the business conference, and growled in frustration when no two pieces of the puzzle fit together.

It was late. I was tired, aggravated, and pissed at the universe for dragging me into another mess that I had no desire to deal with. Okay, maybe I liked solving crimes and putting the screws to murderers, kidnappers, rapists, and the like, but reviewing security measures shouldn't result in the body count rising. This was anything but acceptable, and there wasn't a damn thing I could do about it.

My phone rang, and I glanced at the clock, wondering who would be calling around midnight. Maybe Nick had something useful to share, but it wasn't Nick. That would have made life too simple, and obviously, that wasn't allowed.

- 78 -

"So I left my apartment today. Worst idea ever. I think I'm staying home until you come back," I said in lieu of a greeting.

"What's wrong?" Martin asked.

"Two dead bodies, a police investigation I'm not part of, and a strong possibility the killer might have hired me to prove his innocence." Through the earpiece, there was background noise and traffic.

"Tell your client to go fuck himself. I don't want you to be alone with someone potentially dangerous. Have you called Mark or one of your cop friends? Maybe–"

"I know. I won't do anything stupid. Don't worry," I interjected. "How was the flight? What time is it?"

"It was long and dull, and now it's mid-morning. If you came with me, I know exactly what we would have done for all those hours on the plane."

"Scrabble?"

"That would be such a waste of a private jet," he murmured. "Anyway, I have a meeting to get to, but I just wanted to check in. You seemed off yesterday."

"I'm fine."

"No, you're not." He sighed. "And now I have an actual reason to worry. Do me a favor and leave me a voicemail at least once a day if you can't get a hold of me. I want to know you're all right."

"Martin, I'm a big girl. I can take of myself."

"Humor me, sweetheart."

"Okay," I grudgingly agreed, "but be careful and keep Bruiser close. Some of the places you're visiting aren't particularly fond of wealthy Americans. Fair enough?"

After he agreed, we disconnected, and I rubbed my eyes. With no leads to follow and little information on the police department's progress, I called it a night and went to bed. The dark was oppressive, so I turned on a light. Then the light was too bright. It was hot; then it was cold. Around three a.m., I gave up on the notion of sleeping.

I jogged on the treadmill, did some laundry, cleaned my apartment, made a grocery list, and waited for eight a.m. Finally, when it would be considered a decent hour to make a few calls, I started by dialing Mark Jablonsky. My mentor was a federal agent, and even if the current case was out of his jurisdiction, he could gain access to the information I was lacking.

"Since when do you call this early in the morning?" he asked gruffly.

"Too much time with Martin has ruined me," I retorted. "So I'm calling for a favor."

"I could have guessed as much. What do you want, Alex?"

"My latest gig ended abruptly on account of two dead bodies. One of them was a hotel night clerk who happened to take a few extra day shifts, and I don't have a name for the second DB. To top it off, my ex-boss hired me to work privately for him."

"Prostitution is illegal in every state except Nevada," Mark teased.

"Yeah, well, that's not the biggest problem." I paused, wondering how farfetched it was to consider Eastman a suspect. "The guy that hired me might be the killer, and he wants me to clear his name."

"Since when do you work the other side of the street?"

"I don't. Do you think you can use some of your pull to find out what's going on, and maybe we can meet up tonight for dinner and talk it over?"

"Are you buying?"

"Anything you want."

"Fine." I heard the annoyed exhale. Mark was amazing, even if we occasionally butted heads, so that meant he wouldn't hold back in telling me what was none of my business or what I shouldn't go near. The only problem was I typically failed to heed his warnings. "Just sit tight until I review the information and we have a chance to talk. With Marty away, I'm back to being your emergency contact, and I'd prefer if you didn't need one."

"That would make two of us."

Disconnecting, I dialed the precinct. Jacobs wasn't in. Det. O'Connell and his partner, Thompson, just went off shift and didn't bother to call, and Det. Heathcliff was working on a long-term undercover assignment. Revising my plan of attack, I phoned corporate headquarters for

PDN and talked to someone in charge of the Human Resources department. Perhaps I fudged a few details, but after enough cajoling, the woman on the other end agreed to forward Paul Eastman's personnel file to me. This would give me some sense of who I was working for. With any luck, he wasn't a killer.

Settling onto the couch, I read the security information on the hotel, PDN's plan, the mission statement the Secret Service provided, and researched the point of the international business conference we were hired to guard. The business aspect never seemed important, but it could lend itself to motive and possibly point to a few suspects. Admittedly, this would be quite a bit easier if I had any earthly idea who the second victim was. After searching for today's news stories, my eyelids started to droop, so I shut my laptop and took a nap.

The knocking startled me awake, and I went to the front door. "You look casual," I remarked, opening the door.

Jablonsky eyed the crumpled blanket on my couch. "Anything you want to talk about?" He pressed his lips together and shook his head disapprovingly, going to the counter and putting down a few files. "Didn't we talk about you finding some closure for Michael and Sam's deaths?"

"Mark," I snapped, my tone icy, "I've been up all night, working out theories on my current case. Sometimes, a girl just needs a nap. It doesn't mean shit." He looked sorrowful, and I knew I couldn't hide anything from him, even though my current bout of insomnia had nothing to do with any of that. "Some days, it's still tough. But it's not buried in the recesses of my mind anymore, and I'm getting there. Working helps. Martin helps."

A slight smile erupted on his face. "He's a good man with excellent taste in scotch."

"There's a bottle of Macallan in the cabinet," I replied, knowing the point of the compliment. "He won't mind." After Mark poured a glass, I sat next to him at the counter. "So what's up with the casual dress? I can't remember the last time I saw you in something other than government regulation attire."

"I'm on vacation this week. I figured it'd give me a

chance to catch up on some paperwork, maybe go fishing, and just relax." He narrowed his eyes. "And then you called."

"Face it, you'd be bored senseless without me." Smiling, I retrieved the stack of takeout menus and placed them on top of the files he brought. "What do you say we order dinner, you brief me on what's going on, and we devise a plan of attack?"

"We?"

"Yes, we."

"Well, it's not like I have anything better to do for the rest of the week." He sifted through the menus, finding one for the Italian place down the street with the amazing cannolis. "Manicotti with a side salad, and we can split half a dozen cannolis."

"Three each?" I narrowed my eyes, dialing the restaurant. "Somehow, I think it might turn into a four to two split."

"Wow, you must really have high hopes if you think I'm sacrificing two cannolis to you. Maybe I'll let you have one and a half, but only if you don't tell Marty I'm drinking his scotch."

TWELVE

The body discovered in the tunnels just outside the breached subbasement door was identified as a John Doe. The man was mangled and beaten to a bloody pulp. His fingers were so badly damaged in the attack that prints weren't possible, and dental records could take awhile. The most worrisome part of this mess was the breached door, the same doors that I considered a risk, guarded for half a day, and then forgot about. This wasn't the best way of safeguarding a hotel.

"Hey," Mark nudged my ankle with the tip of his shoe from across the table, "what did PDN hire you to do?"

"Evaluate their plan and protocols to ensure the businessmen and diplomats at the conference were protected."

"Okay." He gave me that knowing look. "And how many of them were actually harmed in the process?"

"None." I rolled my eyes. "But that doesn't make my job a success. There are two dead bodies in the hotel." Before he could interject something ridiculously stupid, like this wasn't my fault, which it wasn't, I interceded. "And I wouldn't put it past the police to assume I had something to do with it, particularly if Eastman is to blame."

"What do we know about him?"

I gave Mark the rundown of everything that happened, leaving no rock unturned or comment unmentioned. Nothing surfaced in any of the background checks. Paul Eastman was just dirty enough to be clean for the murders. There was no confusing him with a saint, but his shit stunk enough for it to be believable.

"Frankly, I don't know enough to determine his level of involvement, but I doubt he's our guy."

"A lot depends on the identity of the second vic," Mark surmised. "The fact that he wants to hire you to clear his name doesn't sit well." He took another swig of the scotch. "Either he's smart enough to realize he's a viable suspect, or he's hoping to pull the wool over everyone's eyes. The problem is you don't trust him, not after he tried to sneak around to gain access to Marty." He leaned back and considered something. "What did Lieutenant Moretti say about this?"

"The police lieutenant isn't one of my phone-a-friends, and I didn't want to overstep and go straight to the big gun when Jacobs is working the case. If it were Nick or Derek, I wouldn't be stuck out in left field, but Nick can't be bothered to call back and Derek's AWOL."

"Oh, so you called me because no one else could be bothered?" I must have looked rather sheepish because Mark let out an exasperated breath. "All right. Fine. Y'know, just because you didn't get reinstated last month doesn't mean you have to avoid the OIO like the plague." I snorted. "Well, you've been avoiding the OIO for the last two years, but it's time you stop." He cast a dark glare at the blanket on my couch. "We'll research the rest of the night. I'll make a couple of calls on your behalf, and tomorrow, we'll begin surveillance."

"Who said you could step in and take over my investigation?"

"You asked for help. You never ask for help, so let's shake off some of that rust that's been accumulating around your deductive skills and see if you still have what it takes to work a case."

"It's the police department's problem," I protested. "And I'm more than capable of working a case, despite what you may think." The last case I insinuated myself into, Mark did all he could to prevent me from assisting, so this was a complete reversal. "Why do you think I should investigate? Shouldn't you be telling me to mind my own business? How much scotch did you drink?" Picking up the bottle, I examined the contents.

"You're an immovable object and an unstoppable force. What's the point? Plus, you need to stay away from the couch."

"Oh, for fuck's sake," I snarled. "You're not my shrink."

"Since when do you seek professional help?" he challenged.

"Well," the smile erupted on my face, "I did call you, didn't I? Now let's cut the crap and get to work." I tossed him the phone. "Start dialing, Jablonsky. We need some solid leads on our first victim, whatever you can find on good 'ol Bernie, and anything scandalous on Paul Eastman."

"Fine," he matched my grin, "but I'm not above calling Moretti." In between placing calls, he met my eyes. "I've missed this."

"Me too."

*   *   *

The next morning, I woke up to Mark snoring on my couch. Normally, I would have been suspicious that Martin orchestrated this so I wouldn't be alone, but since I called Mark myself, that didn't seem likely. Oddly, I was glad he was here to help steer my indeterminate investigation in a more productive direction. I couldn't remember the last time we worked amicably together, and it was nice having trusted back-up.

After showering and working out some of the mental kinks over our lack of useful information, I emerged from the steamy bathroom. Mark was awake, making coffee. He grunted good morning and went to his car to get his go-bag. He never went anywhere without a change of clothes and other necessities. It was one of the helpful tricks of the trade he instilled upon me.

While he was making himself presentable, I left a voicemail for Martin as promised. Then I turned to the pages of notes from the night before. Nothing was useful. Our plan of attack was to spend the day talking to the hotel employees, figuring out who the second homicide victim was, and having another chat with Eastman. This time, it would be unplanned, and maybe he would shed some additional light on everything.

Before Mark emerged from my bathroom, there was a knock at the door. Now what? I sighed and glanced through the peephole.

"Morning, officers," I said, holding the door for them to enter. "Did you forget something on Friday?"

"Ms. Parker," the lead officer looked confused, probably since they weren't the same cops that were waiting for me Friday evening, but I was certain they were here for the same reason, "we need you to come with us, ma'am."

"Why?" It wasn't that I wanted to give them a hard time, despite the fact they called me ma'am, but they could either explain the reason for this or formally arrest me. I spent too many years in law enforcement to go quietly, particularly when I had other plans for the day.

"Your name has surfaced in conjunction with an ongoing investigation."

"Concerning?" Now I was just being a pain in the ass for the hell of it.

"Were you hired by PDN to evaluate hotel security?" the second officer asked, and I heard the bathroom door open behind him. The man spun, surprised anyone else was in my apartment. How he missed the sounds of the shower running was beyond me but whatever. Maybe all the insults Mark had made concerning the incompetence of the police department over the years weren't completed unwarranted. "Sir," the cop addressed Mark, suddenly uneasy, like we were about to jump him, "please remain there."

"What the fuck?" Mark glanced at me. "Now what did you do?"

"I didn't do anything. Apparently, I'm wanted for questioning."

"Too bad." Mark smirked and pointed to the coffee table. "Do you see those credentials?" The cop picked them up and examined them and then Mark. "You'll have to take a number. Ms. Parker is assisting on a case."

"Agent Jablonsky, we're under strict orders to bring her in for questioning," the police officer insisted.

"Is she under arrest?" Mark asked.

"No, sir."

"Then run along, kid." He hid the smile masterfully. "I'll bring her in later this afternoon for your interrogation. If anyone has a problem with that, tell them to speak to Lieutenant Moretti because I'm giving Dominic a call right now." The police officers hedged while I sipped my coffee and wondered how far they were willing to stick their necks out to follow orders. "Go on," Mark jerked his head at my front door, "or do you want to risk impeding a federal investigation?"

The cop glared at me. "If you don't stop by this afternoon, we'll be forced to issue a warrant for your arrest."

"Sure thing." I gave him a bright smile.

After the door closed, I shook my head. There was never a dull moment around here. Mark took a seat beside me at the counter and flipped through our notes from the night before.

"Why do you think they dropped by?" he asked.

"Because they want to cover all their bases."

"And if I wasn't here, would you have gone with them?"

"Eh," I raised my shoulders in a 'who knows' gesture, "too bad they don't want to throw some consulting work my way."

"C'mon," he stood and put his mug in the sink, "we have work to do. And since I've promised to deliver you to the precinct in a timely fashion, we better get started. I would say we could save time by splitting up, but you're likely to go on the run."

"After doing that once, it really isn't all it's cracked up to be." I slipped into my shoulder holster, picked up my purse, and grabbed my jacket. "But just to be on the safe side, you better drive."

First stop was the hotel. Mark's OIO badge packed more of a punch than my P.I. license, and after speaking to a few desk clerks, the shift manager, and a few of the security personnel, we were escorted into an office to await an appearance from the head of security and the hotel manager. It was nice to have access to the big guns.

When the two men entered, I wasn't surprised to learn I hadn't encountered either of them before. It's not like they had to deal directly with PDN, just the Secret Service and whatever foreign security the delegates might have. After a brief round of introductions, the man in charge took a seat across from us while the head of security remained standing next to him.

"What can we do for you, Agent?" Gordon Russell asked. His nameplate gleamed brightly in the fluorescent lights, and I wondered if he polished it on a daily basis. There was no reason not to take pride in your position, even if hotel manager never seemed that important of a role to me.

"Just dotting some I's," Mark said. This wasn't an OIO investigation, and since the FBI was removed from the case based on lack of jurisdiction, it would be a pretty large leap to justify our presence. "What can you tell me about the recent business convention in regards to the two bodies being discovered on the premises?"

"As far as the investigators have determined, the events are unrelated." Russell leaned back in his chair and folded his hands over his stomach. "It's a shame we lost our best night clerk over nothing more than gratuitous violence."

"Was there any trouble at home or personal problems? Do you know of anyone with an axe to grind?" I asked.

A brief look was exchanged between the head of security and the manager before they both gave a slight headshake. "No one I'm aware of. Business was fine. Alvin acted normally. Hell, he even volunteered to pick up some of the slack since everyone was pulling double duty," Russell responded.

"Are you sure there were no personal issues outside of work?" Mark asked. "I mean the guy volunteered for extra shifts. Did he need the money? Or could he have been avoiding someone?" Jablonsky narrowed his eyes. "Has anyone strange been by to speak with Alvin Hodge in the last couple of weeks?"

"Jason," Russell turned to the man beside him, "can you get a copy of the video surveillance from the front desk for the last," he glanced at Mark, "two weeks?" Mark nodded. "And bring it to Agent Jablonsky."

"Right away, sir."

After Jason disappeared, I scanned the rest of the office. The manager's office was situated adjacent to the elevator on the tenth floor. "What's the purpose of those cables?" I asked, focusing on one very similar to the type Hodge was hanging from.

He turned his head to see what I was looking at and chuckled. "They're consolidated to hold the cable, phone, and electrical wires. They run from room to room, mostly through the walls or floors, but after the latest remodel, the elevators were relocated and a couple of walls were knocked down."

"I see." If someone intended to make a statement, they had to be familiar with the locations where they could leave Hodge hanging. Then again, maybe it was purely opportunistic and not at all planned. Mark shifted, and I knew he was waiting for me to ask another question. "What do you know about the second body that was discovered below the hotel?"

"Nothing." Russell's eyes narrowed as if I suddenly struck him as familiar. "One of the security companies for the conference checked the underground tunnels for weaknesses, but they were ruled safe. When the police asked if anyone on staff could identify the dead man, no one ever saw him before, not that identifying someone beaten up like that would even be possible."

"Did you get a name?" Mark asked. We still didn't have an I.D., but in case the police were playing hardball and choosing not to share with us, perhaps something accidentally leaked to the hotel manager.

"No. I'd like to believe he was a vagrant."

"Did he breach the subbasement doors?" I knew the answer was yes, but it never hurt to test out someone's ability to tell the truth.

"Possibly. The seal was broken, but it didn't appear the door was actually opened. Nothing inside was disturbed, and there was no indication he entered the actual basement."

"Can I see the surveillance on that?" Mark interjected just as Jason came back into the room.

"Fine, whatever you want," Russell sighed, clearly annoyed with our questions and requests, "but I need to get back to work. A hotel can't run itself." He whispered some orders to Jason, and we were led out of the room and to the security office.

"Alexis?" one of the security personnel I dealt with during my stint with PDN asked as we entered the room. Shit.

"Hey," I greeted as Jason whose last name was apparently classified information turned with a glare.

"I thought you were federal agents," he growled.

"I am," Mark piped up. "Parker is consulting for me. Do you have a problem with that?" He never raised his voice, but Mark was excellent at making threats without doing anything overt. I never understood how that happened or why, but Mr. Head of Security deflated slightly, almost like a scolded puppy. "Now, you were about to hand over the surveillance from the basement, Mr. ..."

"Oster. Jason Oster," he admitted. At least we had a last name. At this rate, there was no doubt the police would find the murderer and the DA would have a conviction before Mark and I even determined the identity of the second body or if Paul Eastman was involved. Oh well, like I said in my apartment last night, this wasn't our problem. Except, somehow, it was. "Here's that footage. Now, unless you have a warrant, I believe we're done here. I will show you out."

Mark glanced at his watch as we were led back to the lobby. "Fifteen minutes. That's a new record for cooperation without the 'no warrant, fuck you,' speech," he said quietly.

"See, your people skills are clearly improving," I whispered.

THIRTEEN

After getting kicked out of the hotel by Jason Oster, head of security, Mark drove to the OIO building. It was unexpected, and from the sly glance he tossed my way, I wondered what he was thinking. He was on vacation. Obviously, no one expected to see him in the building, and ever since my disgraced failed attempt at the physical reqs, entirely due to my broken bones, I was too embarrassed to show my face here.

"The tech department owes me a few favors, so I'll have them run the footage through facial recognition and compare it to our known criminal databases," he supplied, parking the car. "I'll also check to see if anyone's heard anything about the second DB in the tunnels. Even if this isn't our problem, occasionally word travels, and with the international conference, someone around here might have a vested interest."

"Since when?"

"Since I said so. Now stay put. I'm doing you a favor, so be nice."

"I'm always nice."

He snorted. "Yeah, right, and I'm the Queen of Sheba."

"Well, don't just stand there, I have an inquisition later,

your majesty," I teased as he shut the door and went to the elevator.

There was no reason for me to follow. I didn't have any pull on this case. My friend, Kate, was a forensic accountant, and occasionally, I could cajole some information out of the Interpol liaison assigned to the OIO, but that was about it. I didn't cultivate too many relationships beyond working individual cases, and after vowing to give up this job only to strong-arm my way on to a case, most people with at least two brain cells avoided getting close to me. It was fine. I wasn't exactly a people person.

While I waited, I dialed Det. O'Connell again. After his out of office message played, I left an apology for being such a pain and hoped he would still consider passing along whatever information he finds since he was still my favorite detective, despite his lack of sharing.

A few minutes later, Mark returned. "Are we set?" I asked.

"Absolutely." He turned the key in the ignition. "I figured the last thing either of us wants to do tonight is spend hour upon hour watching security cam footage and playing spot the crook." Pulling out of the garage, he checked the time. "Let's stop by and visit Eastman. Will he be at work, even though it's Sunday?"

"As far as I know." I ran through what little I knew about him and told Mark about the personnel files I ascertained from the head of PDN. "Hell, maybe it's even early enough in the day for him to be completely sober."

"Do you really believe he's a functioning alcoholic? There was a time in my life people probably thought I had a drinking problem too. And you know Marty, never without his scotch."

"I don't know. It doesn't make a difference. Maybe the suspicion and questioning have just been making him overly nervous, so he's imbibing more." I shrugged. "All I know for sure is his hands were a little shaky, and a few minutes before Alvin Hodge's body was discovered, he came into the control room, smelling like a distillery."

"How did he act after the discovery of the body?" Mark

asked, the wheels turning in his head. "Maybe he was drinking because he just killed someone or was informed of the impending find."

"Hodge was DOA for a while. The Secret Service agent said the body was cold, so that probably means Eastman didn't just kill him, grab a drink, and stop by the control room. But it's possible the drinking was to keep his nerves in check. Hell, maybe it would be better if Eastman has a problem. At least then he won't be the number one suspect for the murders." Thinking about the few facts, Paul Eastman was the prime suspect. Frankly, he might be the only suspect. He knew Hodge personally. They were involved in numerous acts which were at least marginally illegal, and he was nervous before the body was discovered. To further complicate matters, he knew about the weakness in the basement doors, distracted me, and possibly even hoped to keep me out of the loop. By hiring me to clear his name, he might simply be attempting to throw us off the scent. I didn't like it. "Do you think he's playing me?" I asked, turning in the seat to face Mark. "It's happened before."

"I don't know, Alex." He met my eyes briefly before returning his gaze to the road. "What do your instincts say? You know I've always valued them."

"This might sound crazy, but I think Eastman's guilty of something else, not the murders."

"Let's see what he says before you mail him your invoice for all these billable hours." He parked the car and turned off the engine. "Do I get a consulting fee for the assist?"

"We'll see. It depends on what you find, but I'll give you a bonus for sourcing out the video surveillance work."

We entered the PDN building, and Mark flashed his badge to bypass the receptionist and go straight to Eastman's office. The only problem was he was gone. According to his secretary, the police stopped by early this morning and dragged him away in handcuffs. Thankfully, they didn't do the same to me. After asking if we could search his office and being told to leave unless we had the proper legal documentation, we went back to the car.

"I guess it's time to drop off America's most wanted,"

Mark mused. "While you have a chat with Detective Jacobs or whoever wants to question you, I'll see what I can find out about Paul Eastman and what evidence they have against him."

"Divide and conquer?"

"Yep, just don't piss anyone off. I don't know that my vacation status has enough pull to keep you from getting arrested too."

After we arrived at the precinct, I went up to homicide and found an empty chair near Jacobs' desk. Scooting it over, I took a seat and rested my elbow on the edge of the desk. He glanced up from his computer with a glare. Obviously, my cooperation wasn't enough to put him in a good mood.

"Parker," he nodded, "do you remember the first time we met?"

"I can't say that I do." He assisted on the first case I worked with Det. Heathcliff, and he popped up a few times on subsequent investigations and consulting gigs, but none of that seemed particularly notable.

"You were still a federal agent at the time." He sucked some air through his teeth. "I expected you to take over my murder investigation. An ADA was killed." I shut my eyes and inhaled. That was the last case I ever worked at the OIO. It was Agents Carver and Boyle's last case too. "But you surprised me. You didn't step on any toes. You were willing to work with us and share information." He shook his head and smirked. "The first time in history some fed didn't try to run the cops off their own turf. I was amazed and maybe a little grateful."

"I'm not sure I remember getting a thank you card in the mail."

"The reason I'm taking this little walk down memory lane is because every time you've been involved in something, you always do the right thing. It might result in having a bitch and a half of paperwork, but you come through. Hell, even today, you still showed up without further prodding by a couple of bored uniforms."

"I'm not getting any younger, Detective. Can we skip all these compliments since I sense a but coming?"

"Because of professional courtesy alone, it would take a hell of a lot for us to actually arrest you. And there's no hard evidence indicating you're involved in anything, but we brought Paul Eastman in this morning. And guess what we found in his wallet."

"I'll be amazed if you say a magnum sized condom."

"Your business card." He picked up a pen and flipped to a new page in his notebook. "Want to tell me about that?"

"What's to tell? I mentioned on Friday that he was looking to hire me, and we've already discussed everything I know relating to Eastman and the first dead body. I told you all about my affiliation with PDN and the Secret Service, so there's not much left. Friday afternoon, Paul showed up at my office and asked if I would help prove his innocence."

"You could be construed as an accessory." He shook his head, fighting the internal struggle of whether or not I was involved in the two homicides. "It's all because of the damn doors."

"I thought they were a risk, and they were. I know how it looks, but I wasn't there."

"Where were you?"

It was ridiculous that I needed an alibi. What was even more ridiculous was the fact that he didn't even give me enough information to determine what timeframe needed accounting. "You're slipping, Detective. I don't know a damn thing about the second body. Do you have a name? Or a TOD? Or anything?"

"Fine, tell me what you did from the time you left FBI HQ on Wednesday morning until the police stopped by your apartment Friday evening." I narrowed my eyes and saw the slightest victory reflected in his dark orbs. He was relieved that I lacked the pertinent information. "A general account should do for now." So I told him about Martin, my work at Martin Technologies, and my investigation on Friday.

"If you need someone to verify my story, here are some names and numbers." I scribbled Martin's cell, the direct line to the MT security office, and Jablonsky's number on a sheet of paper. "So who do I have to sleep with to get some information on the second body you found at the hotel?"

"I'll make a deal with you. Once I verify your story for the estimated TOD and you are officially cleared from any suspicion, I'll let you read through the open case file. Does that sound fair?"

"I can live with that." I stood, realizing I didn't make much progress, but at least Jacobs was extending a courtesy and didn't plan to put me in holding until my alibi was verified. At least he didn't believe I was the killer. "But do you think you could put a rush on it? Apparently my client's under arrest, and I probably need to get to work proving his innocence before the DA arraigns him."

"Do you think he's innocent? When I talked to you Wednesday morning and again on Friday, you were ready to hang him out to dry."

"Honestly, I'm not sure. I'll let you know what I dig up, but only after you let me read through the file."

"Okay." He made a note and jerked his chin toward the door. "You're free to go, but do us all a favor and don't leave town."

"Yes, sir."

"Hey," he stopped me halfway to the door, "O'Connell isn't calling you back until you're no longer a person of interest. Those were orders passed down from the brass."

"Right," I acknowledged, continuing to the doorway.

Before I even cleared the first flight of stairs, Mark appeared on the landing. He met my eyes. "Are you finished answering their questions?"

"Yep."

"Then let's go." There was something urgent in his voice. "We have to get back to the OIO, the techs just called."

FOURTEEN

"You're shitting me." My head was in my hands, and I was on the verge of a horrible migraine. "No. There's no way. You have it wrong. Someone in this office has it wrong. Maybe the software is acting up." I shook my head vehemently. "No."

"Alex," Mark said patiently, glancing at the tech seated next to us, "you've already made Steve run the algorithm four times. We didn't screw up. Someone at the Secret Service must have."

"Or at PDN," I mumbled. "I didn't see it." I massaged my temples which were throbbing. "Are you sure the date and time are correct?"

"Yes, ma'am," Steve Lawson, the OIO's senior tech advisor, replied.

"Now you're just adding insult to injury. How long has he been on the watchlist?" I asked.

"Stop," Mark berated. "You're acting like Osama Bin Laden waltzed into the hotel, and you didn't notice. This guy isn't some international terrorist."

"No. Instead, he's just on the FBI's ten most wanted list."

"On the bright side, it's all white collar crimes, fraud,

money laundering, embezzlement, RICO violations, and failure to appear. His only violent act involved evading capture. Face it, he's the lesser known Bernie Madoff."

"Oh god, what the hell is up with everyone being named Bernie all of a sudden?"

"His name is Frank Costan," Lawson chimed in unhelpfully. "Ever since Homeland took control of the Secret Service from the Treasury Department, it's been one thing after another. Kinda funny if you think that a money guy eluded some Treasury agents." Giving him a dead-eye stare, he recanted with, "Well, they aren't controlled by the money men anymore, so maybe that's why." After another moment of staring, he excused himself from the room.

"It gets worse." Mark drew my attention back to him. "You didn't hear this from me, and whenever you get the official police version, make sure you act surprised, but he was found in the subway tunnel underneath the hotel. He's our second DB. And before you ask, the basement footage didn't show anyone entering or exiting. Maybe Russell was correct when he said the hotel wasn't breached."

"Aside from the fact that Frank Costan was staying at the hotel and ended up dead underneath it." I rolled my eyes and paced the room. "How could I have not noticed this? From the looks of things, the guy was traipsing around the hotel like he owned the place."

"That doesn't mean you ever crossed paths. Plus, even if you did, you weren't expecting to encounter wanted criminals."

"Well, it's no wonder I didn't recognize him since he's no longer on the most wanted list. Maybe you should print out the updated one before anyone else drops dead."

Mark stood and slammed the door, and the vibrations reverberated in my skull. Blowing out a steady breath, he fought to hold his temper in check. The good thing about all those years being trained by Mark was I knew exactly when I pissed him off. Unfortunately for me, now was precisely one of those times.

"Talk to me," he urged, leaning against the door. "Two men are dead, and since Costan is one of the dearly departed, this is now officially a federal matter."

"Don't give me that. It all depends on cause of death. Jacobs didn't say a word to me about any of it, so it might not be your show just yet."

"It's not my show. I'm on vacation this week, remember?" If steam could come out of his ears, it would. "You and I both know your client," he practically spat the word, "is involved."

"This is a discussion for another place." My eyes darted around the room. "This isn't your assignment, Jablonsky. And I sure as hell am not a federal agent. Shouldn't you be telling me this isn't my business and to keep my nose out of it?"

He came across the room and grabbed my shoulders forcefully. This was the first time he'd ever been so abrupt, and I was taken aback. "I'm sorry, Parker." His eyes pleaded for forgiveness, and surprisingly, he hugged me. "For the past two years, I've been treating you like a yo-yo, and then I get irritated when you can't make up your goddamn mind." He released me and stepped back. "No, this has to stop now. No more fighting. No more telling you when you should or shouldn't work an investigation. I trained you. I trust you. Now let's get out of here so you can tell me what you think we should be doing."

"Mark?" Did he just admit he was wrong? The entire situation was surreal, but he turned as if nothing happened and left the room. Chasing after him, we were back in the car before I had any earthly idea what was happening. "My office," I suggested meekly when he turned, waiting for a destination.

Once we arrived and I opened the door, we went inside. He took a seat in my client chair and waited for an elaboration. I still couldn't figure out the reason for the sudden shift in his attitude. Without a word, I turned on my computer, printed off a copy of all the information the criminal databases had on Costan, and grabbed a dry erase marker from the cup on my desk. Going to the whiteboard, I sketched out the hotel, the tunnels, the location of Alvin Hodge's body, the locations I was positioned, the most likely spots Eastman would have been when he wasn't in my presence, and the routes PDN and the Secret Service were supposedly taking to ensure the utmost level of security during the conference. When I was done, I found Mark skimming through the business section of the paper in search of details on the conference.

"Ta da," I said, drawing his attention away from the paper. "This is it. So in the event I'm arrested as an accessory, make sure you erase the damning evidence from the board." He smiled, stifling a laugh. "All right, so this is what everything looked like. As you can see, I have no earthly idea exactly where Eastman was at the time of either murder, particularly since we don't actually know when either of these two gentlemen was killed. I've told you exactly how the planning phase with PDN went and the background and interviews with the government. The only thing I haven't mentioned was a follow-up I conducted the other night. Nothing particularly helpful surfaced. I spoke with one of the delegates representing SMI in order to determine what Eastman's obsession with Martin was. I still don't know, but no one seemed to particularly care for Klaus Manufacturing or the claims Bernard Muller was making on their behalf."

"Hodge put Eastman in contact with Muller, right?"

"That's what Paul said." Flipping the board to the other side, I formulated a new theory, and when I was done with my pictorial representation, I turned to catch the proud hint of a smile on Mark's face.

"It makes sense, but face it, you just pulled the entire thing out of your ass."

"Not to mention, it doesn't help us identify the killer or killers either." Working the kink out of my neck, I tilted my head to the side. "Honestly, it could be Paul."

"Talk it out."

"Okay. This was a huge international business deal, so it wouldn't be strange for Costan to make an appearance. From the hotel surveillance, it appears he checked in two days prior to the conference. I can only assume he was there to make some type of deal. Maybe he wanted to pay off one of the rich moguls to smuggle him out of the country, or he wanted to filter some of his stolen funds through a corporation. Who the hell knows? I'm sure we can find a motive easily enough once forensic accountants start digging." He nodded that I should continue. "Whatever the reason Costan was there, I'd imagine someone in the hotel must have known, even though Russell claimed no one on staff could identify the body. Costan is infamous or was, I guess."

"He could have paid a few key players off. We'll worry about the details later."

"So Costan's there, and Alvin Hodge must be aware of this fact. From the way Eastman described him, I'd say he knew everything that was happening inside the hotel."

"If Hodge arranged a meet between Costan and one of the business types present at the conference, it might explain the motive for his murder, maybe both murders. Costan probably didn't want anyone to be the wiser when it came to his whereabouts. Hell, maybe Hodge threatened to blackmail him or sell him out to the feds if he didn't pay through the nose to maintain his anonymity. So maybe Costan was responsible for Hodge's death."

"Paul might have known Frank Costan was at the hotel. He was staying there at the same time, and it sounds like he and Hodge exchanged information like this all the time." Rubbing my temples, I leaned back in the chair and shut my eyes. "But that doesn't explain Paul's sudden interest in Martin or his dealings with Muller."

"Focus. One step at a time. Work the Costan angle first."

"Alvin Hodge must be connected to Costan. It's the only reason to assume they both ended up dead in the vicinity of the hotel."

"Hodge was left hanging out in the open. That reads like a threat," Mark added. "Costan was found after Hodge, and we know he wasn't dead on Sunday because that's when you checked the subbasement doors and the tunnels."

"So we're thinking Hodge was killed first as a message to Costan." I studied the drawing. "Okay, I'll go with that for now. Maybe it was a complicated deal, and Hodge was the middleman. After he was eliminated, Costan either failed to comply or someone couldn't risk being implicated, so they ended him too."

"Sounds plausible. Let's dig up everything we can

possibly find on Hodge. He's the single piece that holds it all together. Whatever his history is and whoever he encountered could be a part of this."

Concurring, I dug through my files and found the notes on Hodge. A few other pieces were still at my apartment, but since the information came from database searches, it didn't seem necessary to relocate the party just yet. "He has two ex-wives. He lives in suburbia. Nothing pointed to him being this guy. He drives a fucking hybrid for god's sakes. How many criminal masterminds drive hybrids?"

"Parker," he chortled, "even the evildoers sometimes care about the environment, and not all of them kick puppies either. Hell, Hitler liked dogs."

"Yeah, well, it seems to me if you're perfectly fine enhancing your pocketbook through questionable means, you shouldn't give a shit about much else."

As Mark read through the information on Hodge's two ex-wives, his financial history, and the other pertinent facts, I paced my office space. There were a million questions I wanted to ask Eastman, but until Jacobs gave the all clear, I couldn't go near him. Now there was an even smaller chance I'd get to talk to him if the FBI took over the investigation on account of Costan's involvement.

"Rachel Romanski," Mark's voice drew me out of my reverie, "she's teaching an advanced yoga class in the morning. How are you feeling? Are you up for some downward dog?"

Glowering and slightly grateful the question was asked by Mark and not Martin, I shook my head. "Maybe I'll skip that one and just go with warrior pose."

"Don't you always?"

"Since that's not for another twelve hours, let's drive past Hodge's place and see if anything looks out of the ordinary."

The trip didn't take very long, and of course, police tape covered most of the area. This wasn't a crime scene, but it might provide some insight into who Hodge's killer was or if the man really was just suicidal.

"Could we be looking at this all wrong?" I asked out of the blue as Mark parked the car, and we stepped out of the vehicle.

"How so?"

"I don't know. My gut says this relates back to the business conference, but I didn't pay much attention to the comings and goings."

"Hey, you're not a tycoon or particularly business savvy. That's probably why you're dating Marty." He cocked an eyebrow. "He delivers on the few aspects you aren't well-versed in."

"Crude humor and business know-how?" I snorted. "He'll love to hear that." Following Mark's lead, we went around the house, checked the garbage can, which was emptied, and attempted to see if any of the doors were left open. "I thought you liked following rules."

"What rules? I'm a private investigator's assistant for the rest of the week. You mean to tell me there are rules? Since when? You never seem to have any."

"Yes, but that's because I don't have a badge that someone can take away. It's already gone." I put my hand on his shoulder. "C'mon, you're staying out of trouble SSA Jablonsky, especially when we need your official capacity to dig up everything you can on whatever the authorities already found in the house. And while you're at it, get a list of items in Costan's hotel room. I'm sure the techs have figured out which room was his by now. Oh, and a breakdown from the forensic accountants on whatever method he used to pay and wherever funds were being channeled would also be great."

"Oh, so now I'm following your orders?"

"You're my self-proclaimed assistant. The only requirement for that job title is to follow my orders."

"This is payback for years of research and paperwork, isn't it?"

"You bet your ass it is."

FIFTEEN

"Very good," Rachel said. "Take a final cleansing breath and relax." The dozen women in the room began rolling up their mats, and various "Namastes" echoed throughout the room. What the hell does that even mean? "Alexis," she called, and I forced my face into a neutral, at peace with the world, Zen position, "did you want to sign up for weekly classes?"

"Maybe." My biggest decision was determining if I wanted to admit my reason for being at the yoga studio in the first place. "I'm not really sure I'm cleared for physical activity just yet." The best cover stories focused on aspects of the truth.

"Back problems?" she asked, offering a sympathetic look. "From your stance and posture, it seems your back's stiff."

"Wow, you figured that out just from my lack of flexibility?" I asked. "It's not just my back. It's my posterior ribs. Last month, I broke five of them in an accident." Okay, so this was where lying met the truth. The accident wasn't precisely an accident.

She squinted, wiping sweat from her brow. Whoever thought stretching and holding ridiculous poses in insanely high temperatures was a good idea was a freaking idiot, or at least that was my take on the matter, mostly since hot weather and I rarely got along. "So why did you come for the introductory class when you're still on the mend?"

"It seemed like fun. Recently, I was at a business conference at one of the nearby hotels, and one of the night shift clerks was telling everyone how amazing your hot yoga class was." Okay, so I had no way of knowing what Hodge's opinion of yoga or Rachel was, but it was worth a shot.

Something flitted across her face. "Alvin."

"And the Chipmunks?"

She laughed. "No. My ex. He works at a hotel. Half the girls in my classes came here because of his recommendations. At least the dickhead did something nice."

"I guess that means things didn't end quite so amicably. No Namaste?" Was she really that cold? Or did the police fail to notify her or ask her to identify the remains? Maybe Alvin had a different emergency contact listed on his employment forms. Still, it was common practice to question spouses, estranged and otherwise.

"Oh, it definitely was Namaste." She rolled her eyes. "In case you were curious, Namaste roughly translates to bowing to your true self which is why it's a greeting and used in departing from class."

"Ah, good to know." She glanced behind us, but the room was empty. "So his true self wasn't the person you thought he was?" I asked.

"That's putting it mildly."

"Hey, do you think we could go across the street and get something cold to drink while I pick your brain about classes and stuff?" Mainly, I just wanted to pick her brain about Alvin. "I'm about to pass out from the heat. How can you stand to do this all day?"

"Come on," she led me out of the room, "I'll explain the differences in types of yoga and the class structure, and you can tell me about your injury and what you hope to achieve. From the looks of you, I'd wager you already have a great regimen. Your previous statement notwithstanding, you appear incredibly flexible and strong. Plus, I'd kill for your legs."

"I run," I responded, but she looked skeptical, "a lot." She still didn't look convinced as we left the studio and went across the street to a sandwich shop. "Mix in some additional cardio, a little strength training, and well," I saw a chance to get back to the topic of Alvin, "a very active boyfriend."

She snorted, her eyes lighting slightly at the comment. "Is he as flexible as you appear to be?"

"Basically. Sometimes, it's like living in Cirque du Soleil." We made it through the line at the sandwich shop and sat at a table in the corner with our bottled waters. "So since Alvin's boasting about your yoga classes, you probably know exactly what I'm talking about."

"He dabbled, but he was more into the clean living, biofuels, organic foods, a million uses for hemp."

"Besides smoking it?" I asked.

A giggle escaped her lips, and she covered her mouth, surprised by her own reaction. "Actually, despite his hippie tendencies and attitude, he was a straight shooter. Well, I thought he was, but I was wrong."

"I hate it when men turn back into toads."

"Tell me about it. He seemed so perfect. Honest, decent, he made me want to be a better person. And then one day, I discover he's involved in lots of questionable stuff."

"What kind of stuff?" Finally, some progress.

She shook her head. "It was mostly because of his job. He's the night manager or whatever, but guests would ask him for all kinds of things." She glanced around the restaurant and leaned in, lowering her voice. "The kinds of things that could get someone arrested. You'd be amazed what people ask for when they stay at a classy hotel." She kept referring to him in the present, so perhaps she didn't know he was dead.

"I'm guessing you're not talking about a few dozen pillow mints."

"Not unless you can put them up your nose." She leaned back and drank her water. "Whatever. I wasn't down for that. He swore it was just a work thing, but some guys showed up at our house a few times, and it didn't matter how in love we were. I couldn't do it." She blew out a breath. "Don't get me wrong. He's not a bad guy, and I'm sure you could tell his depiction of my class was pretty spot on." She forced a bright, phony smile on her face. "So let's get back to business. I'm sorry to talk your ear off. I'm sure you couldn't care less about my failed fairy tale. It's been almost a year since I've seen or heard from him. I guess it just took me by surprise that he was still talking about me. Maybe in another life, he won't be required to deal with such things, and we can be together."

Not wanting to push any harder, I politely sat there while she discussed the different types of yoga classes, the schedule, how expensive they are, and which would be the most beneficial for meditation. I didn't have the heart to tell her after spending six months in a class a couple of years ago, I would rather gouge my eyes out than remain in any one position while searching for inner peace. Obviously, my personality was too volatile and impatient for the benefits yoga gave to so many others. It also reminded me of having to escape a sadist in a Parisian warehouse. Wow, was any aspect of my life not tainted with bad experiences? Probably not.

On my way home, I left Martin a voicemail. The time difference was killing us, but under normal circumstances, we didn't speak every day. We were both far too busy for idle chitchat. After showering, I phoned Mark, and we agreed to meet at my office. Upon arriving, I filled him in on what I learned from Rachel Romanski.

"It sounds like Hodge was dealing drugs," Mark surmised.

"That's what Rachel thought. But it's possible he was brokering other types of deals, and she just assumed drugs."

"Well, it's a reasonable assumption." He picked up the phone and began dialing. "I'll see if my pals at the DEA, ATF, or Customs had him in their sights for anything. If he was under surveillance or if they ran across him while they were surveilling someone else, then maybe we'll know where to go from here."

While he made the calls, I skimmed through Costan's records. Maybe there was a connection between the two deceased prior to the conference. If Costan and Hodge had a common connector or were somehow affiliated, then whatever led to their deaths might have been in the works for quite some time.

When Mark hung up the phone, waiting for one of his friends to get back to him with the information, I asked, "What did you get on the financials and the items found in Costan's hotel suite and at Hodge's place?"

"Financials are being investigated as we speak. It's part of the FBI's investigation, so it's dependent on warrants and subpoenas. You gotta love court orders."

"What about the rest?"

"The PD isn't playing ball. I spoke with Lt. Moretti, but he said his detectives were handling it. Normally, Dom's friendlier, but I think after I spoke so harshly to his rookies yesterday morning, he wants to remind me of my place. He's being a cocky bastard."

"Wow, a guy being macho and cocky. Who would have thought?"

"Shut up, Parker. I don't need you to be cute."

"I'm always cute." He exhaled, releasing a quiet guttural sound as I skimmed my notes for the next best course of action. "Romanski doesn't know Hodge is dead," I mused aloud.

"Okay, so? Whenever I kick, I don't expect my ex-wives to be the first to find out either."

"But wouldn't next of kin have to be notified?" Flipping through the pages, Hodge didn't have any children, his parents were deceased, and his only brother was listed as MIA from the Army. That ruled out family connections.

"Someone will have to claim the body. Maybe he had an emergency contact on file with the hotel or written on one of those cards in his wallet." He folded his hands over his gut and shook his head as if to himself. "Let's refocus. Hodge won't give us answers. Maybe we should take a stab at Costan."

"What's the point?" I threw on my jacket and picked up my car keys. "There's only one way I can prove Eastman isn't responsible for Alvin Hodge's murder, and that's with an accurate TOD. I'll have to convince Jacobs to give me the files on Hodge and Costan and access to Eastman. Do you want to stay here and dig up what you can while I'm gone?"

"Sure." He was buried in notes and barely aware of my departure.

*　　*　　*

When I sauntered over to Jacobs' desk, he glanced up from making notes. The desk phone was pressed between his shoulder and ear, and he was writing something on a sheet of paper. Occasionally, he'd stop to type something into the computer. Apparently he was great at multitasking. He jerked his chin at the back of the room, near the filing cabinet, and mumbled a response into the receiver. Narrowing my eyes, I pointed at myself questioningly, and he nodded, almost losing the phone in the process.

"Good enough for me," I said, opening the drawer and scanning through the labels for something pertinent. Stopping at the label marked Costan, I pulled out the folder and flipped through a few pages. Maybe that's not what I was supposed to be looking at, but Jacobs gave me free rein over the filing cabinet.

Costan was found Thursday morning. The ME placed time of death between midnight and six a.m. I didn't know what Paul Eastman was up to during that time. Making a mental note to ask what time he was released from questioning on Wednesday, I continued reading the information. The body was discovered by a police officer who was conducting a sweep of the area in light of Tuesday's events. From the autopsy photos, Costan was badly beaten prior to death. Blunt force trauma to the skull and thoracic region were thought to have resulted in various bleeds in both the brain and chest cavity. Either of which could have been the cause of death.

"Put it down," Jacobs hissed. "We agreed that I'd share information on Eastman. That has nothing to do with

Eastman."

"Oh, so you're not considering charging him with a second homicide?" I spun, and Jacobs snatched the file from my hand and shut it, tucking it protectively under his arm. "In case you were curious, I actually have an alibi for Costan's murder. I was with someone from the time I left you until eight a.m. on Thursday."

"I didn't think you were responsible for either murder. Weren't you paying attention the last time we chatted?"

"Well, then what's the problem? Can't a girl be curious?" My eyes darted around the room, but no one else was close enough to hear. "I'm guessing Hodge and Costan are connected. Doesn't that give you jurisdiction over both homicides?"

"No." He found Hodge's file and Eastman's and pulled them out, adding them to the growing collection he was holding. "It just means the goddamn feds want to confiscate all the hard work and long hours I've already put in on this case."

"Damn, they're selfish. Who the hell do they think they are?" The smirk was unavoidable, and my sarcastic tone wasn't lost on the detective.

"Any helpful hints to hold off the dogs?"

"First, let me see those files. Then I'll pass along some tips of the trade." He mumbled something about me being similar to the rest of the feds, but it was too low for me to provide a proper retort. "Fine, I'll go first. You should point out Costan was on city property. There is no evidence to suggest his murder has anything to do with his wanted status, and you'll be more than happy to turn over your findings once your investigation is concluded."

"Like that'll work," he huffed, leading the way back to his desk. "Fifteen minutes. That's it."

"Thanks."

"Y'know, I wish you were still on the job. You might have been the only reasonable fed I ever dealt with." He walked away.

"C'est la vie." I opened Costan's file. He was beaten to death, and it looked like a mugging gone wrong. All of his personal effects, even his shoes, were taken. Anything worth something was gone. "Well, it doesn't look like Alvin killed you since he was already dead. But maybe it was Simon or Theodore."

Flipping to the next folder, I perused the information on Alvin Hodge. The ME didn't list a TOD. The cause of death was strangulation, but the bruising and ligature marks around his neck didn't match the pattern left by the cable he was hung from. Apparently he was killed elsewhere and left to hang in the hotel, maybe to cover up the crime. Too bad the killer didn't bother to match the gauge of cord he used. There was a note about the petechial hemorrhaging, and from the photos of Hodge's eyes, I squinted and scowled out of sheer reflex. It looked like something out of a horror film when saints bleed from their eyes. That couldn't be good. Forensics was analyzing his clothing and wound tracks for fibers or trace elements that could lead to a murder weapon or possible location prior to his posed hanging.

Lastly, I opened Eastman's file. It was sparse. Basic information, his mug shot, list of potential charges, and for some reason, someone ordered a blood test. Not surprisingly, there were trace amounts of alcohol in his system and an abnormally high reading of fluoride when they arrested him.

"He's probably more than just a social drinker," Jacobs said, returning from his confidential errand. "Wednesday morning, it appeared he was going through the DTs. Sweaty, shaking, and a little green. He was complaining of nausea and stomach cramps. When I asked him about it, he said he was coming down with something."

"Or coming off of something."

"That's why I ordered the tox screening when we booked him, but no drugs. Just alcohol. Maybe he was drinking mouthwash. It would explain his affinity for fluoride." He shrugged. "The guy's been holding down a job for four years though. He doesn't even have a DUI. It's weird. Normally, there's something. A drunken disorderly, disturbing the peace, indecent exposure, a DUI, but no indication he has a problem. But he does. He has to."

"Maybe he's been taking some very strong cough syrup

to combat the flu or whatever it is he claims to have."

"Right, that must be it." The cynicism wasn't lost on me. "Look, if you want to chat with him for a few minutes, he's downstairs in holding. He looks good for Hodge's murder, and the DA's scheduled his arraignment. But they're pretty sure he'll be released on bail. So there's no reason you can't ask a few things before he's free to go." Jacobs narrowed his eyes. "Y'know, whatever is said inside a police station that isn't considered privileged is fair game once a suspect has been Mirandized."

"I'm not doing your job for you, Detective. I was hired to clear the guy, not sell him out, but if he's innocent, then there's no reason why I can't inform you of his alibi ahead of time and save everyone some paperwork."

"Thanks, Parker. You're one of the good ones."

"Flattery will get you nowhere."

SIXTEEN

"How's the food here?" I asked, startling Eastman who looked rather green.

"Alexis," he closed his eyes and ran a hand through his hair, leaving it sticking up at odd angles, "what did you do?"

"This isn't on me. Whatever shit you're involved in is the reason you're being held. What are they charging you with?"

"Hell if I know." He shook his head. "This is bullshit. They bring me in for additional questioning concerning Alvin's death and someone else they found dead at the hotel, and then they asked if I'd consent to a blood test. I figured what the hell. It's not like I have anything to hide, and now these fucking pigs are trumping up charges against me. It was a fishing expedition, and I need to find an attorney that will hang them out to dry." He sneered. "I hired you to clear my name from any suspicion on the murder rap, not get my ass arrested for some shit they made up."

"Do you know Frank Costan?"

The look of alarm on his face was unmistakable. "The embezzler, Ponzi scheme guy?"

"Uh-huh." I waited, leaning in to the bars, aware that no one was paying a bit of attention, except for maybe the other degenerates in surrounding holding cells.

"What do you think?" he retorted, but I stared blankly at him. "Is he dead?" he asked after a time.

"Why would you think that?"

"That's not an answer." Paul came closer, lowering his voice. "There are two possibilities here. Either he's in custody and has mentioned my name in relationship to Alvin or he's dead and these assholes want to blame that on me too."

"Answer my question. Do you know him?"

"No."

"Unbelievable." I shook my head, took a deep breath, and stared at the ceiling. "I'm walking. I said if you lied to me again, we were done. And now, we're done."

"I'm not lying." He reached through the bars and grabbed my wrist. His palm was clammy, and I pulled free before the nearest officer could intervene. "Hodge said there was a rumor circulating that Frank Costan was at the conference incognito, but I never met him. I don't know him, and I never spoke to him." He gritted his teeth, furious and betrayed.

"You'll put any spin on things that you possibly can. I don't believe a word that comes out of your mouth. You have to give me something to work with. I'm fumbling around in the dark. Bodies are turning up left and right, and the next person that's gets arrested for these crimes sure as hell better not be me. So if you want me to figure out who the fuck is doing this, then give me something," I bellowed.

My volume and the argument were enough to draw the attention of some nearby LEOs who realized there was no reason for a civilian to be questioning a suspect who was currently in holding. One of them came up behind me. "Ma'am, please step aside."

"Right now, Paul. Right now," I warned as the officer addressed me again.

"Talk to Jason Oster. Tell him it's a favor for his pal at PDN," Paul insisted as the officer dragged me away from the bars.

"All right, I'm going," I said to both Paul and the cop equally. The cop let go, and I went straight to the stairwell. Mark and I already spoke with Jason Oster, and that conversation had been anything but helpful. I didn't see how going another round with Mr. Head of Security would result in anything useful.

* * *

"Marty called while you were gone. It sounds like he had a shitty day. Between the traveling and nonstop business meetings, I can see why. However, he was relieved you've actually been phoning every day. I don't think he expected that to happen. Hell, I was surprised. Since when do you let anyone put you on a leash?" Mark asked as I stepped into my office and slammed the door.

"Damn. I'm going to have to give him the clingy speech again." I slumped into the chair and pressed my palms over my eyes. After a moment to regroup, I glanced at my cell which had no missed calls, and then I checked the answering machine which was also lacking in messages.

"When he found out you were busy, he decided it was best that you didn't know he was calling," Mark added. "So pretend I didn't tell you that." He picked up a sticky note. "Next on the agenda, Interpol sent over the files you requested on Bernard Muller and Klaus Manufacturing. There isn't much. It's a fairly new company that's still getting off the ground, and Muller doesn't have any ties to international crime or known terrorist organizations."

"What about to Frank Costan?"

"Nothing that I can find. Also," he picked up a manila envelope and handed it to me, "that's the financial information on Costan's known accounts. There hasn't been any movement in or out, but Kate and the other forensic accountants at the OIO believe that this is a fraction of his net worth, and the rest must be in offshore accounts that we can't access. I did some digging on Costan's hotel reservation and how he paid. He's not listed anywhere on the guest registry, and none of his accounts were used to pay for the room. He probably has a few established fake identities, or he greased some palms to look the other way. Unfortunately, that makes it insanely difficult to determine which room was his or what items were in his possession. Mr. Russell only gave us the security footage for the lobby and the basement, so we can't track Costan through the hotel until he lets himself into a room." Skimming through the pages, Mark found nothing else of interest. "Why the hell do I feel like I'm a glorified secretary?"

"I believe the term you're looking for is personal assistant. And I appreciate the help, but I'm done."

"Really?" He sounded skeptical. "You're done. Just like that."

"Eastman's a liar. I asked if he knew Costan, and he started spouting out way too much information for someone who says he doesn't. His excuse was Hodge mentioned it was a rumor that Frank was around. Some rumor." Rolling my eyes, I put the papers back into the envelope and toyed with the tiny metal clasp. "Paul said to talk to Oster, and Jason would straighten this out." I tossed the envelope down with a resounding thwack. "But we already spoke to Oster. Paul's lying. I know he's lying, at least about knowing Costan." Wondering what else Eastman was lying about, I dialed the courthouse to find out what official charges were being heard at the arraignment.

"That information has been redacted and isn't included in the public record," the clerk responded. How could it already be confidential when the hearing didn't even happen yet? What the hell was going on?

"Do me a huge favor and find out what Eastman is being charged with," I begged Mark after hanging up the phone. "The court said it's confidential. Eastman said he didn't even know what the cops had on him. And Detective Jacobs didn't explicitly state anything, but he led me to believe it was related to Hodge's murder."

"How could that be?" Mark asked, surprised by that announcement. "They're still investigating. Eastman might be a suspect, but he can't be the only one they have. None of that makes any sense."

And it didn't. The case wasn't solved. The culprit wasn't caught. So why was Eastman being detained and what charge was the prosecutor in such a rush to get excluded from the record?

"Holy shit," the possibilities hit like a ton of bricks, "they want to turn him and use him against someone. I'd say Costan's the only player big enough for this type of maneuver, but he's dead."

"But there were plenty of influential people at the conference. Any one of them could theoretically be worse than Costan, and the FBI just hasn't made a case against them yet." Mark's words held an ominous feel. "And since Paul's in the corporate espionage biz, he might have stumbled onto their radar. I'll access the guest registry and run everyone's name to see who might be the subject of a current ongoing investigation. White collar division at the Bureau ought to know, and if not, I'll check with my friends at Homeland."

"This isn't about Eastman anymore, is it?"

"No, it's about whoever's taking Costan's place on the top ten list."

"What the hell was Alvin Hodge involved in?" I blew out a breath and bit my lip. "All right, if there is an official ongoing investigation, I need to know. In the meantime, Paul hired me to find Alvin's killer. So I plan to do just that."

"Two seconds ago, you claimed you were done."

"You ever hear of a woman's prerogative?"

"Yep. Three divorces later, and it's still giving me whiplash." He grabbed his phone and put his jacket on. "C'mon, I'll go with you. Gotta love technology. When I started out, the only way to make calls was by sitting at a desk. Now I can make calls while you drive me crazy."

The trip to the hotel didn't take too long, and from Mark's side of the conversation, I could tell that he was getting the runaround. No one wanted to admit to having a large-scale op on the books when two homicides took place in the immediate vicinity. As a general rule, intervention was sometimes necessary to ensure everyone remains breathing, even if it would sacrifice months or even years' worth of work.

Leaving my car in line at the valet stand and giving Mark strict instructions to prevent anyone from moving it, I went inside to speak to Jason Oster. Maybe he'd be more forthcoming without my federal agent escort. Meandering through the hallways, I knocked on the security office door and found a few of the lower level guards taking a break.

"Is Jason around?" I asked.

"Yeah, hang on, I'll get a location." One of them picked up the walkie-talkie and spoke into it. "Oster, what's your twenty?" Wow, these guys really wanted to be more than rent-a-cops.

"Seventh floor, investigating a broken window in room 709."

"Roger." He turned to me. "He's in room 709."

"Great. Thanks," I replied, pretending that his relaying the message was the first time I heard the news. Clearly, it would have been impossible for me to hear that over the walkie-talkie.

Taking the elevator up, I narrowed my eyes at the security cam and studied the buttons, wondering vaguely how these elevators behaved in the event of a fire emergency. Shouldn't that have been one of the things PDN examined? I thought about the emergency procedures we went through, but I was certain the elevators remained completely functional at all times. Even in the event of a power outage, power was rerouted to backup generators.

Making a mental note to see about a follow-up with Guillot at the MT building, I stepped out when the doors opened and went down the hallway. My eyes were drawn to the cables near the elevator, the exact same cable that Alvin Hodge had been left hanging from on this very floor. Who would have imagined the number seven would be so unlucky?

"I didn't realize broken windows were something only the head of security could handle," I quipped. Jason spun, surprised by my words, and I stepped into the room. The place was trashed. The bathroom mirror was broken, the pictures were askew on the walls, and the television had a shoe protruding out of it. "Domestic disturbance or maybe a tornado?"

"Get out."

"I'm not here about the excellent job you're doing as head of security." He glared at my words, but I pushed on. "Paul Eastman asked that I speak with you about one of Alvin Hodge's acquaintances." He visibly stiffened and looked nervously into the hallway, so I shut the door to give us a bit more privacy. "I'm not here to make your life a living hell, but I need to know what Hodge was involved in and if it's possible Eastman is to blame."

He snorted and rubbed his nose. "Paul's a jackass." He shook his head. "He paid off my guys to feed him tips on the attendees at the conference. He always has a scheme going, and Al felt bad for him. He'd throw him a bone every once in a while, but it was never anything major."

"Do you know whose body was discovered in the tunnels?"

"I've heard rumors. And I can guarantee if Al knew who was staying here, he wouldn't have shared that with Paul. There's not a chance in hell he'd risk a score like that on a pissant like Paul Eastman." Something about Oster's tone made me suspicious.

"Who would Al have shared that kind of news with?"

"How would I know? Al knew some heavy hitters and could make things happen or disappear for the right price, but I'm not sure what he was planning with the guy they found in the tunnels. And I don't know who did it. Nothing was caught on any of the security cams. It's below the hotel. My job is to protect the hotel, not the surrounding area. I believe that's what the police are supposed to do." He looked disgusted. "You'd think with the way they've been lurking around for the last two weeks, shit like this wouldn't happen. And people like that would get caught before making bogus room reservations under the name John Smith."

"So why didn't you take some initiative?"

"I did." He glanced around the room. "I reported it to Mr. Russell, and he said he informed the FBI agent stationed in the lobby."

"Did he tell you what FBI agent?"

"Yeah. SAC Walton." He read the shocked look on my face. "Mr. Russell told me they were aware of the situation, and I was to keep my distance so they could handle it." He rolled his eyes. "This was how they handled it."

"What do you mean?"

"They used this room to maintain surveillance on Mr. Smith, and the next thing I know, the entire hotel is turned upside down because of Al's body, then Smith's body, and investigators are still crawling all over the place. Things finally start to get back to normal, and housekeeping calls down to my office this morning to let me know whoever was staying here trashed the room."

Subconsciously, I shoved my hands into my pockets, not wanting to contaminate a possible crime scene. "Did you call the authorities?"

"Why? They're the ones that trashed the place."

"Don't touch anything. Just," I put my hands up in a stay still gesture, "don't touch anything else. This might be an active crime scene."

He sighed, annoyed. "My day's just getting better and better."

SEVENTEEN

Jacobs was my current dial-a-detective, and he seemed less than pleased by this fact. He slowly surveyed the entire room while shaking his head. This wasn't what he wanted to be doing with his afternoon. It wasn't what I wanted to be doing either.

"Let me make sure I have this right." He shot a glance at Oster. "FBI agents did this?" He lifted the shoe out of the shattered television screen with the tip of his pen. The crime scene guys already photographed the room, so it didn't matter.

"I assume so. According to hotel records, they rented the room."

"Who was the room registered to? Uncle Sam?" I let out an appreciative chortle at Jacobs' remark and earned myself a sly grin.

"Christopher Walton," Oster replied. "Are we done yet?"

"We're done when I say we're done," Jacobs growled. He shifted his focus to me. "Parker, you're done. Your presence here isn't making my job any easier."

"Okay." I went to the door and stepped into the hallway. "Hey, Jason," I called, "are you positive Eastman wasn't in contact with Mr. Smith?"

"No. Paul pestered me practically the entire time he was here. He would have bragged about it."

"You do realize Mr. Smith isn't really named Mr. Smith, right?" I double-checked, making sure Oster knew Smith was Frank Costan.

"Yeah, I got that too," Jason growled, annoyed with the constant questioning.

"You hear that, Detective? You have the wrong guy in custody for murder. Well, at least one of the murders." I sauntered off before any other unnecessary remarks could be made.

Outside, Mark was still waiting in my car. The windows were rolled down, and he was on the phone. I climbed into the driver's seat and turned the key in the ignition. A minute later, he hung up.

"What took so long? And why did two police cruisers and a crime scene van arrive while you were inside? Don't tell me there's another dead body."

"There isn't. At least none they've found yet. One of the rooms was trashed, but I might have a lead."

"Really?" He mocked astonishment. "Me too."

"Have you ever heard anything negative about Special Agent in Charge Christopher Walton?"

"That's your lead?" Mark scoffed. "I thought you had an actual lead, like the FBI's been conducting a sting operation for the last eight months. The reason for the added security and the constant presence by federal agencies was to ensure the protection of the mole and apprehension of the target. Or rather, targets."

"Don't keep me in suspense."

"Hodge was the mole. He's been tipping off the Bureau for years on buys, dealers, and whatever else goes on inside the hotel. From what I've been told, the conference was big enough to lure Costan out of retirement, and they were confident he'd show since his presumed business partner was scheduled to make an appearance." Glancing at Mark, I wondered if I should reroute to the OIO instead of my office. "Unfortunately, since it's an ongoing op, I'm in the dark concerning who their only surviving target is."

"So Hodge was a CI." Biting my lip, I considered his

hanging. It was out in the open. It wasn't as direct as cutting out the guy's tongue, but still, the message was clearly construed and would serve as a warning to anyone else who might consider talking. "If they think Hodge was working with Eastman, then Paul could be the next victim."

"Not if he's under arrest. As long as he's in police custody, he's safe. So if the charges are severe enough, he won't be released on bail, and it'll work just as well as protective custody but without anyone being the wiser." Mark met my eyes. He still didn't know what charges were being brought against Paul, but at least we knew why they were being filed so quickly.

"But I don't think Paul knows anything." His actions made him look like he knew a hell of a lot. "Whatever he knows, he probably doesn't even realize it." My mind ran through other possibilities like Oster, the desk clerks, and the security guards, but jumping to conclusions was impractical. "One of the business tycoons is rumored to be Costan's partner in crime. It shouldn't take too much digging to determine who it is."

During the rest of the drive, I filled Mark in on the trashed hotel room and the few snippets of information that Jason provided. My lead led back to Agent Walton, and Mark promised to check into it quietly. But why would an FBI agent trash a hotel suite? A struggle definitely took place in the confines of that room, and although I didn't want to consider the possibilities, my mind connected it to the condition in which they found Frank Costan's body. He was badly beaten. That must have happened somewhere in the vicinity.

"I can't deal with more internal corruption," I mumbled, parking outside my office.

"Don't jump to conclusions. There are a million reasons the room could have looked like that. Maybe our unknown target tossed the room as soon as the FBI checked out, hoping to find out how much information they have on him."

"Mark," I put my hand on his forearm, "see if you can find out where the surveillance teams were relocated. Since they checked out of the hotel, they must still have eyes on

Costan's partner."

He rubbed his eyes. "You're going to owe me some major favors when this is all said and done. But on the bright side, it appears your client is innocent," he paused before qualifying that remark by adding, "relatively speaking."

Leaving me to piece together the limited facts about Paul Eastman's involvement with Hodge, Oster, and his ramblings to everyone that he was someone who was willing to sell secrets to the highest bidder, I wondered how the moron managed to maintain a job at PDN with that type of boastful attitude. I called the corporate office again to ask if there were any allegations of corruption, espionage, blackmail, or extortion, but the head honcho thought I was crazy. Although, now that I was asking these types of questions, Eastman might be facing a performance evaluation when and if he returned to work, especially after his arrest for murder or collusion or whatever charges the DA's office was intending to use to keep him in custody.

Deciding that remaining within the confines of my office wouldn't clear Paul's name any faster, I returned to the precinct. It was after shift change, so the current officer manning the desk outside of holding wasn't the same one who so thoughtfully escorted me outside this morning.

"Hey, I'm following up on something and wondered if I could have two minutes with Paul Eastman," I said, offering my most alluring smile.

"Ma'am," he glanced up from the computer and grinned, "what are you following up on?"

"It's part of Detective Jacobs' investigation." I held the smile, batting my eyelashes, despite the ma'am comment. Ma'am was not appropriate for a thirty-one year old who liked to believe she could pass for a twenty-something.

"Go on," he jerked his chin down the corridor, "but make it quick. No one's supposed to talk to the perps while they're in holding."

"Thanks, Officer." Finding the place practically empty, I wondered where all the criminals were. Maybe crime was declining like the papers said. "Hey, Paul," I called. He was slumped in the corner of the cell, sweating and definitely green. He looked ten times worse now than he did this morning. "I need to know who's representing you." He squinted as if the light hurt his eyes and pulled himself off the ground, using the bar as support. "Your attorney, what's his name?"

"Um," he swallowed uncertainly and stepped closer, "some public defender. I don't remember." He inhaled sharply and covered his mouth. On the bright side, he managed not to get sick. "Did you talk to Oster?"

"Yeah," I nodded, feeling sympathetic and somewhat guilty for his current plight and physical condition, even if I wasn't responsible, "he mentioned the two of you were close, and you would have shared information about Frank Costan with him. Why didn't you tell the police to talk to your friends and co-workers when they brought you in?"

"I was worried about my side business. Alexis," he slowly sunk back to the floor, too wobbly to stand, "why is this happening? Alvin's dead." He emitted a strange sound and swallowed uneasily. "I knew him for quite a while." He blinked a couple of times. "And now I'm getting pinned for his murder and the murder of one of the most notorious crooks of the day. What's the world coming to?"

"I believe you're innocent." Pressing my lips together, I glanced down the corridor, expecting the cop to remove me any second. "You didn't kill them. We'll figure out who did. After all, you hired me to clear your name. Once this gets sorted out, it should be fine, but you need a real attorney. One that has time to devote to proving your innocence and keeping you safe. I know some people. Should I make a couple of calls on your behalf?"

"What?"

"Focus," I insisted, kneeling on my side of the bars so we'd be closer, "do you want me to find an attorney to represent you? Do you know when the arraignment is scheduled?" He winced and clutched his stomach. "Are you all right?"

"Not really." He found my eyes. "I'm nauseous beyond belief and dizzy as hell. Maybe it's something I ate."

"Or it's something you drank."

"I don't have a drinking problem." He clutched his

stomach and made a face. "It's probably just nerves. Go. Find an attorney and get me the hell out of this mess. I don't think I can take this much longer."

"Okay." I stood and took a deep breath. If whoever silenced Hodge and Costan was loose, Eastman could be next, but protective custody would be preferable to being under arrest. And from the looks of Paul, he wouldn't hold up much longer inside a prison cell. "Has anyone mentioned anything about striking a deal or protective custody?"

"No. They just stuck me in this hellhole and left me here to rot."

"Hang tight. I'll do what I can." On my way out, I stopped at the desk. "Officer, can you keep an eye on Mr. Eastman? He doesn't look so good." The cop smiled and agreed to check on him. In the meantime, I needed to track down a decent criminal defense attorney.

In the stairwell, I brought my phone out and searched for a number that I rarely used. "Ackerman, Baze, and Clancy law offices, how may I direct your call?" the secretary asked politely.

"Hi, is Jack Fletcher in?" Fletcher was a junior partner and one of the few attorneys who didn't make my skin crawl.

"He's in a meeting, may I take a message?"

"Tell him Alex Parker needs a favor." I gave her my phone number and disconnected. Now the waiting could begin.

Before I even made it out of the building, my phone buzzed in my pocket. It was Fletcher, and he promised to make some calls and find someone willing to take Eastman's case since criminal law wasn't his specialty. Instead of wasting another trip to the precinct in order to share the good news with Paul, I went back down the stairs.

"Just one more minute and I promise not to interfere anymore with your prisoners, Officer," I promised. He was no longer smiling, and I feared I lost my flirtatious edge.

"Thirty seconds. No more."

"Okay, thanks." I dashed down the corridor, the soles of

my shoes squeaking when I stopped abruptly outside the cell door. "Paul." He was lying on the bench, turned away from me. "Paul?" A quick glance demonstrated that no one else was inside the holding cell with him. "C'mon, stop being so stubborn. I have good news." There was no response, and fear clutched my insides. "Paul," I yelled loud enough to attract the attention of the few people in the other holding cells and the officer at the desk. "Eastman, answer me."

"Ma'am," the officer was beside me, and I pointed frantically at the prone man in the cell, "step aside." He pressed the radio clipped to his shirt and requested assistance in holding before unlocking the door and cautiously stepping inside. Under different circumstances, I would wonder if it was a trap to isolate and attack a single police officer in an attempt to escape, but Paul wasn't that brilliant. And after the way he looked earlier, he probably wasn't even conscious. Frankly, there was a chance he wasn't even alive. "Shit." He radioed for an ambulance and immediate medical assistance.

Not bothering to stand on formality, I entered the opened cell. "Let me help." We rolled Paul onto his back and checked his vitals. From the bubbly froth at the corners of his lips, it seemed obvious he had a seizure. If he wasn't locked inside a cell, I would have suspected an overdose. Then again, who knew what someone might have snuck inside, except he was alone. "I have a pulse. It's thready, but at least it's there. Is he breathing?"

"Yes," the officer replied. At least we didn't have to start chest compressions or flip a coin on who would perform mouth to mouth. "The bus should be here any second."

Another two officers ran down the steps and burst into the cell, an EMT at their heels. I was pushed out of the way while the EMT set to work. One of the officers began questioning me and the desk officer while the other one kept an eye on Eastman in case this was an elaborately staged attempt at escape. Soon a second EMT arrived with a stretcher. They placed Eastman on the board, handcuffed him to the cut-out circle in the wood, and carried him up the steps with the second officer in tow.

"I found him like that," I muttered.

"Why were you near the holding cell, Miss?"

"Parker. Alexis Parker. I've done some consulting work for major crimes. My current P.I. gig correlated with Mr. Eastman being charged and booked. I just stopped by to tell him to expect a call from his new attorney."

"But you were here earlier too," the desk officer pointed out, but he blushed when he realized that I mentioned Eastman's condition and that he was directly responsible for giving me access to the prisoner. "It doesn't matter." He redirected the conversation to something more appropriate, rather than insisting I slipped Eastman something that would kill him. "Do you know what's wrong with him?"

"I thought you were keeping an eye on him," I accused. "I guess we'll find out." When the EMTs hauled him away, his lips were a bluish color, and as far as I knew, detoxing from alcohol abuse didn't come with discoloration or froth. Something was seriously wrong. Was I too blinded by my preconceived notions to notice before it was too late?

EIGHTEEN

"He's lucky," Jacobs said. After the incident with Paul, Jacobs reported to the hospital, waited for the diagnosis, stationed numerous officers throughout the building, and returned to the precinct. Obediently, I remained at his desk, waiting for him to reappear while the desk officer from downstairs maintained a visual confirmation that I wasn't making a run for it. Apparently we were both in a lot of trouble. "Your pestering might have saved his life." He pointed an accusatory finger at me. "But you should have gotten permission from someone in charge before speaking to him again this afternoon."

"You mean the guy at the desk isn't running the show? Unbelievable. Apparently I learned something new today."

"You're not stupid, Parker. So stop playing dumb. I could arrest you for obstruction." It was a hollow threat, and we both knew it.

"What happened to Paul?" I asked, getting back to the pressing matter at hand. "I'm guessing it wasn't the DTs."

"Fluoride toxicity."

"Seriously? I didn't realize that was even possible. How did it happen?"

"The doctors believe an increased level of fluoride was

introduced five days ago and has continued to build ever since. We'll know more after they get the panels back and analyze whatever they found in his stomach."

"Will he be okay?"

"They think so. They pumped his stomach and ran preliminary blood tests." I shuddered slightly, but he continued on. "Not that this is any of your business, but the current theory is the high dosage was in something he ingested regularly, so if he wasn't in custody, he might not have made it."

"Am I free to go?"

"Yeah, but a word of advice, stop snooping around. There's someone dangerous out there. We have two bodies. Almost three. You need to be careful."

"Can we talk in private for a sec?" Nodding, he led me into Lt. Moretti's empty office and shut the door. "Was it your idea to charge Eastman with a laundry list of crimes in order to keep him locked up?"

"The only thing I had on him was suspicion of murder. The feds claimed to have additional evidence, so the DA's office was bringing additional charges based on their word. Why?"

"Do you still believe Eastman's guilty?"

"No. Jason Oster updated me on the situation. Before the shit hit the fan, I was considering phoning the DA and seeing what the feds had so we could cut the guy loose. It's a little scary how well you do this job."

"It's mostly luck and being a pain in everyone's ass." I attempted a smile. "Look, you didn't hear this from me, but Alvin Hodge was a confidential informant for the Bureau, and they've been keeping tabs on Frank Costan and his alleged partner. I'd assume this unknown partner is the assailant. He probably eliminated Hodge and Costan and thought Eastman might pose a threat. So since I'm sharing, I hope you'll consider passing along the medical findings and any leads that might surface."

"Thanks, but I don't see why you need any of that information. Eastman's clear. Wasn't that your job?"

"I'm not the best at letting things go, Detective." I stepped closer and slipped my business card into his breast pocket. "I would appreciate a call if it's at all possible."

Leaving the precinct, I had a lot to think about. Fluoride poisoning? Who even used poison outside of contrived film and television plots? More importantly, what did Paul regularly ingest that could contain that much fluoride? And five days ago meant Wednesday, the day we were released from that horrible interrogation hell resulting from Hodge's body being found hanging around the hotel. This didn't bode well.

Driving home, I unlocked my door, checked the entirety of my apartment for anything that seemed amiss, and opened my fridge and pantry, glanced at the few items inside, and threw everything into the trashcan. Yes, I was paranoid, but it never hurt to be cautious. After all the potentially contaminated items from my fridge were discarded, my eyes came to rest on the few liquor bottles on my counter. Martin would kill me if I poured twenty-five year old scotch down the drain. So I resisted, wondering just how expensive it would be to replace the bottle. If it were the fifty year old single malt he kept in a sacred place at his house that I was contemplating destroying, they would never find my body.

Instead of doing anything brash, I dialed Mark. "I'm a paranoid lunatic."

"And what else is new?" he responded. "Is this a cry for help?"

"I just spent the last five minutes contemplating pouring scotch down the drain."

"Well, if you're afraid you're becoming an alcoholic, I'm open to taking it off your hands. What's the story? You spent so much time with your client that you think his more peculiar habits are contagious?"

"He's not an alcoholic. Well, he might be, but that's not the reason for his symptoms. He was poisoned."

"Stay put. I'll be right there. And don't eat, drink, or pour out Marty's scotch in the meantime."

"Yes, sir."

"And don't call me sir."

Disconnecting, I glanced into the full trashcan in my kitchen, wondering why my neuroses were always so prevalent. Just because Eastman was poisoned didn't mean anyone broke into my apartment and laced my food. I was careful. I tried to be. After my last case, I had zero desire to relive accidentally dosing myself with high-powered sedatives and hallucinogens, so I made certain everything in my apartment remained completely undisturbed.

While I waited for Mark to arrive, I dialed Martin and was surprised when he answered, instead of letting the call go to voicemail. "Hey, shouldn't you be asleep or working or something?" I didn't feel like figuring out the time zone differences.

"I just woke up in preparation for another early morning meeting."

"How's the trip?"

"Insane. I'll be happy when it's over. Absolutely nothing went right yesterday. I'm just hoping things will improve. We fly to Dublin tonight. Seventeen cities in twenty days sounds like a job for a rock star, not a CEO."

"Clearly, you need to learn to delegate."

"I will. This is all in regards to our recent merger with Hover Designs. It'll be over soon enough, and I shall be exempt from traveling for the rest of the year." His voice held the hint of a smile. "Although, you can persuade me to go anywhere with you."

"And yet, I failed to convince you to stay locked inside my apartment. Strange how there's a flaw in your logic."

"Ouch. I deserved that." He paused, and I wondered if he planned to confess to phoning earlier. "I'm about to jump in the shower. If I put you on speaker, you can join me." His voice was sultry, and I sighed.

"Mark's on his way here. But you'll be happy to know my client has been cleared from the murder charges."

"That's great," he replied, sounding slightly dejected. "Is your job over? You could meet me in Milan on Thursday."

"Not yet. There are still a few more things I need to handle, and I completely forgot to call Luc today. I found a solution to the elevator issue, but it needs to be approved and implemented. With any luck, it'll be done by the time you get back."

"Alex," the water turned on in the background, "it's

hard..."

"Jackass."

He laughed. "Sorry, that's not what I wanted to say. I...being away from you has never been this worrisome before. I know you think I'm overreacting. And I'm sure I am, but ever since I found you on the bathroom floor, I just...it's been a little over a month. I can't shake it. That feeling. The fear that you would never open your eyes again."

"James," I whispered, the familiar pang constricting my chest. My job was dangerous, and I never wanted to put him through this type of torture.

"Don't you dare start using my first name, Alexis. It never leads to anything good. I'll try to chill out about this but cut me some slack, okay? That's why I want to hear from you every day."

"Well, you're not the only crazy one." I swallowed, giving the garbage pail a dirty look. "Your scotch was almost poured down the drain in a moment of insanity, but rest assured, it's fine. And so am I."

"The scotch I can live without. You are a different story."

Our goodbyes were cut short when Mark arrived. We hung up, and when I turned around, he was surveying the contents in the trash. He shook his head and poured himself a glass of scotch.

"What are you doing?" I asked.

"Taste testing. We need concrete evidence that your apartment hasn't been breached and your position hasn't been compromised."

"What position is that? I don't have an official position on anything, do I?" Maybe Mark found a way to get us involved in the case.

"You were hired to clear Eastman's name. I'm guessing the next step will be determining who poisoned him."

"Isn't that a job for the authorities?"

"Yes, but you'll still investigate. Your empty fridge speaks volumes on its own. You want the party responsible. It's how you're wired." He put the scotch on the counter. "It tastes okay to me. Do we have any idea what type of poison was used, how it was introduced, or who might have planted it."

"Fluoride that built up to toxic levels over a five day span. The prelim report suggested it was in something Eastman ingested regularly. If he wasn't in custody, he might be dead."

"It could be in anything. Maybe he was eating his toothpaste. After all, too much of anything can be detrimental." He narrowed his eyes. "Do you think it was in whatever he was drinking each night?"

"Well, it gives new meaning to pick your poison, now doesn't it?"

"Was he still staying at the hotel or was he back home?"

"As far as I know, he was home. After the conference and being questioned by the authorities, he wouldn't have any reason to stay at the hotel." I took a seat in front of my computer. "I don't know much about my boss. For all I know, the guy has a wife or cohabitating girlfriend. We should determine who has access to his house and the contents of his fridge and liquor cabinet."

"Poison is generally thought of as a woman's preferred method of killing, but assuming he doesn't have a wife or girlfriend that wants him dead, anyone he's cohabitating with could become an accidental casualty."

"True." Eastman's basic information popped up on the screen, but there was no mention of a wife. After a few minutes of digging, there was no mention of an ex-wife either. That didn't mean he didn't have a live-in girlfriend or someone close by with keys to his house who might make themselves at home. "I'll call PDN and see what they can tell me about his personal life."

"Alex," Mark stopped me before I reached the phone, "it's after eight. No one will be there this late. We'll try back tomorrow. Plus, I'm sure the police are ripping his place apart to identify the method of delivery. Once we have that information, we'll be able to narrow down the source, and it might lead to our killer or Costan's partner, in the event they aren't one and the same."

"In the meantime, do you want to reanalyze everything and see if we can determine a list of suspects who might have it out for Eastman? Maybe you can figure out who had access to all three men and had an axe to grind."

"And the reason I get this task is because I can call the Bureau and ask for favors," Mark said knowingly.

"Exactly."

NINETEEN

Mark camped out at my apartment again. He claimed he was only here to fulfill his role as Martin's best friend and protect the scotch at all costs. Realistically, it probably had more to do with the fact that he was afraid I was coming unhinged. Normal people don't think they might be poisoned just because of their proximity to a victim. Then again, for me, this was normal behavior.

During the course of the night, I dug through dozens of records, looking for connections between Eastman, Costan, and Hodge. When little information was gained through the normal channels, like law enforcement databases, I became desperate enough to surf through the convoluted world of social networking.

This was one concept I would never understand. Why did people think posting their life stories on something as insecure as the internet was a good idea? There were photos, mentions of trips, and thousands of pictures of family and children. It was asking for trouble. One crazy person, read as stalker, killer, kidnapper, or just your run-of-the-mill psycho, could easily determine where people were, who their loved ones were, and exactly where and when to strike. It was dangerous. And everyone did it. If that wasn't the definition of insanity, then I didn't know what was. Then again, I had to go grocery shopping in the morning, so maybe I shouldn't be throwing stones at any glass houses.

After I made a short list of Eastman's closest friends, I elected to call it a night. It was around four a.m. when I climbed into bed with my clothes still on. Distant ringing woke me, but it wasn't my phone. Glancing at the clock, it was noon, and I heard Mark speaking softly. Obviously, his leads seemed more promising than mine.

"Anything?" I asked, stepping out of my room and leaning against the doorjamb.

"Quite a bit, actually." He scribbled a note on a sheet of paper. "I'm meeting with Walton in an hour, and we'll take it from there. Jacobs called your house phone this morning a little after six. He didn't want to talk to me, but somehow, I convinced him I was your personal assistant. So he left a message."

"Are you hoping the suspense will kill me so you can enjoy the rest of your vacation?"

He snickered. "No, but they determined the fluoride came from the water filter in the guy's refrigerator. So every time he drank the water, he also got an unhealthy dose of fluoride."

"Isn't that in water anyway?"

"Which makes whoever did this kind of brilliant. It might look like an accident, a manufacturing defect, or something wrong with his water filter since it's designed to filter out chemicals, minerals, and impurities. Maybe it was leaking and putting high doses in the water by accident."

"And we're sure it's not an accident?"

"CSU is examining the canister, but it appears to have signs of tampering. Jacobs said they're running additional tests, but given the circumstances, we're hoping something will be conclusive. With any luck, they'll find prints on the casing."

"So anyone could have done it. Well, anyone with access to Paul's house and refrigerator." Considering the possibilities, maybe my foray into the frightening world of social networking might actually have led to some valid suspects or someone who might know who was puttering around in Paul's kitchen and be able to point us in the right direction. "But it's a start."

"Looks like it," Mark agreed. "I'm going home to change before my meeting with Walton. I'm not sure how long that will be, so I'll give you a call sometime later."

"Thanks. I owe you."

His smile was disconcerting. "Yes, you do." Without saying another word or hinting as to what type of payback he was hoping to exact, he left my apartment.

Dutifully, I picked up the phone, left a perfunctory voicemail since we were all a little crazy at this point, and then I changed into workout clothes went for a five mile run, took a shower, and phoned Luc Guillot. Martin Technologies was no longer my bread and butter, but there was a soft spot in my heart for the building and people. After detailing exactly how to fix the elevator, Guillot asked for a Thursday afternoon meeting for further specifications. If approved, the modified procedures could be performed during the weekend, and everything would be running normally by Monday. That was one thing taken care of.

The next was determining who had access to Eastman's house. I ran the names of a few of his friends from his social networking profile through the databases and came up with addresses and phone numbers. The easiest solution would be to visit Eastman in the hospital and ask him myself, but Jacobs wasn't much into sharing. And Paul might still be recovering, so I would just have to put in some legwork.

I decided to start with his neighbors and move outward, hitting the list of seven names on my drive to the office. It wasn't necessarily the best plan, but it was a start. As I suspected, Eastman's property was cordoned off with crime scene tape. It was a small townhouse, and uniformed officers were speaking to people at the surrounding connected properties. So much for starting with the neighbors. Thankfully, I spotted Officer Taylor, who transferred out of vice and was now pulling whatever duty the brass deemed necessary.

"Shelly," I called, stepping out of my illegally parked car, "do you have a minute?"

"Alex?" She spun, surprised to see me while she canvassed the neighborhood. "What the hell are you doing here?"

Glancing around, I didn't spot Jacobs or any other familiar faces, so I figured it was safe enough to ask a few questions. "Paul Eastman's a client. What do you know about the poisoning and people who might have access to his place?"

"I'm not supposed to talk about it." Her eyes darted around to make sure the other cops were out of earshot. "But there's nothing to talk about. The guy kept to himself. Didn't talk to his neighbors, never threw any wild parties, and didn't have any steady visitors, at least not that anyone around here noticed. The detectives are contacting his family to see if they might know something more substantial, like who he hangs out with or if he had any enemies."

"Damn." That wasn't helping me either. "And here I thought the guy had a drinking problem."

"He did. He drank too much water." She shook her head. "I have to get back to work, but if I hear anything major, I'll give you a call."

"Thanks. I appreciate it." She ducked into the next doorway, ringing the bell, while I returned to my car. Apparently my ingenious plan was so brilliant the PD was already enacting it, and they had a hell of a lot more manpower at their disposal than I did.

While continuing my drive to a few of the addresses on my list, I phoned PDN. Instead of starting at the top of the food chain, I questioned the secretary about Paul and his dealings with his co-workers, favorite clients, and any visitors or guests who have stopped by in the past month. There were a few names that I recognized, mine being one of them. The other two were Alvin Hodge and Jason Oster. Pulling onto the shoulder, I scribbled the rest of the list and asked to be passed along to Paul's temporary replacement. From there, I asked to speak to his supervisor, and lastly, I asked to speak to the man in charge. By the end of it, my list had fifteen names.

Pulling back into traffic, I proceeded to the first address, but the unmarked cruiser out front served as an indication I should move on. Not wanting to be thwarted again by great minds thinking alike, I went to my office, ran a check and people search on the fifteen names, and impatiently stared at the computer monitor. Perhaps I should be ecstatic that the police were doing such a magnificent job investigating. After all, we were looking in the same places for the answers.

Deciding to throw caution to the wind, I printed out driver's license photos of the fifteen names the various PDN employees provided, along with the few friends I pulled off his social networking site, and went to the hotel. Maybe Jason Oster or one of the other security guards would recognize someone. Granted, Oster was a potential person of interest, especially since he seemed friendly enough to have access to Eastman's house, but I wasn't sure where to look. On the way, I tried to figure out how Oster could fit into all of this. If he wasn't working for Costan's partner and trying to silence everyone involved, then theoretically, he might become a victim himself. This would be so much easier if I could have another long chat with Paul.

"Knock, knock," I called from outside the open security office doorway. When two guards who were monitoring the cameras turned at the sound of the intrusion, I smiled warmly. "Is Jason around?"

"He's with the manager right now. Can I help you with something, Miss?"

"Do you recognize any of these people?" I let them skim through the photos, but they remained outwardly clueless. "I just really needed to see Jason." A look was exchanged between the two men, and they grinned. "Did I miss the joke?"

"No," a big smile erupted on one of their faces, "not at all. In fact, you have excellent timing. Wouldn't you agree, Bob?"

"Oh yeah, excellent."

"Guys," I hated being out of the loop, "I work with PDN.

I helped review and implement the procedures this hotel used during the recent conference. I need to talk to Jason about a security issue."

"Oh," Bob blushed, "sorry, we didn't realize this was work related. We thought you *needed* Jason for something else." The two exchanged a glance and a snicker before looking at the wall clock. "He should be back from the morning meeting in fifteen minutes. The meeting room next to the breakfast bar is empty if you want to wait for him there."

"Sure. I'll wait." From the way the two chuckleheads were acting, it was hard not to jump to conclusions, but it seemed apparent Mr. Oster had an early morning visitor who needed a service provided which had nothing to do with security.

While I sat in the empty conference room, I pulled out my notepad and reviewed the names and possible leads for identifying Paul Eastman's would-be killer. Frankly, if what Officer Taylor said was true, then not many people had access to Paul's fridge. Could Paul be poisoning himself to throw off any suspicion? No, I shook my head. The FBI wouldn't have encouraged the DA's office to trump up charges in order to protect the guilty party. So who was the guilty party? My mind considered the key players and the only common denominator I came up with was Jason Oster. Unless Oster and Eastman were working together. Shit, conjecture was impractical. It was time to get back to the cold hard facts. I just began my outline when the door opened.

"Parker, what the hell are you doing here?" Detective Jacobs growled.

"Jeez," I threw my pen on the table and leaned back in the chair, "I can't catch a freaking break. Every place I went today was crawling with cops. Stop stalking me."

"What are you talking about now?" He sat across from me and sighed heavily.

"I wanted to get a jump on possible suspects. It seemed something Paul might ask about in the future, so needless to say, everything I thought to check into is already being investigated by police personnel."

"Like me being here."

"Precisely."

"I phoned you this morning. Did your...assistant...give you the message?"

"It was the water filter in the kitchen with the fluoride." It wasn't every day the perfect chance to make a Clue reference came about, so I couldn't let the opportunity go to waste.

"Right, so we're checking into it. I haven't heard anything yet, but it's the most solid lead we have."

"Who thought to check the inner workings of the fridge?" It was something I never would have considered.

"CSU was sampling all food and beverages found in the house, and one of the techs noticed the replace filter light blinking. One thing led to another, and after reading his medical reports and identifying the toxin, it linked together."

My thoughts were on the filter. Why wouldn't Eastman change it if the indicator light was on? Why didn't he notice? More and more questions were presenting themselves, but not a single answer was in sight. This wasn't working.

"Assuming the filter is responsible and intentional, what other headway have you made on determining the motive for poisoning Eastman?"

"None. He's been squawking about his rights being violated, and once he's cleared from the hospital, I won't have anything to hold him on. If he refuses protective custody, there isn't anything I can do." Jacobs' entire focus shifted to me. "Do you think you might be able to convince him otherwise?"

It was time to play hardball. "Perhaps, but it might cost you."

"I'll grant you access to the files on the two homicides and whatever reports we've compiled on the poisoning if you convince Eastman to cooperate."

"Deal." I extended my hand, and as we shook, Jason Oster stepped into the room, glancing nervously at the two of us. "Shall I go first or should you?"

TWENTY

Out of courtesy, I let Detective Jacobs go first. He asked Jason Oster almost all the questions I could think of and a few I hadn't considered. Despite the fact Oster and Eastman were friends, Jason didn't know much about what Eastman did in his private life. The last time he visited Paul's house was a month ago. It was a short trip to pick up a wireless surveillance camera for implementation as added security for one of PDN's clients.

"So you helped him with his off-the-books projects?" Jacobs asked, jotting a note.

"Occasionally. We weren't doing anything illegal, like making celebrity sex tapes or anything. He just wanted to make sure that no one from the hotel was gaining unauthorized access to PDN's clients. A few months back, a complaint was made that jewelry went missing from some singer's belongings. She blamed one of the security guards from PDN, and he blamed hotel security. Paul just wanted to make sure there were no other mishaps."

"Seems unrelated," I concluded, and Jacobs nodded. Nothing else Oster said was helpful in determining who poisoned Paul or why. We weren't ready to rule Jason out as a suspect, but he offered to come to the station later for fingerprinting.

Since Jacobs was out of questions, it was my turn to play. I showed Oster the photos I printed. He identified a few PDN and hotel employees, but he couldn't imagine any of them were involved. Jacobs gave me a look, and I surrendered the dead end leads to him. He probably already checked into everyone's whereabouts and knew who had access to Paul's apartment, but just in case, maybe he'd find something damning since I came up blank. In the meantime, I decided to throw a lit match at the gasoline tank.

"How was your meeting this morning?" I asked Jason.

"Fine. We have them every Tuesday and Saturday. It's the best way for the manager to remain updated on issues within the hotel." He checked his watch, realizing he should be back at work.

"No. I meant your other so-called meeting."

"What meeting?" His eyes bore into me, trying to figure out what I knew and how.

"Do I need to spell it out for you? You could just make this simpler and tell us who she is."

"That's none of your business," he responded vehemently.

"Hmm," Jacobs leaned forward, "it seems like it might be. Particularly with everything that's been happening in this hotel for the last few weeks," he glanced at his notes, "correction, apparently last few months. It might be nice to have some idea of who you spend time with, Mr. Oster."

"It's casual. She's no one serious, so it doesn't matter."

"Name," Jacobs insisted, and the fact that Oster didn't want to provide one made me that much more curious. "Don't make us pull the footage or start asking around. It'll be more embarrassing for you if we have to resort to such measures."

"Rachel." He looked away. "Romanski."

"Alvin Hodge's ex-wife?" I asked. Talk about incestuous relationships. These people really didn't understand not shitting where you eat. Wow.

"Note the ex part," he replied bitterly, standing. "We're

done. I have to get back to work."

"Don't forget to stop by this evening to give us those fingerprints you promised," Jacobs called after him. Once we were alone, he turned to me. "I didn't see that one coming."

"Neither did I."

"How'd you hear about his rendezvous?"

"Men gossip more than women," shaking my head, we continued down the hallway and out of the building, "particularly the bored out of their skulls security guards."

"Well, it's not like it'd be that difficult to get a room." He scanned his notes a final time and halted our procession once we neared his cruiser. "Anything else you'd like to share?"

"I hate yoga."

He squinted. "Okay."

"Yeah. I really hate yoga."

Not bothering to elaborate, I continued to my car, leaving him to contemplate the importance of my statement. It wouldn't take him long to figure out the connection, so I might as well stop by Rachel's class and schedule a few more sessions before the police showed up and ruined my cover.

When I pulled to a stop outside Rachel's studio, I was pleasantly surprised and relieved to actually be the first to arrive. Well, the first when it came to the police department or any other law enforcement agency that wanted to horn in on my investigation. Okay, so maybe it was their investigation, but I had a client. A paying client. Well, at least as long as he remained breathing, which probably meant I needed to figure out who was behind this. If not, it would be hard to collect from a corpse.

"Rachel," I said, zipping my jacket quickly to conceal my side arm, "I've been cleared to return to a regular workout routine. Maybe we could discuss some of those classes again." I glanced at the clock. Her last session finished fifteen minutes ago, and she was packing up to leave.

"Alexis, right?" I nodded, and she let out a friendly laugh. "I'm glad you've decided to give this another try. You seemed utterly miserable last time."

"No more hot yoga for me." Picking up one of the brochures and flipping through the options, I tried to find one with the most class meetings and the least amount of meditative benefit. "I'm still recovering, but the strengthening and stretching will help get me back on track." Blabbering on, I wanted to broach the subject of her morning with Jason, but that required finesse. It might also require a night out with too much alcohol since we weren't friends, but that would be more work and effort than just being blunt. "Are there any men in any of your classes? Maybe I can convince my guy to take a few of these with me."

She smiled. "Mr. Cirque du Soleil?" Giggling, I nodded. "There are a few men that come every once in a while. Although, they normally only come for a class or two. They tend to think yoga is a great place to pick up chicks."

"Is it?"

She blushed slightly. "Sometimes."

Opening my mouth in clearly fake astonishment, I laughed. "Did you let some guy pick you up after one of your classes?"

"Well, I knew him before, but he showed up a few times, asked me to coffee, and well, let's just say he offered to help stretch out my hips." She snickered. "Anyway, what are you thinking?"

I'm thinking Jason Oster doesn't look particularly flexible, but he seemed the most likely possibility. "Um, how about I take the intermediate class and start on Friday. Is that a problem?"

"Not at all." She handed me a contract for six months, which would be added to Paul Eastman's fee, and I filled out the paperwork. "It'll be nice having someone new around."

"Yeah. It's so hard to make friends when all I do is work. It'll be nice to get to know some people."

"Well, welcome to the class." After swiping my credit card, she handed me a few more brochures on deep breathing, meditation, and the schedule. "I'll see you Friday."

"Can't wait." Heading for the door, I turned back.

"What'd you say that guy's name was? It might help convince my boyfriend to get out of the house and join me if I can name off some other guys who might show up."

"Oh," her brow furrowed briefly, and she shook her head, "Jason. There's also Tim, Nathan, and Evan that show up once in a blue moon."

"Great. Thanks."

On the bright side, I was wheedling my way into a friendship which could result in who knows what kinds of important information. For one, at least I verified Jason's story from this morning. Too bad that wasn't really a priority. Unfortunately, this useless tidbit of information also meant I was sentenced to a few more yoga sessions. Somebody shoot me now. Oddly enough, I made it back to my car without a drive-by occurring.

Returning to my office, I ran a thorough background check on Jason Oster and skimmed through the information I already compiled on Rachel Romanski. Then I conducted copious amounts of research on fluoride toxicity and the ease of killing someone with such a common item. Most often, the poisoning would be prevalent within minutes, which meant the filter tampering couldn't have been leaking such a high dosage that quickly. The vast majority of symptoms were gastrointestinal, but it could lead to neurological disorders and heart problems, which would explain the seizure. From the statistics alone, death wasn't something that typically occurred, but if this was intentional, then that was probably the goal. Although, fluoride wasn't the normal method of killing someone or even poisoning them, except for maybe dentists. There were plenty of more common and less easily diagnosed toxins, but this was clever. It would read like an accident, and even now, I was still having some doubts. Was it possible Eastman did this to himself, knowing the chance of death wouldn't be that great?

"Tell me you have good news because I'm spinning my wheels," I said, answering the phone on the second ring.

"Agent Walton has been very forthcoming in sharing his insights with me this morning," Mark said, sounding particularly proud of himself. "Are you at that hole in the wall you call an office?"

"It is an office. And yes."

"Okay. Grab a pen. Are you ready?"

"No, I can't figure out which pen to use." Snarky didn't even begin to describe my attitude toward his infantile instructions.

"Blue." Obviously, someone was in a good mood, or I would have been forced to endure a snappish remark instead. "Costan's believed to be in the pocket of former senator, Rodney Wheeler. Ever since the guy stepped down, his main focus has been venture capitalism."

"I'm beginning to see the connection." It also explained part of the reason for the Secret Service presence at the conference. "Do we know anything else?"

"Like the entire list of attendees from the conference? Yeah, I might know that. I also might know precisely who is being monitored by the current FBI detail."

"Would you like to share that information?"

"I already did."

"Wait." Shaking my head, I let out a derisive chortle. "One agency is guarding the bastard while another one is keeping tabs on him. And people wonder why the economy is going to shit and the government is basically bankrupt."

"I believe the proper pronunciation is corrupt."

"That too."

"Look, pull Rodney Wheeler's records," Mark instructed. "Everything you can find on his appointment, business, et cetera. We need a full workup. I'm getting copies of the surveillance and as much of the current case file as I can. We'll exchange information as soon as I get there."

"You do realize I no longer work for you, right?" I asked, making sure he remembered this fact that oftentimes he seemed to forget.

"Sure." He didn't sound particularly convinced. "Did you get anything substantial out of your morning outings?"

"It's too soon to tell. The head of security is sleeping with Hodge's ex-wife which adds a new dynamic to this." It didn't seem feasible that the events were related to the news about Costan and former Senator Wheeler, but that was a hunch. It wouldn't hurt to look into it. "But Detective Jacobs and I are getting along great, and maybe Rachel Romanski will be my new best friend."

"You really need to cut out the sauce this early in the morning. Is your coffee Irish?"

"Goodbye, Mark."

Hanging up, I searched for information on the former senator. Rodney Wheeler was an oil tycoon turned venture capitalist who was groomed for a political seat by a particular interest group, but once a few of his less than stellar deals and whispers of embezzlement circulated, he resigned and focused his energy on making money. Obviously, his constituency wasn't a top priority.

He served half a term before stepping down, and the powers that be acted swiftly to sweep it under the rug. Since he was a newcomer to the political stage, it wasn't a top news story, and the politicos squashed it before it turned into a media storm. Frankly, Wheeler didn't appear to give two cents about any of it. He was focused on wealth and greed. After all, money begets more money.

So why did the Secret Service waste manpower and agents on protection for an out of office congressman who by all accounts did nothing useful for the country? Oh yeah, policy. Sighing, I pulled up the list of holdings Wheeler possessed. His private assets included a few million dollar homes, majority shares of three different mid-level companies, and various other highly lucrative positions among half a dozen other businesses. Someone must have hired a pretty brilliant accountant.

Fearing I might go into a coma after reading the mission statements and projected earnings for some of his companies, I switched tactics. Searching instead for anyone who was named as Costan's potential associates, there was probably an overlap somewhere. Just as the names started to blend together into one giant, unmatched blur, something interesting caught my attention. It was a tiny footnote at the bottom of Wheeler's financial record. He was part owner of the hotel where the conference was held. How involved was he in the hiring practices? Was he completely removed from the operation, only collecting dividends from the profit? Or did he arrange all of this, including the security hires, the procedures, and making sure Costan was able to sneak in without too much trouble? Who else was on the take? Did his Secret Service protection detail thwart the FBI investigation? And what the hell did any of this have to do with Paul Eastman getting poisoned?

"This is such bullshit," I muttered. More information was leading to more questions and even less chance of finding a solution.

"Well, it's a good thing your fearless leader is here to help." Mark entered my office and sat heavily in the client chair, shoving a file at me.

TWENTY-ONE

Rodney Wheeler had been under federal surveillance for the past year. After being forced to resign his Senate seat, he returned to the word of venture capitalism. The SEC originally wanted to investigate him on a few reports of insider trading and fraud, but his records were clean. There wasn't any evidence to back the impropriety, even though his actions reinforced his guilt. He was a sneaky son-of-a-bitch who happened to be smart enough to hide whatever scheming he was involved in. Hell, maybe Costan gave him a few pointers.

After the SEC let it go, the FBI continued to investigate. The ties Wheeler had to Costan were mostly hearsay, but since Costan's own people were willing to hand over names and business partners to avoid federal charges, they had to earn their keep with reliable information. The name that had been repeated half a dozen times was Rodney Wheeler. Maybe it was a hoax. But Costan was dead, and Wheeler was still under surveillance. So I doubted it.

"What do you think of the black and whites?" Mark asked, flicking one of the photos with his pointer finger.

"Not artistic enough for a gallery opening, but I'd say they qualify for a spread in a nature magazine with some kind of caption like 'animals in their natural habitat'." Giving the information a final glance, I leaned back in the chair and propped my leg up on the desk. "Where was Wheeler when Costan was killed?"

"Agent Walton didn't share."

"Fine, where was Wheeler for the duration of the conference? I'm guessing he attended all the meetings and business functions, but where was he when he wasn't schmoozing and bartering?"

"He didn't have a room." Mark flipped to the guest registry.

"Yeah, but he's part owner of the freaking hotel. He wouldn't need a reservation." I summarized my research, so Mark would be up to speed. "We need to figure out when Costan ended up below the hotel and who turned him into a bloody pulp. He was killed between midnight and six a.m. on Thursday."

"I doubt it was Wheeler," Mark pointed to the most recent photo, timestamped yesterday afternoon. "There's no bruising on his knuckles. He couldn't have beaten the living daylights out of Costan."

"People like Wheeler pay other people to do their dirty work. Have you learned nothing?"

"How could he pay anyone? We're monitoring his financials, and he knows it."

"Yeah. Exactly." Steepling my fingers, I tapped my index fingers against my lips. "What does the protection detail have to say?"

"Nothing. They were stationed in various strategic locations during the conference to ensure no threat was imminent. You know the drill. You were working for the Secret Service on this."

"Who else were they protecting?" I wondered if Wheeler was their sole focus or simply one that they didn't give two shits about. I wouldn't have wasted too much effort protecting someone like him. He wasn't worth it.

Mark skimmed the list again. "Two other congressmen and a state governor." We exchanged a look. "Wheeler probably wasn't their top priority."

"Okay, how about we swing by and have a chat with the

Secret Service brass and see what actions and protocols their agents followed. After all, you have an OIO badge, and I worked as a third party contractor. Clearly, we should be a shoo-in for getting the answers we want."

He picked up my mug and sniffed. "Well, you aren't drunk." He squinted, focusing on my pupils. "And you don't appear to be high. My next guess is delusional and suffering a psychotic break from reality."

"None of the above." Smiling, I collected my belongings and grabbed my car keys. "After this, we'll stop by the hospital and have a word with my actual client, so if you're going to continue to act this demeaning, you'll be introduced as my secretary.

*   *   *

"Miss Parker, we protect all assets equally," the Secret Service agent in charge of coordinating with PDN responded, casting his eyes at Mark. "And Agent Jablonsky, our procedures and protocols were strictly by the book."

"I don't doubt that," Mark replied.

"Seriously, you expect me to believe that a former senator under investigation for a laundry list of crimes is considered just as important as our current political leaders?" I retorted.

His face read the truth, but he wouldn't waver from the company line. "This is not an issue of guarding the President or protecting vital information in the name of national security. We were present at the conference to safeguard our assets and to ensure the delegates from other nations were equally protected. It's a shame that an unrelated crime occurred at the same time. It gives us a bad name and makes our agents seem incompetent when they are not." He stood. "Now, if you don't mind," he gestured to the door, "work waits for no man."

Mark nodded curtly and led me out of the room. "They didn't fuck up," he whispered as the elevator doors closed. "Don't make accusations that might ruin the names of good men."

Rolling my eyes, I let out a sigh. "You really think I'd do that?"

"Not intentionally."

We remained silent until we were back inside my car and on the way to the hospital. Certain aspects still didn't make much sense, and nothing would have pleased me more than to rip the entire thing apart and reconstruct it from the ground up. Unfortunately, we were too far past that. Two dead. One poisoned. And far too many suspects and clues to untangle the information into a usable theory.

"What do you want me to do?" Mark asked, drawing me from my thoughts. "I'm not exactly in a position to evaluate other agencies' actions. This isn't my case or my jurisdiction."

"I don't care about Wheeler or Costan or who Jason Oster's boning. All I want to know is who killed Alvin Hodge and poisoned Paul Eastman."

"That's it?"

"That's it." Pulling into the parking lot outside the hospital, I killed the engine and took a breath. "Eastman's my client. His safety is my only priority. The rest of this mess," I shrugged, "is so far beyond the scope of a guy hanging from a cable near the elevators. Someone screwed up. I don't know if it was hotel security, or PDN, or one of our beloved federal agencies. I also don't know who's pulling the strings. But y'know what, it doesn't matter." My mind settled around this fact. For once, it didn't matter. It really wasn't my concern. Maybe I was finally getting the hang of this private investigator thing. Proud of my new revelation, I opened my car door. "Now I plan to have a lovely chat with Paul and take it from there. Feel free to join me, or you can wait here. It's up to you."

"I'll come inside." He looked skeptical. "That break from reality you're experiencing seems to be getting worse. Maybe you should have an evaluation done while we're here."

Instead of requesting information as to the whereabouts of Mr. Eastman, I simply wandered the hallways until I found a police presence. Being under guard made it pretty easy to locate someone, just follow the uniforms. After ensuring the person under armed guard was in fact Paul and not some Saudi prince or prison break risk, I flashed my credentials. The officer snorted and shook his head.

"Detective Jacobs will vouch for me," I insisted.

"Really?" The cop looked skeptical. "Why don't we ask him and see what he has to say?" He tapped on the door, and a second later, Jacobs stepped into the hallway. "Sir," the officer began, "this P.I. wanted to chat with the man we have in custody."

"It took you long enough to show up, Parker," Jacobs replied, ignoring the running commentary from the officer. "Agent Jablonsky," he nodded to Mark, "is the FBI stepping in again?"

"No," I answered for Mark, waiting for Jacobs to grant permission to enter the room, "he's just here for moral support."

"What the hell." Jacobs pushed the door wide open. "Maybe you can convince Mr. Eastman to remain in our protection. Now that the hospital is discharging him, he's refusing protective custody." Jacobs' eyes communicated the agreement we reached earlier. It was my turn to try to persuade Paul to listen to reason.

"Can't imagine why," I muttered. Inside the room, Paul was on the edge of the bed, tying his shoe. "Hey, how are you feeling?"

"Alexis," he smiled, "from the stories I've heard, I think I owe you my thanks."

"Well, you're welcome." There was no reason to mention the fact that I simply kept an eye on him because I thought he was going through the DTs. "I hear you don't want to stay under armed guard." The sarcasm was obvious, and he rolled his eyes. "Detective Jacobs thinks it would be in your best interest to remain safe and protected, especially after being poisoned."

"Yeah, just like pinning two homicides on me was in my best interest too." He tossed a scathing look at Jacobs. "No thanks. I'm so out of here. And if you plan to charge me with something else, I will have my lawyer file harassment charges to go along with my claims of unlawful arrest. Do I make myself clear?" Jacobs emitted a low growl but remained silent. "By the way, thanks for the high-powered attorney."

Without turning, I felt the icy glare on my back. Thanks for bringing that up at this particular moment, Paul. "Okay, so what are you planning to do?" I asked, focusing on his current dilemma. "You can't go home. Your house is a crime scene, and someone wants you dead."

He shifted his gaze from me to Jacobs and then settled on Mark. "Hi," he stood and offered his hand, "Paul Eastman."

"I'm Parker's secretary," Mark huffed, ignoring the gesture. "And let me guess, you can't answer her question, can you, kid?" He crossed his arms and leaned against the wall. "In case you haven't realized this yet, whatever's going on is much bigger than you. And if you want to keep breathing, you're gonna need protection and probably a new refrigerator."

"Like what I've been telling you," Jacobs added.

"You've done personal security before," Paul said, ignoring the two men and speaking only to me. "It was mentioned on your résumé. So how 'bout I upgrade my service plan?"

"I don't do that kind of work anymore," I replied.

"Come on," his eyes pleaded, "name your price. We need to discuss your changing role anyway. It seems I might need you to look into a few other things, like determining who wants me dead."

"That's what the police department is working on," Jacobs hissed.

Spinning on my heel, I faced the detective. "I'll keep an eye on him." I jerked my chin toward the door. "You can't force someone into protective custody, just like you can't force cooperation."

"No, but I can hold you for obstruction and impeding a police investigation."

"Well, you have my address if you decide I'm impeding, but I don't think that will be an issue. Didn't we find some common ground this morning?"

With any luck, Jacobs would read between the lines. We agreed to work together, and by stepping in as Paul's bodyguard, maybe he'd provide answers to our questions. There was no privilege when it came to information between a P.I. and her client, and I had no qualms about aiding an open investigation, especially if it would lead to tracking down a killer.

"I hope this doesn't go horribly wrong." Jacobs marched out of the room and slammed the door.

Mark let out an audible sigh but didn't move from his spot against the wall. We made eye contact for half a second, and it was obvious he thought this was a bad idea. It wasn't one of my better ones, but it didn't seem that horrible either.

"This is Mark," I said, introducing the two men. "You can speak freely in front of him. He taught me everything I know."

Paul nodded and slumped back against the bed. "Where do we begin?"

"We'll start with finding you a place to stay," I began, leading the way to the door. "Nothing too fancy, but we'll shoot for something nicer than a roach motel. Don't use your credit cards, make any phone calls, or let anyone know where you are. You're staying off the grid until we determine what's going on."

"Okay, but..."

"And you'll do what I say when I say it. No questions. No arguments. And the same goes for anything Mark tells you. If you can't agree to these terms, I will no longer provide you with any type of security and you're on your own. Do you understand?"

"Yes."

Paul walked out of the hospital room behind me, and Mark brought up the rear. It was beginning to feel like we were moving in a convoy. Maybe I should have taken a job with the Secret Service. When we made it to my car, I opened the back door and closed it once Eastman was inside.

"Are you sure you aren't having a psychotic break?" Mark asked, giving me that knowing look over the roof of my car.

"Actually, it seems there's a good chance I am. Feel free

to put me down before I completely lose it."
He smirked, and we climbed inside.

TWENTY-TWO

"Looks like you're all set," I remarked, scanning the room a final time. "No credit cards. No phone calls." Ripping the motel provided phone from the wall might have been overkill, so I didn't resort to the theatrics. "Mark's picking up a throwaway you can use to keep in contact with me and only me. Once he gets back, I'll drop by an ATM and get some cash you can use in the meantime. I'll add it to your billable expenses."

"Gee, thanks." Paul hopped onto one of the beds and propped himself up on the pillows. "So what am I supposed to do now?"

"What do you want to do?" I sat on the other bed.

"Go home, take a shower, put on some fresh clothes, eat a decent meal, watch some TV, and resume living my life."

"Well, the shower's that way." I jerked my thumb toward the bathroom. "Just don't drink the water." He blanched. "Too soon?"

"Alexis," his tone was commanding, like it had been when he was ordering me around at PDN, "I'd like a workable timetable and plan of action for the course of your investigation. And I'd like it ASAP."

"Do you want a PowerPoint presentation to go with it?"

"Only if it'll help illustrate your plan." He swung his legs off the bed and sat up so he could face me directly. "Stop being so abrasive. I'm not your enemy. I'm the only one who has any right to be pissed, particularly after the way you've been acting, but I'm giving you a chance to prove you know what the hell you're doing. I owe you. So here's your perfect opportunity."

"God, you're unbelievable." I ran a hand through my hair. "I didn't ask for this, and hiring me isn't some grand favor. Hell, before everything is said and done, I might end up arrested for obstruction."

"That cop won't arrest you. No one in the precinct will. Even stuck inside that horrible cell, I could still hear the whispers circulating about the sexy private eye."

"Yeah, and my phone number's written on the wall in the men's locker room. What the hell's your point?"

"The point is the cops think you're impressive, and I don't want to end up in the ground because of whatever the fuck is going on at the hotel. Alvin's dead." His face contorted, and he looked away. "That other guy was beaten to death. And despite how convinced you were that I'm an alcoholic, it turns out those were symptoms of fluoride toxicity, which means I'm next unless someone steps in. Obviously, you're my best chance. After all, you found me in the cell. You got in contact with that attorney. And you convinced the police to cut me loose. It would be stupid to change horses mid-stream." His gaze returned to me. "Why do you have to act like this is the worst job in the world? I'm not asking you to do anything illegal. I'm not hiring you to sleep with me or anything, so what's your deal?"

"I'm sorry." There was no reason to act this way, but something about his personality grated on my nerves. It probably had to do with his underhanded business practices and corporate espionage attempts. "I was wrong not to take you at your word, especially after you've been so forthcoming about your questionable activities." The sarcasm dripped from every word.

"Is that what this is about?"

"Truthfully," I inhaled deeply, "I don't know what this is about. Maybe it's that. Maybe I'm still pissed about the

Martin Technologies thing." He nodded, looking contrite. "Or I'm frustrated because there are so many things going on that I'm suddenly aware of, and none of them are good. We have a lot to talk about. And full disclosure, the last time I pretended to be a bodyguard, my client almost bled to death. So don't assume that I'm your best bet."

"I'll take my chances."

Before he could say another word, Mark announced himself and opened the door. He carried a stack of bags and dropped them on the bed next to Eastman. "Here are some essentials. Get yourself cleaned up. We have a lot to accomplish tonight."

Paul picked up the bags and went into the bathroom. Getting up, I went to the door. "Can you watch him while I pick up a few things, phone Jacobs, and catch my breath?"

"Sure." Mark found the remote and flicked on the TV, stretching out on the bed I just vacated. "Grab some snacks and sandwiches." He jerked his chin at the mini-fridge and microwave. "We're gonna need them." Before I made it to the door, he added, "And don't forget, the hospital said Paul needs to get plenty of calcium to counteract the effects of the fluoride."

"What flavor?" I asked, knowing exactly where this conversation was going.

"I'm thinking mint chocolate chip or maybe pistachio."

"Green it is."

Shutting the door, I leaned against the hard surface and stared over the railing at the parking lot below. It was one of the cheaper chain motels. The room was registered in Mark's name, so it was safe. No one would think to look for Paul Eastman here, which gave me time to figure things out. Now the only question was where to begin. First, I needed to figure out which way was up.

"Detective Jacobs, please. Tell him it's Alex Parker," I said into the receiver as I headed away from the motel.

"Parker," he responded a few seconds later, "I didn't expect to hear from you so soon. Has Eastman changed his mind about protective custody?"

"No. And you and I both know after the way he was jerked around that he's not changing his mind. However, the only reason I've agreed to keep an eye on him is as a favor to you."

"Really?"

"Yep. After the agreement we reached this morning, it seemed only fair. So when can I expect those files?"

"Is that the only way you'll trade information?"

"At the moment, yes."

The silence lasted longer than it should, and then Jacobs cleared his throat. "Twenty minutes. I'll send a uniform to deliver copies to your office. Don't make me regret this."

"Have you regretted any of our previous encounters?"

"Well, I wasn't too fond of your unhelpful statement when I questioned you about the recovery of O'Connell's niece a few months back, but you get the job done. Just make sure there isn't reason for me to regret this one."

"I'll call in the morning with an update."

"I'm looking forward to it."

The click sounded in my ear, and I pulled to a stop in front of my office and rubbed the bridge of my nose. There were a couple of things I swore I'd never do. One was returned to the OIO, which was what I recently tried to do. The other was act as someone's bodyguard. On the plus side, I didn't think Paul Eastman would bother to knock me out of the way of a bullet, so there wasn't much chance he'd die saving me. At least there was something to be said for cowardice.

Stepping inside, I dispensed with the mail and messages; then I spoke briefly with the security guards at Martin Technologies. My meeting with Luc was still scheduled for Thursday afternoon, and at the moment, I wasn't positive I'd be able to make it. Maybe with a bit of bribery, Mark would keep an eye on Paul while I explained the recommended system alterations. Why wasn't I getting paid for this? Oh yeah, I screwed up. That seemed to be one of those things that kept happening frequently.

I checked the time. The police files should be arriving in five minutes. Then I'd stop for cash, ice cream, and some basic supplies, and return to the motel so we could get to work. With nothing better to do, I shut my eyes and processed through everything I knew. When the bell chimed above my door, I opened my eyes and smiled.

"I was beginning to think you were avoiding me. Oh wait, that's because you were."

"Sorry, Parker," Detective O'Connell offered, dropping a couple of files on my desk. "Duty comes first. And for some reason, I was ordered to stay away from you." He raised an eyebrow. "I can't imagine why that would be, can you?" He took a seat and studied me. "At least you're no longer a murder suspect."

"If I murdered someone, they wouldn't find the body or have any evidence."

"Yeah, that's what I thought. But for some reason, that doesn't actually help solidify your innocence when corpses start turning up all over the place." He shook his head and snorted. "Seriously, how are you holding up?"

"I'm fine."

"Yeah, and if that isn't a load of bull, I don't know what is." He narrowed his eyes. "I know how you are. We've worked together far too often for you to act like this doesn't bother you." He tapped the folders. "What are you planning on doing?"

"Not much. Are you assisting Jacobs on the investigation?"

He shook his head. "No. Trust me, I think I'd rather be helping him on this than what I'm working. But I had to pass by here, so I offered to stop in, say hello, and drop off the case files. Sorry, I didn't call you back sooner."

"It's okay. I understand." He glanced at his watch. "Get to work. If I don't get back to protecting Eastman soon, Jablonsky's gonna be pissed."

"He's investigating?"

"Not officially. He's on vacation, so he's giving the private sector a shot to see if he can hack it." O'Connell laughed, knowing there wasn't a chance in hell that was actually the case. "And he's watching my back," I admitted. "It's been a rough couple of weeks. Martin's out of the country, and my gig with PDN and the Secret Service blew up in my face. Right now, I'm just hoping Eastman keeps breathing while Jacobs gets things sorted out."

"That doesn't sound like the Alex Parker I know." O'Connell stood. "And for the record, Jacobs is a good cop, but he could use the help." He waved goodbye and left my office.

Not entirely sure what to make of the commentary concerning Detective Jacobs and the possibility that he needed assistance, I skimmed the files quickly, collected everything I compiled about the hotel, the murders, the employees, and everything from my stint at PDN before locking up and hitting the grocery store.

Almost two hours later, I returned to the motel room. Jablonsky and Eastman were lying on the two double beds, watching sports commentary over last night's game. To the untrained eye, Mark's slight movement wouldn't have been noticed, but I knew his gun was underneath the pillow. And the sound of the door opening was enough for him to aim his weapon.

"I come in peace," I said, and Eastman flicked off the TV and sat up. He had changed clothes and looked ready to get to work. "I might have overdone it on the ice cream though." Shoving the cold items into the mini-fridge, I pulled out a chair at the table and laid the files on top. "O'Connell stopped by to deliver these personally."

"Is he on the case?" Mark asked, getting up and skimming the folders.

"No." I met his eyes. "But he said Jacobs could use some help."

"As if you needed the extra prodding," Mark replied.

"I thought you were working for me." Paul climbed across the spread and sat on the edge of the bed closest to the table. "What's all this?"

"It's where we begin." I looked up. "Mr. Eastman, I need to ask you a couple of questions."

"Okay." His eyes darted from me to Mark. "Why do I get the feeling this is an inquisition?"

"And you thought the doctors at the hospital were too invasive," Mark muttered. "Boy, you're in for a surprise."

TWENTY-THREE

The list of individuals who had access to Paul Eastman's refrigerator within the last month wasn't particularly extensive. A couple of guys from PDN, a few neighbors, some of his pals that I already identified from his social networking page, and a couple of ladies who didn't have last names had been his only recent visitors. But he insisted that none of them would want to kill him. These were his friends and flings, not conniving murderers with an axe to grind.

"Word of advice, the next time you pick some chick up at a bar, get a last name," I suggested. "It makes it easier in the event you need an alibi, have to blame someone for contracting an STD, or in case your wallet gets stolen, or your fridge is tampered with."

"Hey, don't I get some credit for remembering first names as well as their other features?" Paul asked. "Plus, I always go to the same few bars. It wouldn't be particularly hard to track them down."

"Give me their descriptions and the names of the bars," Mark chimed in, "and I'll ask around."

After Mark had enough information to identify the three different women, he left the motel, promising to return with a few names. In the meantime, I was back on guard duty. Spreading out the files and information, I grabbed a pen and notepad and began sorting through the mess that resulted in two homicides, an attempted murder, probably some type of financial crime, and the selling of corporate secrets.

"What are you doing?" Paul asked, looking over my shoulder.

"I'm playing connect the dots."

He pulled out one of the two pints of ice cream that I stocked and picked up a plastic spoon. He took a seat and noisily unwrapped the container. After his third lip-smacking bite, I dropped my pen and stared at him.

"Want some? The doctors said I need to keep my calcium intake up for the next couple of weeks, but there's plenty."

"No." I went back to writing, but it was obvious he wanted some attention.

"So, that guy, Mark, he was your supervising officer at the OIO, right?" He swallowed another mouthful and put the lid back on the container. "He's a scary son-of-a-bitch." I shrugged, not bothering to glance up. "He practically threatened me. I don't see why he's involved in this. I hired you."

Throwing my pen and notepad down, I leaned back, annoyed. "He's helping because this is a giant mess. Do you not understand that?"

"I understand that he threatened physical harm if it turns out I'm jerking you around. He's a bit overprotective, isn't he? No wonder you left the OIO. And it's no wonder you're such a hard-ass about everything. You're used to having to keep people in their place. I'm guessing mainly men, given the way you've reacted to me."

"Apparently it's not working."

"I want to help." He returned the ice cream to the freezer and scooted his chair closer to mine. "Tell me what you're doing so I can help. I work in private security for Christ's sake. Investigations aren't some mystical thing that I have no experience with, so stop acting like that's the case. This motel room and the instructions you've given me are right out of PDN's manual. It's common knowledge for people like us."

"Common knowledge. For people. Like us." Wow, he really didn't get it.

"Yeah. Obviously." He cocked an eyebrow, confused by the surprised, halting speech pattern I was using. "And I'm sure if I'm out in public, you'll tell me to disguise my appearance, blend in with the crowd, and not to draw attention to myself. Am I right?" My mouth moved, but no words came out. "See, this isn't some top secret spy shit. This is just how the job gets done."

"How the job gets done?" I was flabbergasted by his attitude and commentary.

"Okay, now you're mocking me on purpose."

"Are you out of your fucking mind? I'm still trying to figure out if you poisoned yourself, killed Alvin, or made some underhanded deal with Frank Costan that led to him getting beaten and killed. You have some kind of connection with Jason Oster, and I don't know if he's involved. He's definitely involved with someone, which is suspicious enough as it is," I rambled, overwhelmed by so many facts.

"I thought you believed me," he said quietly.

"Paul, I don't know what to believe." I got up to pace; there had to be some way to determine the truth. When I was away from him, I wanted nothing more than to figure out who wanted him dead in order to keep him alive, but after reading through the police files, it was apparent they had no solid leads, a lack of evidence, and no real motive for why someone would want to poison him. "Can you prove you didn't do this to yourself?"

"Why would I?"

"Well, fluoride isn't the typical way to go in terms of poisoning." Brushing my hair back, I spun to face him. "Either you're orchestrating this to cast enough dispersion to make sure you aren't blamed for the two deaths, which would be absolutely brilliant, or you're being set up."

"Apparently if I ever actually want to kill someone, you'll be my first phone call to plan it out." After staring him down for the next couple of minutes, he let out a sigh.

"Alvin was my friend. I didn't kill him. And I never met the other guy, Frank Costan. If you're convinced I'm part of this, then send me back to the police."

He reached for the stack of files, and I slammed my palm against the top. "You swore that none of the people with access to your apartment could have done this to you. So what am I supposed to think?"

"How do we know someone didn't break in to my house?"

"Do you have a home security system? A dog? Was there any sign of tampering on the locks, or did you notice if anything was moved inside?"

"No, none of the above."

"And we're back to square one." Removing my hand from the files, I scooped them off the table and onto the extra bed, out of his reach. "Let's try this another way." I tossed him a contrite smile. "From here on out, I'll take you at your word on everything. But if I find out you've lied about anything, regardless of how insignificant, then we're done. I feel like I keep saying this, but you keep lying or failing to disclose some key facts. And if you want me to divulge this information, I will, but if the police or some other entity determines you're the guilty party, it's gonna be really difficult for you to prove that you weren't privy to the details prior to this moment. So are you sure you want to do this?"

"Let's get started." He grabbed one of the blank notepads and sat up straighter. He uncapped the motel pen and stared at the stack of files. "Um...where do we begin?"

Snorting, I shook my head. "With square one. Did you know Frank Costan was staying at the hotel?"

"Not exactly. I heard a rumor from one of the security guards."

"Which one?"

"I don't remember." I gave him a look. "Seriously, I don't. A few of them were talking amongst themselves, and I happened to overhear on my way to meet with Jason. And when I asked Jason about it, he said he didn't know anything."

"Did you ask Alvin Hodge?"

"He told me it was just gossip and nothing to concern myself with. We already had a big fish on the line." Answering my questioning gaze, he elaborated with, "Bernie Muller." All right, so Frank Costan checked in the Saturday before the conference, like the lobby security cam footage showed, and Paul just corroborated that much. Finally, we were making some headway.

Scooting further onto the bed, I leaned my back against the wall. This was so fucking complicated. "Look, you still haven't told me anything about the corporate secrets you were selling, who your clients were, or who you screwed over in the process. I wanted to let it go because it didn't seem relevant, but poison is personal. So it's time for some details. Why don't you start with the most recent and move backward? Maybe something's connected."

Paul audibly swallowed. "Have you ever heard of the SMI Corporation?"

"Out of Minsk?" My night with the Russian might not have been a complete waste.

"I guess they have an office there. I don't know. It's one of these multinational conglomerates." I nodded for him to continue. "One of their representatives was at the conference, and he secured the plans for their newest energy prototype in the hotel's safe. Alvin gave me clearance, and I planned to copy the information." My face must have read disdain because he added, "Yeah, I know. Despicable." He chewed on the inside of his cheek. "But it turned out I already saw those plans before."

"Where?"

"They were the same ones Bernie was hocking at the conference. It was the same design Klaus Manufacturing wanted to use to power the train." He shrugged. "I guess someone sold the plans beforehand."

"Or Alvin lied to you about the information being in the hotel safe. Did you ask Bernie about it? Maybe Klaus made a deal with SMI." Scribbling a note to check the financial section for possible mergers or hinting at a partnership, I blew out a breath and waited.

"No. Bernie just thought I was a middleman, not a corporate spy, so I didn't want to risk losing his trust."

"Corporate spy? Do you honestly think that highly of yourself?"

"Do you think you can be any more judgmental?" he asked. "It is what it is. Companies employ people to infiltrate their competitors all the time. It's a common practice. Just because I do this as a freelance gig on the side doesn't mean I'm any less reputable."

"You're a thief, potentially stealing millions of dollars, depending on the schematics or product. Remind me not to leave anything of value anywhere near you." Briefly, my mind flashed back to his insistence to meet Martin. He was probably hoping to score schematics on the new R&D line or information on the merger with Hover Designs. "Tell me something. Have you ever used or leaked information about your thievery in order to turn a profit in the stock market? Maybe you were paid to sabotage a company's intended earnings in order to ensure the stocks would plummet. If someone pulled out at the right time and invested in the competitor, they could make a killing in the market."

Paul rubbed his five o'clock shadow and shook his head, trying to process what I just said. After an entire minute passed, he dropped the paper on the table and leaned back. "I never thought to do that."

He probably never thought to do a lot of things, but I didn't offer to share. He wasn't a genius. It sounded like he was a puppet who let other people pull the strings. People like Alvin Hodge or Frank Costan or Rodney Wheeler.

"How did you get involved in this corporate spying in the first place? Was it your idea or someone else's?"

The light bulb clicked on, and he looked green. "Alvin suggested it after he paid some favors to me on PDN's behalf. It didn't sound like a bad idea at the time. It was exciting, and it never seemed that dangerous."

"Yeah, until he was found hanging in the hotel." Jerking my chin at the forgotten notepad, I forced him to focus. "Write down the names of every individual and company the two of you screwed over and the companies that profited by your illegal activities. We'll get to the bottom of this and then work our way back up."

"Okay. Do you think this is why Alvin was killed?"

"It's too soon to speculate, but it's a possibility."

Realistically, I felt certain he was killed because someone discovered he was informing to the FBI. My prime suspect was still Rodney Wheeler, but since I didn't trust Paul completely, I wanted to see how far off course he'd let this investigation go. Plus, in the event my assumptions were incorrect, it'd be nice to know who else had a score to settle.

He quieted and wrote everyone he could think of on the sheet of paper. Since he had only been in the secret selling biz for a year, there were only three instances prior to the conference. I'd check into them, but my money was on Frank Costan and the connection to the conference.

"Someone on this list could be responsible for my friend's death and almost killing me." Paul was scared. Reality finally hit him, and it was about damn time.

"That would be my guess," I replied unhelpfully, taking the paper from him and opening my laptop.

Scanning for alleged links between these companies and Frank Costan, the news sources didn't provide much. Mark would have to run it by the FBI and maybe the SEC and see what they could find. The theory and motive were coalescing into something realistic, complex, and not exactly what I imagined when I began looking into this case. After finding nothing of any use, I paced the room. My original assumptions still seemed the most likely.

"Let me get this straight, you think Alvin was using me to sell secrets so we'd both get a cut of the money from the corporations, and then he was buying and selling market shares in order to make even more cash?" He tapped his leg nervously. "Then if he was making millions or whatever, why was he still working as the night clerk at the hotel? Shouldn't he be on some private island?"

"Maybe the scores weren't big enough." Or more than likely, someone else was pulling the strings, but I didn't want to put words in Paul's mouth. "What do you actually know about Alvin? One minute you're telling me he's your friend or were friendly, but aside from scamming people and keeping PDN's nose out of the drugs and the prostitutes, what did the two of you actually do outside of work?"

"Nothing."

"Did he ever go to your house?" I asked, hoping to find a connection. Maybe the party responsible for tampering with the water filter gained access or knowledge from Hodge prior to his death.

"No. We didn't hang out because it would look suspicious." Paul cleared his throat. "Alvin was killed for scamming someone, and since I helped him do it, the same person tried to poison me. That's what you're thinking. It makes the most sense."

"Yes, it does. Who else at the hotel knew what was going on?"

"No one."

"What about Jason Oster? You told me to talk to him about Frank Costan. He must have known what Alvin was doing. Maybe you bragged to him about it." Jason said Paul was a bigmouth, so it wouldn't have taken much for him to report such action to one of the hotel owners. If Jason opened his mouth to Wheeler about Alvin's squealing and Paul's involvement, it would explain the two homicides and how neither of them showed up on the security footage. Plus, Oster is screwing Hodge's ex-wife. There were plenty of reasons not to mix business with pleasure, but since Oster did, they would both lend themselves to motive for killing or assisting in Hodge's murder. I made a mental note to discuss this in further detail with Mark and Det. Jacobs before focusing back on Eastman. "Plus, Jason came to your house to collect some surveillance gear to set up in the hotel to ensure nothing illegal was happening with PDN's clients." Something was starting to stink.

"Yeah, I used my personal camera so PDN wouldn't be implicated in any drug deals or providing escorts. Jason was nice enough to help me with it to ensure additional protection for PDN's clientele and the hotel staff."

"And Jason set it up every time a PDN client checked into a room?"

"Yes."

"Who watched the footage?"

"Jason." His face contorted.

"And what do you think he saw on the tape?"

"Everything."

TWENTY-FOUR

Everything was such an umbrella term. Jason Oster probably had footage containing celebrity sex tapes, drug use, and plenty to make *TMZ* salivate. Dozens of avenues were available for him to profit from pictures and video like that. Blackmail, trashy tabloids, and internet gossip sites would do pretty much anything for a story on a B or C-lister. But, somehow, I didn't think Oster was selling tawdry secrets. He had enough of his own, so it might have been far too hypocritical for him to stomach. That didn't mean he wasn't my prime suspect.

"Was the camera just inside the room, or did the two of you set up additional security cameras elsewhere?" I asked.

"Just in the room since I only have the single unit. It was to ensure that the hotel staff was behaving appropriately. We weren't looking for dirt, if that's what you think."

"Did Jason ever give you any indication that the footage revealed something heinous?" Paul shook his head. "When did you use the camera last?"

"A week or so before the conference." He scratched his chin. "Come to think of it, he never returned it. He said it was in his locker at work, but with all the craziness going on, he must have forgotten about it."

"Right. That must be it." Unless I viewed the actual footage, it was too soon to speculate if it was related to the crime spree that was wreaking havoc at the hotel. "Let's get back on track." Picking up the list Paul made, I wondered about SMI's relationship with Klaus Manufacturing. "Are you positive the schematics are the same?"

"Yeah." He reached into his pocket but realized his cell phone was gone, still at the precinct with the rest of his belongings that were on his person when they arrested him. "The proof's on my phone. I snapped a shot of SMI's plans."

"Did you also snap a shot of Klaus Manufacturing's?"

"No, I have something even better. Bernie gave me a copy of the documents." Giving him a skeptical look, he added, "They're at home. Bernie gave them to me to pass along to someone in charge at Martin Technologies."

An unfortunate snort escaped my lips, followed by barely contained laughter. "If Bernie's handing the schematics out like business cards, then it's not a secret. He probably gave a copy to SMI too." Rolling my eyes, I was no longer concerned with the connection between SMI and Klaus. It wasn't relevant to either murder. At least that was progress.

"Well, if you're so damn smart, why would the rep stick them inside the hotel safe?" he challenged.

"I don't know. Maybe he wanted to root out the corporate spies running rampant at the conference. It was to throw you off the scent." Shrugging and shaking my head, I flopped back onto the extra bed. "How should I know? But it no longer seems particularly relevant." Unless there was something else on the paper besides a copy of the schematics. Getting up, I flipped through the police file on Paul Eastman, but they didn't have a warrant to access his cell phone, so none of the information it contained was cataloged. It was simply listed as part of the item manifest for personal effects taken into custody.

"What?" He looked quizzical.

"Nothing. I'll get your personal effects out of custody in the morning." Continuing with the questioning, I wondered if there were any other possible persons of interest I had yet to consider. "Aside from work, have you made any enemies lately? Or is there someone who stands to gain something significant upon your demise? Did you ever steal and sell water filter prototypes from one company to another and someone's seeking revenge?"

A noise came from outside the room, and then Mark announced himself and opened the door. He gave me a curt nod, and there was a faint sparkle in his eyes. He was on to something.

"C'mon, I'm a likable guy. None of my friends want me dead, and I didn't steal from a water filter or refrigerator company either," Eastman insisted.

"Yeah, you're so likable one of the ladies you described seems to remember being thrown out of your house the morning after. Another one described you as a little, selfish prick, and the third," he winked at me, "seems to really get around."

"What are you talking about?" Paul asked, reddening. "I never threw anyone out. I might have been in a rush to get to work, and I don't like letting people stay in my house unattended."

"Yeah, they might poison your water," I mumbled.

Tossing a glare in my direction, he continued. "And whoever else you spoke to must have been thinking of someone else because I've never been with a hooker."

"They prefer the term escort," I added, helpful as always.

"No, she isn't a working girl." Mark grinned, and I cocked my head to the side, intrigued. "The reason she's so flexible is because she teaches yoga classes."

"Seriously?" I asked, considering the new implication.

"Let's find out." Mark pulled out a folded sheet of paper containing a photo of Rachel Romanski and held it out to Paul. "Is that one of your flings?"

"Yeah, that's Lexie," he said. "Flexie Lexie." Mark raised an eyebrow. "It's a pneumonic device to help me remember her name."

"I'm just curious. Did Alvin Hodge ever talk about his personal life or ex-wives?" I asked.

"Maybe he mentioned them once or twice, but nothing major. Why?" Paul wanted to make sense of my question in relation to Mark's most recent declaration, but there was an apparent disconnect in his brain.

"No reason. Is Jason Oster seeing anyone special?"

"He's boning some chick. She stops by occasionally and meets him in the mornings in one of the empty rooms at the hotel." Paul scratched his head. "At least that's what the other security guards said."

"Did they ever describe her?" Mark asked.

"Yeah." Realization finally dawned on Paul. "No way. There's no way it's the same chick."

"Did you and Jason frequent the same watering holes?" I asked, and Mark grimaced at the unintended pun. Tossing a brief glare, I waited for an answer. Paul appeared to be appalled and incredulous, so it took him a moment to finally realize I was speaking to him.

"We went out for drinks after work sometimes. Fuck. Do you think he knows?"

"That you were enjoying his leftovers?" Mark asked.

"Did she introduce herself as Lexie, or was that what you decided to call her?" I asked, diverting the conversation back to something practical.

"No, she said Lexie," Paul insisted, looking at the photo. "I take it that's not her real name."

"Not even close, kid," Mark replied.

"What is it?"

"That's need to know, and right now, you don't." Rubbing my neck, I stood up and took a deep breath. "This might just be the break we need. Did you call Jacobs?"

"Not yet." Mark glanced in Paul's direction, silencing him before he could interrupt. "It's up to you, boss, but," he was being cute, and I didn't care for it, "I would suggest we tread lightly. They could go to ground if we spook them. The PD tends to be quite loud about things, and we don't need evidence or suspects to disappear."

"I agree," Paul piped up, as if he were actually part of the conversation. Obviously, he didn't understand the grown-ups were talking. "I want you to find my would-be killer, and if you think Lexie and Jason are in on it, that can't be good. It'd be nice to know who my real friends are, so see if you can make that happen."

Gritting my teeth at his comment, I threw another look at Mark. "Do you mind if I hand over babysitting privileges for the rest of the evening while I do some digging and recon?"

"Not a problem. What should I do if he gets fussy?" Mark chuckled, and Paul gave us each a hard look.

"Well, there is ice cream in the freezer. Or you can shoot him if the whining gets to be too much." Smirking at Paul, I went to the door.

"I can still hear you," Paul said, realizing it was a joke, but still not appreciative of our sense of humor. Maybe it was only funny to federal agents, former and current, which he was clearly neither.

"Great. I'd suggest you don't whine too much," I added, letting myself out of the room. With any luck, this was square two.

*　　*　　*

Rubbing my hands down my face, I leaned forward against the steering wheel, stretching my back and cursing how boring sole surveillance was. After I left the motel, I went to my office, ran complete profiles on Jason Oster and Rachel Romanski again, and checked for any known aliases that I might have missed. Of course, they both came off pretty much spotless. It was too late to call around for favors, so I flipped a coin and found myself parked outside Jason Oster's apartment building.

He lived in a second floor corner apartment. It wasn't too swanky. No doorman or intercom system, but it looked much nicer and better lit than a crack house. It was in a pleasant area, devoid of drug dealers and whores working the corners. Shit, it was nicer than my place, and judging from the number of windows, it was probably larger too. However, it certainly wasn't nice enough for someone selling dirty little secrets or involved in insider trading.

Something was bothersome about the Jason/Rachel dynamic, and after two hours of sitting in deafening silence, I realized what it was. There was no reason for her to meet him at the hotel. As far as I could tell, he lived alone. He wasn't married, and neither was she. So why the secrecy? Frankly, going to the hotel wasn't the best way to keep whatever was going on a secret. The security guards suspected Jason was having an affair, and her ex-husband worked there. The chances for getting caught, getting fired, or worse were much greater. Perhaps they liked the danger of being discovered. Crazier things had happened, but it didn't feel right.

Checking the time, I did some quick calculations in my head and dialed a familiar number. "I'm not leaving you a voicemail tomorrow or today, whatever day it is for you. So just accept this as your daily call."

"Okay," Martin replied, confused by my random bossiness.

"Why would you meet a woman at a hotel to have an affair if neither of you were married and lived alone? Let's add the fact that her ex-husband is the night clerk and someone is bound to talk at some point."

"Alexis, just to be clear, no one is having an affair. The only hotels I've checked into have been necessary for work, and unless you think Bruiser had gender reassignment surgery and has an ex-husband stashed somewhere, then I don't have a clue what you're talking about because he's the only one staying in my suite."

"Not you," I laughed, realizing how poor my conversational skills could be, "hypothetically."

"Well, hypothetically, the only woman I'd meet in a hotel for reasons of debauchery would be you."

"Charmer."

"That isn't to say I haven't met many women in hotels recently. For purely business purposes, I assure you."

"Oh, so that's what you call it. I see how it is. It's probably because of that charming attitude of yours that has forced you to pay for sex."

"God, you're in a mood." He laughed. "Any reason in particular you're being this snarky?"

"Just working out some kinks on a case." What other reason would Rachel have to meet Jason at the hotel?

Maybe it wasn't for the reasons everyone thought. Deciding on my next course of action, I turned the key in the ignition. "Thanks for the help. I better go."

"Be careful."

"Yeah, you too. And don't let Bruiser get too frisky."

"I'll do my best, but you did call in the middle of some grab ass."

"Do we need to go over sexual harassment in the workplace again?" I asked.

"Good night, Alex."

TWENTY-FIVE

One of the easiest ways to get what you want is simply to take it. Granted, that often involves breaking a law or two. But asking first requires the acquiescence of too many other people. There was some type of saying about begging for forgiveness instead of asking for permission, and seeing as how I already managed to sneak my way into the employee area of the five-star hotel and was scanning the labels on the rows of lockers for Jason Oster's, now wasn't really the time to ask permission. Plus, walking into the hotel like I owned the place and ordering people with actual hotel-sanctioned positions to give me directions would become counterproductive if I stopped now.

Locating Oster's locker, I performed a quick sweep of the room, noting the absence of surveillance equipment and hotel personnel. It was now or never, so digging out my lock picks, I set to work. The combination lock was the cheaper model that could be purchased from discount retailers or hardware stores, but thankfully, it had a keyhole at the back in case the user forgot the combination or, in my case, didn't know the combination. One quick turn and the lock opened. At least it was easier than having to borrow a set of bolt cutters from maintenance, which had been plan B.

Inside was an extra dress shirt and tie, a pair of running shoes, a few pictures cut out of Maxim taped to the door next to a mirror, and a box with various charging cables for cell phones and other electronic devices. Just as I was prepared to slam the door shut in defeat, I located the tiny wireless webcam at the bottom of the box. It fit in the palm of my hand and was probably the envy of all the other security cams in the building. After determining where the internal memory was, I removed the card, replaced the camera and everything else inside Jason's locker, and shut the door.

"That's not your locker," one of the maids said, entering as I was sliding the combination lock back into place.

"No wonder I can't get this thing to open," I said, tugging ineffectually at the newly relocked lock. "Silly me."

She glared, but I ducked past her and out of the room. With any luck, she wouldn't report me to hotel security. But in case she did, I needed to figure out what was on the memory card before anyone decided to check on my illegal activities.

Exiting stage left, I wandered back down the corridor, past the lobby, and out the front door. The valet smiled and handed over my keys. For twenty dollars, he had been willing to leave my car parked out front for ten minutes. That was a fair enough trade. Considering my options, I returned home, powered up my laptop, and inserted the memory card into the slot.

"Seriously?" I growled. It was blank. I went to the hotel and broke into Jason's locker for nothing. "Goddammit." Glowering at the empty file folder on the screen, I right-clicked and searched for hidden files. Still nothing. Ejecting the worthless piece of plastic from my computer, I wondered if it ever contained any information. It could be a brand new memory card, or the files were deleted. Files, sheesh. I didn't even know what I hoped to find. Evidence for at least one of the recent murders or perhaps evidence of a conspiracy would have been nice. Instead, I ended up with a blank memory card.

Checking the time, I didn't know who was working

graveyard at the precinct, but I could leave a note for Jacobs if nothing else. Halfway there, I changed my mind and detoured back to the motel where I stashed Paul. Implicating myself in a theft in the midst of a homicide investigation wasn't necessarily the best way to win over Detective Jacobs, particularly if the memory card proved to be absolutely useless.

"I'm back," I announced, waking Paul by slamming the door. He squinted and rolled over in bed, deciding I wasn't much of a threat. Mark was at the table, reading through the files and making notes. "Did I miss anything?"

"I doubt it." He finished writing and assessed me. "How'd it go?"

"Superb."

"Oh, that good?" He knew my sarcasm well.

"Oster's home alone. So I did some digging and pulled this out of the camera Eastman lent him." Tossing a glance at Paul, he didn't stir, and I figured he was out like a light. "The damn thing appears to be blank."

"And you want me to get tech to see if it was always blank."

"Thanks for offering." I sat across from him and stared at the ceiling. "The way I figure it, either Oster wiped the card because of what was on it, or he replaced it with a new one because of what was recorded."

"What are you thinking?"

"Room 709 was trashed. It was a few dozen feet away from where Alvin Hodge's body was left hanging, and there were obvious signs of a struggle. Supposedly, the FBI was renting the room to maintain eyes on Frank Costan. At least, that's the story Jason Oster told. I'm thinking either Oster got the room number wrong or things got out of hand while the FBI was surveilling Frank Costan. Either way, something went down in that room."

"Why would you think it's the same room that Oster had under surveillance?"

"Call it a hunch." Thinking back, I knew Oster had access to rooms that weren't in use, whether or not they were registered to guests was beside the point. He knew where everyone was and when. It's probably how he and

Rachel stayed under the radar for their rendezvous. "From what we know, the FBI was conducting an operation for the last eight months to trap Costan and gain enough evidence against his suspected partner, Wheeler. Hodge was tipping off the authorities, and that room was incredibly close to the staging of his body. It can't be a coincidence. Maybe it was a 'fuck you' to the feds, or Uncle Sam rented the room and never used it. You should ask Walton about it. He was running point." I tossed another glance at Paul to make sure he was still asleep. "According to Oster, he claimed that he spotted Costan at the hotel and informed his boss who in turn informed the FBI. Don't you think he'd want to keep tabs on the agents to see what they were doing, especially if he might be implicated in something?"

"Do you have anything solid against Oster besides your gut instincts?"

"Not yet." I jerked my chin at the memory card. "But hopefully, we will soon." I sighed. "Did Walton give you any other useful information?"

"He said they were monitoring the hotel, but he didn't mention additional surveillance cams. My guess would be they planted a couple of undercover agents, a unit or two outside, and some guys strategically placed throughout the lobby, the conference room, and the bar. Y'know, basic FBI tactics."

"So aside from break time or filling out reports after shift change, they wouldn't have been using the hotel room." Realization hit, and I shook my head. "Don't you have the registry info?"

"It's in your office."

"We'll double-check in the morning, but Oster said it was registered to the FBI."

"How would he have known they were FBI? Most ops are registered under a bogus name or some kind of operational phrase." I smiled, and the light bulb clicked on. "Because that's the room he had under surveillance," Mark said, understanding the reasoning behind my hunch.

"Bingo."

"It could be happenstance. Circumstantial." He was deflating my happy balloon with these negative possibilities.

"Unfortunately, it's the only angle we have."

"The more complicated this gets, the more people seem to be involved. At this point, I'd bet they're all in on it." He shot a look toward Paul, who was buried under the blankets, asleep.

"Okay." I made an 'it's possible' gesture. "Can I ask you one thing?" He nodded. "What is *it*? Because we have two dead bodies, half a dozen reasonable motives which may or may not pan out, and an attempted poisoning."

"I don't know. It looks like a double-cross. It probably started out financial and turned violent." He took a deep breath and rubbed his eyes. "We need to figure out what the hell is going on." He looked at Paul, who let out a slight whistling snore. "I thought the only thing you were interested in was protecting your client and clearing his name."

"It was, but my interest has been piqued."

"And there's the linchpin." Mark snorted. "You can never mind your own business." He neatly stacked the files on the table. "I'm gonna get some sleep and run some things by the OIO in the morning." He picked up the memory card and put it into his shirt pocket. "If you give me the keys to your office, I'll stop by and grab the hotel registry."

"You could just break in."

"One of us needs to obey the law." He gave me a pointed look and held out his hand, and I gave him the keys. "I'll see you in the morning."

After Mark left, I paced the room, turning the facts over in my head. Alvin Hodge was murdered and left hanging in the open. That seemed like a warning. Based on TODs, Frank Costan was killed sometime later. Assuming the two were inextricably linked, which was the only thing that made any real sense, Hodge was either killed as a warning to Costan or because he was a rat. Given Costan's bloody, beaten remains, I was willing to venture out on a limb and say Costan failed to comply with his assailant's would-be demands. Those few facts fit neatly into my theory, and the killer was probably a single individual or hired by a single individual to do the job. I'd wager the party responsible for the two murders was Costan's alleged partner, Rodney Wheeler. The same partner the FBI had under surveillance. Too bad Agent Walton didn't want to share leads. Although if Wheeler paid someone to do the wet work or slipped his surveillance and Secret Service protection detail, no one would want to admit they bumbled an op. It was easier to pass the blame than to take it.

More than likely, someone in the hotel lured Costan into an unoccupied room, and a struggle ensued. Jason Oster might have orchestrated the entire thing, or he might have done the deed himself. If he offed Costan on Wheeler's behalf, then it would explain why the memory card I illegally borrowed was blank. But there was one glaringly obvious flaw in my thinking. How did Costan's body get into the subway tunnels below the hotel without anyone noticing if the struggle took place inside the trashed hotel room or even a different hotel room?

Shit. I rubbed my eyes, scooped the files off the table, and spread them out on the extra bed. Maybe something would pop out at me. A clue would be nice. The truth would be better. Instead, the files, photos, and police reports bled into a sea of random musings that were less helpful than my own internal postulating. There had to be a better way of doing things.

Stretching out, I grabbed a pen and sketched an outline of my hair-brained theory. Hodge and Costan were colluding, at least until Hodge decided to turn him in. Perhaps Wheeler found out and was pissed. Maybe he thought Costan was going to turn on him too for a reduced sentence or leniency. Either way, Wheeler needed to remove the problem. Given the Secret Service detail, he probably hired a third party to threaten Hodge. And since Hodge was dead, I'd wager that he probably failed to comply with the threats.

My mind flashed to the caterer who was not allowed admittance to the hotel on Monday afternoon. The man didn't have his security badge. Scribbling a note to check into his actual identity to see if the badge was ever located, I suspected that might have been the in for whatever hired gun Wheeler used. A quick look at Wheeler's phone and bank records might also prove useful in determining how the attacker gained access to Alvin Hodge and the hotel.

After Hodge was killed and discovered, Costan must have panicked. He had to be somewhere on the hotel security footage. The guy wasn't a ghost, at least not at that point. Claxons blared in my brain, and I figured this might be precisely where Jason Oster fit into the mix. He could have maneuvered Costan around the security system and kept him in rooms not in use. Hell, he could have also been the one to move the body from the trashed hotel room to the tunnels below the subbasement if he wanted. He had the know-how, the access, and the ability to erase any incriminating evidence both in the room and on tape.

Closing my eyes, I considered all the flaws with this theory. First, it was only a theory. Second, it didn't explain why anyone would want to poison my client. Sure, it was possible Paul was involved in a lot more than he was letting on, but still, his dealings with Klaus Manufacturing, SMI, and even his job at PDN didn't coalesce with any of these other things. It just didn't fit. And third, it didn't explain Rachel Romanski's role in any of this. Granted, she might have simply been stopping by the hotel for a quick wham bam, thank you, ma'am, but Oster had gone through a lot of trouble to keep her identity a secret. There would be no point unless she was part of the underlying conspiracy and murders, unless of course he had nothing to do with any of that either.

"Ugh," I muttered, burying my face in the pillow. The only way to work through this mess was with actual evidence, and I was sorely lacking in that department. In the morning, I would handcuff myself to Jacobs' desk until I got some answers, and I would suggest that Mark do the same with Agent Walton.

TWENTY-SIX

"Alexis." I let out a grunt. "Alexis, your phone. Answer it," Paul insisted.

Opening an eyelid, I picked up the device, wondering exactly what Det. Jacobs wanted at eight a.m. "Parker," I answered.

"There was a report of you skulking around the hotel late last night. I thought you weren't sticking your nose into my business."

"I thought you were planning to share your findings. The files you sent are worthless. Some actual evidence, realistic leads, and possible suspects would be nice. Where's the copy of the surveillance footage, your interview notes with witnesses and persons of interest, and the rest of the things cops are supposed to do?"

"And what have you given me about Eastman and his involvement?" Jacobs countered. "Sure, he looks clean, but we both know that's not the case. Be at the precinct by noon. Got it?"

"Loud and clear." I hung up and dropped the phone on the bed.

"You like to burn the candle at both ends, don't you?" Eastman asked, sitting up and staring at me.

"I don't use candles. Fire hazard," I remarked, shutting my eyes and shifting off my side and on to my back. Sleeping in a curled up position for an extended amount of time was a bad idea. The paper from the files crinkled as I stretched and winced.

"When I hired you to protect me, I meant it as more of a joke to get that detective to back off about protective custody." I turned and gave him an incredulous look. "While I appreciate this overzealous attitude of yours, get the hell out of here."

"Excuse me?" I sat up, stacking the papers and files into a more manageable heap.

"Don't forget, I get paid to do this exact job. You set up a room under a different name, got me some cash, the essentials, and I know better than to go out and get spotted. But that doesn't mean I need some chick sleeping in my room. No offense."

"Just because you said no offense, it doesn't make that statement any less offensive." Mornings almost always made me bitchy. And after going round one with Det. Jacobs, I was ready for a K.O. with my second opponent. "First, you fired me from PDN. Then you beg for my help. And now you're firing me again?"

"I'm not firing you. And just so we're clear, the only reason I fired you from PDN was because I was afraid that overzealousness you keep exhibiting would lead to discovering my extracurricular corporate dealings after our little spat." I rolled my eyes, but he was undaunted. "Go home, Ms. Parker. I can take care of myself. I won't do anything stupid. I'll call if I need something, and right now, I'd like some peace and quiet and the chance to check out the continental breakfast in the motel lobby."

"Fine, but if you get yourself killed, I'm done working this case. I'll be back this afternoon to check on you, and you better still be here. Alone."

"Roger that." He mimicked a salute, and I pulled myself off the bed, collected everything of importance, and went to my car. Eight a.m. and already dealing with a couple of macho assholes, fuck me.

Instead of going home and going back to bed, which was

precisely what I wanted to do, I went home, showered, changed, brewed a pot of coffee with plenty of coffee and not much water, and considered my options. Mark was checking on the memory card and planned to have a chat with Walton, so I would work a different angle. Checking the yoga schedule for the week, I wasn't scheduled to start class until Friday, but that didn't mean Rachel wasn't teaching classes between now and then. That gave me plenty of time to dig up some dirt on her.

Driving slowly through her neighborhood, it was a quiet, pleasant area. Soccer moms jogged down the street in herds, and everyone's yard was perfectly manicured. Welcome to suburbia hell. The houses were small but probably pricey on account of their location. It seemed a stretch for a yoga instructor to be able to afford a place like this on her salary, but maybe her great aunt left her a fortune.

Since it was a bright and sunny day, my surveillance wasn't going by unnoticed, so after ten minutes, I had no choice but to leave. It would be premature to arouse suspicion when there were no clear suspects, well at least as far as the police department was concerned. Stopping to pick up coffee that actually resembled coffee and not mud, I splurged on a bag of donuts and went to the precinct two hours ahead of schedule.

"Did you bring me a present?" Det. O'Connell asked, eyeing the drink carrier.

"Seems only fair since you dropped something off for me yesterday." I put one of the cups down, handed his partner, Det. Thompson, another cup, and took one for myself. Leaving the last one in the carrier for whenever Jacobs appeared. "And I brought pastries." Snagging the chocolate cake donut for myself, I handed the bag to O'Connell to do with as he saw fit.

"Why do I get the feeling this is a bribe?" he asked.

"Because you know how she is," Thompson retorted, not looking up from his computer screen. "But I appreciate the predictability, Parker." He cracked a slight smile. "Is there a cruller in there?"

O'Connell passed the bag off to his partner. "What do

you want?"

"Complete access to Jacobs' case. The files were basic. Lots of information by the ME and CSU, but not much in terms of persons of interest or interview notes. Care to point me in the right direction?"

"Did you ask Jacobs?"

"Yes. It seems there's been some kind of miscommunication with our understanding." I rested my hips against his desk. "C'mon, there's bound to be something you can do."

"I told you I'm not working this. And I'm not about to dick around in someone else's mess." His gaze shifted around the precinct. "Talk to the LT. For whatever the reason, he likes you. If anyone can get you access, it's him. After all, he's the boss."

"That's the last time I bring you coffee and donuts," I teased, heading for Moretti's office and knocking on the door.

"Enter," Lt. Moretti bellowed from inside. He looked up, surprised to find me in front of him. "No one said we were hiring you."

"That's the story of my life." I rolled my eyes, thinking of Eastman. "Fortunately for you, I must be psychic. It seems Detective Jacobs is in need of my brilliance and expertise, but for some reason, he hasn't been very forthcoming in sharing suspects, motives, and leads."

"You were a suspect. Now you're not. That prick we had in custody until two days ago, he was a suspect too. Turns out he hired some hotshot P.I. to clear his name and protect him. So now we've got nothing." He leaned back in his chair. "Are you seeing the common denominator here?"

"What about Jason Oster, head of security at the hotel?" I suggested. He shrugged, waiting to see if I'd divulge anything else. "Or Alvin Hodge's ex-wife, Rachel Romanski?"

"Oster has an alibi for the time of Frank Costan's murder. He was in the security office. Hotel cameras caught him in the hallway two hours prior to the estimated TOD, and he didn't leave until late that evening. He sat there the whole day. Between the cameras and the other guards, his alibi checks out, and we have no reason to suspect him."

"What if he altered the camera feed or bypassed the cameras?"

"There's no hard evidence to put him anywhere near Costan or the tunnels. You're fishing. Tell me about the woman." After sharing everything I knew, Moretti rubbed his temples. "We'll look into it more thoroughly. What do you think her motivation was for seducing Eastman while she's banging Oster on a regular basis?"

"I don't know."

"Bullshit. You know a hell of a lot more than you're letting on. Your client," he uttered the word with loathing and disdain, "is involved in some complex, shady shit. Even if he didn't off Hodge or Costan, he's connected to this mess. Why won't you tell me how?"

"Because I don't know." Pinching the bridge of my nose, I stood. "I've been up most of the night, trying to figure it out, but I can't. The way it looks is that Costan, Hodge, and former Senator Wheeler were involved in some financial scheme, but Eastman wasn't. And that's why the attempted murder still doesn't make any sense."

"Did you ever think maybe Eastman's been orchestrating this the entire time, and the poisoning was to throw us off kilter?" Moretti asked.

"I considered it, but I don't think that's it. He's involved with Oster in some way, but I don't know how." My mind kept circling back to Paul's plea to talk to Oster in order to get proof so he'd be released from holding.

"Well, let us know if you discover something concrete. The lawyer you found for Eastman is a bear, and unless the department finds some irrefutable evidence, the DA doesn't want to tango with the city's top defense attorney over a whim." He jerked his head toward the door, dismissing me. "You've really screwed us over this time, Parker."

"That wasn't my intention."

"Yeah." Frowning, he shook his head. "Tell Jacobs I told him to read you in. And if Eastman's dirty, you're fucking cooperating unless you want to be an accessory."

"Yes, sir." He grumbled under his breath as I let myself out of the office and shut the door.

"So, how'd it go?" O'Connell asked when I returned to his desk to retrieve my coffee.

"Apparently I've screwed up."

"Happens." He smirked. "Jacobs just came back. He went to drop something off in evidence." He pushed the almost empty bag toward me. "We saved him the powdered sugar, so go earn some brownie points."

"Thanks."

"And try to be pleasant. Surly won't get you very far," O'Connell added, so I flipped him off. "See, that's exactly what I mean."

Placing the cup of coffee and donut on Jacobs' desk, I pulled up an extra chair and waited patiently. Unlike Moretti, he didn't seem surprised to see me. Removing the plastic lid from the cup, he rummaged through his desk for non-dairy creamer and sugar. Once the coffee was to his liking, he sat down, opened the bag, and took a bite of the donut, chewing thoughtfully before swallowing.

"Fine, I'll overlook the fact you were traipsing through the hotel, even though you have an obvious lack of jurisdiction concerning this entire investigation," he said.

"Old habits die hard. Can we start over?"

"Sure. You go first." He took another bite of donut, forcing me to talk while he chewed.

"Whatever happened in that hotel last week is much bigger than this precinct and local law enforcement. That's not meant to be an insult, so don't take it as one. The FBI has a big fish on the hook, and they were hoping to use Paul Eastman to get to Mr. Big Fish. That's why they phoned the DA to trump up the charges. Paul worked with Hodge often enough that they probably assumed he has proof of Frank Costan's illegal activities and could implicate his suspected business partner."

"Does this whale have a name?" Jacobs asked, sipping the coffee.

"Rodney Wheeler."

"The former senator?" Thankfully, he swallowed before I spoke, or I might have been sprayed with coffee.

"That'd be the one."

"Shit." He snorted. "That explains a lot." He typed a few things into the computer and then returned his full attention to me when the magical box didn't provide the answers he was seeking. "What charges are they hoping to bring?"

"I don't know."

"How does Eastman fit into this if he doesn't know anything about Hodge and Costan?"

"I have some suspicions, but nothing substantiated." I took a sip of my own coffee. "Frankly, it still isn't adding up. Off the record, Paul lets everyone push him around. He attempted corporate espionage with Hodge's help, but nothing that resulted in a big payday. My gut says perhaps that tracks back to Costan or Wheeler. Maybe they invested and used the impending corporate leaks to buy and sell stocks to make millions more. Hodge was working with Costan and informing to the FBI about it, but I don't think Eastman was aware of this. Oh, and in case you don't know, Wheeler is part owner of the hotel, so he also had access to Hodge." I let out a breath, and Jacobs swallowed, attempting to digest these facts. "But when Eastman was in custody, he insisted I speak to Oster to get him out of trouble. So I'd say he's running something on the side with Jason. I just don't know what that is or if that tracks back to the Costan/Wheeler/Hodge triangle."

"Does Eastman know Wheeler?"

I was certain I was red with embarrassment. "I didn't ask." Forest for the trees, Parker, and I couldn't see the forest for the goddamn trees.

"Afraid of the answer?" Jacobs asked.

"Actually, I didn't think about it. I was too busy determining Wheeler's connection to Costan and Hodge, and then I was more concerned with figuring out who could be responsible for the two deaths and how Eastman and Oster fit into it."

"Someone should really ask Mr. Eastman about Senator Wheeler," he pointed out unhelpfully. "Want to borrow a pen and make a note? Or can I have another chat with your client?"

"Only if his attorney's present." I didn't necessarily want to play hardball, but it came as second nature.

"Fine. But when you find out, call me." He rubbed his face. "Since you've been so forthcoming, I'll let you read through the interviews from Tuesday night into Wednesday morning when everyone was questioned."

"So my punishment for my helpfulness is being sentenced to death by boredom?" I teased.

"There are a few things you might find useful. Hell, if you let me speak to Eastman again, I'll even clue you in as to what parts of the interview logs might be particularly pertinent."

"Careful, Detective Jacobs, you're this close to becoming my new best friend." I held my forefinger and thumb close together, and he rolled his eyes and led me down the hallway to another room equipped with dozens of monitors.

TWENTY-SEVEN

"Where are you?" Mark asked over the phone.

"I'm in hell. How did your morning with Agent Walton go?" I asked.

"It went. We have some things to talk about concerning the Wheeler angle. Are you at the motel with Eastman?"

"No, I'm at the precinct in transcript limbo. Weren't you paying attention?" I feigned annoyance. "Paul attempted to fire me again this morning. Well, not fire me so much as redefine my entire job role, again."

"Oh, I see he told you he thought the bodyguard thing was a joke."

"It wasn't."

"I know that. And you know that. He isn't smart enough to know that." There was a brief pause. "But you were willing to leave him alone anyway."

"He should be safe. No one has any idea where he is. And if he's stupid enough to blow the location of the safe house we set up, that's not my problem."

"I'll swing by and make sure he's okay. Want to meet me there, or do you need a badge to get you out of the precinct?"

"I'm okay. I'll free myself once I finish reviewing this

new information."

"Take plenty of notes. We'll exchange info in two hours."

"Sounds good." He hung up, and I closed the file from Kenneth Anderson's interview.

Rolling my neck from side to side, I stared at the stack of files I already read. One was the report from the Secret Service, claiming there was no suspicious activity prior to the discovery of Alvin Hodge's body. The other two were from the PDN employees that discovered Hodge. From the way Anderson and Talbot answered the questions and my own recollection of how they acted in the immediate aftermath, I was fairly certain neither of them was involved. So far, reading through the transcripts was a complete waste of my time.

Paul Eastman's interview was the most interesting, and from the notes Jacobs scribbled, it made sense why the police believed he was involved. It was also why I believed he was involved. He was hiding something, and anyone with half a brain would realize it with his cagey responses. Unfortunately, if everything Paul said to me in the last week was to be believed, then what he was hiding wasn't necessarily relevant to Hodge's murder. Sure, it might lead to other suspects and more appropriate questions to ask, but it wouldn't paint him as a killer or directly lead to whoever was.

"Find anything I missed?" Jacobs asked, returning to the room.

"No, but you have excellent penmanship."

He snorted and pulled up a chair. "I want access to Eastman, unprotected, non-privileged access."

"It's a waste of your time. He's not the killer, and he shouldn't be expected to waive his rights so you can put the screws to him again." Frankly, not that long ago, I would have been happy to take a phonebook to the side of Eastman's skull, but that was neither here nor there.

"Why are you protecting him? He fired you, and the guy's a huge pain in the ass."

"Because someone tried to kill him. Don't get me wrong, I don't particularly enjoy being in his company, but," I shrugged, "he's a victim. And you guys didn't give him the benefit of the doubt."

"How many POIs did you give the benefit of the doubt to when you were on the job?" His question held merit, but I chose not to answer.

Picking up the interview notes, I found the one line that still irked me. "Did you even bother to check out the identity of the caterer that showed up Monday afternoon? The one Eastman reported as a security risk because of his lack of I.D."

"We're looking into it."

"What the hell does that mean?" I asked.

"It means everyone was accounted for on Monday. The caterers weren't short a person."

The implication crashed into the forefront of my thoughts. The killer was inside the hotel on Monday. "When was the last time anyone saw Alvin Hodge at work?" I asked, tossing a disgusted glance at the dozen other pages of notes and interviews that the PD conducted of the hotel employees.

"Monday morning."

"And Hodge's TOD?"

"Monday." He blew out a breath. "We're looking into it."

"Look faster. The killer was already on the premises. And one of the hotel co-owners probably gave him the heads up on the employees, the security protocols, the hotel schematics, and the whole fucking plan that PDN devised. That *I* devised."

"Parker," Jacobs began as I stood and slammed the chair into the table.

"Don't." I held up my hand. He was either going to say I wasn't responsible, or he wanted more information. Either way, his usefulness expired two seconds ago when it became apparent he was dragging his heels on bringing in the actual party responsible for the killings. "You want to find a killer, then go find a killer, Detective. It sounds like he was hired to do the job. Subpoena someone's financial records. I gave you a name. Get to work."

"Oh, so now I take orders from you?" he asked, amused.

"Well, it looks like you need some pointers since you have yet to identify the caterer or the killer." I stomped to the door, but a single thought kept eating away at me. "Have you been dragging your feet because you were hoping I'd give you Wheeler and you could score a really grand collar for yourself? Has this just been about posturing?"

"Watch yourself, Parker. You're speaking to an officer of the law, and the last time I checked, you aren't even lucky enough to call yourself that."

"Fuck you, Jacobs."

Storming out of the room, I wasn't certain he wouldn't arrest me. Things between us started out civil. We were working on the give and take, but somewhere along the line, everything went to shit. That partnership we had forged just blew up. Mark would be pissed, and I'd be forced to listen to the 'play nice with others' speech again. I hated that speech. And I wasn't certain that I wasn't to blame.

But the police department's method of investigating wasn't actually getting to the bottom of anything. They wanted to keep me in the dark, accuse Eastman of everything, and not bother to track down the actual culprit because they were hoping to steal the more lucrative collar out from underneath the FBI. And somehow, I would end up being accused of withholding evidence or, at the very least, causing waves. It wasn't fair, especially when I was the only one without a dog in the fight. And that thought was what made everything fall into place.

When I returned to Eastman's motel, Mark was inside, and the two were talking. He looked up, expertly reading my facial expression and body language. He didn't say anything but stopped the conversation and waited patiently.

I let out a bitter laugh and brushed the hair out of my face. "Politics. Goddamn politics. This entire shit situation is because of a pissing contest. Detective Jacobs, Agent Walton, probably that jerk we talked to from the Secret Service, they all want some fantastic collar. And me, being a total idiot, gave the police department Wheeler's name."

"Well, they should have it. Wheeler was behind the two hits," Mark said. Obviously, his meeting with Agent Walton must have resulted in an exchange of factual information. "The accountants are still monitoring his financials. His phone and internet records are being pulled, but Walton's certain he ordered the two hits. The techs are running everyone from inside the hotel through facial rec. Our killer was one of the caterers and bypassed the security. With any luck, we'll be able to find him and use him against Wheeler. The FBI just gained access to all the security footage from the hotel for the last month. It won't be long before arrests are made."

"The killer wasn't really a caterer. Someone misappropriated one of the security passes from a caterer."

"But the badges have photos on them," Eastman piped up, wanting to be part of the discussion.

"Because a razor blade and access to a laminator couldn't fix that in two seconds," I retorted.

"Alex," Mark said my name sharply, and I fell silent, "take a breath. You've helped the police department get to the bottom of this." He bit at his thumbnail. "Do you think the PD and FBI will botch each other's mission? Maybe I should give Walton the heads up."

"No. We're not picking sides. Let the FBI and PD fight it out. If the Secret Service wants to get involved, maybe they can referee."

"What does any of this have to do with me?" Paul asked, defusing some of the animosity and tension.

"You approved the security provisions, provided the passes, and you were colluding with Hodge." I swallowed, squinting at him to make sure I didn't miss something. "Do you know Rodney Wheeler?"

"No." Paul shook his head, but I was too preoccupied to decipher if I believed him or not.

"The FBI and police think you know more than you're saying. Even though you don't know Wheeler, I'd bet he thinks you're a risk too," Mark added, pondering the ramifications of that. "That's probably what led to the attempted poisoning." He tapped the pen against the table. "Oster's probably working for Wheeler," he said, his eyes meeting mine.

It made sense. Oster could work for Wheeler in an

official hotel capacity and perhaps never technically get his hands dirty while still cleaning up any mess or involvement that might have been caught on tape. It'd be nice if everything was just black and white instead of a million different shades of grey.

"What was on the memory card?" I asked.

"It was blank. Nothing was ever on it. Oster must have replaced it," Mark said.

"When was Rachel…Lexie in your apartment?" I asked Paul, hoping to attack the problem from a different angle.

"Three weeks ago. I picked her up at a bar the week before we did the final run-through at the hotel." Some thought flitted through his mind, and he cringed. "I might have mentioned my job and the important role we were playing the following week." I let out an exasperated sigh. "Hey, dangerous shit and obvious bravery work wonders with the fairer sex."

"Careful," Mark whispered to him, afraid I might demonstrate exactly how much fairer my gender was by ripping out Paul's throat with my bare hands. I paced the room, wanting to burn off the anger and frustration of the morning but failing to find an appropriate outlet to vent. "Do you think Oster put her up to it?"

"Probably, but without her cooperation, we have nothing on him. And I doubt any one of these moronic law enforcement officials do either." Even as I said the words, something buzzed in the recesses of my brain. Something was off.

Cheap motels didn't offer much room to pace, so I flopped onto the extra bed and stared at the ceiling. Not that this position was any more productive than pacing, but something wasn't sitting right. I just needed to figure out what it was.

"You think Lexie poisoned me?" Paul asked.

"What are you thinking, Parker?" Mark chimed in, knowing my habits better than anyone. "Talk it out."

"Paul's date can't be responsible for tampering with his water filter because according to his medical report, the fluoride could only have been building up for five or six days." I bit my lip. "Rachel seducing Paul still doesn't make sense," I insisted. "Not with the way she talked about Alvin. It sounded like she would have stayed with him if he wasn't involved in his under the table dealings. She talked about him like she was still in love with him. And when I spoke to her, I don't think she knew he was dead. Plus, she's screwing Jason."

"Okay, who the hell is Rachel?" Paul interrupted.

"You referred to her as Lexie, but her real name is Rachel Romanski," I said, watching for a reaction, but he didn't have one. "She's Alvin Hodge's ex-wife."

"Shit," Paul muttered, dropping his head to his hands. "I didn't know." He lifted his gaze off the floor and focused on Mark. "Why do you think she would use me like that?"

Mark scoffed. "How the hell should I know? I'm not exactly a dating magnet."

"I assume someone put her up to it so they could gain access to your apartment, but I don't know why. Is it possible she made a copy of your house key or you told her what your home security codes are or something?"

"That night's a bit of a blur," Paul replied. "I can't imagine that someone would do something like that. What would be the point?"

"She could have planted evidence or taken something to plant at one of the crime scenes," I suggested.

Mark took the cue and put his jacket on. "I'll be back later. I'll see if anything damning against Eastman turned up at any of the crime scenes. But if you figure something out in the meantime, give me a call so I don't look like too much of an ass at the precinct. I'm guessing you've won the award for biggest ass of the year today, and I have no desire to compete for the title," Mark teased.

After he left, I went prone on the bed. There was a solution. I just wasn't sure what it was or how to find it.

"You do realize there's something you're forgetting," Paul said, sitting on the edge of the bed next to me.

"What's that?"

"I know most of the people at the hotel. I've heard tons of gossip, and I know the bulk of the people involved in this. Why aren't you using me to figure this out?"

"Because you said you didn't know Wheeler."

"That doesn't mean I don't possess other useful information. Let's take it from the top."

"Fine." I sighed. "Let's start with when PDN entered the bidding war for the security conference."

TWENTY-EIGHT

Paul Eastman was aware of PDN's role at the conference an entire month in advance. I was hired shortly after, even before the Secret Service finalized PDN's position as a third party contractor. While I was evaluating PDN's security protocols, emergency measures, and other operating procedures, Paul ran background checks on every single hotel employee, the catering company, drivers, valets, the conference attendees and their personal security details that were considered public knowledge. Most of the delegates kept their own security details quiet, but he had contacts at a few other personal security agencies, and they were willing to trade information with PDN.

No one stuck out as an obvious threat. No mention of Frank Costan ever surfaced during Paul's preliminary analysis. After all of this was complete, he turned over his findings to the Secret Service. I wondered if the point was to source out the menial labor or if they were conducting their own searches and gave this job to Paul to keep him otherwise occupied.

Next, he went to the hotel manager, Gordon Russell, and asked for complete access to the hotel's security system. Russell passed the request off to Jason Oster, whom Paul had dealt with in the past, and the two of them reviewed the security cams and determined the blind spots. Around this time, I evaluated the work Paul had already done, made some suggestions and modifications to the sweeps, and we began conducting our drills.

"Nothing struck me as strange," I said, interrupting Paul's recitation. "Normally, I have a sixth sense when things go wonky, but it all seemed fine."

"The only thing you hit on was the subbasement," he pointed out.

"Did you discuss that with Jason afterward?"

"Yes, the next day, Jason, Mr. Russell, and I met. I wanted to know if the tunnels ever posed a threat in the past."

"That must have been how Wheeler learned of them. Or he already knew. Do you know if the hotel manager ever met with the owners?"

Paul shrugged. "I don't know. Alvin could have answered that question. He heard all the gossip. I never knew how he was so in the loop, but he was."

"I'm sorry for your loss." It was the first time I offered condolences, and it was possible I had been the only one.

"Thanks, Alexis." He offered a wan smile.

"So Alvin knew about everything. He probably knew the owners. He knew Frank Costan was staying at the hotel, and he might have even helped set up an anonymous room reservation for him. Did he tell you about Frank Costan?" Vaguely, I remembered Oster insisting Hodge wouldn't have clued Paul in on anything that big.

"No, he didn't." Paul squinted. "Apparently he didn't tell me a lot of things, like how he was informing to the FBI."

"So how'd you find out about Costan? Did Jason give you a heads up?"

"I don't know Frank Costan," he bellowed. "I've told you this before. I never met him. I have nothing to do with him or his deals or his death. Goddammit." He stomped around the room, collecting himself. "Why can't you get that through your thick skull?"

"You just finished telling me how thoroughly you checked every aspect of the hotel. Hell, you double-checked everything with Oster and Russell. It makes sense that you might have noticed one of the FBI's ten most wanted traipsing through the hotel," I growled, angry at myself for not noticing either. "Why didn't you ask Hodge what else was going on inside the hotel? You knew he was clued in to the less upstanding happenings."

He took a deep breath. "Because when I asked, he told me about Bernie Muller's plight and introduced me to some Russian guy." He pressed his lips together, looking guilty. "I got distracted by the opportunity to make some cash on the side." He slumped onto the bed across from me. "I let this happen. Maybe if I had known, I could have stopped it." He swallowed. "Stopped whoever it was from killing Alvin."

And there it was. The reason he seemed so guilty. He felt guilty, and he hid it at every single turn. He covered it up with fantastically pathetic stories of selling corporate secrets and wanting to be some hero, but he was just a guy that screwed up.

"You're not to blame. Things happen. Believe me." Processing the words, I asked, "What Russian?"

"Huh?"

"You said Hodge introduced you to some Russian. What Russian?"

"The SMI rep. Gorvanskov or something. I don't remember. He spoke English, but his name was one of those long drawn out things. Y'know, it sounds like a vodka brand." He cringed. "And my god, all he wanted to do at our meeting was drink. Two shots in, I had to excuse myself and get back to work. He basically laughed me out of the bar."

I asked for a physical description, and the man he described matched the representative I met Friday night at the hotel bar. That would also explain how Paul knew SMI had access to Klaus Manufacturing's prototype schematics on the new energy source. At least some pieces were falling into place, even though I wasn't sure any of it was even remotely relevant.

"When did you meet with the SMI guy?" I asked.

"Tuesday. SMI's portion of the conference concluded

early that afternoon, and I met with him briefly on my break. It was maybe thirty minutes before I went upstairs and met you in the control room."

"Which explains why you smelled like a distillery." I laughed. "That's also a huge factor as to why I thought you were an alcoholic."

"Gee, thanks." He chuckled. "Guess I deserved that one."

"And you were staying at the hotel during the conference." My brain was pinging on a dozen points at once, and I tried to slow the thought processes to make sure I didn't miss anything.

"I only stayed Sunday through Wednesday. Three nights, I guess. After they let me out of interrogation that morning, I went home. The conference was over, and PDN was done."

"Did you check in under your name, or was it a corporate thing through PDN?" I asked.

"Corporate. They put me up in places pretty often, so I can keep an eye on the security. Why?"

Okay, so his personal information like name and address weren't in the hotel computer, not that this wasn't readily available when most of the employees knew Paul personally. "Did you keep your keys on you at all times?"

"The valet parked my car. He had my keys."

"No. Your house keys," I clarified.

"All of my keys are together on the same ring." He looked around the room. "Speaking of, weren't you supposed to get my stuff back from the cops?"

"That's it." The light bulb burned bright, and I picked up the phone. "That's how they gained access to your house without your knowledge." Dialing Mark, I waited for him to respond while Eastman looked at me like I lost my mind. "Hey, do me a favor and see if they can run prints on all of Paul's belongings that are in evidence. It's probably been too long for them to find anything usable, but his keys were at the valet stand."

"And that's how they got inside his house, accessed his fridge, and poisoned him," Mark said, coming to the same conclusion I did. "Which means maybe Rachel's off the hook." He blew out a breath. "Except she lied about her name, and she's banging Oster."

"We'll figure that part out later. But for now, stop trying to burst my bubble." We disconnected.

"You think that's when it happened?" Paul asked.

"How long have you been feeling like shit?"

"Since Wednesday."

"I really need to consider getting a M.D. attached to the end of my name." I winked. "But you're right; there is no guarantee that's when it happened. So let's backtrack. Flexie Lexie," I rolled my eyes, "a.k.a. Rachel Romanski is Alvin Hodge's second ex-wife. You said he still loved her. Care to explain?"

"Whenever Alvin and I got a chance to talk, exchanging stories of...well...you know."

"Conquests?"

"Yeah," he looked appropriately embarrassed, "he would always bring her up. She was the one that got away. No woman ever compared to her or what they had. Yada yada."

"Do you know when he saw her last?"

"It's been like a year or so." He suddenly turned ashen. "God, he must be rolling over in his grave to think I screwed the love of his life." He rubbed a hand down his face. "Shit." He met my eyes. "You gotta believe I wouldn't have done it if I knew who she was."

"But she must have known who you were." I stood up, recalling my few brief conversations with Rachel. "There was no reason for her to lie about her name unless she was afraid you'd recognize her or realize who she was." I spun on my heel. "And I'm having some issues believing it's because she thought you were going to be the best lay of her life."

"Hey," he sounded annoyed, "you have no basis for that comment." Even though after Mark's account from the women at the bar, I kind of did, but it would have been a cheap shot to take. So I remained silent. "How could she know who I am if I didn't know who she was?"

I pressed my lips together and shut my eyes. Paul Eastman was my client. I was working for him, but it wasn't a position I was accustomed to since I mostly worked as a law enforcement consultant or corporate consultant. Things seemed tricky, and he continued to stare unnervingly, waiting for an answer.

"Jason Oster is seeing Rachel. Apparently it's been going on for a while. The security guards were cracking jokes, and I confronted Oster about it. He didn't deny meeting with her the other morning, and when I asked Rachel if she was seeing anyone, she said there was a guy named Jason."

His jaw practically dropped. "Great, now I'm getting sloppy thirds."

"That's so not the point right now," I hissed.

He frowned. "Alvin must have known. He knew everything inside that hotel, and you said they've been meeting at the hotel." He shook his head as if a fly was buzzing around. "No. That can't be right. You misunderstood, or you're just plain old wrong. Jason's too much of a straight shooter to jeopardize his job like that. If anything, he'd turn a blind eye. That's why I used him to monitor the PDN client rooms with my wireless webcam. I knew he was the only one who wouldn't abuse the power and sell scandal to the tabloids."

"But they both practically confessed." My brief conversation with Martin resurfaced, and I remembered my reason for breaking into Jason's locker. After conceding on an alternative theory, I asked the only question remaining. "What could have been on that memory card that both Rachel and Jason would have an interest in?" But before he could speak, the only reasonable answer surfaced. "What if it was Alvin's murder?"

Paul paled. "Are you nuts?"

"A little bit." Grabbing a pen, I jotted down everything.

"If that were true, why wouldn't Jason have turned it over to the police? And what would Rachel have wanted with me three weeks ago?" Now Paul was punching holes in my brilliance. Maybe I wasn't quite as brilliant as I thought. "How long have they been seeing one another? It was before Alvin died, right?"

I needed to talk to Rachel and maybe Jason too. There

was so much more to this story than meets the eye, but I could feel we were getting close. "Put on your shoes. We're gonna take a ride."

"I thought you wanted me to keep a low profile and hideout," Paul said, backpedaling.

"Okay, new set of rules. One, no matter what, don't tell anyone we speak to where you're staying, even if they flash you or threaten to kill you."

"Hardy har har."

"Rule number two. Do what I say, when I say it." I paused, wondering if there were any other stipulations he should follow.

"That's it?"

"That's it. But if you behave, maybe I'll even let you wear the Kevlar in my trunk. However, if you don't listen, you'll be riding in the trunk. Does that sound fair?"

He chuckled. "You really are nuts," then he offered a genuine smile, "and I'm glad you're working for me."

"Well, that makes one of us," I teased.

TWENTY-NINE

Parking outside Rachel's yoga studio, I found the flyer with the class schedules in my glove box and checked to make sure we didn't miss her. Her afternoon class would be getting out in twenty-three minutes, so in the meantime, I could teach Paul the finer points of conducting surveillance. Five minutes in, he was bored. That was simple enough.

"What are we waiting for? Why don't you just go inside and talk to her?" he asked.

"Because the point isn't to freak her out or tip our hand. Not yet. We're collecting information."

Paul fiddled with the radio while I stared out the window, contemplating her motivation for bedding Paul when she was in some type of relationship with Jason. Plus, if she still loved Alvin, why would she sleep with two of his work friends?

"Sex complicates everything," I muttered, finding myself close to square one again. I hated square one. I wanted to get some C4 and blow it up.

He laughed. "Sex is easy. Relationships are the complex part."

"I wasn't talking in terms of boy meets girl. I was talking

about this case. Seriously, remove yourself from the equation and explain to me why Rachel would screw two guys that work with her ex-husband that she allegedly still loves."

"To get even or to make him jealous so he'd come crawling back."

"But then someone would have to tell Alvin. And she didn't want you to know who she was, so she must not have wanted him to know about her affairs either."

"Maybe she didn't want me to know who she was because of Jason. But why would she meet Jason at the hotel if she didn't want Alvin to find out? That's asking to be found out." He took off his seatbelt and turned to face me. "Are you positive you have all the facts straight? Because those two points are completely contradictory."

"I don't have all the facts. That's why we're parked out here, hoping to discover something useful." Class let out, but Rachel remained inside even after everyone else left. "Give me the cell phone I gave you."

Cocking an eyebrow, Paul handed me the phone, and I dialed my own number and answered my cell, switching it to speaker and hitting voice record in order to have a record of everything that was said. Once it was working, I put the phone in Paul's shirt pocket.

"What are you doing?" he asked, and his voice echoed through my speaker.

"I want you to go inside and talk to her." This was probably a horrible idea, and it would bite me in the ass. Unfortunately, I didn't want to risk blowing my own cover, and there was no other way to get answers. "Don't incriminate yourself. Don't you dare mention me either. Just go inside, say hello, and let the pieces fall where they may."

"That's it? Should I confront her about Alvin or Jason or..."

I cut him off. "Nothing. Just say hello. Don't say anything even remotely related to Alvin's death, or the hotel, or your poisoning. Just say hello. Okay?"

"Fine." He opened the car door, completely confused by my request. "Wish me luck."

"You won't need it. But good luck."

He shut the door and walked across the street. I inhaled deeply, hoping this wasn't the stupidest idea I could have come up with. Already, I could hear Mark's voice telling me what a bad idea this was. Potentially, I was endangering my client, risking the safe house, and possibly tipping off the guilty parties to go to ground, thus ruining the FBI and PD's investigation. It was a gamble, but I didn't see any other way of forcing Rachel to tip her hand. This was the fastest way of getting answers.

"Knock, knock," Paul's voice came through loud and clear, and I stopped musing and focused my attention on the studio. The large tinted windows didn't provide a great view, but I could see two figures inside. "Remember me?"

"Paul," Rachel's voice sounded shaky, but I couldn't be sure since it was slightly muffled from the distance and Paul's pocket, "how have you been?" She stepped backward, away from him, and went behind the counter. From body language alone, she didn't want to be anywhere near him.

"I'm okay. How are you? I haven't seen you since that night."

"How did you find me? Why are you here?" She sounded frightened and suspicious. Was that guilt, or was she afraid of Paul? The phone crackled, and I strained to hear. "I have another class coming in five minutes, so maybe you should go."

"Lexie," he began, and I let out the breath I was holding, relieved he didn't blow it, "I was just hoping we could go out for drinks. Maybe, y'know, get together. How about I take you out on a real date? Dinner and a movie?"

"I don't think that would be a good idea." She seemed panicky. "Would you please leave?"

"What's wrong? Are you pissed about that night? Are you seeing someone?" Shut up, Paul. Any second, he would let the cat out of the bag.

"No." She shook her head. "That night was a mistake. Just go."

"But," he launched into some explanation about why she should give him a second chance, and I realized I didn't give him an exit strategy.

Dammit. I was used to professionals who knew when to walk away. I should have known he didn't have the same instincts, particularly after the way he had pestered me about the meeting with Martin Tech. Fuck. Please don't blow my cover, I thought as I got out of the car and dashed across the street. Opening the door to the studio, Paul turned to me.

"Hey, I was in the neighborhood and had a quick question about the hot yoga," I blurted out, hoping Paul would shut up and leave. I slapped my palm against my mouth. "Sorry, how rude of me. I'm Alex." I offered Paul a friendly smile. "I didn't mean to interrupt. Please continue, my question can wait."

"That's okay, Alex," Rachel gushed. Scurrying around the counter and coming to stand next to me, placing me between her and Paul. "This gentleman was just leaving."

"I guess I was." He looked bewildered but took a step back. "I'm sorry I bothered you. It won't happen again." He pressed his lips together and nodded to Rachel before stepping outside.

"Oh my gosh, thank you so much," she whispered as the door shut behind him.

"What's going on?" I asked, turning so she was forced to face me and couldn't watch Paul leave or see him get inside my car. "Who was that guy? Is that Jake or Justin or...sorry, I'm bad with names."

"No, that's not Jason." A thought dawned on her. "I need to call Jason." She took a step toward the counter where her belongings were sitting.

"Rachel, hey," I put my hand on her arm, "are you okay? What's going on?"

"Nothing. That guy and I almost had a one night stand. I never expected to run into him. It wasn't my proudest moment." She was frantic, not the typical response for a fling. "I have no idea how he found me or why he showed up here."

"Are you in some kind of trouble?" Luckily, in her current state, my questions didn't seem that odd to her.

"I just really need to talk to Jason. Y'know, get some

reassurance that everything's okay."

"If that guy threatened you or is stalking you, we should call the police."

"No," she pleaded, and the only thing reflected in her eyes was fear. "You can't. Please, just forget this ever happened." I hedged, trying to determine if she was in fear for her life or in fear of getting caught. It seemed to me like she was afraid of someone. "Please," she whispered, "you've done enough by getting him to leave."

"Okay," I shrugged, "but if you need anything, think about calling the cops. My friend's husband is a detective, so if you change your mind, I can put you in contact with someone who can help," I offered.

"I won't. But thanks." She took a deep breath, managing to put a smile on her face. "I'll see you Friday?"

"I'm looking forward to it." Before I could say anything else, she picked up the phone, signifying it was my turn to leave. Once I crossed the street, I dialed Mark. "I don't know where you are, but we need eyes on Jason Oster immediately. Paul and I paid Rachel a visit, and she's spooked. She's calling Oster now."

"I'm on it, but in the future, I'd prefer more advanced notice than this," Mark said, disconnecting.

I opened my car door, refusing to focus on Paul who was ducked down in the passenger's seat. At least he was smart enough to hide. I snickered. And Rachel was too flustered to ask what I was doing at her studio, so on the bright side, I didn't have to sign up for any additional classes.

"You said we weren't supposed to spook her," Paul declared, sitting up straight once we were a few blocks away. "She seemed pretty damned scared to me."

"No judgment, but did you hit her?" If the answer was yes, there'd be quite a bit of judgment and some hitting on my part.

"What?" His jaw dropped.

"Does she have any reason to be afraid of you? Did you smack her around or get too aggressive or forceful when the two of you were together."

"No way. I'd never do anything like that."

"No bondage or domination shit?" I queried, already

considering the more likely reasons for Rachel to be frightened.

"No. What kind of person do you think I am?"

"Then why is she so afraid of you?" I mused, speaking aloud to myself. Paul shrugged, and I considered my next destination. My gut said Rachel would go to Jason. Mark should be covering the hotel, so I'd keep watch on our secondary location, Jason's apartment. "She seemed more afraid that you found her than anything else, but I think she was worried that you knew who she really was."

"I called her Lexie," Paul blurted out. "And I didn't say a word about anything I wasn't supposed to." When I remained silent, he mulled over the facts. Maybe he wasn't completely inept at playing sleuth. "Do you think she knows Alvin's dead?"

"She probably does by now. The police might have needed her to identify the body. And even if that wasn't the case, Jason may have told her."

"Unless Jason killed Alvin," Paul suggested, swallowing audibly. "Maybe he's gonna kill her next."

"Stop." I parked my car a block from Oster's apartment. "Even if he did, it seems unlikely that Rachel would be one of his targets. If anything, she's his accomplice."

"Figure it out, Ms. Parker." The authoritarian tone that drove me crazy was back in his voice, and I wanted to slap him. "I'm paying you to clear my name and find out what happened to my friend."

"No shit. Really?" My sarcasm hit with a vengeance. "Because I thought you were paying me to chauffeur you around and try to hook you up with a few one night stands." Something about Rachel's words resonated in my psyche.

"Insubordinate and abrasive," he muttered under his breath.

"We're not at PDN. And because of you, my parting from that company was less than amicable, so shut your mouth." My words made something ping in the recesses of my mind. "Did Alvin ever tell you why he and Rachel split?"

Paul shook his head, obviously fighting off the whiplash

of my barbs mixed in with my questions. "He said they couldn't see eye to eye. She freaked out on him because of work, but he thought if she would just give him another chance, they could get past it."

"She told me that some guys showed up at the house when they were still married. It sounded like she was convinced Alvin was dealing drugs." Paul met my eyes, and I realized we both had the same idea. "Holy shit." I rubbed my face. "She thinks you're working with them."

"Who are they?"

"I'm not positive, but I'd assume Wheeler and his cronies. Do you think Alvin ever mentioned you to her?"

"Doubtful, they split around the time the two of us began working together."

"What about Jason? Maybe he said something to her about you and Alvin. If she was still interested in her ex-husband, she might have wanted updates on him and his job and his friends." Perhaps she wanted to find out what Alvin was really involved in, and that's why she went home with Paul, to get to know him, see where he lived, do some snooping for drugs or weapons or whatever. Although, going so far as to sleep with someone just to snoop was beyond unsettling.

Paul shrugged. "Could be."

"Tell me how you picked her up at the bar." The night they met wasn't sitting well.

"I was boasting about the hotel job," Paul admitted quietly. "Plus, I only started going to that bar with Jason." He paused. "What if he was setting me up the whole time? Like casing my house and sending Rachel to poison me?"

"Doesn't fit." Paul's running dialogue was interfering with my thinking, and I did my best to tune him out. "What exactly happened that night you took Rachel home with you?"

"I'm not gonna kiss and tell."

"Someone wants you dead, so just spill."

He focused on something outside the window. "We had quite a few drinks at the bar. Then we went back to my place, and she said she could go for a couple more. The next thing I know, I'm waking up on the floor next to my bed. The sheets are tangled everywhere. A lamp's broken, and she's telling me how amazing last night was." He snorted. "Wish I could remember it."

"Wow. You fell for the oldest trick in the book. It's amazing your wallet wasn't stolen too."

THIRTY

It was late that afternoon when Mark double-parked next to my car. He rolled down his window, and I did the same. Casting a glance at the apartment building, he leaned in and nodded at Paul, who was eating a pastrami sandwich.

"Is she still inside?" Mark asked.

"As far as I can tell." I squinted, knowing we had a lot to discuss. "Thanks for keeping tabs on Oster. Where is he now?"

"Detective Jacobs brought him in for questioning. A couple of unis will keep eyes on him, so I figured I'd stop by and see what you've learned."

"Quite a bit. Did you know there's a great deli on this street?" I passed a bag through the two sets of rolled down windows, and he opened it. "Philly cheese steak and a bag of chips."

"Thanks." He glanced pointedly at Paul. "And you're letting your client tag along for an actual reason?"

"He might have just gotten us the break we needed." While I continued to keep an eye on Jason's apartment building, Mark ate and I filled him in on everything that transpired today. "Hodge's death is obviously related to

Wheeler and Costan's deal, whatever plan they had. My guess is with the way Paul likes to brag and the things Jason's overheard, somehow word got out that Paul was privy to sensitive information. That's probably how he became a target. It might also explain why Rachel was inside his apartment three weeks ago. She wasn't looking for nooky. She wanted something else. Maybe evidence of the types of people Alvin worked with or what they were involved in."

"But she freaked the fuck out when Paul approached today." Mark crunched on a chip thoughtfully. I let him listen to the recording, but aside from her panic, there wasn't anything useful to gain from it. "Someone's been to see her before and to make a threat. There's no other reason for her behavior."

"So why doesn't she go to the police?"

"She's scared. Maybe whoever it was said they would kill her if she did," Mark reasoned. "She must think Paul's working with them." He narrowed his eyes, working his way through a theory. "Could they have threatened her before any of this happened? Perhaps someone stopped by and told her to find out how much Hodge and his associates knew of the deal, but since she wasn't on speaking terms with the ex, she sought out his associate." Mark jerked his chin at Paul.

"And she didn't uncover anything because Paul doesn't possess that kind of information which might be why they decided to kill Hodge, Costan, and intended to kill Paul. So there wouldn't be any loose ends remaining." It was a decent explanation. "But how would Wheeler even know about Rachel? Do you think Jason gave her up?"

"Employee forms. Health insurance. Hodge probably had her on his policy before the divorce, so her information must be stored somewhere. Even if the hotel's co-owner didn't have direct access, Jason would, and he is her fuck buddy." He raised his eyebrows, indicating I should take this opportunity to connect the dots.

"And we already suspect Jason's working for Wheeler, but this still doesn't get us the proof we need."

"But it makes a whole hell of a lot of sense. Do you think

we could convince her to cooperate?"

"I don't know. She ran to Jason first thing. She could easily be involved. All those warm, fuzzy feelings about Alvin could be faked."

Mark lowered his voice, so Paul couldn't hear, even though he seemed more interested in his own bag of chips than the conversation. "I spoke to Jacobs before they picked up Oster. They like him for this. They're hoping to throw some suspicions and evidence at him and get him to turn on Wheeler."

"Did you tell Jacobs about the camera and the additional surveillance?"

"It's their case," Mark pointed out. "I came really close to telling Agent Walton about it too, but," his gaze went back to Paul, "I didn't like where our conversation went the last time we spoke." I gave him a look. "I'll tell you about it when we're in private. In the meantime, what's your plan to convince Rachel to speak to the authorities?"

"I don't have one. I'll monitor her movements and hope something surfaces."

"Look, if I can swing another unit to keep watch on her, will you call it quits on the stakeout? We have more important things to discuss, and the police can do this much without our help."

"Are you sure? You tend to harp on their incompetence, even though you and Lt. Moretti seem pretty close, and regardless of what you may insist, I know you like O'Connell and Thompson."

"Yeah, fine. Whatever." He picked up his phone. "They're competent. Happy?"

"Not really."

After a few more phone calls were placed, an unmarked police cruiser was sent to keep tabs on Jason Oster's apartment. Mark didn't mention Rachel Romanski or the fact that she was Alvin Hodge's ex-wife. The way he figured it, he couldn't completely do their jobs for them. But when they arrived, he told the detail to keep a tail on the woman inside. They agreed, forgetting that Mark was a federal agent and had no real power over them or their operation. Who knows? Maybe Lt. Moretti told them to follow his orders.

Giving the apartment one final look, I turned the key in the ignition and took a convoluted route back to the motel. Paul remained quiet for most of the ride, and I realized he hadn't said much since the Rachel encounter.

"Penny for your thoughts," I said, drawing him out of his funk. "What's going on in that head of yours?"

"Nothing." He inhaled deeply. "Do you really think she just used me to find out what Alvin was up to?" It was rhetorical, so I kept quiet. "Maybe the whole reason he's dead is because of my big mouth."

"What did you tell her?"

"Not much. I talked about the conference. Y'know, how it was full of international tycoons and diplomats and how incredibly tight security would be. That it was my job to keep everyone safe and devise the best plans and drills."

"Wasn't that my job?"

"I don't have a copyright on it. Feel free to use the same line to get laid. Or almost laid, I guess."

I laughed. "Sorry, but I don't need to use pathetic pick-up lines, so that's all yours."

"I hate to think my embellishment is the cause of this," he admitted. "How the hell was I supposed to know that there were people looking for information on the conference and Alvin?"

"Word of advice, when you're in the security biz, you don't talk about your job. And if you do, you downplay it as boring and tedious. Glorified pencil pusher works well."

He arched an eyebrow. I knew damn well he liked to brag and hoped to receive some fringe benefits for his badass act. But that's not how things worked in the real world. Cops did it too. It was one thing to shoot the shit with your buddies, and it was another when you were sharing stories with everyone you met at a bar. That was a common rookie mistake, and even more seasoned officers could tell tales about how frequently fantastic stories of chasing perps, shooting killers, and arresting dangerous criminals worked to woo badge bunnies at the local watering holes. It was also the easiest way to tell the real heroes from the jokes. People in my line of work didn't relish in these things. Instead, we buried them, sometimes underneath a lot of alcohol or other times deep in our psyches so they'd surface as terrifying nightmares. Yep, that was the real world, and Paul Eastman was one of the phonies.

After walking him up to the room and checking inside for anything amiss, I waited for Mark to meet us. He showed up, performed the same check I just did, and flipped on the television to the news in case there was any information on our case. "Alex and I will pick up dinner. What do you want?" Mark asked.

"I don't care," Paul replied, enthralled by the latest sports scores.

"Okay, pizza it is. We'll be back in an hour or two. Can you stay put in the meantime?" Mark was desperate to talk, and Paul waved us away. "We'll take your car since it was outside Rachel's earlier. It never hurts to be on the safe side."

"What's going on?" I asked as we returned to the parking lot.

"A lot."

I wasn't in the mood to stay in the car any longer than necessary, especially after our earlier surveillance, so I drove to my apartment while Mark collected his thoughts. He wasn't much of a talker, but the lack of chitchat was indicative of something brewing. After entering my apartment, I flipped the lock, made some coffee, and took a seat on the couch.

"Since I've been running from the precinct to FBI HQ, I think I've made some enemies. Walton doesn't believe this investigation is any of my business," Mark began. "He's right, I suppose, but still, it's bad business when you want to pin additional charges on someone in the hopes of getting them to turn over evidence on a much bigger fish."

"We do that all the time."

"Only when the charges are real. I asked him about Eastman's involvement with Costan and Wheeler to see if they had any real proof that he was involved. Walton practically admitted to fabricating all that shit against Eastman, just so he wouldn't get released on bail and get out of a jail cell, even if it was just at the local precinct."

Even though Agent Walton had limited jurisdiction, he'd been in the game long enough to have local friends. They trusted him, and simply by claiming to have irrefutable, damning evidence against Paul, the charges were being filed, at least until I stuck my nose into it.

"What about Jacobs? Is he using this for his own personal gains too?" Since I basically accused him of it, it'd be nice to know if an apology was in order.

"He isn't, but I think he's still hoping for a major bust. Hell, you're on this, which at the precinct translates into a major crime with major fallout." There was no point in denying it. That was kind of my M.O. "But he was willing to cut Eastman loose at your insistence."

"Well, everything they had against him was circumstantial, and he almost died in that holding cell."

"Walton doesn't know what really happened inside that hotel room. There was a surveillance team set up. They were monitoring the hotel security feed and their own security feed, and it was a large enough team that a few infiltrated the hotel staff and guests. However, he said they didn't use that room. I checked the registry. 709 had a bogus name assigned to it, but he said they didn't have a room." Mark filled two mugs, brought me one, and slumped onto the couch. "Unless they fucked up, and he's lying to cover his ass." We remained silent, drinking coffee.

"Frank Costan was killed in that trashed hotel room."

"I didn't say that." Even though he didn't say it, we both knew it was true. One of the reports I read indicated that CSU found blood on the carpet, walls, and throughout the bathroom. Someone died there, and Costan made sense.

"According to Oster, it was registered to Walton, but I checked. And it wasn't."

"So it was registered to a fictitious party which may or may not be a codename the FBI team used."

"That detail is actually a little fuzzy." I narrowed my eyes, waiting for further elaboration. "Walton insists the party responsible for Costan's murder works in the hotel and altered the guest registry to make it look like a government cover-up."

"That's a nice story with a happy ending for everyone, except good ol' Frank," I replied bitterly. "It also means that Walton should have a name and maybe proof. Shit, he should have spotted the killer. Maybe he has a photo or surveillance footage of the man in question. Like Jacobs and I discussed this morning, Alvin Hodge's killer was on the premises Monday. He used the caterer's stolen I.D. Why won't Walton just turn over what he knows?" I was frustrated.

"Until I hear otherwise, I'm doing my best to take Walton at face value."

"But that explains why you're helping Jacobs out instead." I leaned back, closing my eyes briefly and feeling overwhelmed and exhausted. "Jacobs didn't want to pursue Hodge's killer because he thought it'd be more beneficial to his career if he waited to build a stronger case against whoever was pulling the strings, which in this instance is former Senator Wheeler."

Mark snorted. "Yeah, he mentioned that was the conclusion you jumped to this morning."

"Was I wrong?"

"Let's just say he had his orders from somewhere up the food chain. But I had a chat with Director Kendall, and he had a chat with the police brass, and everyone's priorities should be back in order." Mark was great at the double talk. "Jacobs isn't doing this job so he can climb the ladder. He puts his heart into it."

"Great. I guess I owe him an apology."

"I don't like thinking fellow agents are responsible for a man's death or failing to intervene. It makes them look suspicious, possibly dirty, since we're dealing with very rich men who are likely to make a lot more money. But I refuse to bury my head in the sand either. Since Walton hasn't been particularly transparent, you and I are going to rip through Costan and Wheeler's financials." His phone beeped, and he read the message. "The Costan/Wheeler aspect is now part of an OIO investigation, at least since it seems plausible one of them could have made a deal with some foreign national during the conference. Plus, Kendall wanted someone to go over Walton's analysis and work, just in case he was missing something." Mark stood, scooping my car keys off the table. "The files are ready for pick-up. Looks like my vacation just got cut short."

"I don't remember agreeing to consult for you."

"Quid pro quo. We're consulting for each other." He jerked his head at the door, dangling the keys in front of my face. "Come on. We'll grab pizza on the way. Who knows, maybe Eastman will have some valuable insight since he likes to believe he's a whiz at selling corporate secrets and is in cahoots with all the key players."

I rolled my eyes. "Why don't you and your new best friend, Jacobs, look into this?"

"Because Jacobs is busy on something else." He smiled. "He convinced Jason to turn over the actual memory card from the camera."

"How?" I was astonished.

"Tricks of the trade. Let's just say he was offered a deal he couldn't refuse."

THIRTY-ONE

The financial records for Frank Costan were expansive. When Mark said he was getting the files, I believed they were the most recent. Had I realized they dated back to before Costan's arrest and subsequent escape, I would have driven away as soon as Mark stepped out of the car. Thankfully, the financial information on Rodney Wheeler was much more manageable.

Mark and I were sitting on opposite ends of the bed with the stacks of financial information between us. As he skimmed through the transactions, he would call out names of corporations and individuals, hoping something would ring a bell for Paul. We had been at this for three hours, and not a single name was viable. While Mark assessed Costan's information, I flipped through the pages on Wheeler, hoping to find a match or overlap. Granted, numerous federal agents and accountants had already done this, but maybe two fresh sets of eyes would lead to different results.

Frank Costan was an investment broker by trade. He dabbled in day trading and internet stocks until his client list became substantial and he began his own internet startup. The actual company was nothing more than a fancy website, doctored earning projections, growth charts, and a team of allegedly reputable management consultants that boasted of the brilliance and surefire achievements of this startup company. In reality, Costan had defrauded his investors, skimmed off the top, and when his ends failed to meet since he had no product or actual service to provide, he emptied the accounts and fled before the SEC could raid the office building he was leasing. Men like him were weasels. Sure, these high-risk, high-return investments were always a gamble, and he relied on this knowledge to turn his otherwise legitimate skill set into a way to steal from the rich. He was greedy, sinister, and shrewd. No one realized what was going on until it was too late. Everything looked kosher until it wasn't.

When the actual indictment came down, everyone he employed from receptionists to the management consultants was willing to exchange evidence or information in order to mitigate their involvement. Obviously, Costan didn't make any friends, and once the money was gone, no one was willing to cover his back. So how did he manage to escape, and where was he hiding all this time?

"His arrest was almost two years ago," I said, cutting Mark off from asking about another dozen entities that I was sure Paul had no clue about. "He escaped from the prison transport on the way to the courthouse. And he managed to remain hidden until now. No one does that."

"He did," Mark muttered, still scanning the pages for an answer that wasn't there.

"They needed Tommy Lee Jones to find him," Paul blurted out, and I laughed. He winked at me and smiled. "If I were on the run with millions stashed somewhere, I wouldn't stay in this country or go anywhere near some international business conference. Not after two years. I'd buy a private island with plenty of rum and attractive women in bikinis." He glanced at me. "That wasn't meant to sound as sexist as it did."

I shook my head. "An island with ripped men who are willing to fan me and feed me peeled grapes sounds just about right." I crinkled my nose playfully. "Or was that too sexist a comment for you?" Mark let out a huff, and I returned to the task at hand. "Did Costan run out of money?"

Mark rubbed his face, dropping the paper on to the bed. This wasn't leading us anywhere fast. "How should I know? We have a rough estimate of how much he stole, what he was worth prior to the thefts, and what we recovered through money trails. But there are still millions unaccounted for. Maybe he stashed it somewhere local and came back to retrieve it, thinking he could cut a deal with someone in the process." He arched an eyebrow and shrugged.

"Which is where Senator Wheeler fits in," I added.

"Or it could be one of the international moguls," Paul suggested. "Do we have proof Alvin was working with Frank Costan?"

"You mean aside from the fact the two of them were both murdered in the same hotel?" Mark asked, probably not intending to be as harsh as he sounded. Paul shrunk back, busying himself with pulling one of the pints of ice cream from the freezer.

"Why don't we have Hodge's phone records?" I asked. "He must have been in contact with someone damning."

"He wasn't," Mark said.

"He used the hotel phone for his business," Paul replied. "He didn't want any blowback in case things soured."

I looked at Mark as if to say, 'where the hell are the hotel records', but he shook his head. We weren't given access to them. Too much privileged information or not enough evidence to warrant a court order, unless the FBI just didn't want to share.

"But there was blowback. Rachel left Alvin because men came to their house because of his side business," I said. Despite the fact that was over a year ago, it might explain why Alvin changed tactics and why Rachel was snooping into her ex-husband's business. "Someone got to her."

"We know this, Parker," Mark growled, frustrated with the paperwork and the investigating agents, namely Walton. "You said it earlier when she freaked out at the sight of Eastman."

"So someone came to visit her more recently."

"No shit."

"Well, it can't be Oster because she wouldn't run to him if he threatened her. We're working under the assumption that Rachel went to Paul's after receiving a threat, but why wouldn't Jason just ask you about it?" I queried, turning to Paul.

"I don't know. He can't think I'm in on this too, can he?" Paul put the spoon down, contemplating the friendship he had with Jason Oster. "What I don't get is how anyone knew what was going on a few weeks before the conference. PDN just got the contract. You were still evaluating the security protocols. Nothing was set in stone. So that was like the worst time to ply me for information about Alvin's involvement in this stuff. Didn't you say Frank Costan checked in two days before the conference? He wasn't even here when I took Lexie, I mean Rachel, home that night."

"Wheeler would have known about the conference ahead of time. He was probably making a deal with Costan. Hell, he might have arranged for Costan to stay at the hotel undetected. But something spooked Wheeler. Perhaps he spotted the FBI agents or overheard Hodge supplying them with information, so he suspected he would be double-crossed," Mark suggested. "So he sent someone to threaten Rachel for the information."

"But when she failed to give him anything useful, he killed Alvin in order to keep Costan in line, and maybe Costan threatened to turn evidence against the former senator in exchange for some leniency for his own crimes. So Wheeler killed him too." I rubbed my eyes. "And someone else helped him dispose of Costan's body, assuming Frank was killed in the room registered to the FBI."

"Allegedly registered. Like I said, the registry was altered," Mark insisted. "It had to be someone familiar with security and access to the front desk that knew of your little trip to the abandoned tunnels and was able to avoid the cameras or possessed the ability to alter the footage." He didn't have to say it. The facts added up to Jason Oster and maybe an accomplice or two.

"God, it sounds like it could have been me," Paul stated in a hushed tone. "No wonder the cops arrested me." A thought suddenly crossed his mind. "Y'know, PDN is probably wondering where the hell I've been for the last couple of days."

"You can call work in the morning," Mark said. "I'll take you somewhere else and let you use my phone." He turned to me. "Goddamn, your paranoia is contagious."

"Scary, isn't it?" I smirked. "Can we build a profile on Wheeler and call it a night? I have a meeting scheduled for tomorrow that I can't miss and some final touches that I need to revise on my proposal."

"Fine." Mark looked down at the stack of papers. "Let's hear it, Parker."

"Name a financial crime, and there's a good chance our disgraced former senator has been accused of it. Embezzlement, taking bribes, defrauding investors, inflated earnings projections." I shifted around, flipping through the pages. "Not a single accusation has ever been proven, but Wheeler relinquished his Senate seat before any official investigations could be opened. Since then, he's been keeping a lower profile. His name is on the Board of Trustees for various corporations. He owns numerous properties and quite a few businesses."

"Like his partial ownership of the hotel," Paul said, and I nodded.

"The SEC has been keeping tabs, but his portfolio is so spread out, it doesn't seem likely that they would be able to pinpoint precisely where his illegal financial activities might lie. The IRS is digging through his taxes and earnings, but they haven't hit on anything suspicious either."

"Which is why the FBI is investigating." Mark let out a heavy sigh. "They've been monitoring his movements and spending for the last year or so. And from what Walton said, they still don't have enough evidence to make anything stick to him."

"Do you believe SAC Walton?" I asked, earning myself a glare. "Yeah, I know. We don't know enough either way.

But Wheeler has plenty of money, illegal or otherwise."

"Don't say it, Parker," Mark warned. He knew I thought Wheeler paid off his tail to look the other way. "You have no basis."

"Frank Costan is dead. Alvin Hodge is dead. Someone attempted to kill Paul. I'd call that a pretty big coincidence, particularly since the FBI and Secret Service were both on scene to monitor Wheeler."

"So Wheeler kept them occupied, hired someone else to do the deed, and got his buddies in hotel security to cover it up," Mark argued.

This debate was pointless. We didn't have proof of anyone's involvement in anything. It was entirely conjecture, but either the government agents were corrupt or incompetent. And neither possibility bode well.

"Guys," Paul said, breaking the tension, "that hotel has hundreds of employees. And like you said, Wheeler is part owner. He could have handpicked some people, arranged for everything in advance, and made sure the coast was clear. It doesn't necessarily implicate either the agents guarding him or the hotel security staff."

"There weren't any cameras." I blinked, realizing the significance. "The cable that Hodge was...," I faltered, attempting to be more sensitive for Paul's benefit, "that was because some of the walls and ceiling tiles were moved. And there are no cameras in those areas."

"Wheeler must have set it up." Mark met my gaze. "Fucking bastard."

"Do you remember when the hotel made the renovations?" I asked Paul. Since he had been using them for quite some time to host PDN's clients, he might have remembered.

"About three months ago, I think." Paul contemplated that fact while I retrieved the file on the conference. "Somewhere around then. Maybe four or five. But it wasn't longer than that."

"Wheeler knew all along that the hotel was getting the conference, so he altered everything," I muttered, feeling like I was suffering from shortsightedness.

"Talk about premeditated murder," Mark scoffed. "Why

would he think to do that?" He paused briefly. "Unless he was making the arrangements on purpose so Costan could get in and out without detection since the cameras wouldn't be near the elevators anymore." He rubbed his chin, deep in thought. "Everything runs through those cables. That's what the hotel manager said. It'd be easy to cut into them and reroute the feed or have it play on a loop. No one would be the wiser, especially when they are so easily accessible from the hallways and the rooms nearest to the elevator. Remember, Mr. Russell said they run from room to room through the walls and ceiling tiles."

"Shit." I got up to pace. "I think we need to have another chat with Russell. We're going to need complete access to the hotel's surveillance tapes, the hard drives that stored the surveillance information, the list of employees, phone records, everything. If Wheeler orchestrated this, then there is no telling what the plan was or when the tampering began. It's even possible Costan's been staying at that hotel a lot longer than we thought."

"I'd be willing to go out on a limb and say Costan probably passed his hidden funds to Wheeler for protection and safekeeping," Mark surmised. "This is way beyond the scope of your little P.I. business. If you want to step away and let me handle it, I'll take it to Director Kendall, and we can work something out with the PD and other agencies."

"But what if they're on the take?"

"What if they are?" He gave me a pointed look. "Do you remember what happened the last time you investigated corruption? Someone shot you in the back, and they came after Marty too."

"I thought you said the reason your back hurt wasn't because of a bullet wound," Paul interrupted. I had forgotten he was still in the room.

"It's not. That happened almost a year before the broken ribs," I muttered, my eyes never leaving Mark. "Let me talk to Jacobs before you step all over my investigation."

He snorted. "Now it's *your* investigation?"

"It always was. You've met my client." I turned to face Paul. "He hired me to prove his innocence and determine who killed his friend."

"Yeah. I...um...did." Paul cowered under Mark's death glare, but at least he was brave enough to state the obvious. Now all I had to do was convince Jacobs to let me play on his team.

THIRTY-TWO

Mark elected to stay at the motel to keep Paul company. He claimed it was because our killer was still unidentified and on the loose. Realistically, it was so he could ply my client for more details concerning the international conference, Alvin Hodge, and the other hotel staff. I wasn't fooled, but Paul was a big boy. He could fend for himself, and Mark was only doing his job.

After arriving at home, I turned on my computer and reread the proposal I was planning on pitching to Luc Guillot at Martin Technologies in the afternoon. The fix for the elevators in the event of a fire or other emergency wasn't that difficult. It would require a separate system being established for the main elevator banks and a few override functions to be added to the elevator's operation. It was a pain in the ass, but it would solve the problem in this office building and theoretically all the others. However, since MT existed on multiple continents, I was stuck skimming through the fire safety and building codes for a dozen different countries and cities. Why did Martin's company have to be so goddamn expansive?

My mind kept wandering away from the elevators and back to Wheeler and the hotel. At some point, Wheeler and

Costan must have crossed paths, but I didn't know when or where. I doubted anyone did since the authorities didn't have a solid case against Wheeler on any of his financial crimes. If they could connect him to Costan, then they would have had something definitive to hold him on.

"Focus, Parker," I growled, shaking off the questions of murder, money, and how Rachel Romanski fit into any of this. On the bright side, if she was involved, maybe they could arrest her or place her in protective custody before Friday, so I wouldn't have to attend any more yoga sessions. I snorted. So much for focusing on Martin Technologies' current dilemma.

I glanced at the time, exhausted from the unanswered questions, but it seemed doubtful I'd be able to sleep. After attempting to spend another hour on the safety protocols and building regulations, I decided to present my solution and let maintenance and actual electricians and building inspectors deal with the ramifications. After all, I wasn't consulting for MT. That ship sailed. Printing off copies of my final proposal and the information I had been provided, I turned off my computer and went to bed.

Twisting and turning, I couldn't get the two murders out of my mind. Something was gnawing at my subconscious. What was I missing? At three a.m., I climbed out of bed and went into my living room. Flipping on lights, I grabbed a pencil and went to the wall. It wasn't too long ago that I had to spackle and repaint. Luckily, I learned my lesson, and I invested in some poster board. Tacking up a couple of sheets, I diagrammed everyone involved and drew lines connecting people.

Stepping back, the quadrangle of Paul, Rachel, Alvin, and Jason was still confusing as hell, and I scribbled down my question concerning her motivation for attempting to seduce Paul. Then I contemplated how Jason fit into any of it. More importantly, how did Rachel connect to Wheeler? Did he send someone to threaten her for answers, and if he did, then why not run to the authorities? And why the hell did she trust Jason Oster? Were they having an affair like his security cohorts suspected, or were they meeting about something else? Fuck. Or maybe not. At this point, I wasn't sure of my own name.

Grabbing my notepad, I needed to talk to Det. Jacobs and find out everything I could on Jason Oster and his connection to Rachel Romanski and Rodney Wheeler. Next, I needed to pay Gordon Russell a visit and convince him to hand over all the information concerning the hotel remodel, any input Wheeler might have had on it, and exactly what cutting into those cables could control. With any luck, he'd be compliant. If not, Jacobs or Jablonsky would have to pull some official strings, complete with court orders, assuming a judge would believe my insanity was something more substantial than just a fishing expedition. Lastly, I went back to the wall and scribbled Agent Christopher Walton with a big question mark next to his name. He fit in somehow. I just didn't know how. Although, that fit perfectly with everything else that I clearly knew so well, which was absolutely nothing. It was no wonder I couldn't sleep. I was fumbling around in the dark.

* * *

The next morning, I pulled myself out of bed, replaced the bulk of my bodily fluids with a high concentration of caffeine, and went to the MT building to meet with the VP, Luc Guillot. Upon entering the building, I greeted Jeffrey Myers and asked for a visitor's pass. He chuckled and told me to use my security I.D. to go upstairs. He couldn't be bothered escorting me, even though I teasingly threatened to turn over his lack of proper protocol to the boss.

Exiting on the seventeenth floor, I tossed a few silent curses at the elevator for causing all of these problems and went down the corridor. Martin's office was empty, and the space that had once been my office was also vacant. Apparently I was irreplaceable.

"Bonjour, Mademoiselle Parker," Luc Guillot greeted, buzzing me into his office before I could even knock. "Thank you for your continued dedication to this company." He gestured to the chair. "I don't mean to be rude, but James and I are teleconferencing at two, and I was hoping to pass along a plan for our current dilemma by then."

"Absolutely," I smiled, vaguely remembering that I owed Martin a voicemail for the day, but since he'd be talking to Luc, I figured I should be off the hook. Handing over a copy of my presentation, I launched into the various options available, the one I felt was the most accurate, and explained how a separate power supply for the elevator would be useful in the event of all types of emergencies, how it fit in with the pre-existing protocols, and once implemented it would save time and not require a brand new system and additional protocols to be devised in the event of a fire. When I was done, I let out an audible sigh. "That was a mouthful."

He laughed good-naturedly. "It sounds like you've considered everything." He flipped through the pages. "Is there an estimated cost for these changes?"

"Building maintenance provided me with a rough estimate which you can see there," I pointed to a figure on the page, "but obviously, it will depend on what model power generator is purchased, how much the installation is, and if an alternative fuel source will be used instead of electricity. Mr. Martin tends to be as eco-friendly as he can which isn't always the most fiscally responsible choice in the short-term but often pays off in the long run. However, I don't know what he or the Board will decide since this is simply a contingency and not something that will hopefully ever be needed."

Guillot skimmed through the information again. "Just to save you from having to do this again," he picked up a pen to make a few notes in the margins, "worst case scenario happens. The secondary system fails. The elevator is no longer operational since both systems are offline. It's stuck in between floors, and evacuation from the building is imperative. What are our options?"

"Take the stairs." I sat back, considering different possibilities. "If a person is stuck inside the elevator, the doors could be jimmied open. If the car is between floors and the doors aren't viable, then there is a small hatch in the ceiling. Given the height of the elevator car, it would be

G.K. Parks

possible to get on top of the car and pry open the doors to the floor above and exit from there. Also, like we discussed months ago, there are makeshift ladders of sorts within the elevator shaft that could be utilized in the event of an emergency for both tactical and escape purposes."

He made a few notes, but the smile was obvious. "I don't mean this disrespectfully, but it's obvious your training does not come from a corporate standpoint."

"You mean because upon entering your office I already assessed the possible exits, vantage points for a shooter, and decided on the best place to take cover and what standard office items would make the best weapons?" It was true. But it was also a joke, and one that I would have never uttered if I was still collecting a paycheck from MT.

"That and because I read through your uniform security measures and you spent a lot of time focused on tactical readiness."

"Sorry, some things I just can't seem to shake. I do apologize for this flawed system. I should have noticed when devising the original plan. Maybe I should have been less tactically wary and more pragmatic."

"It's been six months since the implementation. No one noticed until now. I don't believe this was an oversight. We shall call it a glitch." He stood and extended his hand. "It's been a pleasure working with you again, Alexis. There's still a place for you here if you ever change your mind."

"Thank you, sir. But my reasons for declining have nothing to do with the work or the company."

"I understand, but," he shook my hand, smiling knowingly, "you don't enjoy corporate work. It's not," he thought back to recall the word I used, "tactical enough for your taste."

"Perhaps." I went to the door. "Have a good day. Say hello to the head honcho for me."

He winked. "I'll tell James you said hello and sorted out our problem." One down. One very complicated one left to go.

After leaving the MT building, I went straight to the precinct. There were far too many unknowns for my liking, and nothing about the police investigation jived. It was

- 239 -

why I jumped down Jacobs' throat the other morning and why I was still chasing my tail in circles. Even if I wasn't consulting or part of any law enforcement body, that didn't mean that my P.I. license shouldn't come with some perks, namely figuring out what the hell was actually going on.

"Jacobs," I said forcefully, ignoring the fact that he was on the phone, "we need to talk."

He held up a finger, and I leaned against his desk, impatiently waiting for him to hang up. After he concluded the call, he pushed away from the desk and leaned back in his chair. "I didn't expect to see you again, Parker." He chuckled. "I should have listened when O'Connell warned me you'd be back. What do you want now? Planning to accuse me of pinning even more crimes on your client or not doing my job properly," he narrowed his eyes, "or maybe this time you'll suggest I'm taking bribes."

"I need your help."

"And I need an apology, preferably in writing, but I was also told I shouldn't expect that to happen either."

"I was wrong," I admitted.

"You were." He opened his top desk drawer and pulled out a file. "Why don't we grab some lunch? And you can try that apology again. I believe the correct word you're looking for is sorry."

"Fine, but don't expect me to pay because that might be considered bribery." He gestured toward the door I just entered, and he trailed me out of the precinct and led me to his cruiser. Once we were inside and the car was in gear, he handed me the file from his desk. "I am sorry, Detective. I get moody when my problem-solving skills go on the fritz."

I opened the folder. "Any particular reason why we needed to leave the station for this?"

"I'm not a pushover. And I sure as hell don't cater to some P.I., particularly one who accuses me of pussyfooting around when it comes to two homicide investigations." He grinned. Clearly, Jacobs was afraid of the flack his fellow officers would give him if he cooperated with me now. "So if anyone asks, you were groveling at my feet, begging for help."

"Yeah, I don't think anyone will buy that. Your story

would be more convincing if you said I held you at gunpoint for the information." I offered a friendly smile. "But then again, that would probably hurt that macho exterior of yours."

He parked the car outside a diner and hit the release on his seatbelt before turning to face me. "I'll tell you the truth." He looked out the windshield, as if to make sure the coast was clear. "After we released you and the PDN employees from questioning on Wednesday, the only lead we had in the case was something strange in Paul Eastman's responses. It was a hunch, and after some digging, his alibis and insistence on where he was at particularly important times didn't add up. I wanted to bring him back in for questioning, very civil, but he refused. After evaluating the evidence again, it was apparent the security measures PDN used were compromised from somewhere on the inside which led to the second homicide. It was enough to arrest Eastman. I only planned to hold him forty-eight hours and then let him go. There wasn't enough to charge him."

"So you were going to run the clock and see if he'd crack under the pressure." The cops had some leeway which often proved useful.

"The DA's office asked what we had, and I told them I was going to let Eastman go if no other evidence turned up and he didn't confess. About two hours later, I get a phone call. Someone at the FBI phoned the DA and said they had evidence of Eastman's involvement in the murder. Whoever it was pulled some favors because they wanted to indict, despite the department's hesitation."

"Since when does anything like that ever happen?" Under normal circumstances, the police would be pushing for charges and the DA would be reluctant to file. This was completely ass-backward.

"It doesn't. The whole thing stunk to high heaven, so I called in a few favors of my own. It was after Eastman almost died in custody. Thanks for the save, by the way." I nodded, not wanting to interrupt. "Anyway, it turns out Eastman was involved in some shady deals with Hodge, and the FBI was hoping he possessed evidence to use

against their big fish since nothing will stick to this whale."
He shrugged. "I know. You already told me as much. Then
I tried to get Eastman to stay in custody. It honestly was for
his protection, Parker," Jacobs insisted. "But I don't blame
him for refusing or you for agreeing with his decision. He's
been getting played." He pointed at me accusingly. "Not
that he doesn't deserve it for the shit he's involved with."

"I never said he was a saint."

"How's he doing? Is he gonna be okay?"

"He'll be fine. But everything gets even more
complicated than what you just told me." And I filled him
in on my suspicions concerning Rachel Romanski, Alvin
Hodge, and Jason Oster.

Then I took a few minutes to read the information in the
file. It was a statement made by Jason Oster. The tale he
told matched Paul's. The wireless camera was used to
monitor PDN clients and ensure the honesty and moral
integrity of the hotel staff. At the moment, the memory
card was being examined, but the files were damaged and
didn't look promising. Oster's cooperation might have led
to another dead end.

"We need to speak to the ex-wife," Jacobs said, finally
opening his car door. "Let's grab some chow and then go
have a chat. Hell, I'll even let you ride along."

THIRTY-THREE

"Why haven't you questioned her already?" I asked as we drove to Jason Oster's apartment. The detail assigned to monitor the woman inside had reported she never left the premises. She stayed at Oster's all day and night. Jason, on the other hand, went to work in the morning as if his life and world weren't falling apart. "Her ex-husband was found hanging in the middle of a hotel. Spouses current and former are always suspects."

"By the time we sorted out whose case it was, enough evidence surfaced so we didn't need anyone to identify the body, and once Frank Costan's remains were discovered, we had no reason to question Romanski."

"That doesn't make any sense," I argued.

"And what part of this investigation has ever made a damn bit of sense?" he snapped. "I knew I was being kept in the dark. The only question was why. But after what I've learned about Wheeler and SAC Walton's questionable investigation, it all makes a bit more sense. Shit, I'm surprised the suits haven't taken away our homicide investigation completely since they're more concerned with identifying and apprehending Frank Costan's replacement on the most wanted list."

"Did Oster give you anything else?" I asked, realizing I still lacked a lot of information. Maybe Jacobs was in the dark, but at least he had a flashlight. I didn't even have that.

"Only access to the wireless camera he and Eastman set up. The techs are sorting through the files now. The thing's been used a dozen times, so the erased files are corrupted. It'll take time."

"Now who's keeping me in the dark?" I growled, smart enough to realize he didn't want to divulge whatever new information he possessed. "Why would Oster erase whatever damning evidence was on the camera?"

"Probably to cover his own tracks. Maybe hide his involvement," Jacobs speculated. "I'd bet he figured we wouldn't be able to recover the files, so he might as well appear to be cooperating." He led me inside the apartment building and to the stairwell. "One step at a time. And let me do the talking. You're a civilian, and she doesn't have to speak to you or answer any of your questions."

"Well, unless you arrest her, she doesn't have to answer your questions either."

Emerging on the proper floor, Jacobs glanced both ways down the hall, probably out of habit, and went to Jason Oster's apartment, knocking on the door. There was no answer, and he tried again. Finally, he called out, "Rachel Romanski, this is the police. We know you're inside. Open the door, ma'am." So much for subtle.

Rachel came to the door still dressed in the outfit she wore the day before. She looked jittery, like she drank too much coffee and hadn't slept. The same way I looked most mornings.

"Alex?" she asked, completely confused. "What are you doing here? I told you yesterday not to involve the police."

"Sorry, Rachel," I said, hoping she would be more forthcoming if she thought the reason for the knock at the door was for her own protection.

"Ma'am, may we come inside?" Jacobs asked, and she stepped back so we could enter. "I'm Detective Jacobs. I'm sorry to bother you this afternoon, but I have some news. Would you mind taking a seat?"

"What's going on?" The realization that we weren't at her apartment must have sunk in because she turned to me with a fierce, defiant look. "How did you know where I was? Who the hell are you?"

"Alex Parker, P.I." If it was good enough for Andy Barker and Magnum, it ought to be good enough for me. Or I needed to stop watching so much television.

"Ma'am," Jacobs intervened, "please, take a seat." Obeying his order, she sat in a chair and shifted her gaze between the two of us. "I'm sorry to tell you this, but your ex-husband, Alvin Hodge, is dead." She looked away but had no obvious reaction. She already knew. "Ma'am, can I ask you a couple of questions?"

"Go ahead." She turned back and stared at me, betrayal on her face. "Maybe after that you should ask Alex some questions since she showed up while the scumbag responsible was at my yoga studio."

I held my tongue and leaned against the wall near the door in case she tried to make a run for it. While Jacobs questioned her about the last time she had seen Alvin, which was almost a year ago, I contemplated her reasoning for why she would think Paul was responsible. Since her answers weren't useful, I decided to throw caution to the wind and ask about more current events.

"Rachel, when did you first meet Paul Eastman?" I interrupted, and Jacobs turned with a glare, seconds away from telling me to leave or shut up. Before he could speak, Rachel surprised us by answering the question.

"I met him when I was visiting Alvin at work. It was around the time of our divorce. But I don't think he remembered. If he did, then he's sicker than I thought." She shook her head, disgusted. "I mean, seriously, who the hell tries to sleep with their friend's spouse, former or otherwise?" Obviously, that was rhetorical, particularly since that was a fairly frequent occurrence according to officers responding to domestic disturbances. She was angry and got off the couch and turned her back to us, staring out the window.

"But you went to Paul's place a month ago. You wanted to seduce him." It wasn't a question, but with any luck, she'd offer a reason for her behavior.

"I didn't have a choice," she hissed, her back to us.

"What do you mean you didn't have a choice?" Jacobs asked, flipping to a new page in his notepad. "Are you saying Mr. Eastman raped you?"

I let out an audible, exasperated sigh. Now Jacobs wanted to add sexual assault to Paul's rap sheet. Unbelievable. He turned to me and arched an eyebrow, wondering why I was annoyed.

"No. We didn't have sex." She placed her palms on the window sill and leaned forward, resting her forehead against the glass. "I think I need a lawyer."

"Ma'am, we aren't arresting you," Jacobs said, attempting to get her to continue. "Why can't you just answer the question?" She shook her head and continued to stare out the window.

"Rachel," I tried again, "you drugged Paul and searched his apartment for something. What was it?" She remained unresponsive, so I tried a different approach. "Why do you think Paul is responsible for Alvin's death?"

"Because he is." She spun to face us with renewed vehemence. "Whatever they were doing, it involved some unsavory people." She stared into my eyes. "I told you this the other day. The reason for my divorce was because people came to my house. Scary people, Alex. They threatened me. They threatened Alvin. I couldn't live like that." She blinked a few times. "Paul's part of it."

"Did Paul Eastman threaten you or your ex-husband?" Jacobs asked, still working to connect the pieces.

"No. Not directly. I don't know who they were. I didn't recognize them. But Paul called soon after, and he and Alvin had a long discussion. I don't remember what they were talking about. It was a year ago, but I just remember thinking Paul was involved."

"So if you thought Eastman was behind the threats or involved in the threats, why did you meet him at a bar a month ago and willingly go back to his place? That seems completely counterintuitive. If you think a man's dangerous, then you stay the hell away from him," I argued. Admit why you were there, my internal voice screamed.

"You wouldn't understand," she said quietly, returning to the chair and picking at a thread.

"How do you know Jason Oster?" Jacobs asked. "This is his apartment."

"Jason's a friend." She met my eyes. "More than a friend, but you already know that."

"I thought you found it deplorable to sleep with your ex's friends," Jacobs retorted.

"Jason and Alvin were never friends. They worked together, but Alvin couldn't stand Jason. He thought Jason was out to get him. My husband was a lot of things, but he clearly wasn't the best judge of character. Jason was just trying to do his job to protect the hotel and everyone inside."

"How did you meet? Company Christmas party?" I asked, feeling like something was missing.

"After I brought the divorce papers for Alvin to sign, I went back to my car in tears. It was hard to say goodbye to the man I loved. When I was leaving, I drove into that fountain out front. It was an accident. I wasn't paying attention, but Jason had to come out and assess the situation. He was a shoulder to cry on." She looked around his apartment. "He still is."

"Ms. Romanski," Jacobs began, but I cut him off.

"Who told you Alvin was dead?" I asked.

"Jason did." Her chin quivered, and she sniffled loudly. "He told me a few nights ago." A squeak escaped her lips, and she started to cry.

Jacobs threw a dirty look in my direction and went to find a tissue. In that moment of privacy, I moved closer to her chair, hoping to appear comforting.

"Does he know how it happened or who's responsible?" I asked in a hushed tone. She shook her head. "Did he tell you to stay away from Paul?" Again, she shook her head. "Rachel, he and Paul are friends." Maybe friends was too strong of a word, but sowing seeds of distrust and doubt might lead to real answers.

Her eyes shot upward, searching for the truth. "Oh god," she managed, inhaling between choking sobs.

"The police can protect you, but you have to tell us what is going on," I insisted.

Jacobs returned with a box of tissues. He had been in the hallway, hoping she'd open up to me. He met my eyes and gave a slight nod as he handed her the tissue box and knelt in front of her.

"Ms. Romanski, since someone threatened you and your husband was killed, you really need to talk to us. Whatever it is, it can't be as bad as you think."

"I don't know what to think," she whispered, dabbing at her eyes. "I just want to wake up from this nightmare." Silence filled the void as Jacobs waited patiently for her to make a decision to talk to us. After she stopped crying, she scowled and turned to me. "You're working with Paul. That's why you showed up right when he did. You're in on this."

"What is this?" Jacobs asked again, getting annoyed with her constant back and forth, but she ignored him.

"Paul Eastman was poisoned. Whoever killed Alvin tried to kill him too. He isn't involved, Rachel. Not with this. He and Alvin had other deals on the side, but he isn't responsible for Alvin's death."

The blood drained from her face. "I swear I didn't poison him." She turned to focus on Jacobs. "You have to believe me. I had nothing to do with any of it. Oh god. Oh god," she continued to mumble, burying her face in her hands.

"Then tell us why you were at Paul Eastman's apartment," I urged.

"Please, ma'am," Jacobs added, "it's my job to find your ex-husband's killer, and right now, I'd love to rule you out as a suspect." He handed her another tissue and put a reassuring hand on her shoulder. "It's also the best way of keeping you safe from the people who've threatened you."

"Jason said he'd protect me." She blew her nose and balled up the tissue in her hands, worrying the edges with her fingers. "But now," she met my eyes, "I don't know what to believe anymore." She leaned back in the chair and collected herself. "About six weeks ago, a man approached me when I was leaving work. I don't know who he was. I never saw him before. He told me that Alvin owed him a lot of money, and he was coming to collect." She bit her lip, swallowing. "I said I had nothing to do with that, and I didn't want any trouble."

"What happened next?" Jacobs asked when the void in conversation lasted a little too long.

"A week or two later, my windshield was smashed and my cat was left dead on my porch." Her lower lip quivered, but she held it together. "The guy was waiting for me the next day. He said my bad luck would stop if I did him a favor." She looked away. "He said that Alvin and Paul were involved in a lot of shady shit, and they ripped him off. If he found out where they stashed his money, he'd leave us alone." She wiped at her eyes again. "He promised he wouldn't hurt Alvin if I cooperated." She swallowed. "So I asked Jason what he knew about Alvin's dealings and Paul Eastman."

"What did Jason tell you?" Jacobs asked.

"He didn't know what it could be, but he said that Paul was a braggart who had his hands in a lot of different things. He didn't necessarily trust the guy, but he thought Paul was harmless." She blinked a few times. "They would go out for drinks occasionally after work. He just thought the guy liked to blow smoke."

"And that's how you found out where Paul would be," I added, and she nodded.

"I went to the bar and flirted with him a little. It didn't even take much for him to open up about his job. I listened to him talk all night about that security firm he works for and how they were in charge of some conference security. It didn't seem relevant, but I wanted to make sure that guy wasn't going to come back and hurt me or Alvin. Hell, he killed my cat, so what was to stop him from doing something worse?" She shook her head. "The guy had given me a listening device, and I planted it in Paul's apartment after Paul fell asleep. I slipped a few ground up sleeping pills into his drink," she added. "I didn't think it would hurt him. I never meant to poison him."

"That's not what did it," I muttered as I attempted to wrap my mind around why anyone would go to such extremes instead of taking matters to the authorities.

"No." Jacobs shook his head as reinforcement. "Where did you put the listening device?"

"Under his desk lamp, near his computer. It seemed like the best spot." She shrugged. "I don't know. That's where they always put stuff in movies."

"Do you think you could recognize that guy if you saw him again?" I asked.

"Probably. But I don't know who he is. I haven't seen or heard from him since that day." She let out a whimper. "I thought," she sniffed again, tears leaking from her eyes, "it was over. I thought Alvin would be safe. That we'd both be safe." She shook her head. "When Jason told me he was dead, I knew what it would look like. And I just couldn't go to the cops. Jason promised he'd take care of everything."

"Will you come down to the station and look through some photographs and make an official statement?" Jacobs asked gently. "We will protect you if you let us."

"Okay."

THIRTY-FOUR

Just when I didn't think things could get any more complicated, Rachel spouts out stories of threats from unidentified men and planting bugs. If this were the plot for a spy thriller, I would find it contrived and overdone. However, it was real life, or maybe I was having one hell of a lucid dream. Either way, I wanted a chance to speak with Jason Oster about these new developments and to scour Paul's house for evidence. Unfortunately, Detective Jacobs tightened the reins and hadn't let me out of his sight. Apparently I was in the doghouse for disclosing certain material facts to a potential person of interest.

"The officers I sent to Eastman's place didn't find any listening devices. A few techs are going to sweep the entire property, just to make sure we didn't miss something, but I don't think they'll find anything," Jacobs said to Lieutenant Moretti while I eavesdropped. "Either Romanski's lying or someone else was inside Eastman's house and removed the alleged device."

"What's Parker still doing here?" Moretti asked, narrowing his eyes, but I saw the briefest amused glint cross his face. "Are you planning to arrest her for whatever dumbass thing she did this time?"

"No, sir. Just making sure I got all the facts straight. We're exchanging information."

"Glad to hear it. Keep up the good work." Moretti went back into his office and slammed the door.

Jacobs slumped into his desk chair and swiveled to face me. "You're a real pain in my ass, but despite that, you still managed to get us some useful information."

"How useful? You can't corroborate any of her story. It could be bullshit. Maybe she and Jason planned the entire thing, painted Alvin as the scapegoat, and discovered where Frank Costan was keeping his stash of ill-gotten gains, and they are going to abscond with it as soon as the coast is clear. Hell, maybe they were afraid Alvin said something about it to Paul, so she went to his apartment to figure out how much he knew and the best way to poison him."

"Why didn't she just end him then?" Jacobs asked, playing along with my runaway theory that neither of us truly believed.

"The timing was wrong. It would cause Costan to go to ground. So instead, she figures out what make and model fridge he has and reports it back to Jason so they can tamper with his water filter."

"Except Eastman would have mentioned if Jason stopped by his place recently enough to have modified the water filter." Jacobs picked up the forensic report on the tampering. The filter lining was laced with fluoride that ran into the water in high doses, but the smudges on the casing didn't provide usable prints unless we had something to compare them to.

"But Paul stayed at the hotel during the conference and left his house keys with the valet. Anyone could have swiped them, particularly someone who worked in hotel security."

"What kind of idiot leaves their house keys with a valet?" Jacobs asked, gleaning some useful information out of our purely hypothetical conjecture.

"Paul Eastman, PDN's head security management consultant."

"Jesus, don't they teach anyone anything nowadays?"

Jacobs rubbed his eyes and glanced across the bullpen at the sketch artist who was attempting to create a reasonable facsimile of our mystery man from Rachel's recollection. "So what do you really think is going on?"

"I think Rodney Wheeler and Frank Costan were working together. Costan had a lot of money, and Wheeler had a lot of connections. The remodeling inside the hotel, the access to the guest registry and security feeds, and basically everything else that was needed to pull off the two murders had to come from an inside man. Originally, I thought maybe it was one of the agents tailing or guarding Wheeler, but if this has been going on for the last six weeks or so, then it's probably some of Wheeler's hotel employees."

"Jason Oster is head of hotel security and is intimately aware of everything pertaining to Alvin Hodge's personal and professional life. From the way Romanski was talking about Oster, I'd say he has her wrapped around his little finger."

"So was Jason playing her, or is she his accomplice?" I asked. We still had no hard evidence against Jason, but he had the access needed. The detective shrugged. "The only way either of us is going to get out of the dark is by sharing resources. Did you retrieve any information off the camera's memory card yet?"

Jacobs had received a message about this earlier, so it was about time he learned to share. "Come on," he stood from his desk, telling one of the officers to keep an eye on Romanski before we went down the stairs to the tech department. "Since the lieutenant doesn't seem to have a problem with you, neither do I."

He opened a door, and I followed him into the room. A few of the computer geniuses were working on different cases, but the information Jacobs requested was in a folder at an empty desk. He picked it up, skimming the contents, and then handed it to me. A few printed stills with corresponding dates and timestamps were included for each of the twelve recordings listed. Most were of what I could only assume were PDN's clientele. Only the last two took place within the past month.

"Not very helpful," Jacobs said as I read through the transcripts. "It's not the smoking gun we were hoping for."

"No. It's not." I lifted up the final photo from Monday night, the day before Alvin Hodge's body was left out in the open. "But can I have a copy?"

"Yeah, fine. Add it to your collection of unsolvable cases," he retorted. He took the photo from me and opened one of the multipurpose printers, scanning and printing a duplicate. "I shared the evidence, so what exactly are you thinking?"

"Well, first, whoever was actually using room 709 wasn't getting paid by the federal government," I pointed to the attire worn by the portion of the man we could see. Granted it was only a shoulder and part of his back, but no self-respecting federal agent, even undercover, would wear a Hawaiian print shirt. "And second, whoever it is knew the camera was there."

"You got all of that from a single still photo?"

"Yeah." I held up the video transcript. "Two seconds after Mr. Mysterious enters the room, the camera went on the fritz. And I don't believe in coincidences."

"It could be Eastman or Oster. Or anyone else for that matter. There isn't much to go on."

"And on that positive note, I'm gonna stop by the hotel and pay Jason Oster and Gordon Russell a visit."

"I'll come with you," Jacobs said. "I need a follow-up with Oster after our morning with Romanski." He stopped to tell the officers to keep Rachel at the precinct and he would be back soon. "What do you want with the hotel manager?"

"He's in charge, so he'll know when and why the renovations were made. With any luck, it'll trace directly back to one of the hotel co-owners, and that might just be enough to get some official answers." I sighed and went to my car. "I'll meet you there."

On the way, I phoned Mark and updated him on Rachel, the information the police obtained from the memory card Oster provided, and my current plan of attack. While I was out, Mark promised to question Eastman about Rachel's visit to his place, if he ever found the listening device, and if he owned any Hawaiian shirts. It wasn't much, but it was more than what we had last night.

When we arrived at the hotel, I pulled Jacobs aside. He looked questioningly at me, and I maneuvered us around the exterior, out of sight of the security cameras. Once we were in the clear, I leaned against the brick.

"What did Jason tell you yesterday when you questioned him about the camera that he and Eastman set up?" I asked.

"Nothing. He said he'd give us the memory card."

"Did you tell him that I broke into his locker?"

"You broke into his locker?" Jacobs was a lousy liar, and he knew instantly I wasn't falling for it. "Look, the guy didn't want to press charges against you, so don't worry about it."

"What did you threaten him with in order to earn his cooperation?" I knew how the game was played, and before we went inside to talk to Oster, I wanted to know exactly what had already been said and done.

"We still don't have any evidence against him, but I might have fudged a few details and suggested we could get a warrant and search everything he owned if he didn't hand over the camera. Now I can mention Romanski's in custody and is willing to speak to us, and maybe that will get him to open up on at least one of the crimes that has plagued this fine establishment." He glanced around, making sure we were still alone. "Frankly, I was surprised when he willing came to the station. He offered up the proper memory card, and he appeared to be helpful and compliant. That typically doesn't happen."

"So either he's civically minded, or he's one cocky bastard." Oster must have known there was nothing damning caught on tape which was punching holes in the possibility that whatever was on that tape was something Rachel would risk meeting him at the hotel for. I guess their tryst was just that.

"My money's on the second one." He jerked his head back toward the front door. "Shall we find out?"

"Absolutely."

I waited a few seconds before following Jacobs into the

hotel. Something didn't feel right. Why go through all the trouble to cover your tracks, alter the security feed, and ditch Frank Costan's body beneath the hotel when the day before Alvin Hodge was left hanging out in the open for everyone to see? It must have led to tightened security and a much more thorough assessment of all security measures. It would have made the insider's job that much harder to smuggle Costan's body out of the hotel, assuming he was murdered inside the trashed hotel room. We were missing a crucial connection, I could feel it.

"Do you think you could page Jason Oster for me?" Jacobs asked, flashing his badge at the desk clerk. She studied his badge as if it might be fake and then picked up the phone and dialed a number.

"Mr. Oster's on his way." She went back to answering phones and booking rooms while Jacobs and I took a seat on the couch in the lobby.

"Why was Alvin Hodge left hanging in the open?" I whispered.

"It was probably a warning. I was surprised the guy's tongue wasn't cut out, but that would have been harder to stage as a suicide." He shrugged. "Who knows? These sickos do all kinds of crazy shit. If the ex-wife is to be believed, then whoever it was must have made it a point to follow through publicly on the threat."

Rachel and Alvin were threatened. Jason knew about this, and he set up a surveillance camera in a room that was used in the beating and murder of Frank Costan. If he was responsible, why would he risk setting himself up to be caught, particularly after more law enforcement officials and private security were on scene in the wake of Alvin Hodge's murder? It didn't fit.

"Are you sure Costan was killed after Hodge?" I asked. The wheels were turning, and I felt close to a breakthrough.

"Yes." Jacobs questioned my thinking. "Hodge was killed at least two days before Costan."

"And the ligature marks on Hodge's throat didn't match the cables running from the ceiling," I recalled. "Do we have any idea what was used to kill Hodge? I'm guessing after Hodge was left out in the open, Costan was beaten and tortured for information on where his money was stashed."

"I'll check with the medical examiner and see if they can narrow down the timeline for us," Jacobs promised, scrutinizing me in the hopes of some additional elaboration. "So you don't think Costan was killed because of a deal going south?"

"Originally, yes, but maybe, instead of negotiating, someone decided to simply take what they wanted."

"Detective," Oster said, startling me from behind, "you wanted to see me?" I spun around, and Oster looked down at me. "Well, if it isn't the woman who broke into my locker." He plastered a phony smile on his face. "First, you confront me about an affair, and next, you're snooping through my stuff. Let me guess, you want to strip search me."

"I'm not sure. Are you concealing any suspicious packages?" I asked.

"Oh, wouldn't you like to know?" He glared, but I remained unaffected by his outward hostility. Considering the fact I was reevaluating his level of involvement, he should be nicer. Instead, he turned his attention back to Jacobs. "Can we please get on with this? I was just about to punch out when you beckoned."

"We can wait," Jacobs offered. "Maybe you should clock out and collect your belongings. Then we can have this conversation at the station."

"Here and now is fine," Oster insisted, not wanting to risk being arrested. "I thought we sorted everything out last night." He glanced down the hallway. "Let's speak in the conference room." He led us to an empty room just off the lobby.

"We've spoken to Rachel Romanski. In fact, we picked her up from your apartment earlier today. It seems you left out a lot of relevant information, even though you insisted you were doing nothing but cooperating to help further this investigation," Jacobs said, taking a seat and waiting for Oster to break.

Jason snorted and remained silent. He wasn't worried

about the police department. He must have known they had nothing on him. So maybe it was time to sweeten the pot.

"Mr. Oster," I said, recalling the importance of being respectful to persons of interest, "your girlfriend's in over her head. She's admitted to some serious crimes, and she's implicated you in a few of them. I can guarantee this will be easier on both of you if you explain to us what is going on."

"You're a fucking P.I." He rolled his eyes. "Hell, you were fired by PDN, and you expect me to be scared of your hollow threats and obvious lies? Allegations like that are just a hair's throw away from coercion, maybe slander. And just because I didn't press charges against you for breaking and entering doesn't mean that I won't hesitate if you keep this up. This is harassment, plain and simple." He turned to Jacobs. "Unless you have something concrete, I'm tired of explaining myself and playing along."

"Who got to you?" I asked, surprising the two men with my brazen question. "We've spoken before. You were cooperating with the police department. And you didn't come after me. I don't think you're a killer, but you know who is. And they got to you."

He swallowed twice, and I knew it was true.

THIRTY-FIVE

"You're wrong," Oster said, his eyes searching the room.

"Are you sure you wouldn't prefer to have this conversation someplace more private?" Jacobs asked. He sensed there was more to the story than either of us realized. "We don't need to muddy your professional career with these unsubstantiated allegations." He stood, hoping to convince Oster to comply. "I need to step outside and make a few calls. Why don't you think about it?"

I never expected Detective Jacobs to turn into a softie, but maybe he was afraid that pushing Oster too hard out in the open would result in a third homicide. Two already occurred, and a third had been attempted. Depending on who threatened Oster, we might actually get a name for our killer, assuming our newest lead didn't end up dead too.

Following Jacobs lead, I stood up from the table. "I need to have a chat with Mr. Russell." I gave Oster a final look. "It doesn't matter what you've done, but you still deserve the opportunity to remain breathing. Talk to us," I whispered as I went past him.

Before I made it out the door, Oster grabbed my elbow and pulled me backward, slamming the door closed. I pulled free from his grip. My training took over, and I stepped back into a defensive position. He didn't seem to notice and stepped closer.

"Is it true that Rachel's in custody?" he asked.

"She willingly surrendered." I searched his eyes, hoping for answers. "She told us about going to Paul Eastman's house, how the two of you met, and that she's been threatened on multiple occasions."

He nodded once and went out the door ahead of me. That encounter only resulted in further confusion. Did Jason ask in order to ensure she was safe? Or was it so he'd know precisely where she'd be in order to silence her? Goddamn. I sent a text to Mark, hoping for reassurance that someone was still tailing Oster. At least we'd know if he planned to make a move on Romanski. The only good news was she was at the precinct, surrounded by dozens of police officers. It wasn't the ideal place to carry out a homicide.

Moving on to my second reason for being here, I went back to the front desk. The woman from before warily glanced up as if to say 'now what do you want?' Before I could even ask a question, I spotted Mr. Russell heading down the hallway. Skipping the formalities, I made a beeline to him.

"Mr. Russell," I called, falling in step beside him, "can I ask you a few questions?"

He turned and looked at me, never breaking stride. "I know you," he said, attempting to figure out when he saw me last. His brow furrowed. "You're one of the investigators, right?"

"Yeah." Private or otherwise, the term was broad enough to be accurate. "Please, sir, this will only take a couple of minutes."

"Okay." He continued toward the elevator, and I followed behind. "What do you want now?"

"Well, I was wondering if you could provide any additional information on when the hotel was remodeled. You mentioned the cable that Alvin Hodge was hung from was only noticeable in certain parts of the hotel because of a remodel. When did that occur?"

"Um," the doors opened, and we stepped inside, "it

wasn't that long ago. A few months maybe. If you need an actual date, I'll have to find the paperwork." He let out a tired sigh. "The old elevator system was part of the original construction. It was half a century old and not very reliable. We had to install a separate pulley system, and it widened the shaft, which is why we had to knock down some walls and leave the cables exposed." He looked up at the illuminated numbers, hoping to flee from this conversation. "I can assure you that it's all within the fire safety codes."

"What runs through those cables? I know you mentioned it before, but I forgot," I lied, hoping to keep him talking.

"Cable, phone, electric." The doors opened on level ten, and he stepped out. "Pretty much everything."

"And your security systems? The CCTV feed?" I asked.

"Everything. It's all on one main system. Was there anything else? I'm a busy man." He was already a few steps down the hall, making it apparent he had no intention of answering any other questions.

"That's it. Thanks for your time, sir."

I remained in the elevator as the doors closed. Those answers didn't necessarily prove anything, and I still didn't get a chance to ask about the hotel's co-owner, but Mr. Russell was in a rush. Or he was intentionally avoiding further questioning. Unsure which was more accurate, I returned to the lobby. Maybe Detective Jacobs would have better luck convincing Jason Oster to talk.

Jacobs was lingering near the front door. He looked up as I approached and tucked his phone back into his pocket. "That was quick," he said, glancing around.

"Yeah, and not particularly helpful. The remodel took place in the last few months, but I didn't get a chance to find out whose idea it was or who authorized it. Russell claimed it was because the old elevator was shoddy and needed to be replaced. They widened the shaft, resulting in tearing down a few walls which exposed some of the cables."

"Sounds like a late night infomercial," Jacobs said, his facial expression remained serious, but I still laughed at the joke. "Do you have any idea where Oster went?"

"Not since he left the conference room." I spun on my heel, slowly surveying the entire lobby, the numerous hallways, exits, stairs, and elevator. "He might have snuck out."

"Great." He walked out the front door, his phone pressed to his ear.

Before I could follow suit, my phone rang. It was Mark, probably getting back to me about the whereabouts of Oster's potential tail. "Do we still have eyes on him?" I asked in lieu of a greeting.

"Parker," Mark's tone didn't bode well, "I'm not calling about that." He paused, sucking some air in through his teeth. "I lost Eastman."

"You what?" Those words made no sense, and my brain couldn't even begin to comprehend what they possibly meant.

"He wanted to make a call to PDN. So I told him we'd go somewhere else, and I'd let him use my phone, just in case. But after he made the call, he said he wasn't feeling so great and ducked into a bathroom."

"And you didn't go with him?" I ran a hand through my hair. "That's the oldest fucking trick in the book. Who the hell are you, and what did you do with the real Mark Jablonsky?"

"Well, I didn't expect him to give me the slip. He hired you to guard him for fuck's sake."

"Shit."

"He didn't call PDN," Mark continued. "He phoned someone at the hotel. At least that was the number left on my phone. He's looking mighty dirty right about now."

"When did this happen?" I asked, wondering how much of a head start Paul had and if there was a chance I could grab him before he did something stupid enough to get himself killed.

"About twenty minutes ago. I've called in a BOLO on him and notified the PD. Units were scrambled to his apartment, his office, and Rachel's yoga studio. The FBI is sending additional units to the hotel, and the current surveillance team is on standby. Any other places I might have missed?"

"Find out who he called. I want to know. Now." I hung up and darted outside. "Detective," I called, chasing after Jacobs who was leaning against his cruiser, "we've got a problem."

"I heard." He lowered his handheld radio. "And you convinced me your client was innocent."

"He might be." Now wasn't the time to argue about this. "He called someone at the hotel." My mind raced as I remembered the things Paul and I discussed the day before. "I'll bet he plans to confront Oster."

"We don't know enough about his involvement. If Eastman confronts him, we might lose our entire case. Hell, Eastman's probably responsible, and maybe he hopes to silence his remaining partners." He radioed to the precinct for added protection to ensure Rachel Romanski stayed safe.

"Or Oster could do the same," I spat. "We don't know who to trust."

"Trust no one," Jacobs replied. He listened to radio chatter, informing him a few units were on the way to our location. "What do you know about Eastman? Is he armed? Dangerous?"

"He wasn't armed when he ducked out on Jablonsky. And there's no record of violence in his history. From the research I've done, he doesn't own any firearms. PDN security is allowed to carry, but Eastman coordinates, not protects."

"So he could gain access easily enough," Jacobs commented. He glanced back at the hotel. "I'd love to lock this place down, but we don't know enough for that kind of action at this point." He checked the time and his phone. "Where the hell is Oster?"

I turned, staring into the glass doors of the hotel. "He's with Eastman."

Paul slipped past us, probably by taking one of the side entrances reserved for employees and staff. He and Jason were standing across from one another in the lobby. It appeared heated words were being exchanged, and without waiting for things to escalate any further, Jacobs and I sprinted back inside.

"You did this," Paul accused. The two men were in the back corner of the lobby, near the elevator and security office. "You killed Alvin. You tried to kill me. And you used Alvin's wife to do it. Who the fuck does something like that?"

"Paul," I said, stepping close and suddenly realizing that Jason Oster was holding him at gunpoint. Shit. "Okay, let's just take it easy," I said, raising my hands slightly. "No one wants to do anything they're going to regret." Jacobs was two steps behind me, and from my body language, he realized what was happening and pulled his service piece.

"It's not me," Oster hissed, waving the gun around as he spoke. "You're wrong, Paul."

"Mr. Oster, drop your weapon," Jacobs commanded, his authoritarian tone was hushed so as not to panic any nearby bystanders. The last thing we needed was a hysterical person encouraging Oster to open fire.

"I'm sorry, Detective, but I can't." He shifted his gaze to me. "Don't even think about it." He jerked his chin at my shoulder holster. "Keep your hands where I can see them."

"Sure, no problem," I replied. "Maybe we could move this little shindig into your office and have a nice, calm conversation." Cops were on the way, an FBI surveillance team was somewhere on-site, so this needed to find a civilized end before the stakes were raised. "Why don't you put down the heavy artillery? No harm. No foul."

I didn't turn, but I felt Jacobs fidgeting. I knew police protocol, and he would request back-up. He was by the book, and this situation wasn't a normal page out of any book. Oster looked torn, and he stepped backward, toward the wall and the security office.

"Alexis, I'm sorry," Paul muttered. "But after what you said in my motel room, I couldn't just sit idly by while he was still out here. He killed my friend."

"Not now, Paul," I hissed, but it was too late.

"You think I killed Alvin?" Oster studied me, flabbergasted. "Why would I do that?" He scoffed at the notion. "We never saw eye to eye, but I'm not crazy enough to kill someone."

"Then why don't you lower your weapon," Jacobs urged. "Prove what you say is true by your actions."

Oster faltered, hesitating as he considered the words, and at the same moment, Paul rushed forward, grabbing the gun and pointing it at the ceiling. The weapon discharged a few times during the struggle, someone screamed, the fire alarm was pulled, and sirens blared outside. Today just wasn't my day.

THIRTY-SIX

When people are placed in difficult situations, human nature tends to rear its ugly head. With the cacophony of the sirens, the screams, and the wail of the fire alarm as guests fled from the hotel, Jason Oster managed to wrestle his gun away from Paul and use the man as a human shield. Despite the fact that my gun was now drawn, there wasn't a clear shot.

"Drop your guns," Jason growled, pulling Paul backward by the arm. "I'm not a violent man, but you're not giving me a choice."

"I can't do that," Jacobs said. Out of the corner of my eye, I noticed the hotel emptying out. The desk clerk was gone, and hoards of guests were now outside in the parking lot as police officers cleared them away from the doors and began to enter the lobby.

"Stay back," Oster screamed, turning his gun to point at Paul's temple. "Tell them to stay out of here, or I'll do it." And now we had a hostage situation.

"Pull back," Jacobs said to the officers entering the lobby. They took an uncertain step backward, their guns drawn. "Mr. Oster, I'm going to reach into my pocket and pull out a radio to tell them to stay outside." Oster nodded, and Jacobs radioed for them to standby. He didn't say stand down, but Oster didn't notice.

"Now go outside with the others," Oster ordered.

"Jason," I said his name, drawing his attention away from Jacobs, "why are you doing this? You said you weren't responsible. What's going on?" He shook his head and refused to answer me. "C'mon, let Paul go. He has nothing to do with this. He isn't in charge of this situation. You are." Hostage negotiation 101, not that I was ever part of HRT, but we all went through the preliminary classes at Quantico.

He shook his head, stepping backward and dragging Paul with him. "If I let him go, someone will shoot me. I didn't get a chance to explain, and now," he used his gun hand to rub his head, "everything's on fucking crack. After you spoke to me, I wanted to come outside and talk to you. I really did." He looked at Jacobs, begging him to understand. "But before I could, this guy," he pushed Paul forward slightly, "runs in here ranting and raving. I thought we were friends, man."

"We were until I found out you used Rachel, killed Alvin, and tried to poison me."

"Paul, shut up," I snarled. Eastman was going to get himself killed, along with Oster, if he didn't shut his mouth. The moron had no idea how to handle himself in a crisis situation.

"I didn't kill Alvin," Oster insisted. "I didn't kill the other guy either." He met my eyes. "It wasn't me. I swear." A thought crossed his mind, and he began dragging Paul backward at a much faster clip.

"Oster, let Eastman go," Jacobs tried again, following pursuit at a reasonable pace, hoping to stop Oster before this situation could get any worse.

"Jason, take me instead. I'm a much more lucrative hostage. Female. Former federal agent. Constant police consultant. They won't risk my life." It wasn't necessarily true.

"Parker," Jacobs growled next to me, "shut up and get outside."

"No." This wasn't the best moment for an argument,

and Jacobs shook his head. Oster's eyes looked pitiful, but he didn't say another word as we helplessly watched him drag Paul into the elevator. Just as the doors began to close, Jacobs lifted his gun and fired three times. Each shot rang out, echoing as it impacted against the steel doors, never puncturing through the shell. "And now we've got a fucking crisis situation on our hands." I stared at the number next to the elevator, waiting to determine what floor Oster was taking Paul to, but the elevator halted suddenly between levels, making that determination impossible.

"Get outside, Parker," Jacobs growled. "You're a civilian, and my top priority is to clear out all civilians."

I rolled my eyes and holstered my gun. "Is ESU on the way?" The radio chirped, and orders for maintaining the perimeter were relayed. "Never mind," I mumbled. "They're at least on six. I'll help clear the bottom levels."

"Fine. Take the odds. I'll do evens. And then get your ass outside."

"Yes, sir." The sardonic tone was not lost on Jacobs, and he threw me an angry glare before radioing for an officer to monitor movement on the elevator and to cover all the exits. As long as they remained halted between levels, the only person in danger was Paul. I didn't like it, namely since I was supposed to be protecting him, but at least it was one guy and not a hundred.

Amazingly enough, the fire alarm actually cleared out the majority of the hotel. The fact that it was the middle of the day and most guests were out only helped matters. After telling a few people to vacate immediately, I took the stairs up another two levels to repeat the process. Why did Oster pull a gun, and what did he hope to accomplish by grabbing Paul? He was threatened. He practically admitted to that fact when Jacobs confronted him earlier. At the time, he wouldn't tell us who got to him. His only concern was that Rachel was out of harm's way.

On the fifth floor, I stopped, rocked by a thought. Oster was going after the people responsible, and Paul got in the way. Maybe if he hadn't shown up, Oster would have divulged some identities and this could have been handled appropriately. Now we were in the midst of a standoff. I glanced at the main elevator, the one Oster had used, but it was still locked down somewhere above me. He didn't have a plan. He was reacting, and now he was stuck. Desperation only led to bloodshed, and Paul Eastman clearly wasn't smart enough to hold his tongue.

"Don't get yourself killed, Paul," I said to the doors as I went back to the stairwell.

"Hands up," a police officer bellowed when I exited the lobby.

I did as I was told, resisting the urge to roll my eyes. After identifying myself, I was ushered into the FBI's tactical van. HRT and ESU were both on scene. The pissing contest was just beginning. Joy.

"Alexis Parker," an FBI agent said, reading my name off my license. He radioed for further information, taking appropriate measures to make sure I wasn't part of this insane conspiracy that had rocked the hotel and led to a few homicides. By the end of the day, there would probably be even more bodies cooling in the morgue. "OIO agent," he muttered to himself. "Fuck it. Walton wants a word with you."

"Little ol' me?" I asked innocently, knowing precisely what was about to happen. A rectal exam would be less invasive than the interrogation I would be forced to endure.

"Parker," Walton barked from the van door, "let's take a walk." I followed him outside and to the staging area he was sharing with the ESU commander. "Every time this place goes to hell, you're here. It looks like you're the commonality, so I suggest you explain before I bring you up on charges."

After explaining my joint venture with Detective Jacobs concerning Jason Oster and Paul Eastman's sudden interruption, Walton rolled his eyes. I spotted Jacobs having a similar conversation with a member of ESU. Lucky for him, no one thought he was to blame for the current hostage situation, even if those were his bullets in the elevator doors. Briefly, I wondered if firing was a breach of protocol and what IA would think of the officer involved shooting.

"I need a full workup on Eastman and Oster," Walton bellowed, turning to one of the techs. "Does anyone have a twenty on Wheeler?"

"Negative. We lost sight of him when the evacuation began. Our surveillance cameras are down too," the tech said, slamming the keyboard in the hopes of forcing it to cooperate through physical violence, but the inanimate object just beeped angrily in response. "We have no idea how many guests are unaccounted for. The desk clerk and a few of the security guards are trying to compile a list of missing personnel. As soon as we locate the hotel manager, we should have a clearer picture of how many might still be inside."

"You lost Wheeler." Smug wasn't the way to go, but I couldn't help it. "Real fine job you're doing, SAC Walton."

"You're one to talk," he snarled. "At this very moment, it appears that Jason Oster is our killer." He narrowed his eyes, stepping closer to me. "And I'm betting that Paul Eastman is helping him." The force of his words sent spittle flying from his mouth. Disgusted, I wiped my face and stepped back.

"That's not true." My words were hollow.

"Then why didn't Oster put a bullet in his head and call it a day?" He glared daggers. "It's because they're working together."

"You have no basis for thinking that," I snapped. I had no basis not to think that. Truthfully, it would have been a brilliant play. Dupe me, create some bogus standoff, escape during the hostage situation, and kill whatever silent partners might remain, namely Rodney Wheeler. Maybe it was a robbery, a way to access Wheeler's money or whatever money Frank Costan might have stashed somewhere in the hotel, and escape while everyone was working to sort through the mess and deescalate the situation before a tactical option became the only viable one. "But if that's true, they need an escape route."

"What the hell do you think demands are for?"

"Have you received any?" I retorted.

"No. We haven't been able to establish contact. As far as

we know, the elevator hasn't moved. They're still inside."

"Maybe it's a murder-suicide."

"Maybe you're their accomplice." His look grew wary. "You are working for Paul Eastman, aren't you? From what Jablonsky's told me and what has leaked out of the police department, you were instrumental in getting Eastman released from lockup and having the charges dropped."

"The charges were bullshit, and you know it. If anyone ought to be accused of collaborating with the killer, it should be you. You pulled strings to make sure Eastman remained in custody supposedly to make some grand bust, but maybe you're Wheeler's inside man. Has anyone performed an internal assessment to figure out how a killer got inside the hotel, axed one of the FBI's most wanted, and let another party be hung out in the middle of the hallway like a fucking piñata, all while the FBI was monitoring the situation? All while *you* were monitoring the situation."

"Get her out of my face," Walton ordered an agent that just joined us, "but make sure she doesn't go far. Right now, she's a prime suspect."

Biting my tongue, I inhaled sharply, letting out a few barely contained huffs. If Walton wanted to play this game, then I'd give him a much better reason to bring me up on charges, starting with assaulting a federal agent.

"Ma'am," the agent said from behind, "please, come with me." He put a gentle hand on my shoulder, and giving Walton a final death stare, I let the agent lead me back to the surveillance van for questioning.

After answering every question imaginable concerning the two murders, my role as security consultant for PDN, my current client, and Jason Oster and Rachel Romanski's connection to every party imaginable, I was left to sit quietly while techs continued to compile information on Oster and Eastman. The surveillance feed inside the hotel had been cut, and it made no sense to me how that happened.

"We can't locate the hotel manager," one of the agents reported while I drummed my fingers against the side of the chair. "We're guessing he might still be inside."

Even though they weren't talking to me, I answered anyway. "Gordon Russell is upstairs. The last time I saw him was ten minutes before the world went crazy. He was on the tenth floor." The agents turned to me. "I questioned him about the hotel remodel." They looked bewildered. "I used to do your job for god's sakes. I'm not an incompetent moron like the guy in charge of your op." One of the two men shut his eyes, stifling a chuckle, and the other walked away. "Have there been any developments?" I asked, hoping the remaining agent might offer an update.

"Not yet. Contact still hasn't been established. We're reviewing phone records now, hoping for a solid lead. We've dialed Oster's cell, assuming it's on him, but he doesn't answer. We've tried Eastman's too, but we get the same results."

"Eastman doesn't have a phone on him." I bit my lip, wondering if Jablonsky ever figured out who Paul called at the hotel before he pulled his Houdini act. "Can I see Oster's sheet for a second?" He glanced around to make sure the coast was clear before handing me the paper. I didn't recognize any of the numbers and handed it back. "Have you tried phoning inside the hotel?"

"We're on it. We've tried the main offices, front desk, conference rooms, but no answer. Like I said, as far as we know, they're still in the hotel."

"Are you planning a breach?" I asked, afraid of the response.

"We're hoping to get eyes and ears inside before we do. But we'll see what happens." His gaze shifted out of the van and at the group assembled under the makeshift tent that was being shared by ESU and HRT. The two commanders were in the midst of a disagreement, and I wasn't positive they wouldn't come to blows over it. With any luck, Walton would try to take charge of both teams and get his ass knocked out.

"Nice pissing match. A word of advice, have a few snipers set up in the surrounding area. They can fire some warning shots when the PD and FBI come to blows."

"The police need to back off," he muttered. "This is our investigation."

"Really?" Honey, not vinegar, I reminded myself, faking interest and turning on the charm. "How long have you been monitoring Jason Oster?"

"We haven't." He paused.

"So who have you been monitoring?" I knew the answer, but it never hurt to have some additional verification.

"Senator Wheeler." His eyes shifted uncomfortably, and he stepped back.

"Do you know if Wheeler's still inside the hotel?"

"We lost track," he stepped out of the van, seconds away from leaving me to die of boredom.

"So how exactly does that make this situation FBI jurisdiction?" Yes, I used to be an agent, but there were too many cooks in the kitchen for this to have a positive resolution. One team needed to back off.

THIRTY-SEVEN

After alienating the one agent who actually appreciated my sense of humor, I decided to risk my personal freedom by sneaking out of the surveillance van. It was funny since the techs inside didn't give a shit where I went or what I was doing, and Walton didn't bother to confiscate my weapon, P.I. license, or any personal property. Obviously, he was ticked off that I was calling him out on his shit, but he had much bigger fish to fry. I wasn't even a blip on his radar.

"Jacobs," I hissed, coming up behind him and leading him to a secluded corner where only a few LEOs were milling about, "what the hell is going on?"

"The shit's hitting the fan," he looked at the group under the tent, "and it's flying every which way." He sighed deeply. "As far as I can tell, they're working on a plan. The bottom levels have been swept. Everything below the stopped elevator has been cleared."

"Why stop there?" I asked. "Have the doors been opened?"

"We don't know." ESU ventured as high as seven and reported the outer elevator doors appeared to be forced open. The adjacent elevator is halted on ten, and the

override code's been entered. So we can't bring it down."
He pressed his lips together. "I shouldn't be telling you any
of this."

"Probably not," I admitted, "but lucky for you, I'm
intimately aware of the building's layout. And since the FBI
is currently considering me a prime suspect, I'm willing to
share my infinite knowledge." I offered a smile. "What else
shouldn't you be telling me?"

"Gordon Russell is probably still inside. We've phoned
his office, and someone picked up the receiver but hung it
up. And now we can't get an answer."

"So you think they're inside his office?"

"Someone is." His gaze shifted to the police
department's emergency services unit that relocated to
their own staging area, away from the FBI's hostage rescue
team. "Have you picked a side?"

"Maybe I should flip a coin. Former federal agent and
police consultant are both on my résumé, and it doesn't
look like Switzerland is a current option." I chuckled. "Do
you promise not to hold me responsible for this shit?"

"Why would I?"

"Good enough for me." I headed in the direction of ESU.
Not waiting for Detective Jacobs to make the proper
introductions, I introduced myself. Diving into the
blueprints spread across the table, I told the commander
everything that I knew of the hotel, the weaknesses in the
security, the measures in place, and every tidbit of
information I had on elevator operation, courtesy of my
stint with PDN and my recent improvements at Martin
Technologies.

"Parker," Commander Torre let my name play across his
lips, "where have I heard that name before?"

"It's common enough." I shrugged.

"She's worked with major crimes off and on," Jacobs
piped up. "Regardless of her private sector career and
attitude, she knows her shit." He tossed a faint smile in my
direction. "Her current client was taken hostage by Oster."

"All right," Torre came to a decision and spread out the
building schematics and called his team over, "we need to
block off all exits and entrances. The only way out has to be

through the front door in the main lobby. We're working under the assumption it is a single hostile acting alone, but our hostage taker is hotel security. It's possible some of the unaccounted for employees are working with him or are hostages. We have no way of knowing." He handed the marker to me. "This is Parker. She reviewed building security, and she's going to tell us where to position ourselves." He turned to me. "It's your show."

"Okay," I began circling side exits, employee-only access points, and drew into question the subbasement with tunnel access, "these are your points of entry. Anything above the third floor isn't a viable option for escape since there are no practical exterior means of exiting. Someone needs to close off the below ground perimeter. As you might have heard, in the last two weeks, it was used to hide a body. Obviously, that means the doors have been breached. If the chatter from the FBI is believable, the hostage taker might also be responsible for that man's death which means he knows precisely how to access the subbasement and get out undetected."

"I want two guys inside those tunnels, and I mean yesterday," Torre snapped, and part of his team disappeared. "Anything else?"

"That's everything on the building." I stepped backward. "I'm sure Detective Jacobs has offered his insight on the hostile inside."

"All right, stay close in case we need you," Torre mumbled, immediately returning to devising a play as another one of his team members began running through a possible upper level breach using roof access and rappelling gear.

Jacobs nodded his thanks, and I wandered through the mess of police and FBI personnel, contemplating the reason for Oster's behavior. He didn't seem unstable. He didn't seem crazy. And he sure as hell didn't seem like a killer, let alone someone who would ever think taking a hostage was a good idea. The only strike against him was the fact he was desperate. Rachel's threats and involvement made him desperate, and desperate led to horrible decisions. The fact that Paul appeared and added insult to injury only exacerbated the situation.

Dialing Detective O'Connell, I hoped he'd be at the precinct. On the third ring to his desk phone, he answered. "I need to speak to Rachel Romanski," I said, not bothering with a greeting.

"Alex, what's going on?" Nick asked. "Jablonsky showed up maybe an hour ago, asking for a number lookup. And we keep getting reports on the current hostage situation."

"Whose number is it?" I asked, hoping for an answer. Paul dialed someone at the hotel and then took off. Whoever he called had something to do with his appearance, and I didn't think he phoned Oster.

"It was a hotel extension for the manager's office," Nick said. "Hang on, Jablonsky wants to talk to you."

"Alex?" Mark asked, sounding like a nervous father.

"I'm okay. Walton might arrest me in the near future, but that's beside the point. Oster and I had a brief chat before this happened. He needed some assurance Rachel was safe. She knows more than she's letting on. We need her to talk if there's any hope of getting everyone out of this mess alive."

"Yeah, I know. A few detectives are sorting through the details as we speak."

"What about the identity of the man who threatened her? When Jacobs and I left, she was working with a sketch artist."

"They're working on an I.D. now. I'll let you know what I hear. Be careful, and mind your own business."

"Too late."

Something gnawed at my thought process. Why did Eastman phone the manager's office? Was he planning on reporting Jason Oster to his boss for allegedly murdering Alvin Hodge? That seemed stupid, and it wouldn't explain why Paul rushed to the hotel. Before I could continue musing, Mark cleared his throat.

"Were you with Eastman at all this morning, Alex?"

"No. I thought you were watching him."

"Yeah, but we decided he didn't need around-the-clock surveillance. I wasn't with him the entire time."

"Do you think he made contact with someone using the

motel phone? Can you get the phone records from his room?"

"I'm on it." And we disconnected.

Maybe Paul was part of this. Maybe Walton was right, and Paul and Jason planned this out. Between the two of them, they probably would have been able to discover the location for Frank Costan's funds and maybe even how to manipulate Rodney Wheeler into assisting them. And since Paul and Jason both worked in a security capacity at the hotel, officially and unofficially, they might know exactly how to escape.

I took a seat on the hood of a police car and buried my head in my hands. If I screwed up again, I would quit my day job and mooch off of Martin for the rest of my life. Without instincts, this job was impossible.

Why did Paul Eastman phone Gordon Russell's office, and why was he inside the hotel? I didn't have answers, but recalling the exchange between Oster and Eastman before the elevator doors closed, I still couldn't believe Paul was working with Jason. He wasn't that good of an actor. I'd called him out on his lies and his embellishments from the moment we met. He honestly believed Jason was responsible.

"Does anyone have a workup on Alvin Hodge?" I asked, wandering back into the throng of LEOs. Practically no one paid a bit of attention to me. A bullhorn would have been nice. After failing to locate Jacobs, I spotted Commander Torre. "Eastman, the hostage, phoned someone in the manager's office twenty minutes before showing up at the hotel to confront Jason Oster."

"How do you know that?" he asked, pulling the earpiece out of his ear so he could concentrate on our conversation without additional voices inside his head.

"Because I had a friend keeping an eye on Eastman, and before he slipped away, he borrowed a phone."

"And how is this helpful?"

A thought was formulating in my brain, and I latched onto the wisps before they could disintegrate. "I don't know yet. But he accused Oster of killing Alvin Hodge."

"Who the fuck is Alvin Hodge?" Torre was a crisis

solver, not an investigator. "Someone get me information on Alvin Hodge. Now." Before he could focus any of that anger or rage on me, I took a page out of Eastman's book and performed my own disappearing act.

For the life of me, I couldn't remember exactly what Paul was thinking the day before. He seemed happy enough just sitting in the car while we monitored Rachel's movements. Sure, we discussed Oster's possible involvement, and it seemed fairly obvious he was involved. But Rachel went to him for protection and comfort. Normally, people had slightly better instincts than canoodling with their ex-husband's killer, unless they were in cahoots.

Rachel thought Paul was working with the man that threatened her, and Paul thought Jason was behind it. Where were they getting these ideas? Despite the fact I had considered each of them a suspect for at least one of the murders, it was becoming painfully apparent that another party was involved. Goddammit, why didn't Oster give us a name when we questioned him?

Retrieving my phone and pulling out a piece of paper, I went back to the start of my initial suspect list from the poisoning – Paul Eastman's social media pages. It only took a few moments before I found a page for Rachel Romanski. Apparently, Jason Oster was the only one smart enough to avoid the security threats the internet posed. Scanning the dozens of friend pages, I hoped to find some commonalities. There were two dozen matching names, all of which worked at the hotel. Scribbling all of the relevant names on to the paper, I was just about to go in search of the employee manifest when Torre bellowed my name. That couldn't be good.

Appearing next to him, I noted the HRT men were positioned nearby. Apparently the two crisis resolution teams had reached an understanding, or they wanted me to referee the upcoming fight. SAC Walton was ten feet away. He looked grim but nodded at me. Resisting the urge to turn around to determine if someone important was behind me, like a five-star general or the President of the United States, I returned the nod.

"Contact has been established," Torre said, turning so he could face me as well as his men. "We have trained negotiators on standby, as does the FBI, but he refuses to talk to any of them." He shifted his gaze to the phone, wired to computers and recording devices. "He's waiting for your call."

"Me?"

"Yes, you," Walton said, defeat etching his words. "I've skimmed your files. Negotiation isn't your forte." Which was obviously true. When forced to speak to kidnappers, I threatened to hunt them down and kill them, which was frowned upon by tried and true negotiation tactics with the main goal of deescalating a tense situation and finding a positive, blood-free resolution. "So be agreeable, buy time, and get as much information on the situation as you can."

"I can't." I shook my head. "I'm a fucking P.I., and I'm pretty sure that if I screw up and get my client killed, that's gonna come back to bite me in the ass."

"Just make the call and see if you can get a list of demands or determine if he's working alone and how many people are in danger." Torre lifted the handset and handed it to me. "I'll be here every step of the way."

Shifting my gaze around the group, I noticed one obvious asset was missing. "Where's Jacobs? We've been working this from the beginning. He needs to be here."

One of the FBI agents disappeared, and a few seconds later, the two men returned. Jacobs looked annoyed, and I saw him stow his phone. He was still working on leads, just like me. Hopefully, one of us would realize something after my impending phone call with Oster.

"Here goes nothing," I muttered, taking the phone while Torre dialed the number.

THIRTY-EIGHT

"Were you telling the truth earlier?" Jason asked, his words guarded.

"Everything I've said to you has been the truth or what I believe to be true. But they aren't always the same thing." Okay, so non-answers seemed to be part of negotiation tactics based upon the round of nods I was getting for my response.

"Are they listening to this conversation?" Jason asked. Even though I was holding the handset, the conversation was being broadcast over numerous receivers.

"Yes." I heard him exhale. "Jason, what are you hoping to accomplish? What do you want?" Torre scribbled the word demands on a sheet of paper and handed me the pen to write out whatever Oster might say next.

"You don't have a damn clue." He slammed the receiver down.

"Told you I wasn't meant for negotiation," I muttered, dropping the pen on the paper. "So what do we do now?"

"We'll wait ten minutes and see if he calls back," Walton said, stepping closer and glancing uncertainly at Torre. "If he doesn't, you'll phone him again."

"He has three chances to answer, and then we're set to

move in," Torre added, and Walton nodded.

Something about the current dilemma brought the two sides closer together. Maybe they should send me to negotiate peace talks in the Middle East since clearly I was an expert, except when it came to getting the actual party to speak to me.

"Dammit, the talking heads are here," Walton muttered. Police officers set up a perimeter and tried to keep the press back, but reporters were parasites that appeared unfettered by being told no. "I'll go issue an official statement. Maybe that will hold them off a little while longer." He grimaced, disappearing into the crowd.

Since I had ten minutes to kill, I pulled Jacobs aside to see if he made any progress on identifying whoever got to Oster. Based on our earlier conversation, someone threatened Oster, and it made sense for him to take action to stop it, especially now that things were so blatantly being blown out of proportion. But Jacobs didn't come up with anything solid either. After sharing my information on the common friends Rachel and Paul had and my suspicions that someone else was feeding them misinformation, Jacobs phoned the IT department to do a thorough internet search for any activity that overlapped.

"What did Oster mean when he asked if you told him the truth?" Jacobs asked while more of our crisis response group disappeared to handle the growing fleet of media that was salivating at the possibility of imminent bloodshed.

"I don't know. After you walked out, he asked about Rachel. Maybe he thought I was lying about her being at the precinct."

"Or maybe he was asking if you were a more important hostage than Eastman." It was the last thing Oster said before disappearing inside the elevator, and it made sense to a certain degree. Obviously, the look in my eye must have been disconcerting, perhaps reckless, because Jacobs stepped closer and studied me carefully. "You're not a part of this. No one would authorize an exchange like that. Don't even think about it."

"No, they wouldn't."

I bit my lip as my mind ran through the possibilities. There had to be some way of getting Paul out, safe and sound. That was my job, wasn't it? Damn, I vowed against bodyguard work, and this was the thanks I get for reneging on my own word. Fuck me.

I checked the time and scribbled some basic instructions on the sheet of paper, ripping it off and folding it before Jacobs could read what I wrote. Then I picked up the phone. Seven minutes, not ten like Torre insisted, but opportunity was knocking. The area was clear of official personnel, and it was my only chance to have a word with Oster without being overheard.

Jacobs watched uneasily, grabbing my wrist before I hit the last digit. "What are you doing?"

"We need answers, and he won't give them to me with a dozen cops listening."

Jacobs released my hand, nodding, and we waited for Oster to answer. On the second ring, he picked up, not surprised to be receiving a call back. He wasn't stupid, despite his current actions. Something else was happening, and I still didn't know what it was.

"I'm alone," I clarified before he could ask. "What were you going to tell us earlier? Who were you going to give us? Rachel's safe. I promise you that."

"I wasn't going to tell you anything earlier." It sounded like a bald-faced lie, but I didn't protest. "Thank you for keeping your word."

"Jason, who else is with you? Is it just Paul?"

"No, there are others." Other hostages or accomplices?

"Is everyone okay?"

"For now."

"You know the police plan to breach if you don't cooperate. They'll probably succumb to any demands you may have, but if you continue to stonewall, it won't be pretty." Jacobs glared at my words, but I wanted the direness of the situation to sink in for Oster. "Please tell me what you want?"

"You won't believe it."

"Try me," I begged.

"I'll only discuss this in person. Face-to-face with you

and no one else." He hung up. He wasn't willing to bend. How could we force him to play a game when he refused to accept the rules? Leaning my head back, I shut my eyes, thinking through my options. We were almost out of time, and from Oster's tone, he wouldn't change his mind.

"Parker," Jacobs said my name, and I opened my eyes and focused on him, "they're professionals. They'll find the safest method possible with the least amount of casualties. You tried. Frankly, you've done more than what most people in your situation would do."

"Most people don't find themselves in these situations." An abandoned handheld police radio sat on the table next to the phone I just used. "Channel four," I said, picking up the radio and tucking it into my jacket pocket. I handed the sheet of paper with instructions on sending a tactical team through the subbasement to breach quietly, working their way up the building once the power was cut. Then I checked that my cell phone was in my pants pocket, and my gun was in my shoulder holster. This plan might get me shot before I even made it inside.

"What?" Jacobs asked, confused.

Without answering, I sprinted across the expanse from the police barricade to the hotel. Jacobs screamed my name, and a dozen police and FBI agents turned, some attempting to thwart my entrance. But since they weren't expecting someone to burst into the hotel, the positions they occupied behind sawhorses and other temporary barricades allowed for a few extra seconds that I needed to clear the front door and enter the lobby. Once inside enemy territory, they couldn't risk a breach to get me out. Now I was either a hostage or a hostile. Neither title was particularly pleasing.

"You've lost your fucking mind," I mumbled to myself, scanning the abandoned lobby. It was still empty. Should I go straight to Russell's office and hope to find Oster? Before I could move an inch, voices came over the radio.

"Parker, respond."

"Hi," I said, holding the radio in my left and my gun in my right. "Looks like you might have to reconsider that breach."

"Get your ass out here. Now," Torre growled.

"Sorry, I can't do that." I heard a few random bursts of static as I began checking the lobby for potential enemies hiding among lots of rooms and plenty of locked doors. The security cameras weren't helpful since their operational status was questionable.

"Parker," Walton must have won the arm wrestling match in order to have obtained the radio from Torre, "since you're inside, we're gonna use you."

"Great." I opened the door to the security office, stepping inside. The monitors were off. The cameras were disabled, and I remembered Oster was outside the security office when he confronted Eastman. He must have switched off the cameras and the system before Paul arrived, which meant whatever he was planning had nothing to do with Paul. "Tell me what to do."

"Clear the building again, level by level. We'll send back-up like you requested, but they'll stay back. No one will know they are there. If you encounter unfriendlies, do not engage unless absolutely necessary. We are working under the assumption Oster is our only suspect with numerous hostages. Get us some numbers and locations for a full-scale breach."

"Affirmative," I replied, leaving the security office and heading for the stairs.

"We're cutting building power. It'll shut down the elevators, leaving the stairs as the only viable means between levels. It should decrease enemy mobility, so no one will be able to sneak up behind you. It'll also disable the security system, which means even if Oster tries to access it, he won't be able to use it to spot us."

"Okay. I'll radio when I know something. Until then, going silent."

I lowered the volume on the radio, tucked it securely back into my pocket and pulled out my phone to dial Jason. Thankfully, I had his number saved, but he didn't pick up. This was seriously screwing with my plan to have a meet and greet.

I continued working my way through the hotel slowly, level by level. The entire situation was reminiscent of the dozens of drills PDN ran. I was really starting to hate this hotel. The hallways were eerie, although no sign of life was better than encountering men with guns or hostages. It was like being in the wild with only two options, predator and prey. Those labels weren't any better than hostage or hostile, but they meant the same.

On the fourth floor, my phone vibrated. Glancing at the I.D., I answered, hoping Mark had a solid lead from earlier. "What did you find?" I asked, hoping for a solution. If he had one, I could still stroll out the front door with my hands in the air and probably not get shot. Hopefully.

"You made the news." His voice was low, not surprised but slightly amazed. "Care to explain what the hell you're doing inside the hotel in the middle of a crisis situation?"

"Negotiating." Obviously, if I was on the phone, there was no imminent danger. "Jason Oster wanted to chat in person. I'm working my way through the building now, so I need to cut the small talk. Any leverage or helpful information could go a long way."

"Paul phoned the hotel manager's office last night from his motel. He received a call from the same number early this morning, and that's the number he phoned again from my cell. A few computer specialists are attempting to access the hotel's security system remotely since the information is stored on two separate servers, one on-site and one off. If not, maybe we can get access to the employee schedule to figure out who was in Russell's office at the time the calls were placed. Since they didn't occur during normal business hours, we phoned Russell's wife to ask if he was home last night, and she said he didn't go to work until eight this morning. The call came in at 5:47 a.m., so it wasn't Russell."

"Where was Wheeler at the time?" I asked, finding a strategically good place in an alcove at the end of the hallway, just in case.

"According to his tail, in his room." He paused slightly to check the information for my unasked question. "One of the executive suites on the upper level."

"Jason was with Rachel at his apartment," I said more to myself than Mark. "Did Paul call anyone else from the motel prior to yesterday?"

"Nope. Phone records are clean. Be careful, Parker. You aren't HRT."

"No, but they're outside. They didn't give me a choice. A breach was imminent, and they planned to go in blind."

"Jesus," he sighed, "you are insane. Why the hell are you trying to protect Paul when he eluded me and got himself into this mess? He looks dirty as shit."

"That doesn't matter. I have to go. If you find something useful, let me know."

Disconnecting, I continued my sweep until the seventh floor. The main elevator was stopped there, and the door was left open. A chair was wedged between the doors to prevent it from leaving this level. The adjacent elevator appeared intact, and I continued to check for signs of life.

Continuing to the stairwell, I tried to open the door, but it was locked. After radioing in the information, I turned my face away and broke the glass with my elbow. The window was small and rather high, but looking down, I saw a makeshift barricade shoved against the door. How exactly did Jason Oster find the time or strength to move a couch from one of the suites to the seventh floor landing of the stairwell? Either he had an accomplice, or multiple hostages moved the furniture while being held at gunpoint. Neither scenario was ideal, and I provided a follow-up over the comms.

"Parker, return to the lobby. You can't go any higher," Walton instructed. "We'll send up the team."

"No." I went back to the elevator bank. Maybe I could take the elevator instead. "Can you flip the power back on?" I asked.

"Parker." Walton was prepared to argue.

"C'mon, I've come all this way. You can either do that or try phoning Oster again and tell him to meet me on the seventh floor."

"We've tried. Oster doesn't answer." The radio emitted some static. "Hold on. We'll get power restored."

The entire building let out a whining hum as the power came back on, and I moved the chair out of the way, stepping inside the elevator. Punching eight, I waited, but the doors didn't close. The button didn't illuminate, and I let out an annoyed snarl. Having spent a substantial amount of time riding elevators recently, I used all the tricks of the trade, but it was DOA. Somehow, Oster must have disabled it.

I went to the second elevator and pressed the call button, but it didn't work either. Informing Walton to cut the power again, I went back to the first disabled elevator and stood on the chair to access the hatch in the ceiling. I hated heights and dark, narrow spaces, but if this was anything like the elevator system at MT, I should be able to get on top of the elevator and get the doors opened for the level above.

Carefully pulling myself on top of the elevator, I felt my muscles pull and strain. Thankfully, my ribs didn't pop. With any luck, they were fully healed and wouldn't break under the physical exertion I was about to subject them to. It had been almost two months since I did any strength training, and it showed as I dug my fingers between the doors, yanking and clawing. Whenever I got out of this mess, I would have to go back to the gym for some indoor rock climbing.

"Come on, open, sesame," I hissed, finally finding purchase and managing to force the outer doors open. "Now don't close on me." I hissed, grabbing the ledge and hoisting myself slowly up. Who knew what was waiting on level eight, but so far, we were off to a rocky start.

THIRTY-NINE

I pressed my back against the wall, using whatever cover position I could find. My gun was poised, and my finger hovered above the trigger. Taking a breath, I cautiously peered down the corridor. The hallway appeared as desolate as the previous seven levels, and I stepped out of the elevator alcove.

This was unchecked territory, and I began a sweep for possible guests, gunmen, and Jason. When nothing turned up, I radioed an all clear and told Walton I'd work on removing the barricade in the stairwell. Before continuing my trek upward, I took the stairs down to seven and struggled to push the heavy couch out of the way. The thing weighed a ton, and I realized it was a sleeper sofa from one of the suites. It definitely took two people, if not more, to move the furniture to its current position. Pushing my back into it, I managed to scoot the couch far enough to allow one door to be opened from level seven. My muscles cramped and ached, but at least there was a viable escape route.

Opening the door to eight, I performed a quick visual sweep and continued to nine. Russell's office was on ten, and my stress level began to skyrocket. I was close. The air felt electric, and swallowing, I forced myself to focus. Halfway through level nine, I heard the stairwell door clang closed. Spinning, I aimed at the sound and met the business end of Jason Oster's handgun.

"Put your gun down," Oster insisted.

"Why don't we both lower our guns?" I asked, wondering why he would think I would obey when he had no additional leverage. As if reading my mind, a man I didn't recognize emerged onto the floor, dragging Paul Eastman with him. Paul was being held at gunpoint, and I eased my finger slowly off the trigger. "You wanted to negotiate in person," I said, holding up my left hand and slowly reholstering my handgun. "But you definitely didn't make it easy to get here."

"I needed to make sure you were alone," Oster said, but his words sounded rehearsed.

"You're not." Pointing out the obvious was an innate talent.

"No," his eyes bore into me as if trying to convey something, "I didn't have a choice."

"Alex, I'm so sorry," Paul muttered, and the guy clocked him with his gun hand. Eastman stumbled into the wall and wiped at his bloody brow.

"Let him go. You can keep me instead," I offered, wishing there was a way to broadcast this conversation to the team who was probably on the fourth or fifth floor by now.

"Take her gun and search her," Oster instructed, and the man shoved Paul toward me.

"Alex," Paul whispered, reaching inside my jacket and removing my nine millimeter, "it's not Jason." The man who was holding him at gunpoint was aiming at the back of Paul's head and barking at him to drop my gun and kick it toward him. Paul complied and then proceeded to frisk me. "He doesn't have a choice."

"What?" I whispered as Paul removed the police radio from my pocket and held it up. The man stepped forward and grabbed it while Jason remained at the far end of the hallway. It looked like he wanted to be anywhere but here.

"Is that it?" the man asked.

"She doesn't have any other weapons," Paul replied, leaving my cell phone in my pocket. Either he was sloppy, or he was hoping we could phone-a-friend.

"She better not," the man snarled. "Or you'll both be dead."

"So can we get back to the topic at hand? Or should we start with some introductions?" I asked, focusing on Oster. He was in charge. "You said we could discuss demands in person."

"Okay, first, I want safe passage and access to my safe deposit box. After my trip to the bank, I want a car waiting outside with the engine running, a full tank of gas, and absolutely no GPS or lowjack installed. No one will follow me or track me. When I'm clear, I'll release Paul at some truck stop."

"Anything else?"

"That's it," Jason said, ignoring his accomplice.

"All right, I'm sure we can make that happen." I looked at the radio that Mr. Accomplice was holding. "What are you willing to give up as a show of good faith?" I glanced at Paul. "Maybe release a hostage or let me make sure no one else is being held against their will."

"I can't lose my only leverage," Jason insisted, and he turned his head to the side to make sure no one was coming up from behind him. At that moment, I spotted the wire from an earpiece running down his neck and to his collar. Either someone else was giving orders, or he had more people helping than the single guy keeping a gun trained on Paul. "Go on," he jerked his head at the stairwell, "go tell them what I want. We'll hang on to the radio, and you can use it to give me an answer."

"Okay." I shot a concerned look at Paul. "I'll get you out of this. I promise." He nodded, wiping at the blood running down his face. Stepping forward, I doubted I'd get my weapon back, and I didn't want to ask. "You'll hear from me soon," I assured Jason, heading toward the stairwell.

He didn't move, but I felt two guns trained on me. Not being suicidal, there wasn't a chance in hell I'd try something, and I walked slowly past Paul and Jason's assistant. Just as I passed Jason, opening the stairwell door, my phone buzzed. Hoping they didn't hear the faint vibration, I continued at the same pace.

"What's that?" the man asked, glowering at Paul.

Jason grabbed my elbow and yanked me backward, locating my phone immediately. He ripped it out of my pocket, glanced at the caller I.D., dropped it to the floor, and smashed it with his foot.

"Wrong number?" I asked, afraid of what was to follow.

He remained silent, motionless before me, and after what felt like an eternity, he blinked. "You can't be trusted, so we're going upstairs."

I heard the sound of flesh hitting flesh, and Paul yelped. I squeezed my eyes closed, choreographing an attack strategy in my mind, but no matter what I did, I couldn't guarantee Paul wouldn't be killed before I could intervene.

"Let me go outside. I can get you what you want," I said, using the authoritarian tone from my federal agent days. "It's the only chance you have of walking out of this alive."

"Upstairs," Oster replied, and he shoved me toward the staircase. "I'm sorry about this."

Not as sorry as you're gonna be, I thought as I slowly took the steps, scanning the area for any sign of life. I stopped at the doorway to level ten and turned. Paul was being shoved up the steps by the unnamed man. The brutality seemed unnecessary, perhaps even a tad personal, and I wondered if Paul knew who he was. Oster pressed his lips together and nodded at the door.

"Fine," I mumbled, "it's your show. For the record, the only reason I came inside was to negotiate. When I don't return in a timely fashion, they will storm this place and resolve matters using extreme prejudice. I don't want to see that happen." I blew out a slow breath, contemplating the possibility of persuading Oster to reconsider. "Be smart about this, Jason."

"Inside," the other man barked, coming to stand a few feet away on the landing.

"Oh, I'm sorry," I turned toward him, "are you in charge? Because if that's the case, I'm only authorized to deal with whoever's in charge."

"Inside," Oster repeated, and this time he grabbed the

door handle out of my grip and shoved me forward.

This level seemed just as lifeless as the others. Despite the fact I was here a few hours ago to speak with Gordon Russell, it had an eerie quality. Maybe it was the lack of electricity and the dim lighting that made it a bit spooky.

Jason pressed the gun barrel into my back and put his free hand on my shoulder, leading me down the hallway to the conference room where we had been sequestered the afternoon Alvin Hodge was found dead. Three people were inside, but Gordon Russell was the only one I recognized. Why didn't any of them try to escape when there were no visual hostiles guarding them? Maybe they were threatened and scared, but still, the chance of survival was much greater if you weren't hanging around in a conference room.

"Take a seat," Oster commanded, and I sat. He took a seat across from me, near the door, and Paul took a seat at the far end of the table. Oster's accomplice remained stationed in front of the conference room door. He pressed his lips together. "Is the FBI outside?"

"Yes." Why was he asking that question?

"Do they know who is still inside this hotel?" he asked, his eyes scanning the room.

"I'm not working with the FBI. I have no idea what they know." It was partially true. "Frankly, it doesn't make much of a difference. They have a rulebook, and they will breach. Extreme prejudice. Bang." I tilted my head. "Unless I'm outside in the next ten minutes, they're coming in."

"Call them off," the man at the door said, stepping forward and dropping the radio on the table. I didn't even acknowledge him.

"Are you in charge, Jason?" I asked, wondering who this guy was who seemed to be calling the shots. Assuming there was some truth to Paul's warning, someone would do something to tip me off. With any luck, a fight would break out amongst the enemy, and I could use it to my advantage. "Because if you are, it's your decision what happens to me and everyone else here."

"Call them off," the man said again, and I looked up at

him.

"It doesn't work that way. I leave, or they come in. That's the only way the tactical assault is stopped."

"Fine," Jason hissed. "Tell them not to breach. Senator Wheeler is still inside, and he's the first one we'll kill if they come within a hundred feet of the building."

"First of all, I didn't bring my measuring tape, but I'd guess they are already within a hundred feet of the building. Second, Wheeler isn't senator anymore, so why would they give a shit?"

"Because he's still under protection by the federal government," Oster declared, "and they wouldn't risk his life. Too much bad publicity."

"You're wrong." I made a show of surveying the room. "Plus, I don't see Wheeler anywhere. How do I know you aren't making it up to save your skin?"

"Get up," Oster growled, but I didn't budge. "Move," he bellowed, coming around the table and grabbing my arm and dragging me out of the room.

This put me in proximity for some close quarters maneuvers, and I moved swiftly, striking and leaving him dazed in order to grab his gun. Just as I wrestled it from his hands and broke free from his grip, the gun aimed at his chest, a door opened behind me, and the metallic sound of a gun being cocked reverberated in the empty area.

"I'll shoot him," I warned, not turning around. "Oster, call off your dogs, or you won't live to see tomorrow."

"I don't care if you shoot him," a voice said from behind, and then the gun went off.

The look of shock and pain registered on Oster's face, and he clutched at his stomach as he tumbled to the ground. Not lowering the weapon, I turned to face the shooter and fired. It clicked ineffectually. That didn't work out the way I hoped. Rodney Wheeler stood with his gun pointed at my chest. And the man from the other room came up from behind, leaving me no choice but to surrender.

"I take it you're the great and powerful Oz?" Glaring, I wasn't surprised that Wheeler was in charge. We suspected him all along. But why was Oster doing his bidding? Why was Jason holding an unloaded weapon? And what additional leverage did Wheeler have on him? Rachel was safe and sound.

He smiled maliciously. "Indeed." He stuck his hand out, and his partner handed him the confiscated weapon. "Drag him into the other room. We don't need him making a mess in the hallway."

"He'll die without medical treatment."

"And you were planning to shoot him." He shrugged. "Aren't you fickle?"

Paul was inside the conference room, and PDN required first responder training for their employees in the event of an emergency. With any luck, he could buy Jason some time.

"Well, at least now I know who's in charge. Do you want to give me your list of demands to pass along to the appropriate parties? Everyone can still walk away from this."

He laughed, an uncontrollable, manic sound. "Why should I worry? I'm untouchable."

"That's not true. They could spin it. You'd be an accidental casualty. Hell, the government lies. You were in Congress, so I'm sure you're well aware of that fact. We could put a lovely PR spin, make you a true patriot. You died heroically while attempting to save the lives of countless hostages."

"It's scary how accurate your depiction is," Wheeler commented, the gun never faltering. "Who do you work for?"

"I'm a P.I. I work for myself."

"Don't screw with me. They wouldn't let some P.I. run rampant into this building. What are you? DHS? FBI? You're not police. They might be cynical and jaded but not to the extent of expertly weaving a line like that."

I smiled like the cat that swallowed the canary. He expected answers, obedience, and maybe even fear. But at the moment, he didn't know who I was, how much the authorities outside knew of the situation, or if they were waiting for my reappearance. He couldn't touch me, not yet. Not until he had some answers, and I was good at this game. But there was no telling how long it might take, and Jason Oster didn't have much time. It was imperative that I work quickly.

"Want to share your list of demands?" I asked, not wavering or dropping the knowing smile.

FORTY

"Fine," Wheeler shrugged, "we'll do this a different way, Ms. Parker." His eyes flicked to the conference room. "Oh, I'm not as clueless as you'd like me to be. Mr. Oster has told me plenty about you, your work with PDN, your job with Paul Eastman, but frankly, I don't buy it." He jerked his head at the open door to Gordon Russell's office. "After you."

Slowly, I entered the room. It was empty, but from the tenth story window, there was a lovely view of the barricades and tents set up outside. He must have been watching the entire time.

"What do you want?" I tried again.

"I've had a tail for the last few months. My personal security guard noticed almost immediately, despite the fact the Secret Service denied it. Why is the FBI monitoring me?"

"I don't know. Perhaps you're suspected of doing something illegal." I glanced at the gun. "Yeah, I'm gonna go with that."

He snorted. "I'm guessing you're FBI. Probably undercover. That's why you worked for PDN, why you supposedly took some gig to protect Eastman, and how you were authorized to burst through the lobby doors and make it look unplanned, even heroic. I didn't realize they had female negotiators. Most tactical units are men, at least that's what my personal security looked like. Is that why they picked you?"

"Well, you were a congressman. Flip on any news station, there is always a sex scandal, so it makes sense why most female agents would want to avoid you." This was wasting time, but I hoped he'd get tired of aiming at me so I could subdue him.

"How much do they know about my business ventures and affiliates?" His voice went deadly. He was done playing, but I remained silent. "Answer me, or I'll start killing hostages." He picked up a radio from atop his desk and spoke a few words. The next thing I knew, Paul was dragged inside by the same goon from earlier. His shirt and hands were stained in blood, and I didn't know if it was his or Jason's. "Last chance."

"Please," Paul begged, his breath coming in panicked gasps.

Shit. "Don't." I couldn't play chicken with someone else's life. "They were tracking Frank Costan and any connection the two of you may have had. His body was discovered below the hotel." I sidestepped, attempting to possibly shield Paul from any incoming projectile. "I bet you killed Costan and paid some people to help you dispose of the body."

"Very good." He nodded to the goon, and Paul was dragged out of the room with much protest and pleading. "Now, I know you won't do anything to jeopardize anyone else's safety. So I want you to get me the hell out of here."

"I can't do that. You took my radio. I have no means of communicating with the outside world. They will breach, and it will be bloody."

"You will get me out of here," he repeated. No wasn't an option. He stepped closer and pulled me to the desk. "Call them," he insisted, pressing the speaker button on the phone. "And if you try anything, Oster's the first person I kill, that is if he isn't already dead. Then Eastman, and I'll just continue down the line, but you'll be the last." I reached out to dial Jacobs, knowing he would transfer the call. "Don't try anything."

"I wouldn't think of it," I mumbled.

The phone rang four times before it was answered. I stepped closer to the window, wondering if I could see the tactical team below. But the makeshift tent blocked everyone from visual range. The power was out, and despite the dozens of news vans I could see hovering at the line, probably broadcasting this breaking news story, at least Wheeler and his pals were in the dark. Unfortunately, so was I.

"Parker," it sounded like Torre, but he didn't identify himself and I didn't ask, "what's the situation?"

"Multiple hostages," I spoke, watching Wheeler. "I'm working on the demands. But safe passage is at the top of the list. We need transportation out of here."

"The same method you were told earlier," Wheeler hissed, and I realized he must have been the voice in Oster's earpiece.

"A car, full tank of gas, no lowjack or GPS system," I repeated. "Did you still want to make that trip to the bank?" I asked, loudly enough that my voice was heard over the speaker. I suspected Wheeler's was too, but Torre was a professional and wouldn't let it slip unless it served a tactical advantage.

Wheeler cut the line and glared. "I told you not to try anything." His face contorted. "I'll have to prove to you I'm not playing." He nodded to the man outside the open office door, and a single shot was fired inside the conference room.

Oh god. I closed my eyes. "You son-of-a-bitch," I eked out. "Just tell me what you fucking want."

"Tell them to leave the car parked two blocks away." He gave me an address. "And have them pull back. No one within a hundred feet of the hotel." He smirked. "I appreciate the planning and work that you put in which exploited the weakness of the subbasement and tunnels. I wouldn't have discovered it otherwise."

I lunged, but he took a step back and fired, narrowly

missing me. I froze. "You make a single move on me, and Sven will kill someone else. Do we understand one another?" At the sound of his name, the goon stepped inside the office. "Don't be a hero."

"Do you see tights or a cape?" Heroes didn't let hostages get killed. They didn't run into a situation and make dumbass mistakes, and they figured out who was to blame before the body count rose. My stomach lurched, but I swallowed the bile. There would be plenty of time for self-pity and guilt later, if there was a later. Seriously, why didn't I call Martin this morning?

"Pick up the phone," Wheeler said, "and tell them what I want."

"Okay." I did as he asked, avoiding giving answers to the questions Torre asked about everyone's well-being or if we needed any supplies or food inside the building. It was standard negotiation, but I was frazzled and couldn't think to form an appropriate response to tip them off without clueing in Wheeler.

"We'll call back as soon as the car arrives. Stay near the phone," Torre said.

Wheeler hit the disconnect, smiling. "See, that wasn't so hard, was it?"

"Why Oster?" I asked, contemplating what the tactical unit inside the building was instructed to do now that the moronic woman pretending to be a negotiator got captured. "Why was he doing your bidding? What did you promise him?"

"My loyal head of security." Wheeler shrugged. "It seems fitting that he would be the perfect fall guy. He had access, know-how, and the drills that were conducted to advance security during the conference were coordinated through him." He seemed pleased to speak about his brilliance to someone, and I identified that as the boastful politician. "Not to speak ill of the dead, but he was too smart for his own good."

"He was on to you?" I asked, not wanting to admit that Oster wasn't the only one, but until now, there was no evidence.

"Apparently he and his little friend decided to rig their

own surveillance. And he overheard something he shouldn't have." He narrowed his eyes. "You're not planning to make it out of this building alive, are you?"

"You tell me." I wouldn't show fear, nor would I go down without a fight.

"Obviously, I would be an idiot to confess to you and then let you live. So tell me, how badly do you want to know the truth?"

"He blackmailed you," I said, not bothering to answer the question.

"He tried. Many have tried. But you can't bullshit a bullshitter. He tried to use it as leverage to guarantee his girlfriend would remain unharmed. Pity, she was too in love with her ex-husband to ever really care about him. And he died for her. That just goes to show, the only person you should look out for is yourself." He smirked. "That's a lesson you should have taken to heart before running inside this hellhole."

"Too late now." The phone interrupted our conversation, and he nodded that I answer. Instead of putting it on speaker, I picked up the receiver. "Is the car ready?"

"We're working on it. It will take some time. How is everyone holding up? Can I speak to Jason?" Torre asked, still reading from the manual.

"No," my voice shook, and Wheeler hit the speaker button before I could say anything else.

"Are you okay? Is everything okay?"

It was now or never. "Two hostiles, Oster's dead, one hostage injured," I rattled quickly before Wheeler could disconnect.

"You bitch," he pressed his gun to my forehead, contemplating pulling the trigger. "That's it. You're gonna personally make sure I make it out alive." He twisted my arm behind my back and dragged me into the hallway. "Sven, plan B."

The man left the conference room and headed for the stairwell. Opening the doors, he went down the steps. Wheeler followed, hunkering behind me so I could be a human shield. We only made it down a few steps before gunfire reverberated in the enclosed, cinderblock stairwell. My last communication had been enough to trigger an immediate breach. Bullets were flying, and anything that moved would be taken down.

"Fuck," Wheeler cursed, yanking my hair hard and pulling me backward up the steps, so he could still hide behind me like the coward he was. "Back in the office."

He made it to Russell's office and shut the door. He flipped the lock and forced me toward the window. The ledge wasn't a feasible alternative escape route, but he was desperate enough to consider giving it a try. As he struggled to keep the gun pointed at me while attempting to open the large, sealed window, I spotted the HRT sniper in the adjacent building. Distract him, Parker.

"Senator," I said, surprising him with the sudden formality, "the roof would make more sense." He looked suspicious. "It's your only chance." He released the window frame and turned to face me.

"Why should I believe you?"

"Because if you don't, we'll both die." I stepped forward, angling slightly in the hopes of having him turn further away from the window as the red laser sight bounced closer.

He pushed me back, cocking the gun and aiming at my head. "The roof, huh? Good call. But you're gonna die either way."

A red laser dot appeared on the side of his head, and I shut my eyes. Would HRT take the shot before Wheeler did? Either way, I didn't want to see it. The crack of gunfire ripped through the silence. It was fierce, and before I could move an inch, the office door was bashed in and a metal canister hit the ground. Diving underneath the desk, I curled into the fetal position, covering my ears and squeezing my eyes closed.

Thank god, it wasn't a grenade or tear gas. The deafening sound and blinding light of the flashbang was disorienting, and I did my best to shield myself from the effects. I still wasn't certain that Wheeler's bullet didn't rip through me. I remained curled under the desk; my breathing was erratic as minutes or hours passed. Noises sounded distant and muffled, and then something tapped against my shin.

"Clear," the ESU guy said, offering his hand. I took it, and he pulled me up.

"Wheeler?" Squinting and trying to think, I wondered what happened to Sven. Replaying the events of the last two hours, I knew there must be a third man. A sleeper. Someone inside the conference room keeping the hostages at bay. But who? "Do you have a back-up?" I asked. The officer nodded, and without asking for elaboration, unhooked the gun from his thigh and handed it to me. "How many did you get? There are at least three."

"Two. One in the stairwell and him." He jerked his chin at Wheeler's body, slumped half in the office chair, his head and neck at a horrible angle. The nausea hit hard, but I pushed it away, scrambling toward the conference room.

"Alex," Paul called, crouching on the floor next to Jason's body, "it was Gordon Russell. That's what I wanted to tell you before." His words weren't making sense, but Russell was no longer in the conference room. Two other hotel employees were huddled in the corner while Paul pressed his palms against Oster's stomach and chest, and ESU secured the rest of the floor for the paramedics to arrive. "I think he's still breathing. I'm not sure," Paul rambled. He was in shock, and he might not be the only one.

"Where'd Russell go?" I asked, not willing to let a single piece of slime escape.

"I don't know," he replied. Three members of ESU returned to the room, and one kept a watch on the alleged hostages while the other two checked Oster's vitals.

Not waiting for permission, I ran from the room and down the hallway. They were clearing from the bottom up, and HRT was in the adjacent building, monitoring suspicious movement. There wasn't a chance in hell Gordon Russell would escape. I still didn't know how he figured into any of this. Nor did I truly believe Jason Oster or Paul Eastman were entirely innocent. At this particular moment, I saw every single one of them as the enemy, and they might be.

"Parker," the ESU guy who lent me his side arm took lead, "stay behind me. Do you know what this guy looks like?"

"Yep," I said, ready to make heads roll. Being held at gunpoint with my life flashing before my eyes for the past hour wasn't conducive to a positive recovery. But considering the fact I still didn't know what the hell was going on, it would be beneficial to keep as many persons of interest breathing as possible. We went up another level, clearing the rooms. A few more members of the team joined the party, signifying that the EMTs and regular police officers were dealing with the remaining situation.

On the penthouse level, the door to Wheeler's suite was open, and Russell was on the floor, searching through the drawers. Everything in the room was tossed, and he was frantic to find whatever he was looking for.

"Hands in the air," one of the men ordered, and Russell complied immediately.

"It has to be here. Just," he looked at them beseechingly, "give me a minute. He had millions stashed somewhere. We can all be rich. When we find the money, you can have it all, if you just let me go."

"Do you honestly believe you can bribe these upstanding law enforcement officers?" I asked, stepping into the room.

"We can all be millionaires. I didn't kill anyone. I didn't do anything. It will be fine. We'll be rich. All of us. No one has to know anything." He continued the gibberish, even as the cuffs clinked into place.

We scanned the rest of the room, the outer balcony, and every nook and cranny on the top floor. "Clear," I called, shutting the final closet door. A couple of the other men checked the roof, but no one else was in the building. Everyone was either apprehended, taken into custody for questioning, at the hospital, or awaiting transport to the ME's office.

"Parker," Jacobs appeared on the top floor as I returned my borrowed handgun to the ESU guy, "this was some mess."

"Tell me about it." I barely managed to make it down the stairs, feeling nauseous and dizzy from what occurred.

Jacobs wanted a statement and facts. Apparently he received a few phone calls from Jablonsky and O'Connell, and some headway was made when they questioned Rachel Romanski again. But I couldn't concentrate. At the moment, I really just wanted to sit down and put my head between my knees.

As soon as we exited the lobby doors, Agent Walton approached. "You nearly got everyone killed. You almost sabotaged a rescue attempt. You thwarted my investigation, and now there are multiple casualties." He pulled out his handcuffs. "Alexis Parker, you're under arrest for interfering in a federal investigation." The metal clicked into place, and he dragged me to his SUV. On the bright side, there was a good chance I was going to be sick, and he'd have to clean it up.

FORTY-ONE

"Did you check her for a concussion?" I heard Mark ask as the door to interrogation opened. "It's protocol when someone vomits in the back of your car."

"She's fine," Walton insisted.

"Is that right, Alex?" Mark asked, and I lifted my head off my arms, pulling back so the fact that I was still cuffed would be apparent. "Jesus." Mark rolled his eyes and immediately dug out his handcuff key to set me free. "Are you okay?" he asked quietly.

"I am now." I rubbed my wrists, hating restraints for more reasons than I cared to count.

"Good." He put a can of cola on the table in front of me. "What the hell is the matter with you?"

"I'd like to know the answer to that question as well," Director Kendall said, stepping into the room. He was in charge of the FBI field office and OIO, and he was the man I had turned in a resignation letter to on multiple occasions, refusing his offers to return to work until the last time when I failed to be reinstated. "You're the only person I know who continually gets arrested or nearly arrested because you still behave like you're on the job, even though you clearly aren't."

"Sir," I said, opening the soda and taking a sip to settle my nerves and stomach, "what can I say? It happens."

"It only happens to you," Kendall growled. He shifted his focus to SAC Walton. "Chris, take a walk. This has no bearing on you or your investigation." Walton looked ready to protest but was too much of an ass-kisser to speak out against the big boss. After the door closed, Kendall pulled out the chair in front of me and sat down. "We can't keep meeting like this."

"No, sir," I replied.

"Strangely enough, the police lieutenant has come to your rescue this time. Not me. Moretti called and said you were helping his detective on something, and you likely became a bit too overzealous in your consulting. While that doesn't mean we still can't bring you up on charges, I suspect you won't be as willing to cooperate and answer our questions if you fear you'll be implicating yourself."

"That could happen," I said, wondering where this conversation was going.

"Here," he placed a form on the table in front of me, "full immunity, signed by the AG and DA." He pulled a pen from his breast pocket and put it on top of the papers. "Be thankful you still have friends here. Two of them are in this room."

"Thank you, Director." I let out a sigh, relieved to no longer be cuffed or under arrest. "I owe you more than I can ever repay."

"When this is cleared up and you finish with the PD, make an appointment to see me. There's something imperative we need to discuss. Agreed?"

"Yes, sir."

"Get some rest. You look pretty wrecked." He went to the door. "And thanks for showing some initiative today, but in the future, you need to learn to follow orders. Understood?"

"I'll work on it." I signed the papers, indemnifying myself, and leaned back. Kendall left the room, and Mark took the seat he vacated.

"Here's what's about to happen," Mark said, glancing at the door. "Walton's been cleared of any involvement. His investigation is clean, and so is he. So be nice. He's coming back inside to interview you. Tell him everything that happened and everything you know. Transcripts will be sent to the police department, and hopefully, you won't have to repeat this process again. Don't ask questions. I'll catch you up to speed tomorrow before you show up at the police station. They're expecting you to consult pro bono, at least that's what Moretti agreed to after I cashed in a few favors on your behalf." He stood up. "The good news is you were never identified by any of the news sources, and after being arrested, I'm sure no one will think you have any actual involvement with law enforcement."

"Why does that matter?" Being more baffled than usual wasn't fun, but after today, I could follow through on a few basic orders. The sooner I got out of here and back to the safety and comfort of home, the better. My nerves were shot, but at least I wasn't.

"It will. But that's not important now. Answer questions, give your statement, and keep the question-asking to a minimum. I'll give you a ride home when Walton is finished with you."

"Thanks, Mark. For everything. I don't think I've ever been happier to see you in my entire life."

"That's what your assistant is for." He winked and went to the door just as Walton was coming inside.

"Parker," Walton took a seat, "sorry about the arrest." It sounded like he changed his tune in the last few minutes. Maybe Kendall had a talk with him. Walton checked his watch. "You probably want to get out of here as quickly as possible." I'd been waiting inside the interrogation room for over six hours, so that was definitely an understatement. "Why don't you start at the beginning and we'll take it from there?"

After telling him about the situation inside the hotel, the information I gleaned from Oster, Eastman, Wheeler, Russell, and the henchman known only as Sven, a thought crossed my mind. "Is Jason Oster still alive?"

"He's in surgery. His odds aren't great. He took two to the stomach." Walton finished making a few notations, asked for clarification on the elevators, the stairwell, and the makeshift barricade that blocked my path to level eight. Then he asked for a recount that led to my frantic message to Torre that signaled the breach and Wheeler's final moments. When it was all said and done, he stood up, extending his hand, and we shook. "Look, you've accused me of some serious shit. I've brought you in for questioning a couple of times. And you vomited in my backseat. Can we call a truce before things get further out of hand?"

"That sounds good." I smiled at him.

"You're free to go. If I have any more questions, I'll phone. If not, do me a favor and try to stay as far from my investigation as you can."

"Deal." He reached for the door handle, but another thought crossed my mind. "Except, I'm consulting for the PD, so–"

"Yeah." He sighed and held the door for me to exit. "Like I said, try."

Mark drove me home, surprisingly not asking any questions about why I acted the way I did or what happened. Maybe the fact that I was still a little green kept him from wanting to further traumatize me. He parked outside my apartment building and turned off the engine.

"Do you want someone to keep you company?" he asked.

"No. I just want to wash the ick of the day off, decompress, and get some sleep. You told me not to ask any questions, but where's Paul?"

"The police have him. Everyone is stuck answering questions for the next forty-eight hours. You're lucky Walton brought you in, or else you'd probably be at the precinct for the next two days." I nodded, reaching for the door handle. "You sure you don't want me to come up?"

"I'm okay." I thought about my smashed cell phone and confiscated handgun. "That creep, Sven, took my nine millimeter. Do you think he used it to kill anyone?"

"Probably not. I'd bet it's somewhere in evidence. You'll find out tomorrow." He watched me curiously since I had yet to open the car door.

"What time is it in Milan?"

"Go call him," Mark insisted. "It doesn't matter what

time it is. He'll want to hear from you."

Trudging up the six flights of stairs, I barely noticed the sticky note on my front door while I dug around in my pocket for my keys. Pulling it off the door, I was puzzled by the words. Was this a sick prank? *I'm inside. Don't shoot.* – *J.M.*

Cautiously opening the door, I poked my head inside. Martin was standing with his back to me, gazing out my fire escape. His suit was wrinkled. An untouched glass of scotch was on the table, sweating and looking like it had been poured hours ago with a layer of water at the top from the melted ice.

"Martin?" I asked, stepping inside. His body remained facing the window, but he turned his head.

"I'll take it from the lack of firearm that you found my note. Are you okay?" His voice was tired and pained.

"I'm fine. What are you doing here? You're supposed to be somewhere. Italy? I don't know. I can't keep up with the happenings in my own life, let alone your travel itinerary."

He pressed a few buttons on his phone before putting it down on the table next to the forgotten scotch. "You didn't call. And you didn't answer. Do you have any idea how many times I tried to call you in the last twelve hours?" He sounded annoyed, frustrated, and relieved all at the same time.

"Would it be enough to officially qualify you as a stalker?" I quipped.

"Don't you dare pick a fight right now." He turned completely around, looking exhausted, and crossed the room. He kissed me and pulled me tightly against his chest. "Even when I travel, I still get local news updates on my phone. I saw what happened. The news coverage was astronomical. What the fuck were you thinking, running inside that hotel? Are you insane? Do you have a death wish? Are you trying to scare me to death?"

"I was assisting in the negotiation. It wasn't what it looked like," I mumbled, not wanting to think or talk about it. Tomorrow, I would deal, but for now, I wanted to forget.

"Then why didn't you answer or call me back? How could you possibly expect me to stay in Europe when I had no way of knowing if you were okay?"

"God, you're shaking. Take it easy. It's okay. I'm okay."

"I thought you were shaking," he said, and I wasn't positive that I wasn't. "Then again, I spent eight hours on a plane, and I don't know how many just standing in front of your window, hoping you'd come home. That you were okay." He inhaled, his body starting to relax. "So maybe it's both of us." He let out a sigh. "The things you put me through, sweetheart."

"You shouldn't have dropped everything. Even if something did happen, there wouldn't have been anything you could do. You shouldn't derail your business trip because of some idiotic news reporter who probably blew the situation completely out of proportion." He seemed about to protest, so I continued explaining, hoping he'd take it as an apology. "My phone was destroyed, and I just got home. But I planned on calling you." I gave him a final squeeze and pulled away. "When do you have to leave? Are you flying back tonight?"

"You're not getting rid of me that easily." He ran his thumb across my cheek.

The only thing I wanted was to curl up next to him and bask in the comfort he provided, but the violence and death were clinging to me. "I need to wash off the remnants of today." He knew my routine and my symbolic need to scour away the horror. "But you should join me." And he followed me into the bathroom, shedding clothing on the way.

*   *   *

The next morning, I woke up. It was early, and I was sore from the physical exertion of prying open the elevator and moving the sleeper sofa, not to mention all the stress of yesterday. Maybe I could persuade a certain someone to rub my back. Keeping my eyes closed, I reached for Martin. Coming up empty, I turned over and ran my hand across the mattress, finding nothing but cold sheets. Did I hallucinate last night? I opened my eyes; the bed was empty. I sat up and looked around the room for some sign that I wasn't crazy.

"I don't care. Give her what she wants." I heard his voice from the next room. "We're selling that line anyway." He paused. "It doesn't matter how much it costs the company. I don't give a shit." Okay, so at least I wasn't crazy. "We're dissolving our partnership with Hover Designs. I made the deal yesterday. Let Francesca handle the sale," he huffed. "Fine. Talk to the Board and call me back this afternoon." He hung up and returned to the bedroom. His eyes were dark and puffy. It was apparent he was exhausted, physically, mentally, and emotionally. He climbed back into bed. "I'm sorry if my conference call woke you. I didn't mean to be so loud."

"It's okay," I murmured, snuggling against the pillow. He kissed me and wrapped an arm around my waist. "What's going on?"

"Nothing."

"Is there anything I can do?" I felt responsible for whatever business decision he made yesterday in order to come home two weeks early.

"Yes. Promise me we can sleep until noon." He buried his nose in my hair and kissed the nape of my neck. "And when we wake up, I want to revisit the idea of never leaving your apartment again."

"Sounds good."

FORTY-TWO

It was always a strange turn of events when I was awake before James Martin. He was one of those rare breeds of morning people who tended to rise with the sun, cheery and prepared to meet the day head-on. However, it seemed we were trading places today. Not that I was rising with the sun or particularly cheery, but it was eleven o'clock, and a million things needed handling. Mark called, informing me he would be by at one to pick me up. My car was in police impound after being left at the hotel unattended. With my luck, they probably decided it was evidence in the hostage situation. Ugh. I would have been better off if yesterday had been a bad dream instead of the mess it turned out to be. I still didn't know exactly what happened or why it happened. I didn't know the final body count, the motive, the impetus, or even who all of the players were. And yet, the police thought I would be instrumental in helping to figure it out, or so Lt. Moretti claimed in order to keep me out of jail. Orange really wasn't my color.

I let out a sigh, slipping carefully out of Martin's grasp. That was another mess. He shouldn't be here. He should be in some foreign country, having business meetings, or dinner and drinks, or whatever the hell he'd be doing at this moment. Arguing with board members and selling off assets wasn't a solution. It was a sign of a problem, and that problem was me. I didn't want to fight. Furthermore, I didn't necessarily want to get out of bed, but there was work to do.

After preparing for the day, I made a quick trip to the grocery store down the street, picked up some basic supplies after dumping everything out of my fridge not too long ago, and began making brunch. I was putting the final touches on an egg white frittata when Martin came out of my bedroom. His hair was unkempt, but he looked rested and relieved.

"Since when did you become domesticated?" he asked, wrapping his arms around me and kissing my neck. "That smells great, but we can eat later. Come back to bed."

"I can't. Mark's gonna be here in twenty minutes." I swallowed. "The police department requires my presence."

"Hmm," he trailed kisses along my shoulder, "so do I. And I'm calling dibs."

"You aren't making this any easier." Reluctantly, I pulled away from him, resisting the urge to respond with the sentiment we both knew was true. He shouldn't have returned early just because of some stupid news story. "Did you eat yesterday? I know I didn't." I grabbed a few pieces of bread and popped them in the toaster.

"Alex," he grabbed the plates from my hand and put them on the counter, "are we going to talk about this? When I left last week, you were annoyed that you lost a job. Then on the phone, you said you were investigating for the guy that fired you. Neither of those things is indicative of what I witnessed on the news yesterday."

"I think we're going to fight about it. And I don't want to fight with you. Not at the moment. We'll talk about this later. Tonight, maybe. Are you positive you don't need to fly back to wherever you were? Because I think you should go." That comment earned an angry, defiant look. "How much did this cost you?" He didn't say anything. "Hundreds of thousands?" I waited. "Millions?" Still nothing. "Tens of millions?" He pressed his lips together. "I have no idea what you're worth or what your company is worth, so I'll just assume it was astronomical. So go. Fix it. I don't want you to resent me for some botched business trip. I didn't ask you to come home."

"No. You never do." He grimaced. "Since you have to leave soon, we won't talk about this now." He picked up the plates and put them on the table. "But I'm not going anywhere. In fact, I refuse to leave your apartment. I was an idiot for not taking you up on your offer a week ago." He pulled some flatware from the drawer. "I just have one question."

"All right." I poured two cups of coffee and brought them to the table, and we both sat down. "What is it?"

"Do you honestly believe that my business trip is more important to me than you?"

"No."

He nodded, and the anger dissipated. We were silent while he wolfed down the food. My appetite had gone to crap after that question, and I nibbled on some toast.

"You didn't have to make me breakfast," he said around a mouthful. "I would have cooked." He wiped his mouth. "But this is fantastic."

"Surprised?" I retorted, hoping for light, pointless banter.

"You've cooked for me before, and it's always good. But this was amazing." His flattery was meant to smooth the waters, so I offered a smile. "Since you made brunch, I'll make dinner tonight. What time do you think you'll be back?"

"I don't know. Probably late. Don't worry about it. I can pick something up at the station." He looked ready to protest, so I decided to ask for his help on a different project. Since he wanted to stay and appear useful, then I could play along. "Actually, if you get the chance, can you pick up a decent bottle of scotch for Mark? You know what he likes. Just keep the receipt, and I'll pay you back."

"It's not his birthday." Martin searched his mind. "And as far as I know, he didn't get married and divorced again. So what's the scotch for?"

"I owe him. He pulled some strings in order to keep me from getting arrested yesterday. If he didn't, I'd still be in lockup." I pressed my lips together, thinking about the hours I spent handcuffed to the table in the interrogation room.

Martin noticed the involuntary shudder and came around the table and pulled me into his arms. "You have no idea how relieved I was when you walked through that door last night," he whispered in my ear.

"I can imagine. It was probably somewhere close to how I felt when I found you waiting inside my apartment." I rested my cheek against his shoulder. "I am glad you're here. But that's selfish and ridiculous on my part. And I know rationally you shouldn't be here. You shouldn't have jumped to those conclusions, and you shouldn't have dropped everything. If," I focused on the windows, refusing to pull away, "I didn't make it out of that building yesterday, there would have been nothing you could have done. So you didn't need to rush home."

"Alex," his voice sounded hoarse. We weren't doing a good job about not talking about the elephant in the room. Thankfully, before things could get any mushier and nauseating, Mark knocked on the door.

I ran a hand through his hair, taming down some of the wayward spikes, and kissed him before stepping away and opening the door. Mark came inside, carrying a bag of donuts and a couple of coffees.

"Where's mine?" Martin asked.

"I wasn't expecting to see you. Alex said she wanted to call you, but I didn't realize she'd ask you to come home," Mark replied, caught off guard. Martin smirked, apparently realizing exactly how much I wanted him here after my comments and Mark's affirmation. Shifting his gaze to me, Mark asked, "Can you cut this love fest short? We've got a lot to sort out."

"Yep." I took my back-up handgun from my gun safe and slipped into my shoulder holster and jacket. Mark watched, wondering why I needed the heavy artillery. "It should just be paperwork, but y'never know," I mumbled in response to the confused glances.

Kissing Martin goodbye, I followed Mark out of my apartment and down the steps. He waited until we were inside his car before he asked the question that was on his mind. "How come Marty's here? Wasn't he supposed to be gone another two weeks?"

"Local news feed was sent to his phone."

"See, I said you made the news," Mark retorted. Thankfully, he changed the conversation topic to Oster's condition, which was still alive but barely. Detective Jacobs was sorting through the mess, and there were numerous breaks on the case based upon the information Mark received and various statements made by the affected parties. "I'm still wondering if your client is clean."

"I guess we'll find out," I said as he parked the car. "What about Rachel Romanski?"

"One step at a time." He grabbed his coffee cup from the drink holder. "It's gonna be a long day. They want to question you about what happened yesterday."

"Well, it's nice to know I have immunity." I smirked. "What do we know so far?"

Apparently while I was getting myself into trouble at the hotel, Mark and Detective O'Connell were hard at work at the precinct. The caterer who lost his I.D. was identified and questioned. The day before the conference, the catering crew came to the hotel to set up for the next day. And when the caterer left that evening, he had an altercation with a man in the hotel parking lot. The caterer thought the guy was drunk and didn't realize until later that night that his wallet was lifted. And then it didn't occur to him until the following morning that his hotel I.D. was also gone.

"We showed him pictures of our persons of interest, both living and dead, but he didn't spot anyone," Mark said, building to that 'ah ha' moment. "But just as he was about to leave, the sketch artist finished with Romanski. O'Connell figured it was worth a shot, and the caterer said it was the same guy."

"Okay, do we know who he is?"

"I brought the picture over to the OIO and ran it through facial rec," Mark said, "and we got a hit on a Sean Svenstak. He works for Rodney Wheeler as his personal bodyguard."

"Sven?" It was probably the same guy. "ESU took him out yesterday. He shot Jason Oster once. Wheeler shot Jason the first time."

"We identified Svenstak among the dead, so I guess so." Mark looked worried. "You can discuss that with the police. Let's focus on something less morbid." He searched his mind for the tidbits of information I was lacking. "Fingerprints came back on Paul's keys. Once again, Svenstak's name came up. I'm assuming he's the guy that broke into Paul's house, tampered with the water filter, and removed the bug that he told Romanski to plant. This guy really got around."

"Yeah, good for him." So Wheeler was pulling the strings all along. It wasn't surprising. But how did Paul and Jason fit into it? And what was Rachel's connection? These were the same questions I'd been struggling with, and it still didn't look like we had any answers.

"The FBI has the memory card from the wireless video camera that Oster and Eastman set up. Although the files seemed corrupted, we found a hidden file on the card that the PD missed. It's encrypted. It will be a while before they can crack it, but maybe it'll prove useful," Mark suggested.

"Wheeler said Oster tried to blackmail him. He wanted to use the video as leverage to protect Rachel." I screwed my eyes closed, recalling his exact words. "Something was overheard. I don't know if that's why Oster established the surveillance in the room or if whatever was overheard was also caught on tape, but it might explain the connection we are still struggling to find."

"I think you're caught up, finally. Unless there was something else you wanted to know before we go inside and hear what the detectives have discovered in the last sixteen hours."

"Are you sure Walton's clean?" I asked. Mark told me that yesterday, but I didn't know how he knew.

"Kendall ordered an expedited internal review. He's clean. He was just following orders. It looks like Wheeler was an expert at thwarting his surveillance. I think Svenstak would run interference for him, so he could come and go as he pleased."

"That's probably added incentive for the hotel remodel. No cameras were near the elevators, so he could take them down to whatever floor he wanted, maybe slip out an employee entrance or exit, and return without anyone being the wiser." Something pinged in my brain. "Do we know who was using the phone in Gordon Russell's office when Paul Eastman received those calls and phoned back?"

"You're thinking it was Wheeler." Mark nodded, agreeing. "But why would Eastman call him or vice versa?"

"Let's go find out," I said, opening the car door.

FORTY-THREE

After repeating everything from yesterday, writing a report, signing the report, and repeating it again, I found myself at Jacobs' desk. He was sifting through the statements and trying to make heads or tails out of what exactly went down and who was involved. The two hotel employees that were taken hostage in the conference room, besides Russell and Eastman, had been cleared of any involvement. Even though the forty-eight hour hold wasn't over, the police brass cut them loose.

"Romanski, Eastman, and Russell are still in custody," Jacobs said, shutting one folder and opening another. "The hospital called and said Oster's still in ICU. It's touch and go."

"Have you told Rachel?" I asked, wondering if she might confess in light of these facts.

"No. It's his medical history; we're not allowed to divulge information like that. His parents flew in from Miami, and we let them have access. But even that was pushing it." He gave me a look. "You want to speak to her?"

"Yes." I let out an inappropriate laugh. "It's Friday, and I missed my yoga class. So maybe I should schedule a chat with the instructor to make up for it."

Jacobs led me down the hall to one of the interrogation rooms and opened the door. "I'll send Detective O'Connell in to assist. Don't do anything I'll regret in the meantime." He walked out, and I knew the real reason behind it.

"Good afternoon," I greeted, walking to the table and pulling out a chair. "How are you holding up?"

She shrugged. "I'm a cooperating witness. They haven't arrested me, and the police keep saying I don't need a lawyer. But that doesn't mean I want to talk to them or you."

"Did you hear about what happened yesterday? The man that threatened you is dead." She met my eyes, searching to discover if my words were true.

Offering a small smile, she nodded. "Am I safe?"

"Yes, but," I lowered my voice and glanced back at the two-way mirror, "Jason fought to protect you. I don't know exactly what went down or how, but the men that threatened you and likely killed your ex-husband shot Jason. They tried to frame him, and when that plan failed, they shot him."

Her eyes went wide, and she looked on the verge of tears. "Is he okay?"

"I won't lie to you. It doesn't look good." I swallowed and scooted the tissue box closer to her. "Paul was with him. He tried to stop the bleeding in order to save him." Since she accused Paul of working with the men making the threats, maybe this would give her the courage to open up about why she thought that connection was accurate.

"I thought he was behind it. That guy said Paul and Alvin stole his money, so I just assumed he was one of the bad guys."

"Did Jason ever tell you about the surveillance camera that he and Paul set up?"

She wiped her eyes, focusing on the table. "When I told him about the man threatening me, he said he'd take care of it. He mentioned there was a tape." She shrugged. "I didn't know Paul had anything to do with it."

"Do you know what was on the tape?"

"Information, something that the police could use to arrest the people responsible."

"Why didn't he just turn it in?"

She swallowed, looking guilty. "It would have cost him his job. He said it involved his boss and his boss's boss. I thought it might have cost him his life. The man who threatened me was a scary son-of-a-bitch. He killed my cat. He killed Alvin. He," she blinked, the tears rapidly falling, "he shot Jason."

"Did you ever see the tape?" She shook her head, too overcome to speak.

O'Connell opened the door. He looked at me and then at Rachel. "We leave you alone for two minutes and you manage to upset this poor woman. What's wrong with you?" I knew he was trying to appear sympathetic in order to keep her compliant, so I didn't bother to respond to the quip. "Ma'am, is there anything I can get you?"

"No." She whimpered and sighed. "When can I go home?"

O'Connell arranged for a unit to take her back to her place and accompany her upstairs. Officer Taylor was assigned to babysit and check her apartment for any evidence that might be out in the open and wouldn't require a warrant while we guarded Rachel from any other possible threats and sorted through the remainder of the mess.

"What'd she say?" Jacobs asked when I returned to his desk. So I filled him in. "Any word on if the feds made headway on that memory card?" he called to O'Connell, who was on the phone. O'Connell shook his head. "It looks like our best chance of figuring this out is breaking through the encryption."

"I'd say our best bet is getting Oster to talk." I swallowed. The pang of guilt in my gut hurt a little more after Rachel's breakdown.

"I hope he makes it." Jacobs looked grim, and I remembered he took three shots at the elevator. We didn't know what was going on at the time. Maybe if we realized someone else was pulling the strings, we could have stopped the situation before it started.

"Oster was going to confront Wheeler before Paul arrived," I said. "He turned off the security system. He had a loaded weapon, and he seemed intent to stop the party responsible."

"That's why he needed to know Rachel was safe," Jacobs added. "Do you think he was going to kill Wheeler or try to force the man to turn himself in?"

"I don't know."

"How does your client fit into any of this?" Jacobs asked as O'Connell hung up the phone and joined us at the desk.

"Paul Eastman is a piece of work," O'Connell began. "He's admitted to countless schemes. Most of which have absolutely nothing to do with the crisis situation from yesterday."

"Sounds like Paul," I muttered. "Can I talk to him?"

"We can talk to him," Jacobs corrected, not wanting me to be alone with Paul. The last time we were alone in a police station, he almost died.

Going into another interrogation room, I took a seat and waited for an officer to bring Paul in. Jacobs remained silent. He flipped through his notepad, reading information so he'd be well-versed for the questioning.

"Alexis," Paul said, obviously relieved to see me, "is Jason okay? I had it wrong. God, I had it wrong."

"Take a seat, Mr. Eastman," Jacobs urged as the officer moved to hook Eastman's handcuffs to the bar in the table. "That won't be necessary, Billy." The officer nodded and left the room.

"Jason's at the hospital. We don't know enough yet," I said.

"It sounds like you've been cooperating with the other detectives," Jacobs began, forcing Paul to focus on something besides the grim news. "You're the only person who knows what happened in that elevator. Would you care to explain?"

"Yeah, okay. I owe it to Jason, I guess." He blew out a breath. "After we fought for the gun, he dragged me into the elevator. He kept saying that he didn't kill Alvin, and he would never tell Rachel to sneak into my apartment. He said he didn't poison me, but he knew what was going on."

"Did he tell you?" I asked.

"Yeah. We got stuck in the elevator. The doors locked,

and we couldn't get out. So while we're inside, Jason tells me that Frank Costan was staying at the hotel and making a deal with the hotel owner. He never told me what the guy's name was, but from what you and Mark were talking about in my motel room, I knew it was Senator Wheeler."

"Go on," I urged, hoping Jacobs wouldn't think too hard about a federal agent discussing an open investigation in front of a suspect. The last thing I wanted to do was get Mark in trouble.

"Anyway, after Jason discovered that Frank Costan was at the hotel, he told Mr. Russell, who said he reported it to the FBI. The FBI was supposed to be staying in room 709, according to what Mr. Russell told Jason. So Jason took the camera and set it up inside to see what was happening."

"Why?" Jacobs asked.

"He didn't say, but I think it had something to do with Rachel." Eastman looked flummoxed. "That part never made much sense to me."

"Did he tell you what was on the tape?" I asked, getting Paul back on track before he went off on one of his tangents.

"He said he had proof that Wheeler was behind Frank Costan's murder, and that he overheard three people talking about killing Alvin and poisoning me. At first, I thought maybe he was just saying that so I'd stop accusing him, but the more I thought about it, the more sense it made."

"Then what happened?" Jacobs asked.

"The elevator lurched. The doors opened, and that big guy was pointing a gun at us," Paul said. "We weren't prepared for that. I wanted to fight him off, and I got a good swing in. But he overpowered me. I thought Jason would jump in since there were two of us, but he told Jason he better cooperate unless he wanted to risk it all." Paul looked bewildered. "He makes us go up to the tenth floor and puts us in the conference room. A few minutes later, that goon and Wheeler come to get Jason, and I didn't see him again until the big guy dragged me down the stairs to talk to you."

Jacobs made a couple of notes. It sounded plausible, but

Paul was leaving out a few important details. Giving him a hard look, I got up from the chair and paced the interrogation room. The silence was oppressive, and Paul began fidgeting.

"What the hell were you thinking?" I asked, my voice echoing in the room. "It's time you come clean. Because if I start asking questions, you're gonna look guilty as sin." I didn't know how much Jacobs knew about the phone calls Paul made and received prior to showing up at the hotel, but he'd find out soon enough.

"Alexis," he shook his head, hoping I'd keep quiet, "I told you what I could."

"You skipped out on Mark." I waited, hoping he'd say something. He bowed his head, appearing like a scolded puppy that urinated on the rug. "Who did you call?" His head shot up. "Or should I ask who you called back? We have the number and the phone records. You used Mark's phone. It's not some big secret. Plus, Mark's name and credit card were on the room. Of course, we have your phone records." The anger was coming through in every syllable, and Jacobs glanced at me, hoping I could keep it under control.

"I phoned Wheeler."

Those words made me sick, and I walked out of the interrogation room. Paul Eastman hired me to protect him, and then he put himself in contact with the man who less than twenty-four hours ago planned to put a bullet through my brain. I couldn't stay in that room. I couldn't listen. Jacobs could fill me in. Once again, Paul lied to me, and this time, it almost got me killed.

Returning to the bullpen, I spotted Mark speaking to O'Connell. Mark grabbed a chair and pulled it over for me. "You don't look so good," Mark said. "Is everything all right?"

"Eastman called Wheeler. That's who he spoke to in Russell's office."

"Fuck," Mark growled. He gave me a quick glance and went down the hallway to the interrogation room.

We had discussed in detail our suspicions on Wheeler and Costan, as well as the FBI's investigation, in Paul's presence. I thought back to that night in the motel room when we laid most of the cards on the table while Paul slept. What if he was pretending? How much evidence and money did Wheeler hide before everything blew up yesterday? Why would Paul call him?

"Are you okay?" O'Connell asked.

"Yeah, I just needed a minute. And now I need to see what excuse Eastman could possibly come up with." I stood. "Care to join me?" We went down the hallway into the observation room and stood on the other side of the two-way mirror.

"I thought I could help," Paul insisted. "You said Alvin was informing to the FBI. I thought if I offered to make a deal with Wheeler, he'd give me some valuable information, and I could use it to turn him in. Alexis said you didn't have any hard evidence, so I thought this was the way to get it."

He rambled on about how he initially called to warn Wheeler that he was under investigation, and then he lied and told the former senator that he had access to some fictitious evidence. Paul offered to exchange the evidence for a significant sum of money. He planned to make the exchange, record the meeting, and use it to finalize the case against Wheeler, finally bringing the party responsible for Alvin's death to justice.

The problem with his idiotic plan was two-fold. First, there was no actual evidence, and second, he let it slip that Wheeler was under suspicion for Alvin and Costan's murders. That's when the former senator put his silver tongue to good use and spun a story of Jason Oster being responsible. That was how the final call between the two ended and why Paul rushed to the hotel to accuse Jason.

"Is that hero worship?" O'Connell asked. "Let me guess, the guy fell head over heels for you and wanted to do something to impress you. And this was his genius move."

"It has nothing to do with me and everything to do with Paul wanting to prove he's something he's not. Hell, he wants to be you, Nick."

"Me?"

"Yeah, he wanted to be a cop, but he didn't make the

cut. So he works private security, gets disenchanted, tries to be a corporate spy, can't hack that, and pulls a dumbass move." I sighed.

"Should I worry about you turning into him?"

"I do stupid things, but I hope I never endanger so many people that ESU and HRT have to intervene." I took a deep breath, aggravated with Paul. "This is what I get for discussing a case with a client. Maybe I'm a failure at the private sector too."

FORTY-FOUR

I arrived home that night to find my apartment turned into a Valentine's Day card. Flowers and candlelight littered the empty spaces on my counters and tables. A lemon drop martini was immediately poured from a shaker and handed to me while I lifted the bottle of Cristal out of the ice bucket and noted the chocolate covered strawberries on a platter in the fridge which were meant for after dinner.

"Did you invite your girlfriend to my place?" I asked, uncomfortable with the over the top sentiment.

When Martin managed to pull his lips away from mine, he smirked. "Don't tell her."

"Is this so we won't fight?" I asked, gesturing around the room. "Because under normal circumstances, this is the type of thing that normally leads to a fight."

"Drink your martini," he purred, returning to the stove to finish heating whatever dish he decided went with the rest of the extravagance. "And for the record, I didn't leave your apartment at all today. I think it's completely possible to stay here forever, just like you wanted."

"So how did the champagne arrive? I know I don't stock those in my liquor cabinet." I eyed a new bottle of scotch with a bow. "What do I owe you for the scotch?"

"Just say thank you."

"Thank you." I hated when he did stuff like this, but there was no point in arguing. "Do you want to tell me what you're planning on doing?"

"First, we're going to eat because you said you were starving this morning and barely ate a piece of toast. Then we're popping open the champagne, grabbing the strawberries, and we're not surfacing from the bedroom for the next few days." He spun, reaching for the serving platter. "And if you need to be a little drunk to agree to those terms, I will keep pouring the lemon drop martinis you love until I get my way."

"That's not what I meant. Plus, you're going to burn down my apartment if you leave these candles unattended for days."

"Oh, things are gonna heat up, but it won't have anything to do with the candles." He tossed a sly grin my way. "Have I mentioned I've missed you?" He let out a sigh. "I still can't believe you refused to come back to bed this morning," he playfully scoffed. "It's why I'm upping my game. I think I'm losing my touch."

"Martin, stop." He put the food on the table, and I decided to eat before we had a real conversation or else I might actually end up starving to death. I loaded up my plate and ate a few mouthfuls. "Delicious." He smiled. "Please, stop pretending everything's okay when it's not. You're not supposed to be here. You can't sit still for two minutes, so the fact that you didn't leave my apartment explains exactly why it looks the way it does."

"Most places deliver," he replied, chewing and ignoring the dig of my words.

"That's fine. I love delivery. But you love work. You're supposed to be on your rock star CEO seventeen cities in twenty days business trip." He wiped his mouth and leaned back. "I heard you on the phone this morning. It sounded like you made a shitty deal."

"Since when do you care about business? It's fine. Don't worry about it."

"I'm worried."

"Yeah, like I was when that unidentified woman ran into a hostage situation? Then I thought maybe I was wrong. Maybe it wasn't you. So I called and called. And I tried to call Mark. And no one answered. So I finished up my meeting in Milan, made a deal to get rid of a product line that has done nothing but cost me time and money since the start, and went straight to the airport. Then I came here, and," his jaw clenched, "I waited." I didn't say anything because there was nothing to say. "I know. You think I'm overreacting and being overbearing."

"I was going to go with clingy." We resumed eating in silence. "So you didn't screw yourself or your company in order to cut your trip short by two weeks?"

"Not any worse than I did when we merged with Hover Designs. Francesca's taking over where I left off, looking for someone else who will absorb the costs of their product line. Eventually, it'll take off, but right now, it's far too costly." He met my eyes. "Don't worry about my business sense. I haven't lost that."

"You won't lose me either," I said, pushing my empty plate away. My mind went to images of Wheeler, the gun, and Oster getting shot.

"I better not." Serious Martin was hard to deal with. I hated it when things got like this, and he knew it. The classic smirk emerged on his face. "And for the record, I didn't screw Francesca either."

"Glad to hear it." I smiled. "Although your ex-fiancée is probably much less insane than your current girlfriend."

"Yes, but I like how the crazy extends to the bedroom."

*   *   *

"Martin," I said a little louder, shaking him, "wake up. You're having a nightmare."

It was ten a.m., and I wasn't accustomed to him having nightmares. That was my deal. He took a deep breath, his breathing stabilizing, and he snuggled against me, not fully waking up. Hoping that I wouldn't have to show up early for additional questioning, I stayed in bed, watching him sleep.

Somehow, a certain key fact had eluded me. I must have realized it a couple of years ago when I first met him, but I forgot about it. He didn't have anyone. Like me, he was alone. No family, a smattering of friends, and a tendency to hide under mountains of work. Maybe I should cut him a break for being worried and occasionally clingy. Possessive was never acceptable, but if he wanted us to spend more time together or talk more often, I could consider it.

By eleven, every phone in my apartment was ringing. My home phone and Martin's cell were going crazy. He grabbed me before I could get out of bed to get the phone. "If you leave for work, I'm calling the company to disconnect your home phone," he teased.

"Except you're just as popular." He reached for his cell phone, and I went to the kitchen and pulled the cordless off the charger.

"The video encryption has been broken," Mark said. "Do you want to meet me at the OIO building to check out the surveillance, or did you have a standing appointment at the precinct?"

"I'll meet you at the OIO. Have you seen the footage yet?"

"No, but from what I hear, it puts everything into perspective."

"I'll be there soon." I disconnected, turning to find Martin searching through his luggage. At least the good thing about his lengthy trip was he still had two weeks' worth of clean clothes in his packed bags. "And what should I do to you if you leave me on account of work?"

He arched an eyebrow, giving me a seductive look. "You can do anything you want, gorgeous."

A half hour later, his driver pulled up and whisked him off to the MT building while I got inside my car, which thankfully was released from impound the previous day. Life was getting back on track. Martin was going to work, and I was getting ready to help close a case. This was how things should be.

Mark was in his office, waiting for my arrival. At the moment, the five-star hotel was being scoured for evidence. Every single guest room, office, and alcove would be searched. And considering how large the building was, this would take some time and hundreds of man hours. With any luck, we'd finally discover which room Frank Costan was using, find irrefutable evidence against any other potential accomplices, and maybe discover where Alvin Hodge was actually killed.

"Ready?" Steve Lawson, the tech from before, asked.

"As I'll ever be," I replied, and Mark rolled his eyes.

The hidden file contained video feed from room 709. The angle was shit, but three people moved on and off screen, Rodney Wheeler, Sean Svenstak, and Gordon Russell. They were discussing something, but the words were muffled. Lawson clicked a few keys and adjusted some of the sound levels. The words became clearer, and from what we could gather, they were discussing eliminating the threats. Alvin Hodge's name was tossed around, and Svenstak agreed to take care of that problem. After that, Wheeler and Russell went into detail about Frank Costan. Apparently they didn't trust Costan since one of his associates was informing to the feds. They planned to find out how much he knew before silencing him.

"When was that made?" I asked. Rachel was threatened weeks before Costan's arrival, and according to what everyone said, Oster didn't set up the surveillance camera until after Costan was already at the hotel, which was two days before the conference.

"That part was dated Sunday," Lawson said.

"The day before the conference," Mark added. "But there's more."

"Goody." I shifted my weight to the other leg and waited. The video footage blanked out and came back a few seconds later.

"This is dated Thursday," Lawson clarified. "It was saved as a single file, but the date's in the bottom corner." He tossed a look back at us. "This one gets a little gruesome."

"Thanks for the warning," Mark muttered.

It was already apparent what was going to happen. Frank Costan was on the ground in the middle of the room, blood dripped from his nose and mouth, and Wheeler kicked him hard in the ribs. I diverted my eyes for a moment, realizing the sniper's bullet was exactly what he deserved. The beating continued for the next twenty minutes until Costan remained motionless on the ground. The entire time, Wheeler questioned him about the FBI investigation and how Costan could sell him out, but Costan denied it. He didn't know anything about Hodge's deals or the FBI surveillance assigned to Wheeler.

"Here's where things get interesting," Lawson said. His voice broke through the morbid silence that settled over the room like a dense fog.

Someone entered from the bottom corner of the screen, glanced around the room, and picked up the hotel phone. When he turned, I recognized the man as Gordon Russell. He spoke a few words, asking to be redirected to the security office. He asked to speak to Jason Oster, and then he gave orders to disable the cameras on level seven and make sure the elevators remained clear.

"Oster helped him hide the body," Mark commented.

We continued to watch the screen, showing the arrival of Sven, some preparation to conceal Costan's body for the short trip to the subbasement, and then the room cleared out. The feed stopped, and the screen went dark.

"Oster helped them dispose of the body," I said, letting out a breath. "And from the recording, there's no way to tell if he did it intentionally. I'm guessing Russell, Wheeler, and Sven would have had no problem saying he was working with them, even if he wasn't."

"Which explains why he didn't go to the authorities," Mark added.

"Well, at least we know." I nodded goodbye to Agent Lawson and went into the hallway, pondering the violence and brutality of the human race. It was sick. We all had that inside of us, but to beat a man to death because of unsubstantiated suspicions was nothing more than malicious. I glanced down at my own knuckles, remembering we assumed Wheeler didn't do it himself, but he did, at least once Costan was already on the ground. "I'm guessing Sven started it, and Wheeler finished it."

"From the ME's report I read yesterday, Sean Svenstak had excessive bruising to his knuckles which was in a late stage of healing, so your assumption seems correct." Mark offered a wan smile. "They usually are. Plus, I heard they found the caterer's stolen I.D. card among Wheeler's belongings. The photo matched Svenstak, so he's definitely our killer."

"Some good that did." The video made thinking about everything else difficult. "I'm gonna head to the precinct and see if they got anything new out of Rachel. Do you know how Jason is?"

Mark shook his head. "Do you want me to find out?"

"If it's bad news, I don't think I can handle it at the moment. So no."

FORTY-FIVE

The precinct had been sent a copy of the footage, and from Detective Jacobs' attitude today, I suspected he was just as disgusted as I was. We didn't chitchat or make small talk. Instead, we got straight to business. Officer Taylor didn't discover anything damning at Rachel's, but a protection detail was still outside her house. There was no need, but Jacobs wanted to make sure she wasn't part of it. Although at this point, that seemed highly unlikely.

"Gordon Russell's been brought up on numerous charges," Jacobs offered. "We're helping in the search of the hotel, but so far, we've found Frank Costan's room. Inside was a key, probably to a safe deposit box. It'll be a few days before we determine what bank it's for and where the bank is. It's all about evidence collection now."

"Do you know when Rachel told Jason about the man that threatened her?" I asked. "Because from the dates on the tape, he might have been in on it. Or maybe she was."

"He helped dispose of the body, but we don't know if he did it knowingly. Only he can answer that, and he can't answer anything at the moment." Jacobs looked grim. "I hope that changes."

"Me too."

Jacobs flipped through the copy of Rachel's statement. "She said after Jason told her Alvin died, she told him about the threat." He shrugged. "So it could go either way, but I think she's clean. An idiot for taking matters into her own hands," he looked up, making sure I caught the double meaning, "but innocent still the same." He skimmed through the various papers on his desk. "Looks like we don't need you for anything else."

"Did you ever figure out what Hodge allegedly did with the money he stole from Wheeler since that was the impetus for Rachel to be threatened?"

"We've checked into his financials and hers. I'd say there was never any stolen money. It might have just been an excuse to manipulate her into giving them information on Hodge and Eastman."

"Speaking of, what's going on with Eastman?" I asked.

"He's being brought up on a few charges. Nothing too major. He'll be able to plead most of them down to misdemeanors, especially with that attorney of his. I'd wager he'll be out on bail by the end of the week."

"Okay." I stood, ready to call it a day. "Let me know what you find and what happens with Jason."

He nodded. "Parker, thanks for the assist. But don't do anything that risky again, especially for someone as questionable as Eastman."

"I didn't do it for him."

"So why'd you do it?" He looked confused.

"I don't know. It's just how I'm wired, I guess."

* * *

It had been about a week, and Martin was still living out of my apartment. On the plus side, he wasn't spending every waking moment there. He was working, signing papers, dissolving the merger he made with Hover Designs a few months earlier, and dealing with the Board. On the plus side, his elevators worked, regardless of fire or flood.

The police department and FBI finally closed their case on Wheeler and Costan. Gordon Russell was facing dozens of serious charges from financial crimes to accessory to murder. He wouldn't be getting out anytime soon. The hotel had been searched from top to bottom. The safe deposit box key that was discovered must have been what Russell was looking for the day of the hostage situation since inside was hundreds of thousands of dollars and information on dozens of overseas accounts. It was the money Costan embezzled and passed to Wheeler. At least that was over with.

Jason Oster was still in the hospital. He was hooked to numerous machines, but he was conscious and able to answer a few questions. From what Detective Jacobs told me, Oster wasn't involved. He confronted Wheeler and Russell about the crimes after Rachel told him of her threat in relation to Alvin's death. Jason hoped to use the files as insurance to guarantee Rachel's safety and his own. Wheeler promised if he turned the information over to the police, that he'd go down for the murders. After all, dating Alvin's ex was motive, and the cord used to strangle Alvin was actually the hotel security's uniform belt. So Jason would have had motive and access to the murder weapon, which is why he didn't cooperate. He looked guilty, even if he wasn't.

I stopped by the OIO to share this information with Mark. He informed me Walton's investigation was concluded, and the FBI was finished piecing together the financial crimes related to Wheeler and Costan. The parties that were ripped off by Costan's scheme would be reimbursed with the funds that were discovered in the safe deposit box. At least someone would benefit from all the murders and mayhem.

"Are you planning to talk to the Director?" Mark asked as I got ready to leave. "You promised you would."

"I did, didn't I?" I sighed. "Fine. I'll stop by. With any luck, he's busy." Something flitted across Mark's face. "What now?"

"Look, when I don't give you the heads up, you get pissed at me. And since you just gave me that nice bottle of scotch, I probably should return the favor. There's been an incident recently involving some of our undercover operatives. Needless to say, a lot of missions had to be scrapped because their identities were compromised."

"Okay, so you need the name for a computer security specialist?" I asked, not understanding.

"No. We're bringing in some inactive agents to take over."

"I see."

"I'll let Kendall explain the rest. But you wanted to come back. So here's your chance." Mark led me out of his office and down the hall. "Go get 'em, tiger."

*   *   *

That night, Martin was still staying at my apartment. He was on the couch with a sea of paperwork. I curled up on the other end, thinking about everything that occurred over the last week. He put down the report he was reading and put a pillow on his lap.

"Come here," he said, patting the pillow.

I sprawled out. "You need to go home," I said. "My invitation for you to hide in my apartment forever didn't actually mean I was asking you to move in."

"Yeah, I know." He ran a hand through my hair. "But we're pretty good at this cohabitation thing. We'd probably be better at it if we weren't stuck in such close quarters."

"And for the last time, I don't want to move in with you."

"Why not?" I didn't have to say it. He had my answer memorized. "Because you think it's too dangerous for me."

"It is."

"Then come back to work at Martin Technologies. You fixed the elevators. You've revamped the security protocols. You're an obvious asset. I'll pay you whatever you want. Hell, you can have the same benefits and healthcare plan the board members have, if you want."

"And that's exactly why I can't work for you. Because you'd treat me like your girlfriend and not like your employee. It's precisely why I don't want to mix work with play."

"So you're going to keep taking these gigs for shitheads like Paul Eastman?"

Martin had overheard my conversation with Paul earlier in the day. I sent him my invoice, and he phoned to say he got it and the check was in the mail. I told him I appreciated it, and in the future, it'd be in everyone's best interest if he lost my number and never mentioned my name again.

"No, I've got something else lined up."

"Is it dangerous?" The worry etched his forehead.

"It's not anything I can't handle." I brushed my fingertips against the stubble on his jaw. "It's not anything we can't handle."

DON'T MISS THE NEXT NOVEL IN THE
ALEXIS PARKER SERIES.

DYING FOR A FIX IS NOW AVAILABLE IN
PAPERBACK AND AS AN E-BOOK

ABOUT THE AUTHOR

G.K. Parks is the author of the Alexis Parker series. The first novel, *Likely Suspects,* tells the story of Alexis' first foray into the private sector.

G.K. Parks received a Bachelor of Arts in Political Science and History. After spending some time in law school, G.K. changed paths and earned a Master of Arts in Criminology/Criminal Justice. Now all that education is being put to use creating a fictional world based upon years of study and research.

You can find additional information on G.K. Parks and the Alexis Parker series by visiting our website at
www.alexisparkerseries.com

Made in United States
North Haven, CT
11 March 2022

17020917R00209